THE MOTH CATCHER

Also by Ann Cleeves

Raven Black
White Nights
Red Bones
Blue Lightning
Silent Voices
Dead Water
Thin Air
Harbour Street

Ann Cleeves

THE MOTH CATCHER

Minotaur Books

A Thomas Dunne Book
New York

This is a work of fiction. All of the characters, organizations, and events portrayed in this novel are either products of the author's imagination or are used fictitiously.

A THOMAS DUNNE BOOK FOR MINOTAUR BOOKS.
An imprint of St. Martin's Press.

For information, address St. Martin's Press, 175 Fifth Avenue, New York, N.Y. 10010.

www.thomasdunnebooks.com
www.minotaurbooks.com

Library of Congress Cataloging-in-Publication Data

Names: Cleeves, Ann, author.
Title: The moth catcher : a Vera Stanhope mystery / Ann Cleeves.
Description: First U.S. edition. | New York : Minotaur Books, 2016. | "A Thomas Dunne book."
Identifiers: LCCN 2016014330| ISBN 9781250105424 (hardcover) | ISBN 9781250105431 (e-book)
Subjects: LCSH: Women detectives—England—Fiction. | BISAC: FICTION / Mystery & Detective / Women Sleuths. | FICTION / Mystery & Detective / Police Procedural. | GSAFD: Mystery fiction.
Classification: LCC PR6053.L45 M68 2016 | DDC 823/.914—dc23
LC record available at https://lccn.loc.gov/2016014330

First published in Great Britain by Macmillan, an imprint of Pan Macmillan

First U.S. Edition: October 2016

10 9 8 7 6 5 4 3 2 1

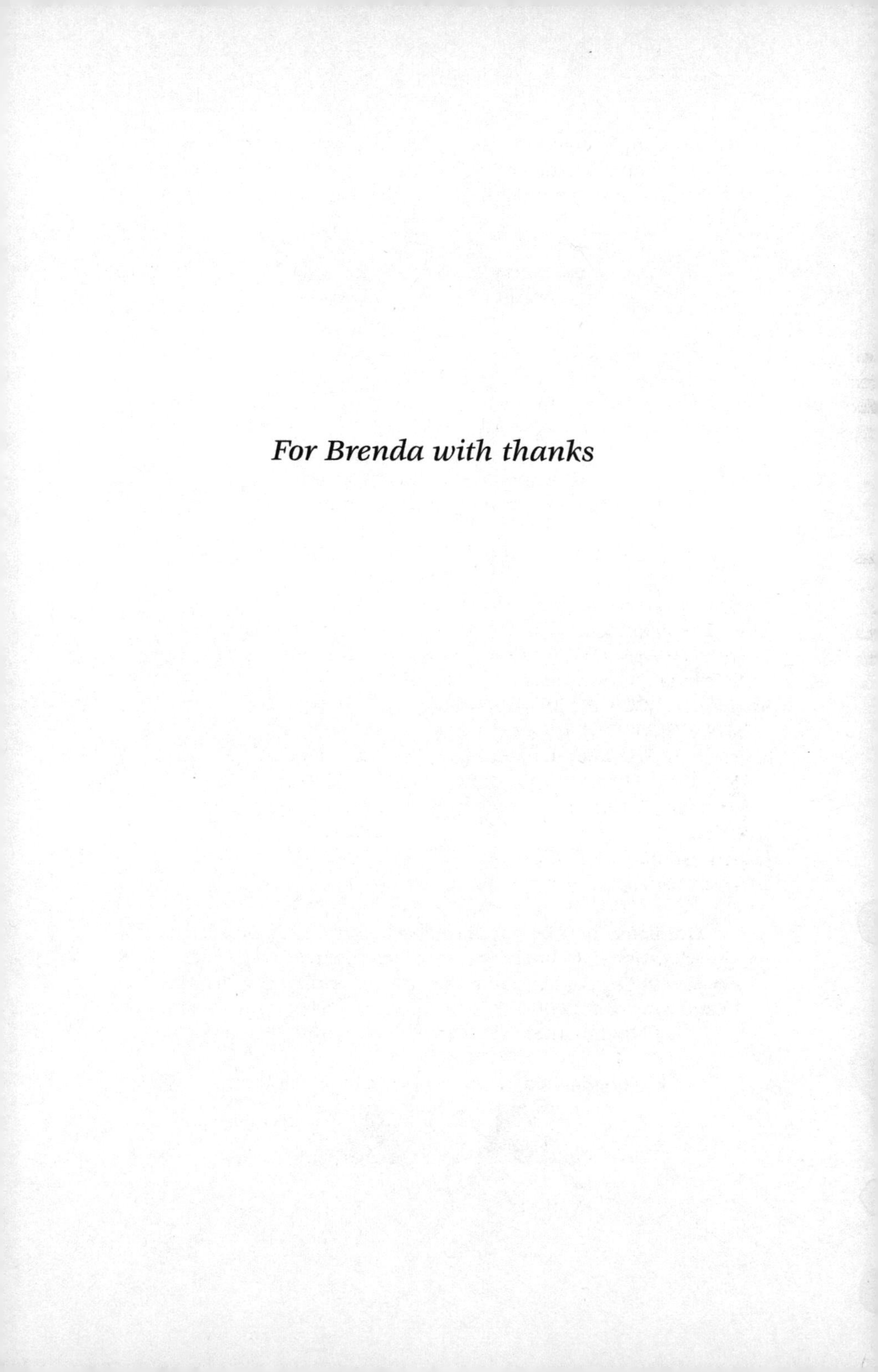

For Brenda with thanks

Acknowledgements

As always I'm grateful to my fabulous agent, Sara Menguc, and to the whole team at Pan Macmillan for their considerable support in the writing of this book. I'd also like to thank Prof. Lorna Dawson, for agreeing to appear as herself. Any mistakes around the soil science in *The Moth Catcher* are entirely mine.

THE MOTH CATCHER

Chapter One

Lizzie Redhead listened. In the prison it was never quiet. Not even now in the middle of the night. The other women in her room stirred, snuffling like animals in their sleep. No cells here. Dormitories that reminded her of school. No privacy. No darkness, either. A gleam from the corridor outside shone through the crack under the door, and though this was a low-security establishment there were spotlights at the walls and the gate, and the curtains were thin. Footsteps in the corridor outside. A screw checking that lass on suicide-watch. Two in the morning.

Lizzie worked in the prison farm, so she had access to fresh air and enough exercise to keep her fit, but that didn't mean she slept well. She'd never needed much sleep. She'd always believed she didn't belong to her parents; had decided when she was quite small that she was a foundling child, secretly adopted. What did they have in common after all? She had too much energy and a very low boredom threshold. Annie and Sam were soft and gentle, big on squidgy hugs and soppy kisses. Lizzie saw herself as hard and metallic. As an adult she'd chosen men like her. Flinty. Flint on flint made fire. Jason Crow had set her alight.

In a week she'd be released, and she was making

plans. She'd become healthy in prison. She'd realized there were better ways to get her kicks than booze and drugs. Jason had taught her that too, though she hadn't believed him at the time. She knew, from all he'd told her, that she was lucky to have ended up in an open institution.

In prison her entertainment was simple. She visited the library and joined the writers' group. She had stories to tell and she needed to find the right words. In the library she'd found a book published by the *National Geographic* and kept renewing the loan until she believed the book was hers. She lay on her bed and looked at pictures of places she wanted to see for herself, felt dizzy at the idea of travelling, had in her nostrils the smell of the rain forest, the salt of distant seas. Huge places, big enough to contain her ambition. Her parents had spent all their life within ten miles of the valley where her father had been born. Lizzie needed tough places to battle with, rocks sharp enough to cut her flesh.

She'd been a cutter when she was a teenager, slicing into her arm with a razor, high on the smell of metal and blood. She still occasionally harboured dreams of steel, sharp blades, blood oozing in perfectly round drops from clean cuts. Her mother had never noticed. Lizzie had always been good at hiding her secrets. Now she was hiding Jason Crow's secrets too. She was haunted by them, but she waited for the time that they might be useful to her.

Chapter Two

Percy steered the Mini down the lane from The Lamb towards the bungalow he shared with his daughter. On the passenger seat beside him sat Madge, a Border-cross and the best dog he'd ever had. She'd win prizes at the trials, if Percy could be arsed to train her properly. Percy's sight wasn't so good these days, so he drove with his nose to the windscreen peering at the road ahead. His daughter said he should stop driving, but hadn't done anything about it. She liked the two hours of peace his time in The Lamb gave her. Besides, the lane didn't go anywhere except the big house and those fancy barn conversions, and at this time of day those people were all drinking too. Susan, his daughter, went in to clean for them, and she said the recycling bin was full of bottles every week. Major and Mrs C from the big house were away visiting their son in Australia, so they wouldn't be driving down the lane. There was nothing else to hit, and the car could find its own way home.

Percy found that his mind was wandering. The beer was strong and he'd been persuaded to take a third pint from one of the youngsters who'd moved into the village. He was late. Susan would be waiting for him, her eye on the clock and his tea in the oven. She liked the washing up done and the kitchen all clean and tidy before the start of *EastEnders*. Her husband had run away with a lass from Prudhoe as soon as their kids had left home, and Susan had moved in with Percy. To take care of him, she said. To have someone to boss around, he thought, though he was used to her now and would miss her if she moved out.

The lane ran along the bottom of the valley. On each side the hills rose steeply, first to fields quartered with drystone walls where sheep grazed and then to open moorland. Close to the road there were trees, a narrow strip of woodland, with primroses now and the green spears that would turn into bluebells. New leaves just starting and the low sun throwing shadows across the road. He was retired, but he'd always earned his living on farms and could turn his hand to anything. He'd liked sheep-work best and this was his favourite time of year. Lambs on the hill and the scent of summer on the way. The sun starting to get a bit of heat in it.

The third pint was sitting uncomfortably on his bladder. That was something else Susan nagged him to go to the doctor about. He was up to the toilet several times a night. Sometimes he got caught short when he was out, pissing himself like a bairn just out of nappies. There was no fun in getting old, no matter what he said to the kids in the pub about having the perfect life. *Me, I've got no worries in the world.* When you got old there was the worry of indignity and dying. He pulled the car as close to the verge as he could get and jumped out. Just managed to get his zip undone in time, the water in the burn mingling with the sound of his own water aimed at the ditch. There was a moment of relief as he did up his trousers and he thought that he would make an appointment to see the doctor. He couldn't carry on like this.

Then he saw the boy's face, half-hidden by cow parsley. The eyes were open and the pale hair drifted in the ditch water like weed. They'd had a dry spell, so the ditch was less than half-full. Most of the face was above the water line. It was unmarked. No lines, no wounds. This was a young man, and he looked as if he'd just gone to sleep. He was wearing a woollen jersey and a waxed jacket, and the clothes that weren't lying in the mud at the bottom of the ditch looked clean and dry. Percy wasn't appalled by death. He'd killed beasts and he'd seen dead people. He'd just been too young to serve in the war, but when he was a child it hadn't been unusual for people to die at home. Now people mocked health-and-safety laws, but there'd been more accidents at work then too. Farm machinery without guards or brakes, foolish men showing off. And he'd been holding his wife's hand when she slipped away. It was a shock to see the boy lying here and it sobered him up, but he didn't want to vomit.

He looked at the face more carefully and took a moment to remember when he'd last seen it. Last week in the lounge of The Lamb. Eating one of Gloria's steak pies. Alone. He'd asked his mate Matty who the boy was, but Matty had no curiosity and didn't bother answering. And Percy had seen the boy again, more recently. Yesterday morning, strolling down the road towards the village. Percy had been up on the hill walking Madge and had meant to ask Susan about him. Susan was more nebby than he was and she knew all the gossip.

Percy walked back to the car and took the mobile phone out of the glove compartment. All around him blackbirds were singing fit to burst. It was that time of year. The time for marking territories and breeding. He always missed his dead wife most in the spring. Not just the friendship, but the sex.

Susan had given the phone to him so that she could keep track of him. She'd called him earlier this evening to remind him he should be on his way home, and that was why he'd headed straight to the car from the pub, without going to the Gents first. It didn't do to cross his daughter. He'd never used the phone before, but Susan had talked him through it when she gave it to him. The figures were big, so he could read them easily. His first call was to the bungalow. Susan had a temper on her; she could chuck his tea in the bin if he was late, and now that he was sober he was hungry. Then 999. The person on the other end of the line told him to stay where he was. Percy found a bar of chocolate in his jacket pocket and he waited. Doing what he was told for once.

He'd been expecting a police car or an ambulance. No siren. There was no rush after all; the bloke was quite clearly dead and cold. Percy had been thinking about it. At first he'd assumed some sort of accident. But if the lad had been knocked into the ditch by a car he'd have been lying on top of the vegetation, not hidden underneath it. The same would be true if the man had been taken ill. He might be walking on the verge to keep out of the way of a car or a tractor, but he wouldn't be that close to the ditch. Percy had come to the conclusion the bloke had been put there. Hidden. Even a walker in the lane wouldn't have seen the body unless he'd scrambled through the undergrowth like Percy, who'd been trying to retain a bit of his dignity by getting away from the road. Then he heard a vehicle, an old vehicle, coughing and spluttering. Madge had been asleep, but she woke up, gave a little growl until Percy put his hand on her neck. It was a Land Rover, so mucky and bashed that it was impossible to make out the original colour, and there was a woman at the wheel. He got out of his car to tell her that she was on the wrong road and this was a dead-end, and anyway she wouldn't get past him here, but she stopped and got out. He wondered how her knees managed the weight of her on the deep step down to the tarmac. She was big. No beauty. Bad skin and bad clothes, but lovely eyes. Brown like conkers.

'Percy Douglas?' A local voice.

He thought he might have seen her in The Lamb. Not a regular, but occasionally. The size of her, you wouldn't miss her even if she was sitting on her own in a corner.

'Aye.' It still didn't occur to him that she was here because of the body.

'I'm Vera Stanhope. Detective Inspector. I don't get out of the office much these days, but I live not far off, so I thought I'd come along.' She groped in her pockets for a moment, as if she was planning to show him some ID, but in the end all she pulled out was a half-eaten tube of mints. She gave up. 'Are you going to let me see this body of yours?'

'Nothing to do with me.' But he started down the lane.

'Hang on. I'd best dress the part or the CSIs will cut me up into slices and stick me in one of their fancy microscopes.' She reached into the Land Rover and pulled out a packet wrapped in plastic. There was a white paper suit with a hood, and white boots to go over her shoes. 'I know,' she said, when she was all dressed up, 'I look like the Abominable Snowman.'

She made him stay on the lane and point her in the direction of the body. She stood on the bank and looked down into the ditch. 'How did you find him? You can hardly see him, even from here.'

Percy felt himself blushing.

'Call of nature, was it?'

He nodded.

'I get taken short myself these days. Not so easy for a woman. You should thank your lucky stars.'

He could tell she wasn't thinking about what she was saying. All her attention was on the lad in the ditch.

'Do you know him?'

He shook his head. 'I've seen him about. In the pub in the village once. Walking down the lane a couple of days ago.'

'Where do you live?' Her voice friendly, interested.

'In the bungalow further up the lane. I built it when I first got married. Major Carswell let me have a bit of land. Most of my work was on the estate farms.'

She nodded as if she understood how these things worked. 'A bit odd then – you not knowing the man. If he was local.'

'He doesn't live in the valley.' Percy was sure about that. 'He's a visitor maybe.' He paused. 'Susan would probably know.'

'Susan?'

'My daughter. Lives with me.'

There was the sound of another vehicle. This time a police car with a couple of uniformed officers inside. Vera Stanhope climbed back to the lane. 'The cavalry,' she said. 'Just in time. I'm gasping for a cup of tea, and you'll be starving. Why don't you make your way home and I'll follow you when I've chatted to the workers. Your Susan can tell me what she knows about the lad in the ditch.'

She turned up half an hour later. Percy and Susan were still at the table, but the cottage pie had been eaten and they were onto tea and home-made cake. His Susan had always been a lovely baker. There was no sweetness in her nature these days and Percy had the sudden notion that it all went into her cakes and puddings. The detective knocked at the kitchen door, but didn't wait for anyone to answer. Just inside, she pulled off her shoes. Percy thought that was a smart move. Susan couldn't abide anyone bringing dirt into the house.

'I hope I'm not disturbing you.' And with that, the detective was at the table, and Susan had already fetched another cup and saucer. Tea was poured and a slice of cake had been cut. The bright conker eyes were looking at them.

'Percy here told me you'd know all about the lad he found in the ditch. We've got a name for him now, at least. There was a wallet in his jacket with a credit and debit card. And a driver's licence. Patrick Randle. Does that mean anything to you?' She bit into the cake.

Susan was enjoying every minute of this. Since Brian had left and the kids had gone away – Karen to university and Lee to the army – gossip was what brought her to life. Malicious gossip suited her best, and she'd upset most of the women in the village. It pained him that she had so few friends. 'Patrick,' Susan said, 'that's the name of the house-sitter at the Hall.'

Vera looked at her without interrupting, and Susan continued.

'When the major and his wife go away to stay with their son in Australia, they bring someone in to look after the house. Well, it's more to look after the dogs really, but they feel happier knowing there's someone onsite at night. When they're away I still go in a couple of times a week – it's a good chance to give the place a good clean – but I wouldn't want to stay there or walk those great slobbering Labradors.'

'Is it always Patrick who stays, when they're on holiday?' Vera had finished her slice of cake. Without asking, Susan cut her another.

'No, it's usually a woman, middle-aged. Name of Louise. This time she was unavailable and the agency sent them the young man. I wasn't sorry. Louise acted as if she was lady of the manor, all airs and graces. She was the hired help, same as me.' That bitterness showing itself again.

'How long has Patrick been here?' Vera reached out for the teapot.

'Just a fortnight. He arrived on the Tuesday and that's one of my cleaning days. Mrs Carswell asked me to show him round and settle him in. There's a flat in the attic where their eldest Nicholas lived, before he went off to Australia, and the house-sitters always stay there.'

'What was he like, this Patrick?'

Percy was tempted to leave the women to it. This time of the evening he usually put on the television, and he never liked his routine disturbed. And he thought Susan would show herself up and say something nasty. But there was such a connection between the women, such concentration, that he was scared of moving in case he broke it.

'He seemed pleasant enough,' Susan said. Percy felt relieved. 'Easy to talk to. Relaxed. I asked why he was house-sitting. It seemed an odd way for a bright young man to earn a living.'

'And what did he say?'

'That it suited him just at the moment. He was between projects and he was enjoying exploring the country.'

'Projects?' Vera squinted at her. 'What did he mean by that?'

'I'm not sure. But that was what he said.'

'Where did he come from?' The questions were coming quickly now. Percy thought the fat woman would surely have an address, if she'd found his driver's licence, so what could that be about?'

'He didn't say.' Susan sounded disappointed. He saw that Vera Stanhope was providing her with attention, and she didn't get much of that these days.

'But you might be able to guess,' Vera said. 'From his voice, the way he spoke.'

Susan thought for a moment. 'He had a voice like a television newsreader. A bit posh.'

'From the South then?'

Susan nodded.

'When did you last see him?'

'Yesterday afternoon. Today I work for the people who live in the barn conversions. There are three houses at the end of the valley.'

'What time yesterday?' Again the question was fired at speed. Percy thought the woman found it hard for her words to keep up with her brain.

'About four o'clock. I was in the kitchen and he came in with the dogs.'

'Did he seem okay? Not anxious about anything?'

Susan shook her head. Again she seemed disappointed because she couldn't be of more help. She had no juicy bit of information to pass on. The detective got to her feet and that seemed to break a kind of spell, because Percy found that he could stand up now too. At the door the fat woman wobbled a bit as she struggled to pull on her shoes, and Percy put out his hand to steady her.

She turned to Susan and smiled. 'Have you got a key to the big house? Could I borrow it?'

For a moment Susan was flustered; she'd never been any good at taking responsibility. 'I don't know. Perhaps I should call the Carswells and ask their permission. They left me their phone number, in case of emergency.'

'Why don't you give me that, as well as the key, and I'll sort it all out for you?'

So Susan handed over the bunch of keys and the piece of card with the number neatly written on, and the detective left the house.

They stood at the window and watched her walk out to her Land Rover.

'Nice woman,' Susan said. 'You'd think she'd want to lose a bit of weight, though.'

Chapter Three

When Vera arrived back at the scene, Joe Ashworth had turned up. He was talking to Billy Cartwright, the crime-scene manager, and they'd taped off the road.

'You here already, Vera?' Cartwright said. 'There's something ghoulish about the pleasure you take in your work.'

She thought he was probably right, but she didn't deign to give him an answer.

'What have we got then, Billy? First impressions?' Billy might be too fond of the lasses, but he was good at his job.

'This isn't where the lad was killed. You need to be looking elsewhere for the murder scene.'

'It *is* murder then?'

'Not my job to tell you that, Vera my love. Paul Keating's on his way.' Keating, a dour Ulsterman, was the senior pathologist. 'But I can't see that it was an accident. He was put in the ditch because it was close enough to the road for someone to get him easily out of a car. And he was hidden. He might have lain there unnoticed for weeks.'

If Percy Douglas hadn't been caught short. And, by then, the rats and foxes would have been at the body and that would have made life more difficult.

'Tyre tracks on the verge?'

'One set, very recent, most probably belonging to the chap who found the body.'

She nodded and thought there was nothing she could do here until the experts had finished poking around. And she was restless. She'd never been good at hanging about. No patience. 'Joe, you come with me. I know where our victim lived, or where he'd lived for the past fortnight at least.'

He started to climb into the passenger seat of the Land Rover, but she called him back. 'We'll walk, shall we? It's not far and I could do with the exercise.'

He seemed a bit surprised, but he knew better than to question her. Vera liked that about Joe. He could be as bolshie as the rest of the team, but he picked his battles and didn't make a fuss about the trivial stuff. That got her thinking about Holly, who made a fuss about everything. 'Has anyone told DC Clarke what's going on?'

'Aye, I let her know as soon as the call came through. She said she'd make her own way, but she'd be a while.'

They walked in silence for a moment. Vera was pleased it was just her and Joe. That was how she liked it best. She couldn't imagine being any closer to a son. There was grass growing in the middle of the road and, once they were out of earshot of Billy and his team, it was very quiet.

'What is this place then?' Joe wasn't a country boy and Vera sensed that he was out of his comfort zone. Joe aspired to a new house on a suburban executive estate, somewhere safe for the kids to play out. His ideal neighbours would be teachers, small-businessmen.

Respectable, but not too posh. Vera's neighbours were aristo hippy dropouts who smoked dope and drank good red wine. And worked their bollocks off on a smallholding in the hills that could hardly provide any kind of living.

'I'm not sure what they call it. The nearest village is back on the main road. Gilswick. And that's nothing but a few houses, a church and a pub. Maybe this valley doesn't have a name of its own.'

They turned a corner and came to the entrance to a drive. Crumbling stone pillars half-covered in ivy. No gate. No house name. Vera had seen it on her way to chat to Percy, but she hadn't stopped. The drive led through wild woodland underplanted with daffs, and at this point there was no sight of the house.

'This is a grand sort of place for a young man.' Joe was tense, a bit anxious. His dad was an ex-miner and Methodist lay preacher. Joe had been brought up to think that all men were equal, but had never quite believed it.

'He didn't own it!' Vera gave a little laugh, but her second-hand impression from Susan was that Patrick Randle *might* have come from somewhere like this. An idle young man with time to laze around in someone else's home. Enough money not to bother with a proper job. 'He was the house-sitter.'

'What's that?'

'Someone who looks after a house when the owners are away.'

They turned a corner and the house was in front of them. Not a huge mansion with pillars and turrets. This was compact and square. Old. Solid stone. A pele-tower at one end, long fallen into disuse. One of the fortified farmhouses that had been built along the border, to see off the Scottish reivers. In the last of the sunshine, the stone looked warm. 'Nice,' Vera said and felt a momentary stab of envy. Hector, her father, had grown up somewhere like this. The third son with no claim to the land, and anyway he'd upset everyone and the family had disowned him. Then she thought of her little house in the hills – she couldn't keep that clean and maintained; she'd have no chance with something like this.

They walked on. To the side of the house there was an old-fashioned kitchen garden. Fruit bushes covered with netting, vegetables starting to come up in rows. Everything tidy. Susan hadn't mentioned a gardener, and Vera thought she would have done if the family had employed a man. So this was the Carswells' work. They loved this place, and they must surely be retired to devote so much time to it. Beyond the garden the hill rose steeply to a rocky outcrop. They stood for a moment and heard sheep and running water.

Susan's key let them into a big kitchen. An old cream Aga at one end and a drying rack over it, empty except for dishcloths and tea towels. Beside it stood a basket containing a fat black Labrador, and a blanket on which lay another, thinner dog.

'Shit!' said Vera. 'We'll need to get someone to take care of the animals.' She wondered if she might persuade Percy to take them until the family got home. Though it might be more a case of persuading Susan.

There was a big scrubbed pine table. The kitchen was tidy and everything gleamed, but it wasn't *Homes & Gardens*. None of the chairs matched and the crockery on the dresser was old and some of it a bit chipped. The rug on the tile floor was made of rush matting. Presumably the cleanliness was Susan's work. If Randle had lived in the flat in the attic, Vera supposed that he'd have his own kitchen there.

They wandered on through the house. There was a formal dining room, which felt cold and looked as if it was hardly ever used. Dark paintings of Victorian gentlemen in dull gilt frames. French windows led to a terrace of flagstones and then to a lawn. Vera wondered if cutting the grass was part of the house-sitter's job description. Then a family living room. A fireplace with bookshelves in the alcoves on either side, old sofas scratched by generations of dogs, photos on the mantelpiece. One of a handsome young man in uniform standing next to a young woman in a floral dress; others of the same people as they got older: with two children on a beach, standing outside a college at a son's graduation, in smart clothes at a daughter's wedding. The last picture must be recent and showed the two of them sitting on a white bench outside this house. They were probably in their mid-seventies, but wiry and fit. The man looked at the woman with the same adoration as in the first picture.

'The portrait of a happy marriage,' Joe said.

'Man, that's a bit profound for you.' Vera kept her voice light, but she was moved too. A tad jealous. She didn't have any personal experience of happy families. 'It's easy enough to be taken in by appearances.'

A wide polished staircase led to the first floor. The bedrooms were big and airy. Old-fashioned furniture, sheets and blankets and floral quilts. None of that duvet nonsense, with cushions on the beds that you only had to throw off before you went to sleep. Two double rooms and two twins – the twin rooms still decorated for children. One with a train set on a big table and a moth-eaten rocking horse. Vera wondered if there'd been grandchildren. There'd surely have been photos, and they hadn't seen any downstairs. Perhaps the Carswells were waiting in hope for their children to produce offspring. They found one family bathroom with a deep old enamel bath, and a more recent shower room, built in what might once have been a cupboard in the main bedroom. The only gesture towards modernization. No toiletries in either room to indicate they were used by a young man. And still there was no sign of disturbance, nothing that could be considered a crime scene.

'Where did our victim live then?' Joe was getting impatient, but Vera didn't mind taking her time over this stage of the investigation. It was getting the feel of the place. Like setting a scene in a story. You learned a lot about people from the place they lived, and the Carswells might have been halfway around the world when this man was killed, but he was staying in their house.

Joe looked across the bannister and down to the hall below. 'I mean, you said he lived in the attic, but I can't see any way up.'

He was right. There were no stairs leading from the first floor. But there definitely *was* an attic. Vera had seen the windows from outside. 'They'll go from the kitchen,' she said after a moment's thought. 'The staff quarters. You wouldn't want to see the minions in the main body of the house. Not when this place was first turned into a domestic residence.' She hoped the

Carswells wouldn't hold that attitude. She liked their house and had a picture of them as friendly people. Open-minded. Though, as she'd told Joe, appearances could be deceptive and she needed to keep an open mind too.

They found the stairs in the kitchen, hidden by what they'd thought was a cupboard door. It was painted white, like the door leading into the walk-in larder on the other side of the range. Behind, steep and very narrow stairs twisted their way up. There was a switch inside and a bare bulb screwed into the wall gave the only light. Perhaps once there'd been access to the first floor, but it seemed that must have been plastered over. Vera thought the work had been done when they'd installed a shower in the cupboard in the main bedroom. But now the stairs continued up and the light hardly reached here. The passage was wider, but still, because of her bulk, she had the nightmare thought that she might get stuck in one of the tight twists, that she'd suffer the indignity of Joe trying to pull her out.

She was starting to feel panicky and claustrophobic by the time she reached the top. The crime-scene suit didn't help. Behind her Joe was breathing evenly, but she was already out of breath. Another white wooden door. She pushed against it and nothing happened. She pulled it and had to squeeze against the wall because it opened towards her.

'The maids must have been skinny little things in the old days.' She gave a little laugh, trying to make light of her discomfort, stepped into a cramped hall and stretched. Bare whitewashed walls. A pair of wellingtons. A scarf and a duffel coat on a hook. The only light came from a small window in the roof. Joe joined her and they took up all the space. She paused for a moment before opening another door into Patrick Randle's flat.

It was big and light and must have stretched over half the house. This had more the feel of a city loft apartment than a home in the country. The walls sloped, but big windows let in the last of the evening light. The floorboards had been stripped and polished and the doors were open, so Vera could see right to the gable end. There a window was open and they heard the outdoor sounds of woodpigeons and water. Close to the entrance there was a small bathroom. A crumpled towel on the side of the bath. An electric razor on the shelf over the sink. Vera caught her reflection in the mirror and turned away quickly.

The rest of the space was divided by one wall. A large open-plan kitchen and living room took up most of it. In the kitchen section a fridge and a slim cooker. A cup and two plates washed up on the draining board, two more mugs still dirty in the sink. Did that mean that Patrick Randle had entertained a visitor? The rest of the room was furnished with cast-offs from downstairs: a squashy sofa and a scratched dining table. The room wasn't a mess, but there was clutter. Last week's *Observer* on the arm of a chair, a couple of books on the table.

Vera walked on towards the open door that led to the bedroom. The room faced west and it was bright, inviting. It seemed to glow. She stood at the door, aware that Joe was opening drawers in the room behind her, making a first check of Randle's possessions. Inside the room there was a double bed, low to the floor. The mattress very thin, so she thought it'd be hard to get a good night's sleep. In one corner a huge, heavy wardrobe. She thought that must have been built up here; you'd never get it up those narrow stairs. In fact all the furniture must have been in place before the door to the first-floor bedroom had been plastered over.

Then she thought it was odd the way your mind worked, because as soon as she'd looked into the room she'd seen the man lying on the floor under the window. So why had she focused on the trivial matter of the furniture? Why had her attention been caught by a monstrous wardrobe? She forced herself to look again. To concentrate, because sometimes first impressions were the most important. In shock you picked up details that you could miss later. This was an older man. Middle-aged. Grey hair, grey suit. A civil servant of a man. He lay on his back and his spectacles were still in place on his nose, though tilted so that he would only see through one of the lenses. His white shirt had been slashed into shreds by the sharpest of knives. The shirt was no longer white, but reddish-brown, and what looked like blood had soaked into the stripped wooden floor beneath him.

Joe must have sensed that something had shocked her because he came up behind her.

'Stay there!' It came out as a shout, and she hadn't intended that. But she was thinking that this was a nightmare. She and Joe had walked from one crime scene to another and any defence lawyer would have a field day about contamination. At least Joe had made her put on the fresh scene suit before coming into the house.

And while all those thoughts were rattling around in her brain something else was going on too. An excitement. Because this was a new case that was different from anything she'd ever worked before. Two bodies, connected but not lying together. And nothing made her feel as alive as murder.

Chapter Four

Vera waited in the big house for Paul Keating. She'd given her orders, rattling them off to Joe Ashworth until she'd confused him and had to start again more slowly. Then she'd spoken on the phone to Holly.

'Where are you, Hol?'

'On my way, Ma'am.' The voice sounded as if she was speaking through a piece of hosepipe. She must be using the hands-free set in her car. But, even so, Vera felt a stab of anger. Why did that *Ma'am* always sound as if her DC was taking the piss? Cocky and resentful at the same time.

'Well, don't stop at the cordon in the lane. I'll leave instructions for them to let you past. Come to the big house further up the valley. The drive is the first on the left after you pass the crime scene. I'll be waiting for you.'

'You don't want me to help out at the scene?' She sounded offended. It took very little to offend Holly.

'Not at the scene in the ditch. There's been another murder, and I need someone fresh here. We don't want any further contamination.' That shut Holly up.

Vera waited outside the house, sitting on the white bench where the photograph of the owners had been taken. It was cooler now, with the sun only just over the horizon, but there was the smell of cut grass that always made her think of summer. She loved this time of year. She'd sent Joe back to the station to start making calls and pulling together information. And to organize all the extra personnel they'd need for the following day. She'd already talked to Billy Cartwright on the phone. They'd need a different team at each locus, and she wanted him to supervise both, so he'd need to bring in another manager for the lane as well as for the house. Paul Keating was the only Kimmerston pathologist on call. He'd said he'd try to pull in a colleague to help with the post-mortems, but he wanted to look at both scenes himself. 'Don't worry, Inspector. I'll change before I head up to you. We're aware of the dangers of cross-contamination.' She'd known him for decades, but he'd never used her first name.

There was the sound of a car on the drive. Holly's Nissan. Very new and very sensible. No fun. The young woman got out, slender legs first.

Am I just jealous? Because she's young and bonny and organized? Am I being unfair?

'You said there was a second murder.' Holly was already struggling into the paper suit, pulling bootees over her shoes and tucking her hair into the hood.

'A middle-aged man in the flat where the house-sitter was staying. It looks as if he's been stabbed, though there was no sign of a knife on my first quick search. No sign of a break-in, either, so it's possible that he was known to our first victim.' Vera thought that an intruder would be unlikely to wander into the flat in the attic without prior knowledge of the building's layout. Any valuables would be in the main part of the house, and it had taken her and Joe a while to find the entrance to the staircase in the kitchen. But those speculations could wait.

'ID?'

'Nothing yet. I've sent Joe back with a photograph to circulate. Our victim looks the sort who'd be reported missing, though. Respectable. You know.'

Holly gave a brief nod.

'The first victim is Patrick Randle. Aged twenty-five. He was employed by an agency to stay in the house while the owners were away. I'm presuming they wanted someone to walk the dogs and cut the grass, and they could afford to pay an outsider to do it, but we'll need to check the details. Joe will phone them from the station.'

Holly nodded again.

'Shall we go up then?' Without waiting for an answer Vera went inside the house. She locked the kitchen door behind them, then opened the painted door by the side of the Aga. 'You go up first.' She didn't want Holly following her up the stairs, muttering when the progress was slow. 'There's a small passage-way at the top. Wait for me there.'

Randle's flat was in shadow now. Vera flicked a switch and spotlights fixed to the beams in the sloping ceiling lit the rooms. For a moment she wondered if she'd imagined it all. She'd look into the bedroom and there'd be no body on the floor. The stripped pine boards would be clean. But the middle-aged man was still there, caught in the pool of artificial light.

Vera stopped at the doorway and moved aside so that Holly could see into the bedroom. 'I don't want to go in there. I saw the body from here and haven't been over the threshold. This is a fresh scene suit, but I was out near the ditch to look at Randle. We don't want a defence lawyer screaming further down the line that we didn't keep everything separate.'

'You want me to go in?'

Well, I didn't bring you out here for your scintillating company. Vera took a breath, told herself again that she was probably just jealous. No other reason why this woman should get under her skin. 'Yes please, Hol. It'll take Billy a while to get a separate team of CSIs here and I'd like to see if there's any ID on the body. And while you're in there, have a look for the weapon. I'd say we're looking for a very sharp knife and it might have been thrown under the bed or a chair.'

Holly walked into the room. She made her way to the far side of the body so that Vera would have a good view of what she was doing.

She's bright, Vera thought, *considers everything.*

The younger woman squatted by the side of the body, taking care not to move it or touch the skin, and reached into the pockets on the suit jacket. First the outside pockets, and then she lifted the cloth so she could get into those on the inside. She shook her head. 'Nothing.'

'Try the trousers.'

'I can only get to the front pockets without moving him.'

'That'll do.' Vera thought that only younger men carried important things in their back pockets anyway. Or middle-aged men in jeans. This man would have his wallet inside his jacket. A wallet and his keys. And that led her to wonder how the victim had got here and, if Patrick Randle had owned a car, where it might be kept. There had been no vehicles parked on the gravel outside the house. She was still thinking about that when Holly stood up.

'Sorry, Ma'am. Nothing. That's unusual, isn't it?'

'His pockets have been emptied,' Vera said. 'To delay identification, or for some other reason.'

Holly kneeled again to look under the bed. 'No sign of a knife.'

Downstairs in the big kitchen Vera was on the phone to Joe. 'Can you get me the registration details of Randle's vehicle? We found a driver's licence on him. There was nothing on the grey man's body, so an ID for him would be brilliant.'

'The grey man?'

'The man in the flat.' That was how she was thinking of him. As a grey man. Anonymous. She waited on the line while Joe dug out the details of Randle's car. A small VW, only a year old. Would a young man be able to afford a car like that? Unless he had wealthy parents? She wasn't sure. The young had always been a mystery to her, even when she'd been one of their ranks. She'd understand the grey man better and felt more sympathy for him, without knowing anything at all about him.

They went outside. 'There are some buildings at the back.' Vera's feet crunched on the gravel, slightly muffled by the paper overshoes. 'I'm assuming one of those has been used as a garage.' The light had thickened into dusk. A bat skimmed over their heads. Vera waited for Holly to scream, but she gave no reaction.

There were two garages. One was a small open-fronted barn, rickety and in need of repair. Against one wall stood a neat stack of logs, depleted after the winter. That was where they found Randle's car. 'We won't be able to get into the vehicle,' Vera said. 'There was a bunch of keys on Randle's body, and Billy has those.' Holly put on new gloves and tried the handle. The car was unlocked. Was that carelessness or a sense that crime would be unusual out here in the valley? Again Vera thought that the boy must have money, if he cared so little about security. They looked through the windows, but didn't get into the vehicle. There were two empty Coke cans on the passenger seat. In the back a brown Manila file was stuck in the side pocket.

'I want to see that,' Vera said, 'as soon as the CSIs have finished with it.' She paused. This was where the gravel ended and the vegetable garden began. There was no sign of another vehicle and the second garage was locked. So how had the older man arrived at the house? The nearest public transport would be the bus to Gilswick, and she guessed they'd be as common as hens' teeth. Then there'd be the walk down the lane. A good two miles, possibly more. In his grey suit and his city shoes. Someone would surely have seen him if he'd made the journey during daylight. Otherwise he must have got a lift. That would have been organized in advance. The grey man wouldn't be the kind to hitch-hike. Or a taxi. Or – and as Vera considered the possibilities, this seemed most likely – Randle had brought him here. And that meant there must be some connection between the two men. They'd arranged to meet.

The second garage was more solid, stone-built to go with the house, but put up more recently. A padlock held the two doors together. Vera tried the smallest key on the bunch given to her by Susan and it opened as smoothly as if it had just been oiled. Inside there were two cars: a new Range Rover and an elderly Morris Minor estate, obviously much loved. The women stood at the door and looked in.

'The family that lived here had money,' Holly said.

Vera nodded. *Money, but class. Nothing too showy here. Nothing ostentatious.* Then she remembered that nobody had spoken to the Carswells yet. She needed to know that they really were in Australia, and they might have more information about Randle. She'd had the impression they'd already left when the house-sitter arrived and that Susan had managed the hand-over, but one of them had probably talked to Randle on the phone. She called Joe again and left him more instructions. 'See if any of the local taxi firms brought our second victim to the big house. Have you talked to the Carswells in Adelaide yet?'

'I've tried, but there was no response. It was still early morning there then and they might have been asleep. I was going to give it another hour.'

'I'd like to know what contact they had with their house-sitter. Did they meet him before he started work? The cleaner settled him, so the Carswells weren't here when he arrived.'

Suddenly the garden was flooded with light. Two lamps on black iron stands set along the drive and one fixed outside the main front door had switched on. Presumably they were on a timer or had a light sensor. Was that a security measure or just about convenience? Holly was walking away from the garage and back towards the house. A tawny owl started calling from the trees behind them. It seemed to have become night very quickly.

'Ma'am.'

That word again. Vera remembered a line from one of the cop shows that she pretended never to watch on the telly. *Don't call me that! I'm not the bloody queen.* She took a breath. 'Got something, Hol?'

Vera walked over to her colleague. Holly looked as insubstantial as a ghost, but Vera's shadow was very sharp in the white light. Sharp and even bigger than usual, because she was still wearing the scene suit. Holly was looking into a small pond. It was surrounded by flagstones, slippery with lichen. The water looked black and oily. Everything monochrome. Now there was a half-moon and that was white too.

In the mud at the side of the pond, only visible because one of the lamp stands stood right beside it, was a knife. Thin-bladed, with a black handle. Vera thought it was similar to the ones she'd seen in the kitchen of the flat, slotted into a wooden block.

'What do you think?' Holly sounded very pleased with herself. 'Could this be our murder weapon?'

Before Vera could answer, before she could shower Holly with the praise the DC obviously felt was her due, headlights swept across the black grass. This would be Paul Keating and the new team of CSIs. Again, the cavalry arriving just in time.

Chapter Five

Tuesday night. Annie was ready to go next door for the drinks party. They were supposed to take it in turns to host, but somehow they usually ended up at Nigel and Lorraine's house. And this was unusual, a midweek celebration because it was Lorraine's birthday. Sam had made a rabbit terrine and a pudding, a chocolate tart that managed to be rich but not too sweet. One of his signature dishes from the old days. He'd much rather cook than have his home invaded. The food was standing on the bench in the kitchen, and Sam was in the kitchen too, waiting for her. Annie wasn't sure what he made of their Valley Farm social whirl. When they'd had the restaurant she'd always done front-of-house and Sam had never seemed to need friends. Now every week it seemed there was an excuse for a party. She knew she should go downstairs to see him, because he fretted about being late. Waiting made him nervous.

Instead she went into Lizzie's room. Lizzie would be home soon, but they didn't talk about her. The silence had become a wall between them. Their daughter had been the only cause of stress in their marriage. Now, Annie thought, Sam preferred to pretend that she'd never existed.

It was almost dark and there were lights in the

valley. Strong white lights, which enabled her to see that there were cars parked along the lane close to the entrance to the Hall. Annie thought the others at Valley Farm would be interested to know about that. In the quiet days of their retirement they all loved a drama. She took Lizzie's last letter out of her bag. It was written on cheap lined paper, with the name of the prison stamped on the top. It would have been an ugly object, but for Lizzie's writing, which was strong and rather beautiful. Annie read it again. There was nothing much of significance. News from the farm, which was more like a smallholding, where the prison grew vegetables for its own use and kept a few rare breed pigs. Then: *I'm looking forward to seeing you both*. Had she ever expressed any affection for her parents before? Annie certainly couldn't remember. Lizzie had been prickly even as a baby, turning her head away when they tried to stroke her hair to make her sleep, lying rigid under the pretty quilt when they leaned over the cot to kiss her goodnight.

'Are you ready?' Sam had moved to the bottom of the stairs and was shouting up. Wanting information, not grumpy or impatient. He was the most patient man Annie had ever met.

'Just coming!' She returned the letter to her bag. When it had first arrived in the post she'd left it on the kitchen table for him to read, while she went out into the garden. If he *had* read it, he hadn't said. Perhaps he was still angry about the way Lizzie had behaved. Perhaps he only contained the fury by shutting down all his emotions.

He'd packed the food into a wicker basket and covered it with a clean tea towel. Very WI. Annie thought he'd make a much better member of the institute than her. There was a bottle of good red under his arm. Outside in the clear air they heard distant noises, shouted voices from the cars on the track.

'What's going on?' Sam sounded mildly curious.

'I don't know. I saw it from upstairs. Perhaps some TV company filming?'

'Don't tell Nigel,' Sam said. 'He'll drag us all down to be in it. You know how he loves to be the centre of attention.' He had the slow, soft accent that belonged to that part of Northumberland; sometimes she thought his voice was unique to the valley, and that he was the only one of them who truly belonged here.

They paused for a moment outside the farmhouse window and looked inside. Nigel and Lorraine were already playing host, pouring Prosecco into tall fluted glasses. They did love their fizz. The professor, another of the neighbours, was there already. A big presence. Hair still mostly dark, despite his age. Eyes that were almost black. Lorraine had once said, 'John O'Kane looks like a poet, don't you think?' Speaking with something like admiration in her voice. Annie had wondered if there could be an attraction there. Nigel was lovely to Lorraine of course, but certainly not poetic. You certainly couldn't describe him as soulful.

As they watched, the professor's wife Jan appeared in the room. She must have come in through the back door. She was wearing a dress that she might have owned when she was a student: long, with flowery prints in blue and green, frilly at the neck and very Laura Ashley. Now it didn't suit her. Her hair was wiry and curly and streaked with grey and she looked like an eccentric Edwardian grandmother. John looked at her, not exactly with disdain; more like disappointment. Annie wondered how she would feel if Sam looked at *her* like that.

Sam had already knocked at the door. He wasn't comfortable with the Valley Farm residents' habit of letting themselves into each other's houses. Nigel Lucas came to answer. He was a short man. Of all of her neighbours, Annie thought he was the hardest to get to know and wasn't sure how else to describe him. She thought he was ambitious and a social climber, but very kind.

'Come in!' Below the voices in the room beyond there was music. Jazz. A double bass, insistent like a heartbeat. 'You know you'd be welcome, even without Sam's delicious offerings.' It seemed Nigel couldn't speak without flattering, and it came to Annie that he was less confident even than Sam. Nigel was desperate to please, but Sam didn't really care what other people thought.

As they walked into the living room a phone rang in the distance. Lorraine Lucas went to answer it, shimmying to the music, the silk of her loose trousers catching the candlelight.

When she returned she stood inside the door. They fell silent and looked at her. She had that kind of presence.

'You'll never guess.' Her eyes were huge. 'That was Susan. She heard it from her father. There's been a murder in the valley.'

Chapter Six

The three detectives met up late that evening at Vera's house. It was just across the hill from Gilswick, closer than the police station in Kimmerston, and Joe was summoned to bring pizza and beer on his way home. He caught the takeaway-pizza place just before it was closing and had to pay over the odds for beer in a small convenience store. He was surprised to see that Holly was there, sitting in the chair that he thought of as his own. He couldn't remember her ever being invited to Vera's house before and she seemed uncomfortable, a bit nervous. There was a wood fire in the grate, but the logs must have been damp because it soon fizzled into nothing and Vera made no move to revive it.

Holly sat in her coat and nibbled at a slice of pizza. She'd refused the beer and now held a mug of instant coffee. He couldn't see her drink from it; perhaps the mug hadn't reached her standards of hygiene. He hadn't really wanted alcohol, either, though he took a bottle to keep Vera company. To prove his allegiance? He still felt weird, disengaged. Two murders in a valley where nothing happened, where smart people lived. He couldn't take it in.

Vera was talking. She seemed to have a personality transplant when they were in the middle of an investigation. To become younger and more energetic. She stopped grizzling about her health, her itchy skin and the aches in her legs. Joe thought that Billy Cartwright knew her too well: there was something ghoulish about her passion for her work; for suspicious death and other people's tragedies.

'We have ID on the boy in the ditch. Patrick Randle. Joe, what do we know about him?'

'He only registered with the house-sitting agency six months ago. He looked after a place in Devon for a month and then a flat in Hampstead.'

Holly looked up. 'That's in London.'

'Yes, Holly, we do know that.' Vera was at her most imperious. A pause. 'Do we know if Randle was offered the Carswell job just by chance? Or did he ask to come to Northumberland?'

Joe thought Vera had a knack for making them all defensive. 'Oh, I'm not sure. The woman I spoke to didn't seem to know the details. The agency owners were out for the evening.' He realized that he sounded like a schoolboy making excuses because he hadn't done his homework. 'But I did find out a bit more about Randle and the agency.'

'Go on.'

'The owners of the agency are a couple called Cunningham and the company's based in Surrey. As I said, Randle had only been on their books for six months. Because the house-sitters are put into a position of trust, they're all vetted pretty carefully. They need a CRB check, at least two references and an interview. Randle had no criminal record and he provided two good referees. One was the supervisor of his

PhD and the other was the priest in the village where he'd grown up.'

'Which was?'

Joe checked his notes. 'A place called Wychbold in Herefordshire.'

'Is he still a student then?' Vera finished the beer in her bottle and set it on the floor beside her chair.

'No, he recently completed his doctorate and was taking some time out, before heading straight back to academia for postdoctoral research. A bright lad apparently.'

'What subject?' This was Holly, who seemed to be feeling left out.

'Ecology.'

'Family?' Vera asked.

'Mother, still living in Herefordshire. The locals have informed her of her son's death. Randle was an only child, and his father died when he was a teenager.'

Vera smiled at him, the closest she'd get to telling him he'd done a good job. Then she lay back in her chair and raised her eyes to the ceiling, which was nicotine-brown and hadn't been decorated since her father, Hector, had died. Smoking was one of the few vices in which she didn't indulge. 'Of course it's important that we find out if Randle asked to come to Northumberland. We need to find out if he had a specific reason for being in Gilswick, or if this was random.'

There was a moment of silence.

'Could it have been a burglary gone wrong?' It had crossed Joe's mind that some of those paintings downstairs in the big house might be valuable, and there could have been bits of jewellery in the master bedroom. His Sal made him watch *Antiques Roadshow* on a Sunday night and he was always astounded at the value put on stuff he wouldn't give house-room to.

'Well, that might work, if Randle's was the body in the house and we didn't have a second corpse.' This time Vera made him feel like the stupid kid at the back of the class. 'Besides, I didn't get the feel that anything had been taken, and there was no sign of a break-in.'

Holly shot Joe one of her superior looks.

There was a moment's pause.

'Do we know anything about the older man?' Vera asked at last. 'The man in the flat. Anything from the second CSI team, Joe? Holly didn't find anything in the pockets that she could get to easily.'

'Still no ID,' Joe said. 'They've taken fingerprints, but there's no match yet. And when I left the station there'd been no missing-person report that could have been him.' He was starting to think of the older victim as the 'grey man' now too. Grey and almost invisible.

'And no information on how he actually got to the house?' Absent-mindedly Vera reached out for another beer.

'No, but we haven't canvassed the neighbours yet.' By the time they'd got a team together, most of the villagers would be in bed.

'That's a priority for the morning then. Let's talk to Percy Douglas and his daughter again. Then apparently there are some fancy barn conversions at the end of the lane. The victim wouldn't have passed them to get to the big house, but the residents might have been out and about this afternoon.'

'It couldn't have been a murder followed by suicide?' Holly was tentative, worried about being shouted down.

'You mean Randle killed the older man, then himself?' Vera didn't dismiss the idea out of hand, but she sounded sceptical. 'Have we got a cause of death for Randle yet, Joe? Dr Keating was at that locus first.'

'He says they'll do both autopsies first thing tomorrow; after working two scenes he needs a break and doesn't want to start tonight. He'll bring in a colleague to help, but he'll supervise both. He'll move on to the grey man once they've completed the forensic capture on Randle.' Joe paused for a moment. 'He said he'd go for a seven o'clock start. He hasn't got much on just now, so the place will be quiet.'

'Did he tell you how Randle died?' Vera sounded impatient. Joe thought that, unlike the pathologist, *she* wouldn't need a break. If she had her way, they'd be in the mortuary now, working through the night. 'Keating must have some idea! Was he stabbed, like the older man? I couldn't tell from the top of the bank. If he *was* stabbed, it must have been in the back, because there was no disturbance to the front of the clothes. And it looked to me as if he was placed under the cow parsley. I can't see how he could have done that himself.'

'A double-killing then?' Joe stretched. He supposed this would mean big-style overtime. Sal liked the extra money, but not the fact that he wouldn't see the bairns awake until all this was over.

'Though Hol found a knife in the pond at the big house.' Vera ignored him and continued her train of thought. She was like a tank when she got going. Relentless. Nothing would stop her. 'If we assume that it was the murder weapon and that Randle was stabbed too, it makes sense that the young man was killed somewhere near the house. Otherwise the killer would have had to go back to the house to chuck the knife in the pool. Joe, will you organize a proper search of the garden tomorrow. The big cheeses won't make a fuss about resources, not with two deaths and the press going ape.'

Joe could tell her mind was sparking and fizzing and she was still considering the possibilities. He thought she would probably be up all night, working through multiple scenarios. He hoped Keating had switched off his phone; otherwise he'd get no rest, either. She'd pick at every thread until one led to real information.

'But the only blood in the flat or the rest of the house was under the older man, so we definitely need the search team in for the garden. I can't see that Randle was killed *in* the flat.' Vera looked up at him. 'Did you get through to the Carswells, the home owners?'

'Yes, I spoke to Mrs Carswell, just before I left the station.'

'On the landline number I gave you? Not a mobile?'

He smiled, understanding the way her mind was working. 'They're definitely in Australia. There's no way they could be our murderers.'

'And? Had they met Randle?'

'No, but they had chatted to him on the phone.' Joe looked at his notes again. 'Mrs Carswell said he was well spoken and very pleasant. They were reassured that he'd be perfect for what they needed.'

'How did she take the news that we found a body in her attic?' Vera still had the energy of a hyperactive three-year-old.

How do you think she took it? A complete stranger was stabbed in her home. Joe kept his voice even. No point winding her up even more. 'I described the dead man, but she said it didn't sound like any of her acquaintances. She would ask her husband and get back to me if they had any thoughts.'

'Are they planning to come home immediately? That'd make life complicated. It's useful to have the big house empty.'

'Nah. Their son's girlfriend's expecting a baby. The first grandchild. They'll stay on until after the birth.'

Vera nodded.

Joe shut his notebook and then remembered something else. 'She said not to ask Susan to look after the dogs. Apparently the woman hates them, but she's the best cleaner they've ever had and they don't want to lose her. Mrs Carswell said that there's a family in one of the barn conversions – Professor and Mrs O'Kane – who'd take the dogs in. I've spoken to the team on the ground and asked them to sort it out.'

Joe stood up and made it clear he was planning to leave. His toddler was going through a nocturnal phase and, though she didn't work outside the home, Sal made it quite clear that he should take his turn. He was shattered already.

Vera finished her beer and set her glass on the table in front of her. 'So we have three priorities for tomorrow.' She held up a fat thumb and two fingers of her right hand in order, as if she was counting. 'We need to find out where Randle was killed, and at least get a name for the older man. And talk to the neighbours in the valley.'

Holly seemed relieved that Joe was making a move and started packing her iPad into her bag. He knew she thought this sort of discussion was a waste of time and preferred structured briefings in the police station. He sometimes wondered why she wanted to rush home. As far as he knew, there was nobody waiting for her. He'd never been invited into her flat in Gosforth, but she hadn't mentioned a partner. Her sexuality was the subject of curiosity at the station, but maybe that was only because she'd made it clear that she didn't welcome advances from male colleagues.

Vera got to her feet to see them out. The empty pizza boxes were on the floor and she picked up a scrap of crust from one of them and stuck it in her mouth. 'Are you okay to do the post-mortems with me, Hol?'

'Yes, sure.'

Joe was glad not to have the early start, but felt abandoned. Vera usually liked him with her in the mortuary. She'd once said that Holly was like a puppy needing a run. 'All that energy. I find it distracting. And it doesn't feel respectful in the presence of a corpse.'

They stood for a moment with the door open. Below them a string of lights marked the village that represented Vera's nearest civilization. They'd nearly reached the cars when Vera shouted after them, 'And for Christ's sake, Joe, get a decent night's sleep. You're no good to me looking like a washed-out dishcloth.'

He didn't like to say that it would be his turn with

his youngest child, if she decided to wake in the night. Vera might be all for gender equality at work, but she thought Sal's sole purpose in life was to prepare *him* for work with her.

In the end the toddler slept well until nearly six. Then Joe made coffee and switched on the television. He'd wake Sal at seven and still get to the police station before Vera and Holly returned from the post-mortem. He took his coffee into the lounge. The bairn was on the carpet playing with a stack of blocks. Happy as Larry, so Joe switched from CBeebies to the breakfast news to see if there was anything on the Gilswick double-murder. Nothing on the national news, and only a brief piece on the local. It would have been too late the night before for the press office to get out a media release. He carried on watching anyway. There was a feature about immigration, a reporter in the street asking passers-by what they thought about border controls. Usually the journalist got the answers he was hoping for: bluster and bigotry. As Joe looked, the reporter approached a man walking down the pavement towards him. The man just shook his head and hurried on, ignoring the fact that the reporter was calling after him, 'Surely you must have an opinion, sir.'

Joe grabbed the remote, pressed a button to pause the piece and then played it again. No doubt; the bloke who'd refused to answer the journalist's question was their second victim, the middle-aged man in the grey suit. He thought Holly would be a Radio 4 person. She might not even own a television, and anyway she'd be in the hospital, helping Paul Keating with the forensic capture of Patrick Randle's body. Holly wouldn't be the person to deliver news to the boss that might lead them to their older victim's identity. The thought cheered him up and carried him through the changing of a stinking nappy.

Chapter Seven

Vera stood in the mortuary with Holly, Billy Cartwright and Paul Keating. Randle was lying on the stainless-steel table and, as his clothes were cut away, Billy was bagging them. Holly was taking notes. Vera was trying to contain her impatience. She understood that Keating was meticulous and hated being forced into speculation, but still she found this waiting for a cause of death impossible. She would have preferred to be with the search team in the valley at Gilswick, looking for the place where Randle had died. Or in Percy's bungalow, talking to him about life in the tiny community, asking if he'd seen her grey man the day before.

But she tried to focus. Patrick Randle's clothes would tell them something about the man, and Holly knew all about clothes. 'What do you think, Hol? Can we tell the sort of chap he was by what he's wearing?'

The DC looked up from her notebook. She always seemed surprised when Vera asked her opinion. 'I'm not sure. Waxed jacket. Barbour. That wouldn't be cheap. It's a good-quality shirt, but something that an older man might wear in the country. Is that a stain on the back?' Billy Cartwright shifted the clear plastic bag so that they could all see. 'It's certainly well worn and rubbed at the neck. On top of that, a jumper. Round-necked. Hand-knitted.'

'Is it?' Vera hadn't noticed and she was surprised. When she'd been growing up sometimes bairns wore hand-made clothes, but it wasn't so common for adults. These days she couldn't remember the last time she'd seen a man in a hand-knitted top.

Holly continued. 'Jeans. Levis. Underwear from M&S. Shoes. Very good-quality, leather soles as well as leather uppers. Well polished and well looked after.'

'So what does that tell us, Hol? A typical student, do we think? Doesn't sound like it to me.'

'It depends which university he went to. Maybe he'd fit into one of the smarter ones.' She sounded unsure.

'Oxford or Cambridge, do you think? Joe didn't tell us where he did his PhD.' Vera was feeling out of her depth. When she was young, all students had looked the same – as if they'd bought their clothes from the church jumble sale. 'We'll get Joe to find out.' Her frustration spilled over. 'Any chance of getting to the cause of death, Doctor? Sometime this month would be good.'

Keating looked up from his work. 'Patience, Inspector.' Friendly enough. 'The younger man's death was caused by a blunt-force trauma blow to the head. I think one blow, because of the lack of spatter on the clothes. There's just that small stain on the shirt.'

'And you couldn't tell me this last night? You must have been able to tell he'd not been stabbed, as soon as you moved the body.'

Keating didn't answer immediately. 'I thought you deserved your beauty sleep, Inspector.'

His assistant muffled a giggle. There was an awkward silence. Vera continued, 'But there's no stain on the jumper.'

'Apparently not.'

'So he was just wearing a shirt when he was attacked?' She was running through various scenarios to explain the fact. Why would a killer add extra clothes to the victim's body after death?

'I think that's a logical assumption.'

'Why was one victim stabbed and the other bludgeoned to death?' Vera's mind was racing. 'If they were both killed at the same time, wouldn't the same weapon be used?' She turned to the pathologist. 'I'm assuming they both were killed at the same time.'

Keating shrugged. 'You should know by now that we can't pin down the time of death with that kind of pinpoint accuracy.'

'But Randle might have been killed in the flat, with the middle-aged man?'

'That's entirely possible.' This time Billy Cartwright joined in. 'The search team only made a start yesterday. We're stretched. Of course we'll be checking for blood stains, anything that places Randle there after his death.'

But I didn't see anything. There was no blood, except under the older man.

'Then why move him!' She realized the words had come out as a cry. 'Why dress him up in a jumper and a jacket and risk being seen carrying him into the ditch?'

'I do bodies,' Keating said, 'not mind-reading. I'm afraid I can't answer that for you.'

'And I'm not saying that Randle *was* killed in the

flat in the big house.' Billy Cartwright seemed to be enjoying her discomfort. 'Not yet. Just that it is a possibility.'

'Can you tell me anything about the knife Hol found in the pond?' Vera thought this was just too complicated. She'd assumed a double-murder, both men killed with the same knife.

'We're pretty sure it's one of a set from the kitchen in the flat. You noticed yourself that one was missing from the block on the counter. We can tell you later if it matches the wounds on the older man.'

'So the killer didn't come prepared,' Vera said. 'Not into the flat, at least.' Possibilities flashed into her mind, but nothing made sense.

Later they were in the briefing room at Kimmerston. Vera had left Holly to be present at the second post-mortem. There were already photos on the whiteboard: close-ups of Patrick Randle and of the chap Vera called the 'grey man'. Pictures of the ditch and its vegetation, the outside of the manor house and inside Randle's flat. On the desks where the team was sitting a pile of bacon sandwiches, half-eaten, and torn sachets of brown sauce. Bodies never put Vera off her food.

'We know nothing about this man.' Pointing to the second victim. 'Nobody's got in touch overnight to report him missing. I've just checked. And precious little about this one.' Jabbing a ruler at Randle. 'Joe, have we got a bit more from the agency?'

'It seems Randle *did* request a placement in Northumberland when he first joined up with them, so they put him in for the Carswell job and gave him two short-term contracts while he was waiting to start it.'

'Do we know why he was interested in coming to Northumberland?' It seemed to Vera that this made the killing less likely to be random, or the work of some delusional mad person.

'He told the agency he was interested in natural history and this was an area he hadn't explored yet.'

'I suppose that could be true. If he had an ecology degree.' But Vera thought the request lay at the heart of the case. They needed to know exactly what had brought Randle north.

'I've spoken to the mother.' Joe's voice was sombre. He was a great family man, a bit too soft-hearted for a policeman, in Vera's opinion; but then she thought Holly was heartless, so perhaps she was never pleased.

'And?'

'She's older than I was expecting, in her late sixties. She said Patrick came when she'd given up having another child. He read directly from his notes. "But not an afterthought – a consolation."'

'I thought he was an only son.' Charlie looked up from his sandwich.

Vera gave a slow clap of her hands. 'So you're awake after all. And listening! I was wondering.'

'There was another boy,' Joe said. 'Simon. He'd have been nineteen years older than Patrick. Apparently he committed suicide. When he was a student.'

'Oh,' Vera was moved almost to tears. 'The poor woman.'

'Patrick did his first degree in York and his Masters and his PhD in Exeter.'

'Not one of the posh ones then?'

'Posh enough,' Joe said. 'Apparently. I asked Sal. She's already been reading up on unis. We've got high hopes for our Jess.' There was a moment of silence and Joe looked up at Vera. 'The mother would like to come up to view the body.'

'Oh,' Vera said again. She thought that would be a job for Joe. He was good at all the touchy-feely stuff and he'd know how to handle it. Though maybe Holly needed the practice. 'Well, I suppose that saves us having to make the trek down to chat to her.'

Vera perched on a desk, her fat legs swinging. She was wearing square lace-up shoes and her feet banged against the table leg. She was aware that the team was waiting for her to speak. 'So we're starting to build up a picture of the youngest victim, but we still don't know anything about the older man.'

Joe stood up. She realized he wanted them all to take notice of him, and that wasn't like Joe. He waited until he had their full attention before he spoke. 'We know where he was yesterday morning.'

Vera turned slowly to face him. She stopped her legs from swinging. 'And where was that?'

'Kimmerston Front Street. A BBC *Look North* reporter was canvassing opinion about immigration from the EU, and our second victim was one of the people stopped.'

'And you know this how, Joe?'

'I saw him on breakfast telly and called the BBC in Newcastle as soon as I got in. The reporter isn't at his desk yet, but they could tell me where the film was made.' Joe tried not to grin.

Vera began to chuckle. 'You spawny git, Joe Ashworth. Better to be lucky than to be smart any time. I don't suppose the reporter asked for his name?'

'I don't know yet, but I'll soon find out.'

Chapter Eight

Back at his desk, Joe called the BBC in Newcastle and was put through to the reporter, who sounded older and more experienced than he'd looked on the screen.

'So you're saying that one of the guys I interviewed was the victim in the Gilswick double-murder?' In his head the man would be imagining a spot on the national television news. Fame at last.

'That's not information that we'd like to make public at this point. Not until we can be sure of his identification, and his family have been informed.'

'Of course.' So the man was responsible at least. He knew he'd still be able to use the clip, once they gave permission, and he'd get credited then.

Joe took a deep breath. 'Did you take his name?'

'I didn't get a chance. I don't like to hassle people and I wouldn't have spoken to him, but he walked straight towards me on the pavement. I thought he must be interested in getting his face on the TV, and most of the punters I'd spoken to were younger, so he'd be a good contrast. Maybe bring a different perspective. That was why I pushed it, when he refused to engage.'

'Why did he approach you then, if he didn't want to be interviewed?' Anyone in the street with a clipboard and Joe immediately crossed to the other side.

'I don't think he noticed me. He seemed completely preoccupied, wrapped up in thoughts of his own. I think he was startled when I spoke to him.'

'Is there anything else you can tell me?' Joe was starting to think that he wasn't being so lucky after all.

'He walked away up Front Street and I'm fairly sure that he went into an office on the corner.'

Joe shut his eyes and pictured the scene. Front Street had a row of traditional shops and then there was a newer place. Ugly. Glass and concrete, with the concrete disfigured with damp. Pale-green paint. It had a shop with cards in the window, and inside a row of computers that looked more like gaming machines. And perhaps getting work in Kimmerston was a bit of a lottery. 'The Job Centre?'

'Of course! That's it. Yes, he went into the Job Centre.'

Joe thought his luck must have held out after all. If the man was a claimant, they'd have all his details on file. And if he'd made an appointment or spoken to an officer, it would be easy enough to get a name. Though it was more likely, Joe thought, remembering the grey suit and the old-fashioned specs, that their victim worked there. He looked like the stereotypical civil servant.

'What time were you recording in Kimmerston?'

'I started just after midday. We waited for the clock on the market square to finish chiming before we began. Finished about thirty minutes later. We didn't need much to go with the news report.'

So their grey man could have been out of the office for his lunch-break. Joe pulled his jacket from the back of the chair and went out. The Job Centre was only five minutes away and Vera always said that face-to-face interviews were more valuable than the phone. He took with him the head-shot of the victim.

It was another sunny day. In the street a couple of young mothers sat at tables outside the coffee shop in the square, chatting as toddlers in buggies snoozed. Elderly women were taking their time shopping, stopping to greet friends and catch up on gossip.

In the Job Centre Joe waited in the short queue at reception. A woman scarcely looked away from her screen. 'Yes?'

He held out his warrant card. 'I'd like to speak to a manager.'

'Oh.' She scurried off. Joe looked around and thought the place was depressing. Lots of grey people. An overweight man studied one of the computer screens and walked out, apparently disappointed, letting the door slam behind him.

A woman with a baby in a buggy was having an argument with a member of staff. 'So what am I supposed to do about childcare?'

'I'm sorry.' The officer was young and seemed close to tears. 'I don't make the rules.'

Not much of the joys of spring here.

A middle-aged woman appeared through the door that said *Staff Only*. 'Come through.' Brusque, no wasted words. Well-cut hair, a black pencil skirt and black jacket. A woman with ambition. She led him through a large open-plan office and into an interview room.

'How can I help?' The tone of her voice made it clear that her time was precious.

'I wonder if you can tell me who this man is?' He laid the photograph of the grey man on the desk in front of her.

He was so certain that the grey man had been a colleague that he expected an immediate response. But her only response was a question. 'Why do you want to know?'

'We suspect that he might have been the victim of an incident last night, and we need to inform his family.' *Incident*, he thought. *A useful catch-all word.*

'I don't recognize him.' The woman was staring at the photo. 'But I don't spend much time on the floor. You'd need to ask the customer-service staff.'

'He doesn't work here?'

'Oh no!' As if it were impossible that someone working in the Job Centre could be involved in any sort of incident at all.

Downstairs the war of attrition between the young officer and the single mother was continuing, though it seemed to be reaching a climax. 'I can't be doing with all this now, you stupid cow – I need to get the bairn to the health visitor, or they'll have the social onto me for neglect.' The mother was screaming at the top of her voice, her face red with anger and embarrassment. Suddenly she stood up and walked out.

In the room there was no reaction at all, except for a small sigh of relief from the young officer. Joe approached her. 'Is it always like that?'

'Nah,' the woman grinned. 'This is one of the quiet days. And to think I joined up because I thought I could make a difference.'

He introduced himself and then held out the photograph. 'Do you recognize this man? He was in yesterday lunchtime.'

'That's Martin Benton.' She didn't have any curiosity at all about why Joe would want to know. 'He's just been assessed as fit to work, after a long time on invalidity benefit. We've been helping him back to the job market.'

'He had an appointment with you yesterday?'

'Yes, the initial interview, so I could explain the process and the responsibilities of the jobseeker. But when he came in he'd already decided to take the self-employment route.'

'Did he say what work he intended to do?'

'I don't think so, and really it wasn't relevant for our purposes. He'd decided not to claim benefit. That was all we needed to know.'

'But you'll still hold all his details. His address and previous work record.'

'I'm not sure I can give you that information. Data protection.' The room was quiet now and the sun was streaming through the windows, making it feel very hot.

'Well, I can get a warrant of course, but your supervisor said you'd be able to help.' Joe nodded towards the door that said *Staff Only*. He thought the people upstairs in the open-plan office had it easy.

The young woman shrugged, tapped a few keys and hit the print button. 'I'm leaving anyway,' she said. 'So sod it – it's their responsibility. I'm going back to uni to do a social-work course.'

'This'll be good practice.'

'Aye,' she said. 'That's what I thought.'

She held out two printed sheets.

In the cafe on the square Joe drank milky coffee and read the life history of Martin Benton. The facts, at least. It seemed to Joe that there was little here to bring the man back to life. He'd been forty-eight when he died and he lived in a suburb of Kimmerston. He'd gained eight GCSEs at reasonable grades and three A levels, then got a degree in maths from Northumbria University. He'd done a postgraduate teaching year and had worked in a number of local high schools for fifteen years. There was no explanation for his decision to leave teaching. His most recent employment had been three years before, when he'd worked as an admin officer for a small charity. After that he'd been registered for invalidity benefit until, under the new regime, he'd been assessed as fit for work.

There were some gaps in Benton's employment record: a couple between teaching posts, and a longer spell before he began work for the charity. If he'd been a different kind of man, Joe would have suspected criminal activity. Spent spells in prison wouldn't necessarily have to be declared. His record could be checked, but it seemed unlikely. Qualified maths teachers didn't usually become petty criminals.

There were no details of Benton's family history. Joe found himself hoping that in the house in Laurel Avenue there would be a wife waiting for him – that the grey man hadn't been a loner. He pictured someone soft and comfortable, with an easy smile, and began to imagine reasons why she might not have reported her husband missing the night before. Then he told himself that such speculation was ridiculous and he should check out the address to see.

Laurel Avenue was a quiet terrace on a hill on the edge of the town. Neat little Edwardian houses with identical porches, and a footpath that separated the homes from tiny gardens. At the back, yards and a narrow street for cars and bins. Joe preferred new houses that took no maintenance, but he could see the attraction of living here. The kids could play out, because there was no traffic at the front, and there was a view of the hills. It felt as if you could be in a village. Some of the gardens were planted with raised beds of salad leaves, wigwams for runner beans, but number twelve held the traditional square of grass with flowerbeds round the edges. The lawn could have done with a cut, but the place wasn't overgrown or neglected. At the bottom of the garden stood a square plywood box that, from a distance, Joe took to be a hutch for a small pet. Curiosity took him over the grass to look, but there was no animal inside; instead an aluminium funnel and a large bulb. Joe was none the wiser.

There were three steps up to the front door. He rang the bell and waited. Pressed it again and listened to make sure that it was working. No response. Perhaps the comfortable wife of his imagination was out at work.

He was thinking he'd go round to the back and see if he could find a way in, without breaking a window, when a neighbour appeared. Elderly, plump. White hair in tight curls. She looked like Benton's imaginary wife, but thirty years older.

'Martin's not in.'

Joe stepped over the low wall that separated her front step from number twelve. 'Has he got any family?'

'Who wants to know?' She gave him a lovely smile, but her words were sharp.

'Police.'

'Come in then, and we can talk. They're a nebby lot round here.' Another smile. 'As you can see. I'm Kitty Richardson.'

Inside the place was polished. Every surface in the small living room gleamed in the sun that came through the bay window and smelled of lavender. In a corner a yellow budgie sat on a perch in a cage on a stand. Joe thought little had been changed since the house was built.

'You've been here a while?'

'Since we were first married.' She settled on a high-backed chair facing the television and nodded for him to take the sofa. 'My Arthur passed away on my seventieth birthday, but I stayed on. No point moving when my friends are all here.' She nodded towards the partition wall that separated her house from Benton's. 'Elsie was like a sister to me.' A pause, then a confession. 'When she went, I missed her more than I did Arthur.'

'And Elsie was?' The reflected light was making him blink.

'Martin's mam, of course.'

'Did he always live with his mother?'

'On and off.' She looked up at him. 'He was never a strong man. Always had trouble with his nerves.' There was a moment's silence. The budgie squawked. 'What's he done?'

'Nothing.' Joe hesitated and then thought that the news would get out soon enough. 'Martin's dead. He died in suspicious circumstances. I need to notify his next of kin. And get into the house, if I can.'

'Did he kill himself?'

Joe thought of the body that had been lying on the polished wooden floor in the attic of the big house. The slashes of the knife ripping at the shirt, and through the skin and bone. That certainly hadn't been the result of suicide. 'No!'

'It wouldn't have been surprising,' Kitty said. 'Elsie didn't go into details, but I think he tried. Once or twice.' She paused. 'I don't know about next of kin. His father died just before Elsie. There weren't any other children.' She looked up. 'Sad, isn't it? I can't think of any relative who might be interested.'

'Can you tell me about him?' A Vera question, open-ended.

'He was one of those quiet, sickly bairns. I was a nursery nurse before I married and I knew the sort. Given to asthma and feeling sorry for himself. It didn't help that he was an only child and his mother loved the bones of him.' She hesitated and Joe knew better than to jump in with another question. 'He's always been a loner. Never had a woman, as far as I know.' A pause, a sly look and a grin to show how enlightened she was. 'Or a man. He was canny enough, though. Kind. He took other people's problems to heart. He was at the front door every five minutes collecting for some charity or other.'

'Where did he live when he wasn't at home?'

'I believe he got himself a flat in Newcastle when he did his teacher training. I thought it would be the making of him. He'd have pals from the college and he might meet a nice lass. But it didn't last and he was soon home.'

'He was a teacher?'

'Elsie's idea. Her man had been down the pit and she didn't want manual work for her boy. I never thought he'd have the constitution for teaching, though, not with the way bairns are these days.'

'And he went along with the idea?' Joe couldn't imagine his children doing anything he suggested without a battle.

Kitty shot him a glance. 'That was part of his problem. He'd never been brought up to think for himself.'

'But he stuck at teaching for quite a long time.'

'Aye, but the stress of it was killing him and he moved around a lot. Every time he changed jobs his mother had an excuse: the head teacher didn't like him, or they were a cliquey bunch in the staffroom. Nothing was ever Martin's fault. Truth was he just didn't have the personality to control the classes.' She sighed. 'One of my pals had a grandson in his class. Apparently it was a riot. But they're short of qualified maths teachers, aren't they, so he always seemed to get a job. He never learned to drive, but he had a bike and he got to work on that.' She paused.

'Did he still have a bike?' Joe was wondering if that was how he'd got to Gilswick the day before. It'd be quite a stretch, but not impossible if you were used to riding long distances.'

'He did. He went out on it yesterday, early afternoon, and he never came back.' She looked guilty. 'That's why I was looking out when you turned up. I was wondering if I should tell someone he wasn't home. But why would anyone be worried? A grown-up man.' Another pause. 'But Elsie would have been worried. She'd have had the police out as soon as it got dark.' A young woman pushing a buggy walked past the window and Kitty waved as if they were old friends.

'You said Martin lived at home "on and off". What did you mean by that?'

She looked awkward. 'He spent a bit of time in hospital. St David's. You must know it.'

St David's. The psychiatric hospital on the outskirts of Kimmerston. The name still spoken in a hushed tone. When Joe had been growing up it had been a place of legend. The ogre's castle. 'If you don't stop playing up, Joe Ashworth, you'll end up in St Davey's.' He nodded.

Kitty went on. 'I don't think he minded it so much in there, and it gave his mam a break, whatever she said. They gave him pills and they seemed to work for a while, but then he'd get poorly again. Depressed. Maybe he stopped taking the medication. I don't think it helped him being next door with Elsie fussing all over him, treating him like a bairn. She liked it when he was off sick from work. He was company for her. I said so a few times, but she didn't like me interfering and I decided it wasn't worth falling out over.'

'How did Martin get on after his mother died?' Joe wondered what that must be like: to be sheltered and pampered and then find yourself alone, with the freedom to make decisions for yourself. It'd surely blow the mind even of a sane man.

'He had a bit of a breakdown,' Kitty said, 'and ended up in hospital again. I think he realized he was ill and took himself off to the doctor. Since he's been back he's seemed better than I've known him for years. He gets a bit of company from some lad that visits every couple of weeks.' She broke off. 'I suppose he's the closest Martin had to a friend – you'll need to tell him.'

'Who was he, the visitor? A community psychiatric nurse?'

Kitty shook her head. 'Martin had one of those when he first came out of hospital. A lass. Didn't look much like a nurse to me. Fishnet tights and a skirt that barely covered her behind. Enough to give a healthy man palpitations.'

'So who was the lad?' Joe was starting to feel that he was losing the plot.

'Name of Frank. Maybe he was a teacher with Martin, though he didn't look like a teacher. Big lad. Tattoos. Or perhaps they met in hospital.'

'Do you have a second name for him?'

Kitty shook her head.

'According to the Job Centre, Martin was planning to become self-employed rather than go on Jobseeker's Allowance. Any idea what that was about?' Joe thought maybe Benton had set up as a private tutor. There was plenty of call for people to give a bit of extra coaching, especially in maths. And surely it'd be easier to deal with one child than a rowdy classroom. But why would that have taken him to the big house at Gilswick? There were no kids there.

'I never really talked to him once Elsie died,' Kitty said. 'He was always pleasant enough. Took in my parcels if I missed the postman. A good neighbour. But if he confided in anyone, it wasn't me.' She paused.

'He wouldn't have been completely without money, if they stopped his benefit. Elsie and him never spent much at all, and his father left him a little nest egg. But maybe he felt he wanted to do his own thing – after years of trying to please his mother, maybe he wanted a bit of independence.'

Kitty gave Joe a key to the back door of Benton's house. She'd had it since Elsie had died. Joe stood in the Benton yard and phoned Vera. 'What do you want me to do?'

There was a pause. 'Well, it's not a murder scene, is it? We know Benton was killed in the flat at Gilswick Hall. We'll get the CSIs into his house as soon as they can make it, but it wouldn't hurt for you to have a look first. I just need something to link Benton to Randle, and we've got bugger-all at the moment.'

He waited before opening the door and took time to look around the yard. A washing line with a shirt and a pair of socks dangling in the sunshine. Did that mean Benton was planning to come back the night before, to take them in? Joe had never done his own washing, but Sal would never leave laundry out overnight. A shed, very tidy. Tools hanging on nails, a stepladder. In the yard a couple of pots with daffs, dying now.

Joe unlocked the door and stepped into a back kitchen. And back into time and his nana's house. A sink and a twin-tub washing machine. Then a step into the kitchen proper. If Benton had been pampered by his mother, there was no sign here that he hadn't been able to care for himself. No dirty pots. The small gas cooker was so clean that it shone, and a tea towel had been folded on the rail. He opened the elderly fridge to find a carton of milk, four eggs and a supermarket packet of bacon. Then a row of small jars. All clean and all empty. Joe stared at them for a moment, but couldn't think what they might be for. The house was long and narrow and seemed squashed by the houses on either side. At this point the only light came from the small scullery window.

He walked through to a dining room, gloomy and stale. Joe wanted to open a window and let in some air. A dark wood table and four matching chairs and a sideboard. Clean enough, but dusty. There was a gas fire in a tiled surround that looked so old Joe wouldn't have wanted to try lighting it. None of the rooms had central heating. He thought that this room hadn't been used since Elsie had died. Maybe not even before that.

Opening the door to the small living room, Joe blinked because of the sudden light. The sun flooded in, as it had in Kitty's house. No sofa, but two chairs covered in a shiny floral pattern facing a large TV. Nothing unusual. Nothing to add character to the man who'd spent his life here. Had it been as if he was a lodger in his mother's house, frightened of upsetting her, of disturbing the family home?

Upstairs. The door ahead of Joe opened into a bathroom. Deep enamel bath, stained and chipped. No shower. To the left, a separate lavatory. There were three small bedrooms. The largest held a double bed, pink candlewick quilt and the smell of old woman. Talcum powder and lavender, on top of something less pleasant. And next to the bed there *was* still a commode with a social-services stamp on the back. Joe shut the door quickly. Let the CSIs check in there.

It seemed that Martin Benton had taken the other bedrooms for his use. The smaller one was just big enough for a single bed, small wardrobe and chest of drawers. The bed was made. Sheets and blankets, army-style. The clothes in the chest and the wardrobe were mass-produced. What struck Joe as strange was that they were all very similar. Jogging bottoms, all black. Polo shirts. Two grey fleeces. Two pairs of trousers of the sort that old men wear to work and a few folded shirts, all white. It seemed that Benton had only possessed one suit and he'd been wearing it when he died. Why had he been wearing his suit for his trip to Gilswick? It suggested something formal. An interview? Had there been a parent in Gilswick village, wanting him to tutor a child? That still couldn't explain his presence in the valley. And would Benton really have cycled all the way from Kimmerston to Gilswick in his suit? Joe thought they still needed to find out how he'd made his way to the big house.

The second room looked out over the yard and was a revelation. It was kitted out like an office: a large desk against one wall, one main computer and a laptop. Next to the window was a filing cabinet and on a shelf above the desk a row of reference books and academic textbooks, all related not to maths, but to natural history. The impression was more of a gallery than an office. The walls were white and hung with photographs. Beautiful photographs of butterflies, moths and other insects, all blown up so that every detail could be seen. Joe's attention was caught by a picture of a caterpillar on a laurel leaf. Every vein on the leaf was sharp and clear. There was a raindrop, a shimmering prism like a tear. It seemed to Joe that if Benton had intended to set up his own business, it would surely have been as a photographer. A camera that Joe guessed had taken up six months' invalidity benefit was hidden in one of the filing-cabinet drawers.

If Benton had been in Gilswick to take photographs of the house or the gardens, why hadn't he taken his camera?

The camera was in the bottom drawer of the filing cabinet; the other two drawers were conventionally arranged. Each drop-file was neatly labelled with a letter of the alphabet, but all of them were empty. Joe suddenly felt a wave of depression. He imagined Benton preparing his office for business, excited perhaps; but he had been killed before he could start out. If he'd gone to the big house for work, it must have been the first contract of his self-employment and might have marked a turning point in his life. Joe checked the desk for a mobile phone. There was nothing. The landline phone was in the hall downstairs. No messages. He dialled 1471 and a disembodied voice gave him a mobile number. He made a note of it and then went outside into the sunshine, closing the door carefully behind him.

Kitty was still sitting in her bay window. He tapped on her door and she answered at once.

'Do you know what that contraption is, at the bottom of Martin's garden?'

'Oh, aye,' she said. 'That's his moth trap.'

Chapter Nine

When Holly got back from the post-mortem, Vera left her in the police station and headed out to Gilswick. She knew that was the wrong way round, and that she should be the person coordinating the action from a desk while her subordinate should be doing the legwork. But it was spring and being the boss should carry some perks. With the first real sunshine of the year, she couldn't bear to be inside. She'd parked outside the big house and was watching the search team walking through the woodland between the road and the manor when Joe phoned to say that he'd got a name for the grey man. Martin Benton. An anonymous kind of name for an anonymous man.

She ended the call, waited for a moment and then started the car. It was time to get to know the other residents of the valley. The lane wound past Percy Douglas's bungalow and ended in a small development. Three houses converted from a farmhouse and two barns. Vera supposed that the buildings had once been a part of the Carswell estate. All over the county farm tenancies were being relinquished and buildings converted to residential use. It was hard to make a living in the hills.

All the houses faced into a paved square, which

had probably once been the farmyard. The stone farmhouse had a small front garden, with more land at the back; the barn conversions led straight onto the yard. Fancy cars were parked outside each of them. There was a view of the valley and the hills beyond. It would be as exposed as Vera's place in the winter and she wondered how all the glass in the barns stood up to the weather. Would you get a window cleaner to come all the way out here? She thought someone must have seen her car coming along the track, and she stayed in the Land Rover for a moment. There were three households here and she needed to speak to the most inquisitive resident. She didn't have to wait for long.

The door of the farmhouse opened and a squat man appeared. Late fifties or early sixties. A bit of a beer belly and a rolling gait that made her think of a sailor. He came up to her and she opened the car door to greet him.

'Can I help you?' A southern English voice. Not posh. Jovial enough, but making it plain all the same that she'd strayed onto private property.

She smiled. 'I hope so, pet. I'm after information.' Laying on the accent, because she'd taken an irrational dislike to him and wanted to mark this out as her territory, not his. She climbed out of the vehicle. 'Inspector Vera Stanhope. Northumbria Police.'

'Ah, we saw all the activity at the Hall.' His manner had changed from suspicion to interest. He'd be one of those ghouls who'd want all the details of the killings. He held out his hand. 'Nigel Lucas.'

'You'll have heard rumours, no doubt.'

'Well, we got a phone call from Susan Savage, old

Percy's daughter, last night and she said that the Carswells' house-sitter had been found dead in the ditch. I must admit we went upstairs to look at what was going on down by the burn.' Vera wanted to slap him. And remind him that the lad had a mother who was grieving for him.

'I've got a few questions,' she said. 'Can I come in?'

'Of course, Inspector.'

The interior of the house had been torn apart and rebuilt. Once there would have been small rooms, easy to heat. Now there was one L-shaped open-plan space. The door opened into one of those kitchens that you'd be scared to cook or eat in. All granite and stainless steel, more laboratory than home. Vera found herself wondering where they kept their boots and the vacuum cleaner. There must be hidden storage space and she was distracted, looking for where it might be. But Lucas was leading her on through an arch into a living space, the width of the house, where the original flagstone floor was scattered with rugs. The walls were eggshell blue and covered with paintings. Watercolours. Vera recognized some of the scenes as local. There was a giant television screen, a glass coffee table and two white leather sofas. Not much else. She sat on one of the sofas and hoped she wouldn't leave a mark from her greasy coat when she stood up. Or at least that nobody would notice.

'Can I get you something to drink, Inspector?'

'I'm on duty.' She wondered why she couldn't be more gracious, why she found the man so intensely irritating.

He gave a little laugh. 'I wasn't thinking of alcohol. It's not quite wine o'clock, even in the Lucas household. And we had a bit of a session here last night. But I could do you a coffee.'

'Thank you,' she said. 'That would be lovely.'

The man shouted up the polished wooden stairs that twisted from a corner of the room. 'Lorraine, we've got a guest. Are you ready for a break?'

There was a muffled reply.

'My wife,' he said. 'She took up watercolours again when we retired, and she's ever so good – she did all these . . .' He nodded at the walls. 'But she usually takes a breather at about this time.' He sounded very proud of his wife, and for the first time Vera felt herself soften. *Good God, woman, don't despise the man because of the way he's decorated his house. You're turning into a snob, like your father.* Hector was always sneering about the nouveaux riches who bought property in the country without understanding its ways.

Lorraine turned out to be slender and pale, with high cheekbones and hair that was almost white. Vera thought she was younger than her husband by at least ten years. She wore jeans and sandals and a loose silk top. Was that the style they called hippy-chic? Silver earrings. Make-up. Vera wondered if she was on her way out to a special lunch or if she always made the effort. It was clear that her husband doted on her. Vera thought for a moment that *she* might have found a man if she'd scrubbed up a bit better, then decided that no man was worth the time it took to plaster stuff on your face in the morning, when you could have an extra cup of tea instead.

'How can we help you, Inspector?' Lorraine had the same accent as the husband, but gentler. He'd disappeared into the kitchen and there was the sound of grinding beans, cups being put onto a tray. A performance for the audience on the leather sofa.

'Patrick Randle . . .' Vera looked at her and waited. No response. 'He was house-sitting for the Carswells.'

'Ah yes.' A small frown to indicate sympathy. 'Susan said there'd been an accident and that he was dead. Terrible.'

'Someone killed him. Hit him over the head with a blunt instrument.'

Lorraine looked horrified. Vera thought she was upset not so much by the young man's murder as by the fact that Vera had been so forthright.

'Percy found him in the ditch by the lane,' Vera went on, 'and then there was another body in the attic flat in the big house. A middle-aged man named Martin Benton. Ring any bells?'

Lorraine shook her head slowly. 'We moved here to escape all that. Robberies. Violence. We spent all our lives in the city, and when we retired we thought: "Why not live the dream?" We'd been to Northumberland on holiday. We put in an offer on this place online. We hadn't even seen it then.'

Vera was tempted to say that they'd have been unlikely to come across a double-murder even in the city, but decided that wouldn't help. 'How long have you lived here?'

'Two years. It's taken us this long to get it as we want it. Nigel project-managed it all himself. He had his own business, with offices all over the South. Lucas Security. You've probably heard of it. He's used to running a big show, so this was a doddle.'

So he got craftspeople in and bossed them around. 'And you don't get bored?'

Nigel walked in then, carrying a tray with a coffee pot, a milk jug and a plate of home-made biscuits. *You must be bored, pet. Someone like you doesn't bake biscuits unless you need to fill your day.*

Lorraine was about to answer, but Nigel got in first. 'We don't have time to be bored, Inspector. There's something going on in the valley every day. Life's one big impromptu party, here in the farm conversions. One of our neighbours calls us "the retired hedonists' club". We all took early retirement. Kids flown the nest. Those of us who had kids . . . We all have reasonable occupational or private pensions. This is the time of life when we can enjoy ourselves.'

Lorraine had been staring out of the window, but looked back into the room. 'Perhaps we shouldn't speak like that, Nige. Not when there's been a murder.' She paused. 'Two murders. The inspector says they found another body in the house-sitter's flat.'

There was a moment of silence. Vera thought they were trying to find a suitable response. Something tasteful, after Nigel's boast of indulgent pleasures. She almost felt sorry for them.

'The man in the big house was middle-aged,' she said. 'Grey hair. Glasses. His name was Martin Benton. Does that mean anything to you?'

Again it was Nigel who answered. 'We don't mix much with the Carswells. I mean, they're pleasant enough when we meet them in the lane. But they're almost aristocracy, aren't they? Their family has had that place for generations. We might have got them out of a fix financially by buying the farmhouse, but they're not going to ask us down to the Hall for dinner.' There was a brief hint of resentment and then he smiled again.

'I don't think Mr Benton was a friend of the family, either,' Vera said. 'You didn't see anyone of that description in the lane yesterday?'

'No.' Lorraine had the coffee cup poised between the tray and her mouth. 'But we probably wouldn't. He wouldn't come past here to get to the Hall.'

'Where were you yesterday afternoon?'

They looked at each other. 'I went into Kimmerston to do some shopping,' Nigel said. 'Stocking up. It doesn't do to run out of milk all the way out here.' As if he lived in a remote community halfway up the Amazon.

'And you, Mrs Lucas?'

'I was here,' she said.

'In the house?' Vera was about to ask if there'd been any phone calls to the landline, any visitors to corroborate the story.

'No. Outside. The garden at the back leads onto the hill. I was sketching the view across the valley.'

'So you'd have seen anyone driving up the lane? Or out walking?'

'I suppose so.' Though she seemed uncertain. Everything about her seemed a little unfocused. Vera wondered if she had a hangover, or if she was taking prescription drugs. 'I get lost in my work.'

'Well, did you see anyone at all?' She tried to keep the impatience from her voice.

There was a beat of hesitation, the little frown again. 'No. No, I don't think I did.'

Vera got to her feet. 'One of my colleagues will be along later today to take a statement. If you can remember anything else – even if it seems to have no importance at all – please let us know.'

They walked out through the grand kitchen and Vera paused there for a moment. 'Your neighbours, the other members of "the retired hedonists' club". What can you tell me about them?'

Nigel rubbed his hands together. Vera wondered if he was real. Surely there was more to the man than this caricature who seemed to have stepped out of a 1970s sitcom.

'The O'Kanes are in the house to our right. John's a retired academic, a history professor. She was a kind of social worker. Divorce-court mediation – something of the sort. You know the type. *Guardian* readers. They keep hens. She's a veggie.' As if there was nothing more for Vera to know. He paused for a moment. 'Lovely people, though.'

'And the house on the left?'

'Annie and Sam. They ran their own business in Kimmerston, before they sold up and moved out here. They're local. Know everyone in a ten-mile radius of Gilswick. Great if you need a plumber in a hurry.' Another pause. 'Salt-of-the-earth.'

Outside, Vera sat in the car to phone Joe and Holly and catch up on their news. She was aware of Nigel and Lorraine Lucas staring at her through their huge picture window.

Chapter Ten

Annie Redhead was making biscuits. A fat woman in a dreadful coat had just come out of the Lucas house and was sitting in her car making a phone call. Annie wondered if she had anything to do with the death of the Randle boy. Surely she must do. Could she be a reporter? They'd been bothered by the press a few times after Lizzie was sent away.

The biscuits were made with dried ginger and golden syrup and the kitchen was full of the smell of them. She lifted a tray out of the cooker and prised each biscuit onto a wire tray to cool and harden. She and Sam couldn't possibly eat them all and she'd give most of them away to the neighbours, but baking reminded her of the old life, before they'd come back to Gilswick. When they'd run the restaurant, she'd made tiny pieces of shortbread or brownie to go with after-dinner coffee. Otherwise Sam had never allowed her into his kitchen.

There was a sound of an engine. She looked out of the window again, but the woman was still there, still talking into her phone. The sound was made by Sam's car turning into the yard. Every morning he went down to the village to soak up the news and collect his paper, and now he was back. He must have seen the stranger, but he didn't acknowledge her. He'd never been one for confrontation. That was why they were living here, miles from anywhere, and why Annie was making biscuits for entertainment.

The door opened and Sam walked in as if he didn't really have the right to take up the space. The way he always walked into a room. She stooped to put another baking tray into the oven and felt the strain on her hip as she stood up. She should lose some weight. If it came to it and she needed a hip replacement, it wouldn't do to be carrying all this fat. 'All right?'

He smiled. 'I met Gordon in the shop. He sent his love.'

'That's nice.' Gordon had been the postman when they'd first married and lived in the valley the first time. He'd seemed ancient even then and it was hard to believe that he was still alive.

'Percy was there.'

She looked up sharply. 'Any more news about what's been going on at the Hall?'

'Perce reckons there are two people dead. The lad that he found in the ditch and another in the house.'

'Not the major? Or Mrs C?'

Sam shook his head. 'Can't be, can it? They're visiting their boy in Australia.' He folded his newspaper on the table so that he could read it. He did the same every morning, and Annie switched on the kettle for tea. That was their ritual. Tea and the crossword.

Sam looked up. 'Who's in that car in the yard?'

'I don't know. She's been in next door.'

And that was when the doorbell rang and, glancing through the window, she saw that the fat woman was standing on their step.

Annie went to open the door. She thought again that she'd always done the front-of-house. That had never been Sam's style and she was quite surprised to see him, still in his seat, when she led the strange woman into the kitchen. She'd almost expected him to have scuttled upstairs.

'Eh, this is a lovely house.' The woman was even bigger than Annie. She stood in the middle of the kitchen and, unlike Sam, seemed to expand to fit the room, to suck all the extra space into her body. 'Cosier than that great palace next door. I'm Vera Stanhope. Northumbria Police. You'll likely have been expecting me.'

'Aren't you Hector's daughter?'

The women turned to look at Sam. Clearly the question had surprised them both.

'For my sins,' Vera said. 'Did you know him?'

'Knew of him.'

'He didn't have many friends,' the detective said. 'Lots of acquaintances. Through his business. You weren't one of those?'

Sam shook his head slowly.

'That's all right then. *They* were an unsavoury lot.'

Annie looked at them for some explanation, but none was forthcoming. She'd have to ask Sam later. She made tea and put some of the biscuits that had cooled onto a plate. Remembered just in time to take the others out of the oven.

'So how can we help you?' Annie realized that her voice was sharp, but she wanted this over. Vera Stanhope seemed to have no urgency, and Annie didn't like having the detective in her house. It made her uneasy.

'Two murders,' Vera said. 'Not what you'd expect in a place like this. A disturbing time. I'm sure you want to help.' Then she fired a question at Sam. 'What business *were* you in then, before you retired?'

'We had a little restaurant,' he said. 'On the square at Kimmerston.'

'Annie's!' She beamed. 'Of course. I ate there myself a couple of times. If there was a special occasion. You had a great reputation with the foodies.'

Annie found herself smiling. She knew this fat woman was trying to get her onside, but she couldn't help herself. 'That was Sam. He was the chef.'

Sam shrugged. 'It's all in the ingredients.' Which is what he'd always said when he got a compliment for his cooking.

'Why did you sell up?' The detective again. As much tact as a tank.

Annie got in before Sam had to answer. 'It's a tough business,' she said. 'Long hours. We wanted some time for ourselves before we got too old.'

'Very sensible,' Vera said, though Annie couldn't imagine *this* woman would ever retire. Vera paused for a moment to drink her tea. 'Did you ever meet the dead lad? They called him Patrick Randle and he was the house-sitter at the Hall.'

'I met him a couple of times,' Sam said. He didn't usually volunteer information and Annie thought he wasn't as intimidated by the detective as she was. Perhaps that was because he'd known Vera's dad. He was always more comfortable with folk who'd grown up in the hills. 'In the post office in the village. We got talking. You know how it is, waiting in the queue.'

'What was he like?'

'Nice enough.' A pause. 'Canny.'

'Eh, man, that doesn't tell me anything. I've never met him and it'd help to have your opinion.'

Sam tried again. 'Just the sort of lad the Carswells would ask to look after their house. Pleasant and polite. He could have been a friend of their son's.'

'Was he a friend of the son's?'

'Not as far as I know. But they could have mixed in the same circles. Posh school. University. You know.'

Vera nodded. 'You got kids?'

'A daughter,' Annie said, not looking at Sam. 'Lizzie. She's working away at the moment.'

Annie felt Vera's eyes on her. They seemed to bore through her skull and into her brain and her memory. Annie held her breath, expecting more questions about Lizzie, knowing that she'd find it impossible to lie to this woman again. Besides, the detective would be able to find out all about their daughter, if she really wanted to know. *Lizzie,* she thought as she had so many times before, *where did we go wrong?*

But the inspector had a different question. 'This Patrick Randle, did you ever meet him, Annie?'

'Not to speak to. I saw him a couple of times in the lane, walking the dogs.'

'There was a second murder,' Vera said. 'A bit of a mystery. We can't imagine what the victim was doing in the flat in the big house. His name's Martin Benton, a middle-aged chap. Apparently he'd lived in Kimmerston all his life. Worked as a teacher most of the time. Single. Does that mean anything to you?'

Annie shot a look at Sam.

'I don't think so,' he said, 'but as I get older, names don't mean so much.'

Vera barked, a sound that was a cough mixed with a laugh. 'I'm just the same, pet. It's a nightmare in my work. But have a think, will you? Ask around.' She paused. 'We're wondering if Patrick Randle might have employed Benton in some capacity. It seems as if he'd just set up his own business. Any idea what that could be about?'

Annie shook her head. 'Maybe the major wanted some work done in the house while they were away? Decorating or plumbing? So it wouldn't disrupt the family too much when they came back.'

'Aye, that makes sense.' But Vera didn't sound convinced and she changed tack. 'I suppose all these buildings belonged to the big house at one time. When did the family sell up?'

'Five years ago,' Annie said. 'About that time. After the financial crash things got difficult for the tenants. Some clung on longer than others. The major sold the barns to a developer, and he hung onto the place before doing the conversions. Maybe he had problems raising the capital. The Carswells kept the house where the Lucases live, and put that on the market at the same time as the barns went up for sale.'

'So you bought your place from the builder, but the Lucases bought theirs straight from the family?'

'That's right.' Annie thought there couldn't be much wrong with the inspector's memory because she wasn't making any notes. Annie experienced the anger that lit a little fire in her brain every time she thought of their move to the valley.

'Did you all arrive at the same time?'

'More or less.' Annie reached out and took another biscuit. She always ate when she was stressed. 'Lorraine and Nigel camped out at The Lamb for a few months while their renovations were being done, but we were here within six months of each other.'

'And you all get on.' It wasn't exactly a question.

'We've got a lot in common,' Annie said. 'Similar sort of age and newly retired. We have different interests, of course. Janet's into natural history and she's the leading light in the Gilswick Walking Festival. Lorraine has her art. I volunteer a couple of days a week at the first school in the next village. Listen to the kids reading. We're not in and out of each other's houses all the time, but we socialize. Meet for drinks on a Friday night. It kind of brings a bit of structure to the week, now we're not working.' She bit her lip, realizing that she would never have dreamed up that idea for herself. It was probably something the Prof. had said and she was just repeating it like a parrot.

'Good that you keep so busy. You wouldn't think there was so much to do out here.' Vera smiled. 'Nice view, though.'

There was a moment of silence that lasted long enough to become awkward.

'I have to ask what you were both doing yesterday,' Vera said at last. She gave an apologetic smile. 'I'm sure you understand. So where were you from early afternoon?'

'Of course.' Sam sounded very reasonable and Annie was proud of him. She knew he'd hate having this woman in their house as much as she did. 'A tree came down at the end of the garden in the last storm and I was sawing it up. Logs for the wood-burner. We built a workshop at the back of the house when we first moved in and I was there all afternoon.'

'And you?' Vera turned to Annie, caught her in the process of nibbling another biscuit.

'I was at the WI in the village.' The crumbs made her throat feel very dry and it was hard for her to speak. 'Janet O'Kane gave me a lift. There was a lecture on Neighbourhood Watch.'

'Very appropriate.'

Annie had the feeling the detective was making fun of her, but when she looked, Vera's face gave nothing away.

'The meeting started at two-thirty,' Annie said, 'and once we'd had tea and caught up with our friends, it was probably five o'clock by the time we got back here.'

'Did you pass anyone on the lane?' Vera's voice was easy, almost uninterested, so Annie guessed this was an important question. 'Anyone walking down the valley? Any parked cars?'

Annie shrugged. 'We were talking,' she said. 'Gossiping, I suppose. I don't think that I'd have noticed.'

'You might have noticed if there was a vehicle coming in the opposite direction.' Vera's tone was sharper now. 'There are hardly any passing places, and you'd have to back up.'

'I don't think we passed anyone,' Annie said. 'But I wasn't driving. You're probably best asking Janet. It might have registered with her.'

The detective levered herself to her feet. 'You're probably right,' she said. She paused with her hands still on the table. 'What was the gossip about?'

For a moment Annie's mind went blank. 'Oh,' she said, 'other WI members. Committee politics. You know what it's like when you get a bunch of women together.'

'I'm not sure that I do, pet. Most of my colleagues are men, and I don't really do girlie chats.' She flashed another smile and made for the door. Annie followed her and showed her out.

Back in the kitchen, Sam was standing by the window looking out. 'She's still there, sitting in the car.'

Annie joined him. Vera Stanhope was leaning back in the driver's seat and seemed to have her eyes shut. For a moment Annie wondered if she was ill, if she'd had a heart attack or a stroke. The woman was so big she'd be a candidate for a stroke. Then she shifted and seemed to be writing on a scrap of paper. So perhaps she did take notes after all.

'Come away,' she said to Sam. 'We don't want her to think that we're bothered.'

Chapter Eleven

Holly sat in the big open-plan office and let the buzz of phone conversations and chat fade into the background. The sunshine lay on her desk in stripes, filtered by the blinds at the big windows. She needed to concentrate. To her left she was vaguely aware of Charlie talking to a taxi company about any bookings they'd taken to Gilswick the day before, but in her head she was back in the mortuary with Paul Keating and Billy Cartwright. They were working on the second body, stripping the clothes away, a strange kind of ritual. Vera had already lost patience and disappeared. The care that was taken in the removal of the garments was almost loving and the voice describing the process into a recorder was rhythmic and gentle. Like a prayer. Keating was a religious man, and not even Billy Cartwright managed to be too flippant in his company.

Holly had held the bag while they slipped the victim's shoes inside. Keating was still speaking. 'A bit of mud and what might be gravel in the tread. It would be worth letting Lorna Dawson from the Hutton work her magic.' Professor Lorna Dawson, Keating's favourite forensic soil scientist, should be able to provide information about where their victim had been just before he was killed. Then the suit had been removed.

Marks & Spencer. It looked timeless, but it might be possible to track down when it was bought from its style, small differences in stitching. It gave no sense of the personality of the man, except that he was someone who wouldn't have wanted to stand out. Holly could see why Vera called him the 'grey man'. There was nothing in the pockets, not even a tissue or loose change.

It was when they cut away the underwear that the thought had flashed into her mind. Subversive, an epiphany. *I don't have to do this. I don't have to live in a northern city with people who despise me, helping strange middle-aged men undress the dead. I'm smart and young enough to make a change. I can do anything I want.* And following on from the first flash of revelation: *I don't want to end up old and single and married to the job, like Vera Stanhope.* So now Holly was sitting at her desk trying to recapture that moment of excitement and decision, that instant of courage. Her phone rang. Joe Ashworth.

'I've got a name for the grey man. Can you find out everything you can about Martin Benton?' Then Joe gave her a list of facts. The man's age and address. His last known employment at a charity in a small town in south-eastern Northumberland. 'I'm just going to check out his home. See if I can track down any relatives.'

'Sure,' she said. 'I can do that.'

Holly went to the office where Benton had last worked, without calling in advance. That wasn't her usual style. Generally she was happier talking on the phone. She hated to think how much time Vera wasted, drinking tea and listening to idle chat that had no relevance to the inquiry. But today she wanted to be away from the station. She'd always been ambitious about work. Now the police station, with its banter and apparently meaningless routines, made her think those goals might be worthless. She was better away from the place for a couple of hours.

Martin Benton's most recent workplace was in Bebington, a former mining town a few miles south-east of Kimmerston. Terraced streets scattered with 'To let' or 'For sale' signs. The main road a selection of charity shops, pawnbrokers and bookmakers. A convenience store with a handwritten notice in the window advertising cheap booze. Cheap spelled 'cheep'. A million miles away from the valley at Gilswick, with its big house and primroses. Though hardly any distance at all, as the crow flew.

The charity where Benton had worked as an admin assistant was called Hope North-East and its base was a little house in a rundown street just off the main drag. The front door was open and she walked into a narrow lobby. To her right she looked through a glass door into a social space with a kitchen area beyond. There it seemed that a discussion group was taking place. Half a dozen people, mostly men, were sitting in a circle on beaten-up chairs. In the middle of them was a low table holding mugs. Nobody was smiling and the conversation seemed very intense.

Just inside the front door a laminated sheet of paper had been fixed to the wall with a drawing pin. It said 'Office' and an arrow pointed up the stairs. Holly followed it and came to an empty reception desk. She hesitated for a moment when somebody shouted from a room to the right. 'Can I help you?'

Holly followed the voice into an untidy space. Two desks piled with files, a couple of computers that looked as if they'd been there for a decade. And two women, one large and confident, one skinny and nervous. A window looked out towards the main street and there was a background rumble of traffic.

Holly identified herself. The skinny woman looked even more nervous. Holly heard Vera's voice in her head: *You shouldn't read anything into that, Hol. In some communities bairns are brought up to see the cops as the enemy. It doesn't mean they've got anything to hide.*

Still, Holly couldn't help feeling suspicious. 'Hope North-East. What's that?'

'We're a registered charity,' the skinny one said, too quickly. 'We're all above board here.'

Holly didn't answer and turned to the larger woman. She had an official-looking name badge that read 'Shirley', and wore smart black trousers and a blue silk top. Holly thought she'd get more sense out of her.

'We provide support and assistance for offenders newly released from prison or young-offender institute.' The words came easily. Shirley had given the same explanation many times before. 'We also give help to the offenders' families.'

'What kind of service do you provide?' Holly felt more confident now. Shirley was a professional and she could relate to her. 'Specifically.'

'Sometimes all people need is information. If the wage earner suddenly disappears from the scene, partners flounder when it comes to applying for benefits.

Just the business of organizing visiting orders and transport to the prison can be a nightmare. And you can find that your friends suddenly disappear, once a family member is sentenced. When offenders are first released, we try to provide friendship and company. Practical help with housing and money. In prison it's easy, in lots of ways. The inmates get fed, clothed, and if they're lucky they're given work. When they first come out some people flounder.'

'What's going on downstairs?' Holly thought the victims could do with a bit more support, and these do-gooders should direct their efforts in that direction.

'A support group for people who have a problem with alcohol. The traditional AA approach doesn't work for everyone. Our approach is a little less formal.'

'Did a man called Martin Benton work for you?' Holly took the photograph of the dead man and placed it on the desk in front of Shirley. The skinny woman stood up to look too, more curious now than worried.

'What's happened to him?'

Holly didn't reply immediately. 'You do recognize him?'

'Yes,' Shirley said. 'That's Martin.'

'He died yesterday in suspicious circumstances.' She thought the information would be all over the news by that evening, and besides you could tell from the photo that the man was no longer hale and hearty. 'We're trying to piece together as much information as we can about him. I understand that he worked here with you.'

There was a moment of shocked silence, before Shirley started speaking. 'He came as a volunteer first. Then we put in a funding bid, so we could update our

IT. When I first started, it was a nightmare. Everything on card indexes, no attempt at data protection. Martin applied for the admin post and got the job.'

'Were there any problems?'

'None at all. He was a dream employee.'

'What do you mean?' For the second time that day Holly found her attention wandering. *I don't have to do this. I don't have to be in a scuzzy office in a scuzzy town asking questions about a man I don't care about at all.*

'He was punctual, reliable and very effective. A whizz at anything to do with the computers. In the end he was helping the clients. He ran a series of workshops for us in the local library, showing people how to register online for work and for benefits. Lots of them don't have computers at home.'

Automatically Holly took out her iPad and began to write notes.

'How long did he work for you?'

'He was here on a six-month contract,' Shirley said. The skinny woman had moved back to her desk, but made no pretence of working and was listening to every word. 'After that, our funding dried up and we couldn't afford to keep him on. He still came in once a week to help out as a volunteer. I'm the only paid worker in the place, and I'm on the minimum wage.'

'What's your background?'

'I did a social-work diploma and worked as a probation officer for twenty years,' Shirley said. 'But I didn't fancy working for a company more interested in profit than in befriending clients, when the service was reorganized and put out to private tender. Here I'm doing what I'm good at.'

Downstairs the group seemed to be breaking up.

There were shouts as people wandered out into the street. The buzz of more animated conversation in the room below.

'Did you know that Martin collected moths?' Holly wasn't sure how that could be relevant to the man's death, but Joe had made a big deal about it.

'Sure. He was very quiet. Shy. But when he talked about moths he seemed to come alive. Moths and computers. The loves of his life.' Shirley smiled.

'There was nobody special then?'

'He never mentioned anyone. But then he probably wouldn't. As I said, he was very shy. Anyway, he found dealing with people tricky. Martin ran the taster computer sessions with clients because he knew they were useful, but he was happier tucked away here in the office.'

There were footsteps, heavy on the bare stairs, and a man stood just inside the office door. Middle-aged and enormous. Shaved head. Tattoos. Hands the size of shovels, with dirt ingrained under the fingernails. 'This is Frank,' Shirley said. 'He's just been running the group. Another of our regular helpers.'

They sat in the window of a cafe. Frank drank a double-espresso and asked for a Coke to go with it. Holly had tea, too strong for her taste. Frank did most of the talking, a continuous monologue fuelled by caffeine and sugar. 'I've got an addictive personality. Better coffee than booze. That's why I got into bother when I was a kid. I wasn't into thieving because I needed stuff. It was the buzz, the excitement. Knowing that I might get caught.'

'And you did get caught.'

'Of course I did. I was stupid. Detention centre, young offenders, prison. I worked my way through them. Didn't stop me stealing, though, and by then I'd found other stuff to give me a buzz. Heroin. I got into that inside. By that time I was needing to thieve to pay for it.'

'But you're straight now?'

'Yeah. Clean and straight. I've got my own little business. Gardening. I was never going to be any good working indoors. And I help out at Hope when I can.'

Holly wasn't sure how to react. She'd never been convinced that people changed so dramatically. 'You got friendly with Martin Benton?'

'He was a gentle soul, Martin. He needed someone to look out for him.'

'You supported him when he came out of hospital after his mother died?' Holly was still struggling to think of this man as a guardian angel.

'Then, but also when the Job Centre got him assessed as fit for work. The stress of teaching had made him ill and he was still getting over the last breakdown. No way could he go back to that. So I suggested that he'd be better registering as self-employed. That gets the bastards off your back, you know. He was a clever guy. He had some savings in the bank to see him through until he got set up. And he had skills.'

'Moths and computers.'

'And photography! Have you seen inside his office? All those beautiful pictures. He just needed the confidence to go it alone.' Frank drained the Coke and fidgeted in his seat.

'What business did he decide on in the end?'

For the first time Frank seemed hesitant. 'I don't know. He wouldn't tell me. Not in detail. He'd met some guy who wanted him to do some work. He wouldn't tell me any more than that.' There was a pause. 'I wondered if he was getting ill again. When he was really ill he heard voices, you know. Got paranoid. Dreamed up weird conspiracy theories. He said he'd been sworn to secrecy.'

'And you thought he was psychotic?' Holly decided that this was a nightmare. Vera would want facts, not news of a madman who heard voices.

'I don't know. I'm not qualified to tell. I'm not a doctor, am I? Martin seemed sane enough, but his stories didn't hang together. Why would he turn setting up a new business into such a mystery?' Frank was drumming his fingers on the table.

Holly saw that she wouldn't keep him here for very much longer. 'Can I get you another coffee?'

He shook his head. 'I've got work.'

'Can you tell me again what Martin said about his business? Where did he meet the man who offered him the work?'

Frank got to his feet, leaned over the table towards Holly. 'He wouldn't tell me. Nothing. "It's not that I don't trust you, Frank, but I'm sworn to secrecy." And his eyes were kind of glittery, so I wondered if he was on something.' He looked directly at Holly. 'Then he said that I'd be proud of him. "You, of all people, would understand." I asked him what he meant, but he just smiled.'

Chapter Twelve

Vera was hungry. Biscuits were all very well, but she hadn't had a proper meal since the pizza the night before, and pizza never seemed very filling to her. More like a snack. She was thinking she might slide back to the village for pie and chips in The Lamb, when the door of the barn conversion on the other side of the farmhouse opened. The two Labradors she'd seen in the big house burst out, followed by a middle-aged woman. The woman was fit. Not an inch of spare flesh. She wore specs and had curly hair that looked like a Brillo pad. She wore wellingtons, jeans and a T-shirt. No coat or jersey.

'Janet O'Kane?' Vera was only halfway out of the car and had to shout above the sound of excited dogs.

'Yes?' The woman stopped, but the dogs bounded off.

'Inspector Vera Stanhope. Have you got time for a chat?'

'If you don't mind a walk.' She nodded after the Labradors. 'They're used to a big garden and they're going stir-crazy in the house.'

'It was good of you to take them on.'

'I'm not sure what my husband makes of our new house-guests but, really, it was the least we could do.

Two people dead! I can hardly believe it.' She paused and they walked down the track for a little way. 'I'm pleased that you can join me. I was a bit anxious about going out on my own, even with the dogs. Ridiculous, I know. John said he'd come, but he's not been well and I could tell he'd rather not.'

She set off down the lane.

'I'd usually go up onto the hill, but there are lambs, so it's probably better to avoid there today. Wren's very well behaved, but Dipper's a bit of a bugger. He's her son.'

It took Vera a moment to realize that she was talking about the dogs. 'Do you look after them very often?'

'If the Carswells are only away for a weekend I go down to the house a couple of times a day to feed them, let them out – you know. I'd love to have a dog of my own, but John's not keen.'

'It's a lovely place to live,' Vera said.

'Isn't it? John was an academic at Newcastle University and the plan was always to retire early and find somewhere with some space to breathe. Live the good life. Maybe it's a bit daft, but it works for us.' Her voice was very bright.

She took a footpath that led from the lane and onto a narrow bridge over the burn. The dogs nosed through the undergrowth. There were wood anemones, celandines and all around them birdsong. It occurred to Vera briefly that she should get out more, take a bit of exercise as the doctor had advised. At least it would stop Joe nagging, and she might even enjoy it. 'How well do you know the Carswells?'

'I met Helen when I was walking and she was out

with the dogs. I didn't realize who she was at first. Since then we've been down to the big house for drinks a few times, and John and Peter seem to get on very well. Both history geeks. Helen calls in for coffee if she's walking our way. She's a very sympathetic woman. I miss her company while she's away.'

'Very chummy.' Vera wondered about that, if the close relationship between the O'Kanes and the people at the big house caused resentment among the other residents of Valley Farm. 'And you get on well with your closer neighbours?'

There was a brief pause. 'Oh, we do. We're very lucky.' She threw a stick and watched Dipper chase after it. 'Sometimes I think this period of our lives is a kind of regression. We have no real responsibilities. The six of us at the farm are of an age when we should be caring for elderly parents or grandchildren, but coincidentally we're all free of those ties. It feels a bit like being a student again. We have nobody to worry about except ourselves.'

'The retired hedonists' club.' Vera was feeling a little breathless and wished the woman would slow down. She sat on a fallen tree and Janet came to join her.

'Ah, somebody told you about that. John's little joke. Though the pedant in me thinks it's not quite right. It sounds as if we used to be hedonists and now we've stopped. In fact we're hedonists who happen to be retired.'

'And what form does the hedonism take?' Vera had never been very good at grammar at school. Hadn't seen the point, as long as you could make yourself understood, and now she was just confused.

'Oh, nothing very dramatic! We don't go in for orgies or hallucinogenic drugs. We probably drink too much. Eat too much. Enjoy each other's company. Take the occasional trip into Newcastle or Kimmerston for the pictures or the theatre. A weekend away. Perhaps it's not so much regression as a kind of desperation. We see time trickling by and want to enjoy life while we can.' She stopped abruptly.

'But the Carswells aren't members?' Vera remembered Nigel Lucas's resentment when he spoke of the people in the big house.

'Oh no!' As if the idea was unthinkable. 'And they do still have responsibilities. Peter's chair of the Country Landowners' Association and sits on lots of committees. Helen is something to do with the hospice in Kimmerston and a trustee of any number of charities. Annie and I are involved in the community too, but not to the same extent.'

'The Carswells don't have grandchildren?' Vera remembered the photographs in the living room of the big house. No babies there.

'Not yet! But there's one on the way.' Janet got to her feet. It seemed she was eager to continue with the walk. 'That's why they're in Australia.'

Of course. Joe had provided that information.

'What did your neighbours do before they retired?' Vera knew she should move on to the detail, to questions more relevant to the investigation, but she'd always been a nosy cow.

'Lorraine and Nigel Lucas? Nigel had his own business. He made a fortune when he sold it. Money's definitely not a problem in that house. Lorraine was a teacher. Not in a school. She taught art to troubled youngsters and in prisons.'

Vera blinked and had to reassess her image of Lorraine Lucas. Vera had seen her as a trophy wife, attractive but with little personality. It was hard to imagine her dealing with young offenders. 'They never lived locally before they retired?' Vera tried to remember what the couple had told her. Joe had passed on the information that Martin Benton had worked for a charity that helped offenders and their families, and she was desperate to make connections.

'I don't think so. I'm sure they were based in the South. The Midlands somewhere, I think.' She spoke as if the South was a mysterious place with ill-defined boundaries.

They began the walk back towards Valley Farm. Vera had to walk very fast to keep up. 'Did you know Patrick Randle, the Carswells' house-sitter?'

'Well, I met him. Helen asked me to call in the day after he arrived, to make sure he was okay. Susan, their cleaner, was going to let Patrick in and show him the ropes, but Helen thought it would be nice if I dropped in, to welcome him to the valley. And introduce him to the dogs, of course.'

'What did you make of him?'

'He seemed very pleasant. Polite. Charming even. He took me up to the flat and made me tea. I said that he'd have to come to dinner one night, but we didn't fix anything definite. I gave him our phone number in case he needed anything. That was all. I thought we'd have a couple of months to get to know him.' Janet paused. 'It's still not really hit me that he's dead.'

They climbed out on the lane, so now they could walk side by side.

'The second victim was a man called Martin Benton,' Vera said. 'Did the Carswells mention anyone of that name to you?'

Janet shook her head.

'He was found in the flat at the big house. Any reason for him being there? For example, were the Carswells planning to get any work done on the house while they were away?'

'I don't think so, and Susan would probably know more about that than me.' They'd reached the houses and the dogs were chasing around the yard.

'I've got a few more questions,' Vera said.

There was a brief hesitation and Vera sensed something. Panic? Hostility? Then Janet smiled. 'Of course. Come in. Meet John and have a coffee.'

They sat in a room at the back of the barn conversion. It seemed rather shadowy. There was a view of a long, narrow garden that ended with a drystone wall and then the open hill, but the sun was behind the house. John O'Kane was dark-haired and dark-eyed. Vera could see he would have been handsome when he was young, imagined him as a new lecturer, adored by his students. He was wearing cord trousers and a big sweater. He'd taken a chair in the window and had a box of tissues on the floor beside him. There was a bowl of boiled sweets on a table and he sucked them throughout the conversation. His words were interrupted by fits of coughing and sneezing. Vera thought he was one of those men who couldn't be quietly ill. The room was a comfortable clutter of books and papers, quite different from the magazine-perfect style of the house next door. Vera wondered what the two couples could have in common, couldn't quite imagine them sharing drinks on a Friday night and laughing at the same jokes.

'Could you both tell me what you were doing yesterday afternoon and evening?' She was sitting at a scrubbed pine table. There was a jam jar of daffodils, a seed catalogue and a scattering of the Sunday papers from a couple of days ago.

'I was at WI in the afternoon,' Janet said. 'I went with Annie. Lorraine says it's not really her thing, though I'm sure she'd enjoy it if she gave it a try. It's not all jam and Jerusalem these days.' She seemed aware that she was talking too much and her voice tailed off.

'Mr O'Kane?' Vera turned to the man.

'I was here all afternoon.'

'You didn't go out at all?'

'I've not been well.' He sounded fractious, like a difficult child. 'And besides, Janet's the one who feels the need for fresh air. I was reading.'

'John's working on a book.' The woman managed to sound proud and apologetic at the same time.

'The history of the Border Reivers,' he said. 'My subject.'

'Fascinating.' Vera turned her attention back to Janet. 'Did you notice anyone in the lane when you were driving back from the WI?'

'I've been thinking about that, of course. Annie phoned to say you'd asked her. But no, I didn't see anyone.'

'Does the name Martin Benton mean anything to you, Mr O'Kane?'

'Who's he?' The professor scowled.

Vera thought O'Kane had been pandered to throughout his career and couldn't quite get used to being a retired old git without a secretary or fawning students. Then she decided she might be bored and demanding, if she'd just retired. 'He's the man who was found dead in the attic of the big house with multiple stab wounds to the chest.'

There was a pause. 'No,' the professor said at last. 'I've never heard the name before.'

'And later in the evening?' Vera asked. 'What did you do then?'

'At about eight o'clock we went next door for drinks,' John said. 'Usually we only meet up on a Friday night. It's something of a weekly ritual. Nigel prides himself on making the best G&T in the North, and I wouldn't disagree. It marks the beginning of the weekend for us retired people who no longer work away from home during the week. Last night was a bit special, because it was midweek and Lorraine's birthday.'

'How did you get next door?' Vera was starting to lose patience with him.

'I might be ill, Inspector, but I was perfectly able to walk a few yards.'

'Did you go this way, through the garden or through the front door?' She found herself glaring at him. Something of his arrogance reminded her of her father, Hector.

Again there was a moment's silence and this time Janet answered. 'John was ready before me, and he went in by the front door. Our Friday socials are quite formal, in a tongue-in-cheek kind of way. We make an effort, dress up a bit. And we did exactly the same last night for Lorraine's party. You know how it is.' Vera didn't and Janet continued. 'We were going to eat next door too and I'd made a pudding, so I just went out the back way and let myself into Lorraine's kitchen. I'd made a cheesecake and it needed to go in the fridge.'

'Their back door wasn't locked?'

'No, none of us lock our doors during the day, if we're in.'

'Did either of you notice anything unusual while you were on the way to the farmhouse?'

'If we'd seen a stranger brandishing a knife, I really think we might have mentioned it, Inspector.' The professor again. His face seemed very red. Vera couldn't tell if he really had a fever or if the questions were making him angry or anxious.

'There might have been an incident that seemed insignificant at the time.' Her voice was bland. 'A car on the lane. A walker down by the burn. It would help if you could remember anything of that sort.'

He shook his head. 'I'm sorry. I didn't notice anything out of the ordinary at all.'

'Mrs O'Kane?'

Janet took more time to consider. 'No,' she said at last. 'I was in the garden for a little while because I shut the hens away before going next door. We lock them up at night because of foxes, and I knew I wouldn't want to do it later. I don't remember seeing anyone on the hill. I'm sorry. I wish I could help.'

In the silence that followed Vera could hear the hens at the bottom of the garden. She thought they sounded like old women gossiping. *That's all I am. An old woman who gossips.* She stood up and sensed the relief in the room. It was physical, like a smell.

John O'Kane gave her a little wave, but made no move to get to his feet. Janet walked with her to the door. 'Call in again, Inspector. Any time.' A polite formula that certainly wasn't sincere.

Vera got into the car and drove down the lane. There were messages on her phone, but she didn't want to read them until later. She thought all the residents of Valley Farm were watching to make sure that she'd driven away.

Chapter Thirteen

When Vera arrived at The Lamb they'd already stopped serving food, but the landlady took pity on her. Vera found herself alone in the small bar with a plate of reheated shepherd's pie. No alcohol. She needed a sharp brain. There were missed calls from Joe and Holly. She called Joe first.

'What have you got for me?' The words slurred because of the pie. The phone in one hand and a fork in the other.

'I've found a connection between Benton and Randle.' He sounded jubilant. She thought he'd been waiting for her call so that he could pass on the information.

'And?'

'Moths.'

'You'd better explain, lad.'

'Randle did ecology at university and his PhD was something about moths. I checked with his supervisor. I couldn't quite grasp the detail. Something about moths being an indicator of global warming.'

'And?' The prompt was automatic. Her plate was empty and she pushed it away from her, took a scrap of paper and a pen from her jacket pocket.

'Benton was into moths too. There was a trap in

his garden in Kimmerston and his office was full of photographs. He might have been an amateur, but you could tell he knew what he was on about. The woman at the charity where he'd worked said he had two passions: computers and moths.'

'Do we have a record of any communication between them? Phone calls? Emails?' Vera was struggling to understand how an interest in Lepidoptera could lead to murder. Hector had never been into moths. His obsession had been for larger, more macho creatures: buzzards, peregrines, goshawks. She imagined moth-trapping as a gentler occupation, old-fashioned. The pastime of elderly clerics and schoolmasters. One of her father's friends had been a collector. Like Hector, he'd seemed more interested in dead beasts than live ones, and there'd been drawers of insects pinned onto boards.

There was a sudden flash of memory. Vera and Hector had stayed with the collector one night in a house close to Kimmerston. The place hadn't been as grand as Gilswick Hall, but had been large and shabby, surrounded by farmland. She remembered the mercury-vapour bulbs of the moth trap in the garden sending shafts of light into the sky, and the chug of the generator that powered them. Then, at dawn, examining the contents that had collected in the egg boxes at the base of the trap. The two men poring over them, excited as children taking part in a lucky dip. Later Hector had been dismissive: 'There's something distasteful about a grown man fiddling with the genitals of a small insect to make an identification.' But at the time he'd been caught up in the excitement of discovery. Vera decided he just hadn't had the patience for such detailed work.

Joe's voice brought her back to the present with a start. 'We haven't found either of the phones yet. We're trying to track down the service providers. Randle's mother will have a number for him, but she's on her way north and I don't want to disturb her unless I have to. The last call to Benton's landline was from a mobile number.'

'What time are we expecting the mother?'

'Holly's meeting her train at Alnmouth at six. We've found accommodation for her at Kimmerston and we've arranged for her to see Patrick's body first thing tomorrow.'

'Tell Holly to take Mrs Randle out for a meal. I'll join them if I can.' Vera thought the last thing a recently bereaved woman would need would be to be alone all evening in a strange hotel. But perhaps making conversation to strangers would be even worse. 'If she'd like to, of course. Give her the option. We can talk tomorrow, if she'd rather.' She paused. 'What about emails?'

'The techies have got Martin Benton's computer. Nothing yet, they say. He seems to have deleted all his communications as he went along. Almost as if he was paranoid about security. And Randle didn't have a laptop in the flat. At least there wasn't one there when the search team went in.'

'Seems a bit odd.' Vera thought that if Randle was planning to continue his academic research he'd want to keep up with the latest scientific publications. To write. Even if he'd had an iPhone for calls and emails, surely he'd need a computer too.

'You think the murderer took his computer?'

'Well, we're assuming the same person killed both men, even though the cause of death was different, so we know they were in Randle's flat.' She felt suddenly tired. It was the food and the warmth. *I'm not much younger than the folk at Valley Farm. They'll be relaxing at home or pottering in their gardens. Perhaps I'm past my sell-by date.* But she knew that was ridiculous as soon as the thought floated into her head. She was as sharp as ever. 'I'll be driving back to the office shortly. Let's get together before Holly heads out for Patrick Randle's mam. I want everything you can dig out on the three couples who live at that small development at the head of the valley. Sam and Annie Redhead. They used to have the classy restaurant on the square at Kimmerston, but they seem a bit young for retirement.' *Younger than me?* 'Find out why they sold up so suddenly. Nigel and Lorraine Lucas. They lived south, somewhere in the Midlands. He had his own security business and she was an art teacher. And Professor and Mrs O'Kane. He was a historian at Newcastle Uni and she was some kind of social worker. All ladies and gentlemen of leisure, but there's a weird feel about the place.' Vera tried to remember how Janet had described it. 'A kind of desperation.'

Later they sat in her office drinking the lethal coffee that she'd brewed to keep her awake. In the open-plan room beyond the glass door there was a buzz that reminded her of the hens at Valley Farm. Muttered conversations on phones and the hum of the printers. Late-afternoon sun flooded through the windows. She perched on her desk so that she was looking down at

Holly and Joe. 'So,' she said, 'what can you tell me about our victims? Hol, you checked out Benton's workplace. Any motive there?'

'He seemed a gentle sort of guy.' Holly was choosing her words carefully. She was always anxious about getting things wrong. A perfectionist. Better say nothing than make a mistake. 'Nobody mentioned him losing his temper or annoying people in the office. He was negotiating his way through the benefits system, but he was luckier than most claimants moved from sickness benefit. He'd inherited the house from his mother, so there were no housing costs, no worries about the bedroom tax, and he had some savings. He'd been in and out of mental hospital, but once he'd given up teaching his health seems to have improved too.'

'Apart from one episode immediately after the death of his mother,' Joe said.

'Yeah, apart from that.' Holly was concentrating so hard on her narrative that the interruption failed to throw her. 'It's almost as if he saw the withdrawal of his benefit as an opportunity. A chance to follow his dreams for once.' She looked up. 'Sorry, that sounds daft.'

'Not daft at all.' Again Vera thought of the tiny community at Valley Farm. This case seemed to be all about people following their dreams. It had appeared a bit self-indulgent to her. 'But we still don't have any idea what his business might have been?'

Holly shook her head. 'He had one friend at the charity. An ex-offender called Frank Sloan. Martin told Frank that he'd approve of the work that he was planning, but gave him no more details.'

'So why the secrecy?' Vera looked at Joe. 'I hope you've got something for me, because we've got bugger-all to work on so far.'

'I know how he travelled to Gilswick yesterday.'

'So?' Vera stretched and pretended not to be pleased. It didn't do to have favourites.

'He left his bike chained up at the bus station and got the bus. It left Kimmerston at two-thirty and arrived into Gilswick an hour later. It stops everywhere.' Joe paused. 'I spoke to the driver. Most of his passengers are regulars coming back from Kimmerston after shopping – Tuesday's a bit busier than usual because it's market day – so he noticed the stranger. He described Benton exactly, down to the suit. I got uniform to check, and the bike was still in the racks in the bus station.'

'And how did our grey man get from the village to the big house?'

'Randle picked him up in his car. The bus stops at Gilswick for quarter of an hour before heading back to town. The driver went into the post office to buy a can of pop and saw Benton get into the VW.' Joe allowed himself a brief grin. 'The guy described Randle's car perfectly.'

'And we know that both men arrived at the big house, because Randle's VW was found there.' Vera was trying to work out where everyone else in the valley had been at the time. Janet and Annie had been in the village hall for the WI, Nigel had been in the supermarket at Kimmerston and his wife had been painting at home. Vera had lost track of Percy Douglas and his daughter, who lived in the bungalow. She'd get Hol to knock up some sort of chart or spreadsheet for witness movements. It was the sort of thing she was good at.

'What I don't understand,' Joe was saying, 'is how Randle came to be in the ditch. We can assume that both men went into the flat. There were two mugs on the draining board. How did they come to be separated?'

'And why was Benton wearing a suit?' Holly surprised herself by speaking without having considered the words first and coloured slightly. 'I mean, if they intended going out into the garden to look at moths, wouldn't he wear something more casual?' She looked at her colleagues.

'Of course he would.' Vera wondered how she could show that she was pleased with Holly's contribution without sounding patronizing. In the end it was easier to do nothing. 'So we've ended up with lots more questions.'

There was a silence. In the main office the hum of conversation continued. Outside there was the rumble of rush-hour traffic.

Holly looked at her watch. 'I should get off to the station to meet Alicia Randle. I want to be there when the train arrives. I haven't booked anywhere for dinner. Any ideas?'

'What about Annie's, that restaurant on the square?' Vera thought there was nothing wrong with killing two birds with one stone. 'Haven't they got a private dining room? We went there once for the boss's leaving do. I'll see if that's free. We'll see you there, Hol. About seven?'

It was a kind of dismissal and Holly went. Joe and Vera were left alone. There was another moment of silence and then Joe got to his feet too.

'Just a minute.' Vera thought more clearly when he was there. Her brain was muddled with detail, but Joe was straightforward. He could see the wood for the trees. She poured more coffee into both their mugs. It was thick like drain-sludge. 'Do you really think the interest in moths is what links these men? I just can't see that as a motive for murder.'

'I think it was what brought them together in the first place.' Joe tried the coffee, pulled a face and stuck the mug on the windowsill. 'There'll be a website, won't there? Online contact between moth-obsessives. It's too much coincidence to think they never had any contact.'

'We'll get Holly to look into that in the morning.'

'They might have become friends,' Joe went on. 'Of a sort, at least. An online relationship. Benton was shy, socially awkward. If this was their first meeting, perhaps the suit was about him wanting to make a good impression.'

'So the meeting in the big house might not have been about work.' Vera wondered if she could be described as socially awkward. Once she retired, would all her contact with the outside world be made online? 'It might have been about friendship. And if that was the case, why did both men have to die?'

Chapter Fourteen

Annie stood at the window in the bedroom and watched until she saw the detective's car disappear down the lane towards the village. The house faced south and the valley seemed a lake of sunshine. It was only as the car joined the main road that she felt the muscles in her neck and face become relaxed. She realized how tight her whole body had been while Vera Stanhope had been prowling around their territory, prodding for answers, intruding into their space.

There was a moment of euphoria, like bursts of sunlight in her brain. Of course there was nothing to worry about after all. She was tempted to call Lorraine and Jan and suggest an impromptu bottle of wine. A girly gossip and some fizz to celebrate having Valley Farm to themselves again. Then she remembered that two men were dead and that although she couldn't see into the big house because of the trees, there would still be people there. People in paper overalls and masks and they'd be searching for physical evidence, just as Vera Stanhope had been searching for connections in their own small community.

She heard footsteps on the bare wood of the stairs and Sam stood behind her. 'She's gone then.'

'Aye.'

'I was thinking we should go away,' he said. He looked pale and he had a bit of a paunch. She thought, as she always did when she saw him face-on, that he could do with more exercise. Walk to the shop in the village if the weather was nice, instead of taking the car. Sometimes she panicked at the thought that he would die before her; then she decided that the worry was ridiculous. *You're the one to talk. A size sixteen these days! If anyone's going to have a heart attack, it's you.*

Sam came up behind her and they looked together down at the burn. 'We always said we'd do a cruise when we had the time, didn't we? Let's just go for it. Book something last-minute. The Med. The Caribbean. It doesn't matter where it is.'

Oh yes! She imagined herself dressed in something silk and floaty, standing on the deck of a sleek white liner. Then she thought she'd done enough running away, and she turned slowly so that she was facing Sam and put her hands on his shoulders. 'Let's do that later,' she said. 'When all this is over. I couldn't enjoy it properly now. Besides, there's Lizzie to think about. She'll be home any day. We can't let her come back to an empty house.'

He shrugged and she could tell he was disappointed. The holiday had been his big idea for making her happy. A sacrifice, because he was never really happy away from home. His comfort zone had distinct geographical boundaries: the Tyne to the south, the North Sea to the east and the Scottish border to the north. He'd venture west into Cumbria if he was pushed, but he didn't really enjoy it.

She tried to explain. 'I'm such a control freak. I

know I can't control the police investigation, but at least we can be here, watching what's happening. Seeing what dirt gets dug up and thrown around. I'd be a nervous wreck if we were too far away to get any information.' He hadn't responded to her comment about Lizzie and she decided not to push it. The glass wall that was their daughter still stood between them.

'You're paranoid,' he said, but his voice was gentle.

She stroked his cheek. 'And you're very, very kind.'

There was a noise in the yard below them and they saw Lorraine emerge from the farmhouse. She carried a satchel over her shoulder; inside there would be her paints and brushes. She was wearing jeans and a sloppy hand-knitted jersey, and from this distance she looked about eighteen. Annie felt a stab of jealousy. Sometimes she and Jan speculated that Nigel's wife had had work done on her face. A tuck or a lift, or Botox. And how could she stay so skinny? But really there was no sign of surgery; it must be down to genes or luck. Something must have made Lorraine aware of them looking down at her, because she turned and waved. Annie opened the window.

'I'm just going to catch the last of this light.' Lorraine sounded childishly happy. Annie wondered if she'd been drinking already, or if Vera Stanhope's disappearance had caused her to relax suddenly too. 'Isn't it fabulous?'

'Should you be going out on your own? The police don't seem to have caught anyone yet.' Annie could see what Lorraine meant about the light, though. It was seductive. She felt she could walk into it and drown.

'I'm not going very far, and I'll stay on the lane.

You'll hear me if I scream.' Lorraine gave a little giggle, but Annie shivered at the thought of anyone screaming alone in the valley.

'Come in for a glass of wine when you've finished, so we know you're safe. We'll get Jan to come along too.'

But Lorraine was already heading down the track and Annie wasn't sure if she'd heard her.

Sam was cooking supper when Lorraine called at the house. She knocked at the back door and then came straight into the kitchen, still carrying the satchel. She looked radiant. Annie sensed Sam stiffen. The kitchen was his workspace and he didn't like anyone other than Annie there. Not even a woman as bonny as Lorraine.

'Come through,' Annie said. 'It gets cold when the sun goes down. I've just lit the wood-burner.' She reached into the fridge for a bottle of Prosecco and followed Lorraine out.

In the living room Lorraine sat on the floor in front of the stove. The sun was low now and the room was in shadow.

'Did you finish your painting?' Annie twisted the bottle until she felt the pressure behind the cork and poured the wine into the glasses.

'Not quite.'

So it would be no good asking to see it. Lorraine never showed her work until it was done. Annie had once asked how she'd got into the painting. Lorraine had said she'd run art classes in prison and it had grown from there. Now it seemed to have taken over all her life. As if any minute not painting was wasted.

'Shall I send Jan a text?' Annie said. 'See if she wants to join us?'

'No point.' Lorraine grinned. 'I walked past her house and she's fast asleep in the rocking chair with those great dogs at her feet. I could hear her snoring from outside.'

Annie opened the door of the wood-burner and pushed in another log. She had to reach across Lorraine to do so. Even close to, the woman's skin was smooth and flawless.

'What did you make of that detective?' Lorraine had almost finished the first glass of wine.

'Quite a character.' Annie decided to be non-committal.

'A bit of a monster, I thought, but clever. She makes you think that she's really stupid, then comes out with a question that surprises you because it's so perceptive.'

'Yes!' Annie thought just then that *Lorraine* was one of the most perceptive women she knew.

'What do you think was going on down there in the big house?' Lorraine narrowed her eyes. 'Nigel thinks it was what he called "some random loony", but I'm not so sure. You wouldn't just wander into the valley by chance, would you? So what actually happened there that led to two murders?'

'The detective asked us about an older man – the second victim – who was killed in the attic flat.' Annie found herself being drawn into the conversation despite herself. She'd been terrified of dying since she was a child. Not the reality of pain or illness, but the idea of the world going on without her. She still had nightmares about suddenly disappearing, being swallowed up by the dark. Yet she found herself fascinated by these sudden deaths. Was it because, although they'd happened so close to home, the people involved were strangers? She felt like an extra in a TV drama. It was hard to believe the situation was real.

'Martin Benton.' Lorraine reached out and poured herself more wine. 'The name's on the BBC news website now. I checked before I came out. The police are asking for information about him.'

'Did Vera Stanhope question you about yesterday evening?' Annie could imagine Lorraine giving quite the wrong impression. She could be flippant, and was given to exaggeration. *We were all pissed, of course! We always get pissed on party nights. It's the only entertainment there is out here.*

But Lorraine shook her head. 'She was more interested in earlier in the day. The late afternoon and early evening. Percy found Patrick Randle's body when he was driving home from The Lamb at teatime, so they think both murders must have happened before then. The police won't be bothered by a few pensioners partying later that night.'

'No.' But Annie thought the fat detective would be interested in everything they did. She was that sort of woman. She allowed her eyes to glance at the clock on the wall. Sam took food seriously. He'd get moody if he thought the meal he'd prepared was spoiling.

Lorraine must have noticed because she stood up and set her glass carefully on the coffee table. She wasn't always so tactful. 'I must go. Nigel might be worrying about me. I'm surprised he hasn't phoned to check that I'm okay.'

Annie thought Nigel would know exactly where

Lorraine was. He watched her. He kept binoculars in the upstairs den and pretended they were to look for birds and animals in the woods, but Annie knew better than that. Sometimes she thought it was lovely that he obviously adored his wife, that he couldn't let her out of his sight. Mostly she thought it was creepy. It occurred to her that if anyone had seen a stranger in the valley the afternoon before, it would be Nigel, staring out of his upstairs window keeping track of them all.

Annie let Lorraine out of the front door so they wouldn't disturb Sam in the kitchen. On the stone step Lorraine paused for a moment.

'I know it is horrible,' she said. 'Two deaths in the valley. The police nosing about. But it is interesting too, isn't it? Thrilling to be so close to violence and sudden death. I can't help being excited by it.'

Chapter Fifteen

Holly drove slowly through Kimmerston, held up by heavy traffic. Roadworks in the middle of Front Street. Stopped at temporary lights, she was close to a cafe where tables had been set out on the pavement for the first time that spring. An elderly woman was sitting there. She was alone and presumably her companion was inside ordering coffee. She had round spots of rouge on her cheeks and her lipstick had seeped beyond her lips into the face powder. Her clothes were bright: a blue coat and a pink scarf. She was holding a rag doll on the table and bouncing it like a baby, talking to it. Holly had her window shut and couldn't make out the words, but watched with embarrassment and fascination as the woman stopped bouncing the doll and cradled it in her arms and stroked the hair.

The woman obviously had dementia. Alzheimer's, perhaps. There must be a carer somewhere, because surely it wasn't safe to leave her alone there so close to the road. A thought flashed unbidden through Holly's mind. *Why do they allow old people like that out in the community? Wouldn't she be more comfortable in a home somewhere?* Knowing that it wasn't the woman's comfort that she was thinking of, but her own. Horrified that she could be so cruel and judgemental, that this reminder that even *she* might end her life being frail and mad, made her suddenly sick with disgust.

The traffic started moving again and Holly drove on without glancing back at the pavement. She arrived at the station early and waited on the platform for Alicia Randle's train. The sight of the old woman from the pavement cafe was still troubling her. She'd always considered herself without prejudice, open-minded and fair. How could she have such an appalling reaction to someone who was obviously ill?

Boxes had been planted with flowers all along the platform and there were ornamental cherry trees, white with blossom beside the track; the air was heavy with the smell of them. Holly sat on a bench, suddenly tired. She must have fallen asleep and was only jolted back to consciousness by the screech of brakes as the train arrived. Alnmouth was a small station and few passengers alighted. A woman with very short white hair who'd been waiting further up the platform greeted a friend. They kissed and walked away arm-in-arm. Holly tried to remember the last time anyone had greeted her with such affection. Then she saw Alicia Randle. Tall and elegant, dressed in well-cut trousers and a tweed jacket. Classy. Only a big leather shoulder bag for her overnight stay. As she got closer, Holly saw how pale she was, her eyes red-rimmed.

'Mrs Randle.' Holly held out her hand. 'I'm so sorry.' What else was there to say? 'I'm Holly Clarke. We've been speaking on the phone.'

The woman's hand was very cold and dry. She was older than she'd seemed at a distance, certainly in her late sixties. Holly remembered that Patrick had been a late baby, a consolation.

'It was good of you to meet me.' Manners would matter to Alicia Randle. Politeness was probably holding her together. It wouldn't be good form to break down in front of strangers.

'Let me take your bag and I'll drive you to your hotel.'

Holly had found a small hotel for Alicia close to the park in Kimmerston. The owners brought them tea in a conservatory at the back of the house. The door was open and the sound of birdsong seemed very loud. Too cheerful for the occasion.

'We wondered what you'd like to do this evening,' Holly said. 'My boss suggested that you might like to have dinner with us, but really if you'd rather stay here on your own, that's fine too.' She didn't want to inflict Vera, with her size and her brash questioning, on this grieving woman. 'There's no restaurant here, but I'm sure they'd make some sandwiches for you to have in your room, and I can pick you up in the morning.'

'That's very kind.' The politeness seeing Alicia through again. 'Though I would like to meet the inspector, if that wouldn't be too much trouble.'

'It wouldn't be too much for you?'

Alicia blinked and briefly the mannerly mask cracked. 'I've lost two sons and a husband, Ms Clarke. I'm sure that I can survive dinner with the women who will, I hope, bring Patrick's killer to justice.' There was a brief moment of silence filled by birdsong, before she spoke again. 'Forgive me. I didn't mean to be rude. You were just trying to be kind.'

*

The private room in Annie's was too big for the three of them and it felt cold and unused. The only natural light came from a narrow window. They sat at one end of a large table. In the main restaurant there seemed to be a sixtieth birthday party, three generations celebrating, and whenever the waitress opened the door laughter and children's voices spilled in. Vera had made an effort. Her hair was combed and she was wearing the suit that she kept in the cupboard at work, in case she was called to court. She was there before them and stood up to greet Alicia Randle. 'Eh, pet, I'm so sorry.' Holly thought Vera might attempt to take the woman into her arms, but she sensed in time that the physical contact might not be welcome.

The service was slow and they spoke as they waited for the food. Vera offered Alicia wine and she accepted, so there was a bottle on the table. Holly never took alcohol when she was driving, not even a small glass, so the older women drank it between them. They carried on the conversation too. Holly thought she might not have been there.

'Tell me about your son.' A classic Vera opening line. She was spreading butter on a warm roll and was looking at that, not at the woman on the opposite side of the table. Not wanting to make this sound like an interrogation, though the way they were sitting each side of the table reminded Holly of the interview room.

'Patrick was a joy from the moment he was born. I was already in my forties and never thought I would have another child. Simon . . .' Alicia looked at them to check that they knew she'd had another son, 'was born while I was still a student and he died not long after Patrick was conceived. Perhaps it was because I was already middle-aged that Patrick was so calm and relaxed. My husband was considerably older than me and he died when Patrick was a boy.'

'And now you're on your own.' A statement of fact.

'I have friends, but Patrick and I were very close. I didn't think anything could be worse than losing Simon, but I was wrong. Losing my husband wasn't so terrible. He'd been ill for a while when he passed away, so it wasn't a shock.' She paused. 'But this is horrible. Nobody should have to suffer in this way. I'm not sure I'll get through this intact.'

'Of course you will.' It was Vera at her most bossy. 'You're strong. I can tell that.' She paused for just a beat. 'Did you find another man, after your husband died?'

Holly almost gasped at the bluntness of the question, but Alicia gave a little smile. 'Yes. A widower. He's really rather special. We were planning to get married in the summer. Now? I don't think I can face it. Not just yet. It's not a time for celebration.'

'Did you not want to bring him with you today?' Vera was poised with the bread close to her mouth.

'No. This was something I had to do on my own.'

Vera nodded as if she quite understood. 'You were telling me about your boy. Patrick.'

'He was an easy child. Self-contained. He could spend hours lying on his stomach on the grass staring at bugs. He did his homework without being asked, and he never went through that teenage time of rebellion.' Holly could tell she loved talking about her son. She was grateful to Vera for giving her the time and the space to do so. 'I even liked his girlfriends. Simon was much more normal.'

'He *did* go through the teenage rebellion thing?' Vera reached out for more bread.

'Well, you know, he slammed a few doors in his time.' She paused. 'Actually it was worse than that for a few years. He mixed with kids I didn't really approve of. He even had a brush with the law. Drugs. Though I never told Patrick that. Patrick always thought of Simon as some sort of role-model. And Simon did pull his life around. He got into Oxford. He was very bright. Very ambitious. In the end, I think that was what caused the suicide. He could never live up to his own expectations. He'd only been there six months when he died.' A pause. 'I was careful not to put Patrick under any pressure academically.'

The waitress came in with their food. They ate without noticing what was on the plates.

'You said that you liked Patrick's girlfriends,' Vera said. 'Was there anyone special at the moment?'

'He'd been in a relationship for three years. All the time that he was doing his PhD in Exeter. She was a medical student. Rebecca. They were living together, and I was imagining that they'd marry. I must admit that I'd started to think about the wedding, hoping for grandchildren.' Alicia put down her cutlery and sat for a moment staring into space. There would be no grandchildren now. 'Then a little while ago they separated.'

'What happened?'

'I don't know. Patrick wouldn't talk about it, and that wasn't like him. He came home for a month before he started house-sitting. He seemed a bit withdrawn and moody, but he didn't even tell me that the relationship was over until I asked when Rebecca was coming to stay.' Alicia paused. 'I supposed that she'd finished with him, found someone else perhaps, and that he didn't want to admit that he was hurting. The male-pride thing.'

'We'll need to talk to Rebecca,' Vera said. 'You'll have her contact details. Perhaps you could give them to Holly here, when she drives you home.'

Alicia nodded. 'I was tempted to speak to Rebecca myself when they separated. I even thought about coming up to Durham to meet her. But I knew Patrick would hate it if I interfered. And really it was none of my business. I just hated seeing him so unhappy.'

'Was he still unhappy?' Vera had finished her meal before the rest of them and sat back in her chair. She poured the last of the wine into Alicia's glass. She wasn't usually so moderate in her drinking, so Holly supposed Vera would be driving later. At least she wouldn't have to taxi Vera home. 'You'll have been in touch with him since the two short contracts he did for the house-sitting agency. How did he seem?'

'Better,' Alicia said. 'He was home for a month before he came north to Gilswick. He sulked around the house for a couple of weeks and spent hours in his room on his computer, but then he seemed to snap out of it. Become the old Patrick again. Though perhaps not quite. I asked him what the problem had been, but he didn't want to talk to me.'

'Did he catch moths when he was at home?'

'Yes! He's been doing that since he was about eight years old. We set up some traps in the orchard. One of the masters at his school was very keen, and a group of them became interested. I think Patrick's the only one who's maintained the passion.' She gave a sad little smile. 'I thought even when he was boy that he'd make a career of it, become an academic and continue his research.'

'The second victim, an older man called Martin Benton, was passionate about moths too,' Vera said. 'It's the only connection we can find between them. Do you recognize the name?'

'No, but I wouldn't do,' Alicia said. 'Patrick seemed mostly to communicate with other enthusiasts online. He had his own website and visited other people's. There are separate lists for the different counties. It's all rather esoteric. I could never get terribly interested, especially in the tiny moths – the micros – and they were Patrick's favourites. Hard to identify, and a challenge.'

'Martin Benton was a photographer.' It was the first contribution Holly had made to the conversation. 'His images are rather beautiful.'

'I think Patrick was more interested in the science than the aesthetics,' Alicia said. 'He took pictures to help in identification. He'd put the moths in small jars in the fridge, because they're still when they're cold and easier to photograph. Then he let them go in the garden. He had no interest in collecting.' She seemed lost for a moment in her memories. 'But I suspect that he would have met Mr Benton, at least online. It's a very small community.' She looked up and her expression changed. Again the veneer of politeness shattered. 'I need to know why somebody would have wanted my son dead. It's the randomness of the brutality that makes it so hard to understand. I don't even want vengeance. I just need to know what happened, and why.' Her voice was scratchy, as if she had a throat infection or had been screaming.

'And that's what we want too.' This time Vera did make contact. Alicia's bony hand was lying on the table and Vera covered it with her big paw. 'Can you let us have Patrick's mobile number? We haven't found his phone.'

'Of course.' The woman reeled off the number without having to check.

Holly looked in her notebook. It was the number Joe had taken from Benton's landline. She caught Vera's eye and gave a little nod.

Vera gave Alicia's hand a little pat. 'You'll be tired with all that travelling. Holly will take you back now and we'll catch up in the morning.' She stood up and, obedient as children, both other woman followed.

It was dark outside. Vera came with them to the door, but didn't follow them out. Alicia Randle took her place in the passenger seat and sat in silence, gripping her handbag on her knee, until they'd almost reached her hotel.

'I'm glad that I met your boss,' she said. 'I think she's a good woman.'

Holly thought for a moment. 'She is.' She paused. 'And she's a very good detective.'

Holly sat in the car outside her flat, overtaken by the exhaustion that had hit her at Alnmouth station. She felt as if she could sleep here in the street and not wake up until morning. At last she roused herself and climbed out of the vehicle. She let herself into the flat and stooped to pick up the post. In the kitchen she switched on the kettle.

The flat was new, in a recently built block on the site of a former fire station. Low-rise and discreet, its dark-red brick had been chosen to match the surrounding Edwardian houses in one of Newcastle's more fashionable suburbs. Her apartment was at the back and looked over a cemetery. Most of the graves were old, covered with lichen and sheltered by mature trees, but occasionally there were funeral parties; elderly women dressed in black coats and hats shaped like mushrooms gathered around the newly dug hole in the ground, like crows around a roadkill rabbit.

Holly made some camomile tea and moved into the living room. It was square and uncluttered and she loved it. It had taken years of saving to get the deposit for the mortgage, but usually when she arrived here after work she didn't begrudge a penny. This was where she could be calm and free from the irritations of work. She liked the silence, the lack of traffic noise, the sharp edges of the newly plastered walls and the sharp folds of the ironed linen sheets. She'd moved to the North-East because she thought a challenging place would be good for her career, and since moving to the flat she hadn't considered leaving. Until now.

She seldom invited friends here. She preferred to meet in one of the restaurants and wine bars close to her home. Her friends were people she'd met at university or at the evening classes she took. She kept her distance from her colleagues. She enjoyed her own company. She set her tea on the glass table and went to close the blinds at the window. There was a moon now and the white light was shining on the marble headstones in the cemetery. It occurred to her that, at work and at home, she was surrounded by the dead.

Chapter Sixteen

Vera stood outside the restaurant, waiting until Holly had driven away, and then she went back in. The birthday party was over and the main dining room was nearly empty. Vera wasn't surprised. She thought the place was still trading on the reputation it had achieved under the old management. There'd been no imagination or flair to the food they'd eaten that evening. At the bar she ordered coffee and the bill and returned to the room where they'd sat for the meal. It was cold in there. She didn't take off her coat, and felt as if she was sitting late at night in a station waiting room. The room was wood-panelled and dark.

An older woman who'd been in charge in the restaurant carried in the drink, the bill and a card machine. She seemed to Vera very glamorous in the dim lighting, like a film star from a former era. Her big eyes were lined with black and she wore heavy mascara. Her white blouse had one fewer buttons fastened than was entirely decent. Something about her was familiar. Vera paid and, as the woman was walking away, remembered where she'd seen her. 'Weren't you here under the old regime?'

The woman stopped and turned into the room.

'Who wants to know?' The voice went with the

look. Husky. A badge pinned to her blouse had the name-tag Paula.

What was it with the fashion for name-tags? *It's as if we're all dogs*, Vera thought. *As if we can't explain who we are, if we get lost*. She smiled. 'Detective Inspector Stanhope. Have you got time for a chat?'

'Let me just check what's going on in the restaurant. They've employed a bunch of kids. Cheap, but crap.'

'Not like the old days?'

Paula looked sharply at Vera, but didn't answer. She returned a little later carrying a mug of tea.

'I've told them to lay up for tomorrow and then let themselves out. I can lock up later.' She nodded towards Vera's coffee. 'Do you want a real drink to go with that?'

'Nah.' Vera spoke quickly before she succumbed to temptation. 'I'm driving.'

'So are you just nosy,' Paula took Alicia Randle's seat at the table, 'or do you have a reason for asking your questions?'

Vera paused. 'Well, pet, I've always been nosy . . .'

'But maybe you have a reason for talking to me too?' Paula tossed back her hair, but it had been lacquered into shape and hardly moved.

'Maybe.' Another pause. 'You did work for Annie and Sam, didn't you? I'm sure that I've seen you in here.'

'I worked front-of-house with Annie. As you said: the good old days.' Paula set the mug on the table in front of her and stared into it. She might have been reading the tea leaves. 'We were classy in those days. Great food. Nice atmosphere. The new owners just couldn't carry that off. Headed downmarket. As if there aren't enough cheap bars and restaurants in Kimmerston. There's no way they can compete on price and they've got another place in Morpeth, so they're hardly ever here. They're just playing at it. I'd hand in my notice, but I suspect it'll go under soon enough anyway. I might as well hang on, so I get paid my unemployment benefit as soon as I stop working. No point getting penalized for resigning.' She drank tea. Her fingernails were as long as talons and painted scarlet.

Vera wondered what it would be like to have nails like that. *Fun*, she thought. *It would be fun!* She imagined waltzing into the incident room all glammed up, fingernails and cleavage flashing, and pictured Joe's face. She felt a moment of regret. She'd never gone in for anything theatrical, even when she was young. She'd never been into anything fun at all. And it was all too late now. She became aware that Paula was staring at her.

'Do you know why Sam and Annie sold up?'

Paula hesitated for a moment. 'It was an important decision. Something they had to sort out for themselves. They weren't going to discuss that with the hired help, were they?'

'But you might have guessed what was going on.'

There was another hesitation, and Vera thought the woman was preparing to confide in her, but in the end her response was bland, almost meaningless. 'They said they wanted to enjoy some quality time together before they got old.' Which was what they'd told Vera.

'Tell me about them.'

Paula stared at Vera across the table. 'What is all this about?'

'There was a double-murder in the valley beyond Gilswick. Naturally we're interested in everyone who lives there.'

'You must be joking!' The waitress began to laugh. It started as a bewildered snigger, then became hysterical until she was choking. Vera couldn't tell if she found the idea of her former employers as murderers genuinely amusing or if the laughter was a reaction to stress. At last Paula dabbed her eyes with a napkin and started speaking. 'Annie and Sam are the gentlest people I've ever met. They adore each other and think the best of everyone. There is no way that either of them could be a killer.'

'So there's no problem in telling me a bit more about them then, is there?' Vera leaned back in her chair. 'How long did they run the restaurant here?'

Paula considered. 'I remember the tenth anniversary,' she said. 'A glorious night. That wasn't long before they sold up.'

'What did they do before they took this place on?'

'Sam was a farmer. His dad was a tenant of the Carswell estate, before the major sold off most of their holdings. It's tough scraping a living from the hills. You know that. They kept going by diversifying and ran the farm as a B&B, and later they set up a shop and tea room – Sam's baby. That was where the idea of this restaurant came from. The menu in the tea room was all about local food, simply cooked. When his father died, Sam knew he'd rather be a cook than a farmer. He gave up the tenancy and set up this place.'

'What's Annie's background?' Vera loved this part of the investigation: the excuse to satisfy her curiosity, to dig her way into the suspects' lives.

'She and Sam were childhood sweethearts. I think she grew up on the coast. Blyth perhaps? I'm not quite sure how they met, but it was while they were both at school. Then they separated and she went away to university. When she came back to Northumberland she was engaged to be married to someone else, but the week before the wedding Sam tracked her down. He turned up at her parents' home one day and persuaded her that she was making the worst mistake of her life. He said that he was her one-and-only true love.'

'And she went for that?' Vera wondered if *she'd* be taken in by a gesture so flash and corny. Probably. But she was middle-aged and overweight, and occasionally desperate not to be left alone.

'Trust me.' Paula smiled. 'Showy romance really isn't Sam's style. Annie must have known he'd only have spoken up if he meant every word.'

'Have they got any kids?'

'A daughter.' Paula snapped her scarlet lips shut.

Vera looked up sharply. 'Problems?'

'All kids have problems of one sort or another, don't they?' Vera didn't answer and Paula continued, 'And they certainly become problems for their parents. Mine were a nightmare as soon as they hit thirteen and didn't become civilized until they were old enough to buy me a drink.' She looked up at Vera. 'Have you got any?'

Vera shook her head.

There was another silence until Paula continued.

'Elizabeth, their daughter's called. Known to everyone as Lizzie. Wild from the beginning. I think she was chatting up middle-aged men from her cradle.'

'Is she still getting tangled up with the wrong sort of bloke?' Vera tried to work out where this was leading, but was caught up in the story now and didn't care if it was relevant to the case. Annie had told her that their daughter was working away, and Vera hadn't bothered checking.

'When Lizzie was still at school she had a relationship with one of the teachers. Got him sacked.'

'Not her fault that!' Vera shot back. 'Especially if she was underage. The only guilty party was the man.'

'I'd have thought just the same.' Paula paused for a moment to finish her tea, though it must have been cold by now. 'Until I met her. Lizzie has no boundaries. No limits. She goes for what she wants without any worry about the consequences, especially if the consequences are for other people.' There was another hesitation. Outside in the street a couple of drunks were shouting to each other. 'Sam and Annie were always bailing her out. I used to dread it when there was a phone call at work and it was from Lizzie. Sam would drop everything in the kitchen and rush out to rescue her from whatever scrape she'd made for herself. He'd bring her back here – they had a flat over the restaurant for a while – and she'd be pissed or stoned. Or just mad. Laughing like a drain, or in floods of tears.'

'Did they try to get her some help?'

Paula shrugged. 'I don't think they wanted to admit that there was anything seriously wrong. Not then. Annie made excuses for her. She was always saying that Lizzie had finally turned a corner and they'd arrange for a new college course for her, or pay off someone she'd had a go at.' Paula fished in her bag and pulled out a cigarette, lit it and took a drag.

'This is a public place, and that's illegal.' But Vera trotted out the words with no force. Everyone had the right to their own vices.

'You know what?' Paula said. 'I don't fucking care.'

Outside in the street the drunks had started yelling some football chant. The end of the season and at least their team wasn't going down.

'Is that why Sam and Annie sold the restaurant?' It was a big leap in the logic, but Vera thought Paula's antipathy to Elizabeth was personal. She hated the girl, because she hated working for the new owners. 'Was it something to do with Lizzie?'

A silence. 'I don't know. Like I said, they didn't confide in me. Why would they? I'd only worked my guts out for them for about twelve years.' Now the bitterness was obvious. 'I only asked Annie to be my fucking bridesmaid.'

'But you might have guessed?' Vera's voice was as gentle as a mother's. 'You strike me as a woman who understands things. Who'd know what was going on in that family. You and Annie were close as sisters.'

'They found Lizzie a job,' Paula said. 'Pulled some strings. I don't know how. Or perhaps Lizzie arranged it herself. Fancied the boss and made promises she was only too happy to keep. Rumour has it he fancied her rotten anyway, so perhaps the attraction worked both ways.'

'And the name of the boss?' Vera's voice was as

quiet as a whisper. Paula was in full flow and she didn't want that to stop.

'Jason Crow.' Paula made it sound like a swear word. 'Builder. Developer. Local wide-boy.'

The name was familiar. Vera had come across it through work. Crow had been charged with threatening behaviour, and then the case had been miraculously dropped when the victim had decided not to press charges. She said nothing, though, and Paula carried on talking: 'Lizzie worked in the office. She did the filing. Sent out bills. Looked glamorous when the customers turned up. Kept the boss happy in her spare time. But it seemed she wasn't as stupid as we all thought. She found some way of fiddling the payroll, siphoning a bit off every month into her own account. It took Jason six months to find out what was going on. It had made him look ridiculous and that was unforgivable. He was going to make an example of her.'

'He threatened to go to the police?'

Paula looked up and gave a slow, wide smile. 'Oh, that would only have been the start.'

'Go on, Paula. Make the connection for me.' The same encouraging mother's voice.

'The new owner of this place is Jason's little brother. He already had a wine bar in Morpeth and he wanted to expand. Go figure.' Paula stubbed out her cigarette on the side of her mug.

'So Sam and Annie sold the place to Jason, to stop him having a go at their daughter.'

Paula shrugged. 'I don't know how much they got for it, but I bet it was nowhere near the market price. And it didn't do any good, did it? That's the fucking irony. The lovely Lizzie managed to get into quite enough bother, all by herself. And now she's safe from Jason and all the Crows.'

'Why? What happened?'

'Nine months ago she got into a fight in a Newcastle nightclub and stuck a bottle into another lass's face. Only just missed her eye. She's in prison.' Paula looked around her at the cold and dusty room. 'Annie and Sam sold up for nothing.'

Chapter Seventeen

Eight o'clock in Kimmerston police station. A weekday morning, but still the street outside was quiet. Sal had been on overnight toddler duty, so Joe felt refreshed, ready to take on the day. Ready to take on Vera. She was there before any of them and he wondered if she'd been in the building all night. Occasionally he'd found her asleep in the chair in her office at the start of the day. But she too looked bright and rested. No Holly. She'd been sent to take Alicia Randle to the hospital mortuary, so that she could view her son's body. Even Charlie seemed awake. His daughter had moved home recently and he'd lost the air of depression and neglect that had lingered over him since his wife had left.

Vera had pinned a large-scale OS map on the board and started talking them through the geography, summing up for the new members of the team, who'd been drafted in to help. 'This is the village of Gilswick. A pub, a church and a post office. Some older residents who've lived there for years, and lots of newcomers who commute to Newcastle or Kimmerston. Still, it's a place where strangers are noticed, and I want all the houses canvassed. Let's aim to do the whole community, even if it means repeat visits to catch folk in this evening. We know that Martin Benton arrived on the bus and Patrick Randle picked him up. Was anyone else seen in the place? We're especially interested if they made their way down this valley.' She pointed with a ruler to the map and looked around the room to check that she had their full attention.

'This is where Randle's body was found by Percy Douglas.' Another stab at the map. 'And this is the big house where Randle was the temporary house-sitter and where Benton's body was found.' A pause. 'Joe, fill us in on what we know about our victims.'

Joe stood up. At one time he'd been nervous about taking centre-stage, but he thought Vera had cured him of that.

'Patrick Randle. Only son of Alicia, who's a widow. There was another boy, Simon, but he died before Patrick was born. Suicide. Patrick's family was affluent. He went to an independent boys' school and a good university. Graduated with a first, and went on to do a PhD in Exeter. Area of study was moths as an indicator of climate change. After the doctorate he decided to take a year out, before settling back into academia.' For the first time Joe looked up from his notes. 'Apparently that's unusual. If you get offered a university post you grab onto it, before they change their minds. There's fierce competition.'

'So why did he take the year out?' Vera could never keep quiet for very long in these sessions. 'And why not do something a bit more exciting than house-sitting in rural Northumberland? It seems he separated from his long-term girlfriend at around the same time as he left university. Was that why he wanted to get away? Or was it a sign of some other crisis in his life?' There was no answer in the room and she looked over at Joe. 'Go on then! We don't want to be sat here all day.'

Joe went back to his notes, though he knew the details off by heart. 'The second victim is Martin Benton. Also the only son of a mother who doted on him, but from a very different background. Local comp, Northumbria Uni, before training to be a teacher. Suffered periods of work-related stress, before signing on for long-term sickness benefit. He was recently reassessed and found fit for work. But instead of registering for Jobseekers' Allowance, he decided to go self-employed. We have no indication of what kind of business he set up. We know he was a whizz with computers and a skilled photographer, but we can't find any promotional material or business plan. In fact there's very little of interest on his PC – he seems to have been an obsessional deleter. The IT guys are digging around in it now. And although he set up a filing cabinet, there are no labels and all the files are empty. Maybe it was all still in the planning stage.' He paused to catch his breath and Vera jumped in.

'That reminds me,' she said. 'There was a Manila folder in the back of Randle's car. Has Billy Cartwright still got it?'

The question was directed at Joe. He thought, *Why am I supposed to be the person with the answer?* 'I suppose so,' he said. 'I haven't seen it.'

'Track it down, will you? It might be important.' Vera looked up sharply. 'And get on with it, Joe. Let's have a sense of urgency here.'

Joe glared at her, but Vera only smiled.

'Benton wore a suit for his trip to Gilswick and it's possible that his meeting with Randle was work-related, that he'd found his first client.' Joe took a breath. 'Apart from a vaguely similar family structure, the only thing Benton had in common with Randle was an interest in moths. He was a keen amateur entomologist.'

'Uh?' Charlie's first contribution.

'Someone interested in insects.'

'Thanks, Joe.' Vera flashed him a smile, the only praise he was likely to get for his presentation. She turned back to the map. 'After the big house, the lane follows the valley for about a mile and a half. The next house you come to is the bungalow where Percy Douglas and his daughter Susan live. She moved back with her dad when she got divorced, and her life's work is to keep him on the straight and narrow. She cleans both for the Carswells and for all the residents of the Valley Farm development, which is here.' The ruler hit the map again. 'As you see, the track peters out into a footpath after the houses and then forks – one path leads down through the trees to the burn, and the other goes onto the hill and circles back to the village. It's a popular route for walkers, and we could do with a media release asking anyone who was there on Tuesday afternoon and early evening to come forward. We'll get Hol to work with the press office on that, when she's seen Alicia Randle safely onto her train.'

Vera tracked her ruler back down the map until it rested on the blocks of colour that marked the house and barn conversions at Valley Farm. 'Yesterday I spoke to all the folk who live here. An interesting group. All recently retired and relatively well off. Too much time on their hands, and nothing to think about but good works and getting pissed. So it seemed to me. First, in the barn conversion, we have Sam and Annie Redhead. They used to own and manage the restaurant in Kimmerston, but sold up in rather interesting circumstances.'

Joe listened to the information she'd gained from Paula the night before, and thought Vera was some sort of witch. How had she learned so much from a brief chat at the end of dinner?

'Annie told me her daughter was working away,' Vera said. 'But having a daughter inside is probably not something you'd boast about to a stranger.'

'I know Crow,' Charlie said. 'Teflon man. Nothing sticks to him.'

'Capable of murder, do you think?' Vera's eyes were bright. Joe thought she was in terrier mode, sniffing out more leads.

'Capable of anything. He's famous, Jay Crow, for being a cold and ruthless bastard.' Charlie stared at her. 'But I can't see what the motive might be. Why kill a couple of geeks who have nothing to do with his business? Who are no threat to him.'

'Quite. I think someone should have a chat with Lizzie Redhead, though. Joe, can you do that? She's being kept out of harm's way in Sittingwell Prison. Apparently she likes the men, so see if you can charm some information from her. Find out if she's ever had any contact with our victims. I don't quite see her as a woman with a passion for natural history, but we need to check.'

Joe nodded, but felt a sudden gloom. He disliked prison visits. It wasn't the smells, the catcalls from the inmates or being locked up. He knew he was a daft bugger, but it was coming out at the end of the session and hearing the door shut behind him, knowing that the people he'd just interviewed were still inside. 'It might take a while,' he said. 'You know what they're like these days about visits.'

'This is a murder inquiry.' She shot the words back at him. 'Tell them you need to see her today.'

Sittingwell was an open establishment. Joe had checked out Lizzie Redhead's records with the prison department. She'd spent a month in a local dispersal prison and then been sent here. Middle-class and first-time offender, so it had been decided she posed no security risk. Once Sittingwell had been a grand house. Victorian Gothic. Then a home for 'fallen' women, then a sanatorium. It still had the trappings of the original grand house. There were tennis courts in the grounds, but the nets had been removed and grass was growing through the hard surface. The lawns were mowed, but most of the flowerbeds were overgrown, with occasional patches where they'd been freshly weeded. A high wall surrounded the place, but there was no razor wire, no clanging gates. In reception Joe handed over his phone and signed in, then waited in a small interview room for Lizzie Redhead to be delivered to him.

The room might once have been the hospital's office. It had a high ceiling and a large sash window. The prison was pleasant enough in late spring, though it still had the institutional smell of disinfectant and overcooked greens. In winter Joe imagined it would be unforgiving; an easterly wind would rattle the draughty windows and the big trees would be bare and gloomy. Outside a work party was pushing bedding plants into a patch of soil close to the main door. The women seemed happy enough, chatting with the prison officer in charge, breaking out into an occasional burst of laughter, but most of them were of an age when they'd have small children and his thoughts were with the kids. Sittingwell had a mother-and-baby unit, but once the children were toddlers they were sent away to live with relatives or foster parents.

The door opened and Lizzie was brought in. Joe stood up and held out his hand. Vera had told him to charm her. Even in her uniform denim and ill-fitting jeans she was stunning to look at. Coppery hair and white, flawless skin. Not too skinny. Sal was always on a diet, though Joe had told her she looked better when she was eating properly. Lizzie took a seat at the little table and looked across at him. He felt flustered and for a moment forgot how he'd planned to start the interview. She didn't speak and there was a silence that he found awkward, but it didn't seem to bother her at all.

'What am I supposed to have done now?' she said at last, her voice amused. She leaned back in her chair. Her accent was classy and he wondered how she fitted in here. Even in an open prison, she'd be out of place.

'There have been two murders near to your parents' home.'

'Well, you can't blame those on me.' When she smiled he saw that her teeth were small and very white, oddly sharp. A carnivore's teeth. There was something about her that reminded him of a fox. 'I've been in here for three months.'

Joe felt like a new officer. His brain had turned to

sawdust and he'd lost control of the interview already. 'Jason Crow,' he said. 'He doesn't like you much. He's not the sort to take kindly to people who steal from him.'

'I'm sure he hates my guts.' She paused and gave a brief smile. 'But he wouldn't kill two strangers just to inconvenience my parents.'

'Were they strangers?'

'What do you mean?' Lizzie was playing for time. Or just playing with him.

'Did you know either of the victims? You'll have a telly in here. You'll have seen the story on the news.'

'I don't watch television much. Most of what's on is drivel.' She looked up at him. 'Remind me.'

'Patrick Randle and Martin Benton. Patrick was a student. Not local. Martin was a teacher a while ago.' Joe had a sudden thought. 'Maybe he taught you?' The timings would fit.

She paused for a moment. Thinking. Or pretending to think. 'The names don't ring any bells. I hated school. I've tried to forget all that.'

'You didn't come across those names when you were working for Crow?'

She shook her head. 'I don't remember them.'

There was another silence, broken this time by Joe. 'What's it like in here?'

She seemed surprised by the question. 'All right,' she said. 'Some of the screws are okay.' She paused. 'My parents sent me away to boarding school when I was thirteen. They said all I needed was a bit of discipline, and to get away from the bad crowd in Kimmerston. That was much worse than being inside. Everyone hated me. I was only there for six months.

The same sentence as I got for nearly blinding a woman. Here everyone's screwed up and I'm one of the sane ones. Almost responsible. It makes a change to be one of the good guys.'

'Do you know anything about moths?'

'What?' She looked at him as if he was mad. He'd have bet a month's salary she wasn't acting this time.

'Never mind,' he said. 'It was just a long shot.'

Outside the gardeners were moving on to a different flowerbed, piling tools onto a wheelbarrow. He could hear another peal of laughter, remembered the tabloid papers' descriptions of open prisons as holiday camps and pushed the thought away.

'How are my mum and dad?'

'Don't they come and visit?'

'My mother does. My father can't bear to. He loved the restaurant and he blames me for having to sell up.' She stared at the women outside. 'Quite right too. It was all my fault.' She stared out of the window. 'Sometimes I wonder what's wrong with me, why I can't be like other people. It's boredom mostly. I've always got bored so easily.' Another pause. 'I've got less than a week to go before I'm released. Full remission. Like I said, I've been a good girl.' She didn't sound delighted by the prospect of leaving prison.

'Will you go and stay with your parents?' Joe thought if Lizzie had been bored in Kimmerston, the house at the end of the valley would drive her to madness in a matter of hours.

'For a while,' she said. 'I suppose. Until I get myself sorted out.'

'You could see it as a new chance.'

She grinned, showing the sharp fox's teeth. 'You sound like my social worker.'

'Aye, well, my boss always says I'm a soft touch.' As soon as he spoke he thought that instead of charming Lizzie Redhead, he'd been charmed by her. Vera would have been better sending Holly, who was never taken in by anyone's sob-story.

He stood up and opened the door to tell the prison officer outside that the interview was over.

'So you can't help about these murders?'

She shook her head and got to her feet, but the officer gestured for her to stay where she was.

'You've got another visitor. Popular today. You might as well wait here.'

So Joe left on his own, without really having a chance to say goodbye to her. He turned to look as he was led away, but Lizzie had her back to him and was nibbling her nails and staring into space.

In reception he had to wait while a smartly dressed woman was let in through the outer door. He listened while the officer behind the glass signed her in. Her name was Shirley Hewarth and she said she was from the charity Hope North-East. When she'd passed through into the prison, Joe spoke to the officer on the gate. 'Any idea who she was going to visit?'

He thought the man would refuse to answer, but he only sounded bored. 'The same lass as you. Elizabeth Redhead.' He looked up briefly from his paperwork. 'Bloody do-gooders, eh?'

Chapter Eighteen

Lizzie watched the detective leave the room. She'd been surprised to see him there when the screw had brought her in. She'd been expecting Shirley Hewarth. Joe Ashworth hadn't seemed much like a detective to her. He was too gentle. Good-looking enough, but not her type. He talked more like a doctor or a priest. He'd be no real match for her. There'd be no steel in him. No fire. Nothing to hit against.

She looked out of the window while she waited for her new visitor to arrive, imagined Ashworth walking out through the main door, getting into his car and driving through the gate. She thought she'd soon be there too. Outside. The women talked about *Outside* as if it was a different place in a different universe. But lots of them were at Sittingwell because they were working towards a release date after years inside a high-security prison. Lizzie had met murderers here. Women who'd killed their kids. Their men. Of course they'd be daunted to be leaving. She didn't think *she'd* find it so hard to adjust to the outside world. She had plans.

The policeman's visit had been a shock. She couldn't have anticipated a double-murder in the valley. She was running through the implications of the news when the door opened and Shirley Hewarth came in. The woman always looked very smart. Professional. Lizzie liked that about her. She thought appearances mattered. Shirley had brought a bag of sweets and opened them on the table, nodded for Lizzie to take one. Lizzie took a sherbet lemon. Her favourite. She liked the sharp burst of sherbet on her tongue when the hard lemon case was shattered.

'So, Lizzie. Only a few days until your release. We should be thinking of your future.'

Lizzie nodded. She thought any screw listening in to the conversation would be completely misled. The conversation sounded just like any other pre-release interview between a social worker and an offender. They would never guess that Shirley and Lizzie shared secrets. And, sure enough, there were footsteps on the parquet floor in the hall outside as the officer moved away to sit at the desk in reception.

'I'm going to chat with your mother,' Shirley went on. 'Is that okay with you?'

'Why do you need to talk to her?' Lizzie looked up sharply.

'You'll be staying with her, won't you?'

Lizzie thought about that. Her parents didn't feature in the pictures she held in her head. But she was suddenly surprised by a wave of emotion as she thought how it would be good to spend some time with them. Inside, she'd come to enjoy the ritual of daily life. The calmness of the expected. Her parents would provide that for her too. It would be a good place to make decisions and set her up for her next big adventure.

'You won't tell them about Jason,' Lizzie said. She

thought she'd shared too much with the social worker. Shirley had been a good listener and she'd seemed to understand. Lizzie hadn't meant to pass on Jason's secrets. They'd spilled out when Shirley had asked her about her experience of prison.

'Everything between us is confidential. You know that.'

'There was a murder in the valley. A young man called Patrick Randle.' Lizzie realized that she was moved by the thought. Although she'd never met Patrick, she pictured a good-looking young man lying on a table in a mortuary. White and waxy. Some of the women in Sittingwell knew about violent death and had described the procedure. Even those inside for less serious crimes were fascinated and borrowed books about famous killers from the prison library. They told her all about the process, about the crime-scene investigation and the post-mortem, forensics and DNA. She knew where the pathologist cut into the body. She looked at Shirley, expecting a comment, but none came. 'And an older man.' Lizzie had no interest in picturing *his* body.

'You've heard about that?' Shirley spoke at last. She seemed surprised. Upset.

'Were you going to tell me?'

'Of course!'

Lizzie looked at the social worker. She thought Shirley Hewarth had secrets too – so many secrets that they might get confused in the woman's head.

'How did you know about the murders?' Shirley sounded shaken, uncertain. Lizzie thought she seemed tired, with that deep exhaustion that comes from several nights without any sleep.

'I've just been interviewed by a detective.' Lizzie looked up. 'He asked me about the murders. Because they happened close to where my parents live. He thought Jason might be involved.'

A silence. Outside someone was walking on the gravel path beyond the window and they both waited until the sound moved away.

'What did you tell him?'

'Nothing,' Lizzie said. 'There was nothing to say. Two strangers were killed in the valley. What could that have to do with me or Jason?'

'Of course.' Shirley wiped her hand across her forehead and Lizzie thought again that she looked exhausted. 'We'll have to think about finding you work,' Shirley said, her voice suddenly bright and professional. 'I thought the hospitality industry might suit you. You're articulate and present very well, and you'll have picked up a lot from your parents. You might consider a college course in September, but it would be good to get some hands-on experience before that.'

There was another silence. Lizzie couldn't imagine working in a restaurant. She'd never been any good at taking orders. She had travel in her head. Wide spaces, to contrast with this place. Huge grasslands and orange deserts. Once she'd made her peace with her family and raised the funds, she'd disappear overseas. She'd joined the creative writing group in Sittingwell and had secret dreams of writing a book to capture her travels. Didn't writers make money?

'I've been thinking I should go to the police.' The social worker's voice burst into Lizzie's dreams. 'Explain about Jason. This is murder, after all. The things he told you might be more relevant than you realize.'

'No!' Lizzie forced her voice to be calm. 'You promised. Everything we discussed was confidential. I trusted you.'

Shirley didn't reply.

'I'll be out soon and we can discuss things properly. Will you at least wait until then?'

'I can't stop thinking about it,' Shirley said. 'It's making me ill. There are things you don't understand. Martin Benton, the older victim, used to work for me.'

'Do you know who killed him?' Lizzie felt another tingle of excitement. She could understand why some of the women inside loved those true-crime books. The ones with pictures of blank-faced killers staring out of the pages. There was something compulsive about the sadism. The sexual violence. She remembered again Jason's words, his hard laughter and his scorn at her tears. The books the women read were all about pain and humiliation.

There was another long silence before Shirley spoke again. 'I don't think so.'

'So you've nothing to tell the police.' When she was a child and hadn't been able to persuade her friends to do as she wanted, Lizzie had thrown tantrums, pulled hair and dug fingernails into soft flesh. Now she'd learned to be more subtle, more reasonable. 'What can you contribute to the investigation? You'll just be another crank with weird stories to tell.'

'I suppose that's true.' Shirley was about to stand up.

'The older dead man,' Lizzie said. 'The one who worked for you. What's his role in all this?'

'I don't know.' Now Shirley did get to her feet. She began to walk towards the door to call to the officer sitting at the reception desk in the grand lobby that she was ready to go. 'Really, I can't see how he might have got caught up in this business at all. I don't understand any of it.'

Watching from her chair, Lizzie thought Shirley was lying.

Chapter Nineteen

Holly stood beside Alicia Randle in the mortuary and tried to put herself in the older woman's place. Why had Alicia felt the need to travel north to look at a dead body? There was nothing of the young man left inside the grey skin but bone and muscle. A white sheet reached to his neck. Alicia stretched out an arm. Holly was afraid that she was going to pull back the sheet to reveal Paul Keating's dissection. Instead the woman touched her son's forehead. *She needed to be certain,* Holly thought suddenly. *All this time she's been carrying the hope that there was a mistake, that her boy wasn't the victim.* She twisted her body so that she could see Alicia's face without seeming to stare. The woman was crying. No sound. Even in her grief she felt the need to maintain a certain dignity.

'That *is* Patrick?' The Carswells' cleaner had made the formal identification, but Holly felt now that she needed to ask.

'Oh yes. Or it *was* Patrick.' Alicia stroked the forehead again, bent to kiss it lightly and then turned away.

She was booked on a train later in the morning and Holly drove her into Alnmouth for coffee, instead of leaving her to wait on her own at the station. They sat in the window of an old-fashioned tea shop. In the car there'd been no conversation, but now Alicia seemed to feel the need to talk.

'I found Simon,' Alicia said. 'My first dead golden boy. He'd hanged himself. Tied a belt round a bannister and dropped into the stairwell. I still have nightmares. I don't think he meant me to find him. Of course his father was alive then, and I was supposed to be spending the day with friends. But I got bored and came back to the house early. It was this time of year. Simon was home from Oxford for the Easter holidays and I wanted to spend some time with him. I could tell that he was stressed. My husband had high expectations of both the boys. I've always thought Simon planned for his father to find the body. A petty act of revenge and quite unfair.' She was dry-eyed now, but the words flowed instead of tears. 'Suicide can be a kind of violence too, don't you think? It hurts the people left behind. It took me a long time to forgive Simon, but I understood even at the time how desperate he must have been. At least I can grieve for Patrick without those complications. Without blame.' She paused and sipped the coffee. The cups were very small and painted with flowers. Vera wouldn't have got her fat fingers through the handle.

Holly didn't know what to say. Usually she was confident and decisive at work, but this case seemed to be undermining her judgement. 'We can't find any motive for either murder,' she said at last. 'You don't have any idea why someone would have wanted to kill Patrick?'

'In the last year I felt as if I'd lost touch with him.'

Alicia poured more tea. Her hand shook a little and there was a spill on the tablecloth. 'We'd been so close, especially after my husband died, but more recently if he'd had problems, I don't think I'd be the person he'd come to. Perhaps he disliked the fact that I'd fallen in love with another man, though he always seemed to get on well enough with Henry.'

'Can you think of anyone he might have confided in?'

Alicia shook her head. 'At one time I'd have said Rebecca, his girlfriend, but as I told you last night, they'd separated. There were colleagues, people at the university. I don't think he was particularly close to them, though. They shared a passion for Lepidoptera, but not much else.'

'Does Rebecca know that Patrick is dead?'

'Not from me! I suppose she might have seen it in the media. Of course I should have phoned her.' The woman seemed distraught. 'How dreadful not to have thought of that!'

'I'm sure she'll understand,' Holly said. 'Would you like me to tell her?'

'Oh, please do. Pass on my apologies. Tell her I'll be in touch. She might like to come to the funeral.' Alicia's voice tailed away.

'Have you had any thoughts about that?' Holly thought how hard it must be to plan a funeral for a child. Somehow it was unnatural for a son to die before his mother. Two sons.

'I'll bury him in the churchyard in the village, next to his brother,' Alicia said. 'They never met, but I know that's where Patrick would like to be.' She looked at her watch. 'The train won't arrive for half an hour, but would you mind driving me to the station, please? I'm afraid I'm not very good company, and I'd rather be there in plenty of time. Punctuality has always been an obsession. Patrick used to tease me about it.'

At the station Holly got out of the car and shook the woman's hand. With anyone else she would have been less formal, put an arm around her shoulder, taken a hand, but she knew Alicia Randle wouldn't want that. 'Shall I wait with you?'

'No, no.' It sounded as if the woman was horrified by the thought and Holly understood. Alicia was close to tears and wanted to sit on the empty platform and cry in peace.

Back in the police station in Kimmerston, Holly tried to track down Rebecca Brown, Patrick's ex-girlfriend. The number that Alicia had given them over dinner was unavailable. She was about to call the university in Exeter when Vera wandered up to her desk. 'Can you sort out a media release, Hol? I'd like to get it out for the lunchtime news. If there was a stranger in the valley, somebody must have seen him, and the canvassers have come up with bugger-all so far. Let's appeal to all the nosy stay-at-homes in the surrounding villages and the people who were walking on the hills or along the burn. We need details of any unfamiliar cars or people. I've still got teams out there, but we need a wider hit.'

Holly nodded and replaced the phone. The call to the university would have to wait.

'How was Alicia Randle?' Vera leaned against the desk. The fat on her backside spread inside her

Crimplene skirt, made it bulge. Holly found herself fascinated by it.

'Very brave,' Holly replied. 'She said it was easier to grieve for Patrick than for her first son. Less complicated. He couldn't be in any way to blame.'

'Let's hope that's true.' Vera slid away from the desk, leaving Holly to wonder exactly what she meant.

Later, when the media release had been sent to the press office for approval, Holly tried again to track down Patrick's former girlfriend. The woman at the end of the phone in Exeter University's school of medicine was cautious. 'Give me your number and I'll call you back. You could be the press.'

The phone rang half an hour later and the university admin officer had all the information Holly needed. 'Rebecca Brown's at home with her parents in County Durham.' She read out the address. 'It's still the Easter holidays and she won't be back at the university until the middle of next week. This is her mobile number.' She finished the call without asking any questions. Holly couldn't tell if she was very busy or very discreet.

A male voice answered Rebecca's mobile. 'Who is it?' Then, without waiting for an answer, 'Becky's not up to talking now.' He sounded angry.

Holly supposed this meant that Rebecca had seen the news about Patrick's death and had been upset by it. She introduced herself. 'And who are you?' Keeping the question polite.

'I'm her brother. The press have tracked her down. So-called friends must have told them she knew Patrick. It's been a nightmare. We're worried that if someone doesn't answer her phone, they'll just turn up on the doorstep.'

'We'll need to talk to her, I'm afraid. Can I come there?'

There was a pause and Holly heard a muffled conversation in the background. 'When do you want to come?'

'Now,' she said. 'If that's all right.' She thought again that she'd be glad to escape the office and Kimmerston.

The young protector at the end of the phone agreed and gave directions.

The Browns lived in a small market town on the edge of the Durham moors. Once it must have been prosperous. There were grand Georgian houses and an impressive town hall stood on the market square. Now, though, many of the shops in the main street had been closed and were boarded up, and even in the sunshine it had an air of desolation. The Browns lived in one of the big merchants' houses close to the square. By the time Holly arrived it was late afternoon. The market was closing down, the stallholders folding tarpaulins and clearing tables. Cauliflower leaves and overripe tomatoes littered the cobbles. There was no sign that the press had tracked down Rebecca's address, and the street outside the house was quiet.

The door was opened by a young man who must have been close to Patrick Randle in age and a little older than his own sister. 'I'm George. Mum and Dad are out. Dad's a GP and he's still at the surgery. Mum's just gone into town to visit a friend. Becky's in here.'

It was a big family kitchen looking out over an untidy garden, and a young woman sat in the window-seat looking out. She was big-boned, tall and blonde. When she saw Holly she stood up. Her eyes were red from crying, but she managed a smile. 'Sorry I'm in such a state. I can tell George thinks I'm being a bit of a drama-queen. It sounds like something out of a women's mag, but Patrick really was the love of my life. I can't believe he's dead.' A pause. 'That someone killed him.' She sat back down, but now she faced into the room.

'Had you heard from him recently?' Holly took a kitchen chair. The room looked as if it had been furnished by individual purchases from auctions. Lots of beautiful pieces, but nothing coordinated. Holly thought she wouldn't have been able to stand the clash of colours and the clutter. It would bring on a migraine. She'd need to clear the place and start from the beginning.

'There was a cryptic text a week ago.' Becky pulled out her phone. 'I've saved it, of course. It says: *Nearly fit to be your friend again. If you can forgive me.*'

'What did you take that to mean?'

'That whatever project had taken up the whole of his head for nearly a year was complete.' Becky looked up at her. 'That he was planning to come back to me.'

'And you'd have had him back?' Holly wouldn't have considered returning to a failed relationship. It would never work and anyway she had too much pride.

'Of course. I've told you he was the love of my life. But I couldn't be with him as he was. Semi-detached. Obsessed with strange conspiracy theories.'

'What sort of theories?'

Becky shrugged. 'At first I thought it was about his work. Some scientists are haunted by the thought that another researcher will publish before them or steal their data. And Pat's stuff was quite topical. There are still climate-change deniers, and his findings would have made their position seem even more ludicrous. He was always passionate about his work.'

It seemed unlikely to Holly that research into the habits of flying insects could provide a motive for murder, but she kept quiet.

Becky continued, 'Then I thought it was something entirely different that was eating away at him. Something to do with his family. It seemed to start when his mother took up with another bloke, but the timing could have been coincidental. Or perhaps that triggered his desire to know more about his close relatives. Anyway all his spare time was taken up digging away in old newspaper reports and family-history sites online. And his attitude to his mother changed too. They'd always been very close, but suddenly he was cold when he spoke about her. It was as if visits home were just a drag. I hated the way he was with her. It wasn't the Patrick I'd known and loved.'

'He'd discovered something about Alicia? Something he disapproved of?'

'I don't know what he'd found out, because he wouldn't talk to me about it. That was why I broke off with him. He seemed to be going faintly loopy, but I didn't split up with him because I thought he was losing his mind. If I'm going to be a GP, I'll have to deal with that and I knew he wasn't really mad. And it wasn't because I thought he was totally crazy to give up the chance of an immediate research post, when that was what he wanted since he was about twelve. I dumped him because he was being so bloody secretive. I only know that his family had anything to do with his obsession because I caught him digging into past copies of his local newspaper online. He seemed to be brooding over his father's obituary. And even then he wouldn't talk to me. He said he'd tell me the whole story when he knew it himself.'

'What's the name of the newspaper?' Holly thought it was a long shot, but Vera Stanhope liked detail.

'The *Hereford Times*.'

'So you were the one to end the relationship?' Holly was trying to make sense of this. The boss would love it. She enjoyed complication, stories of past feuds and tensions. In Holly's experience, murder was usually much simpler.

Becky nodded. 'And, you know, I think Patrick was almost pleased. Because that would give him a free hand to carry on with his research. Or whatever it was that was keeping him awake all night.'

'Was anyone helping him? There was another victim. An older man called Martin Benton.' Holly was already imagining taking all this information back to Vera, but it would be even better if she could find a connection between the two men.

'The name doesn't mean anything.' Becky had turned back to face the window. Outside an old apple tree was in blossom, the flowers the colour of candy floss. 'But. as I said, Patrick didn't talk to me about it.'

'Do you know if the Randle family had any connection with Northumberland? Did the county have a special meaning for him?' Holly thought the man could have come north to continue his research. 'We still don't know why he chose to come to the area.'

'Well, it wasn't to see me.' Becky stood up. 'I thought I might phone him, you know. After I got that text from him. I was going to offer to meet up. I kept planning the words in my head. *We're only forty miles apart. Let's get together for a drink. In Newcastle maybe. That's kind of halfway.* But in the end I decided against it. I thought I had to let him come back to me when he was ready. And that's what's really hurting. I could have seen him, changed things. He might even still be alive. It's not just grief that's kept me awake since I heard he'd died.' She paused and looked directly at Holly. 'I feel so bloody guilty.'

Chapter Twenty

Vera sat in her office and brooded. Joe had come back from the prison with news of his conversation with Lizzie Redhead. He'd achieved precious little and she thought that she should have gone instead. Joe was at the time in his life when his judgement could be clouded by a bonny lass. The only useful information he could offer was that the woman from the prisoners' aid charity had visited too. What was that about? Lizzie would have plenty of support on the outside and a home to go back to. Vera thought there were people who needed Shirley Hewarth's help more than Lizzie Redhead.

A wasp was buzzing against the glass of the window. Vera opened it, letting in a sudden roar of traffic noise, and set the insect free. Wasn't it too early in the year for wasps? She stood up, grabbed her bag and went out. In the car park she passed Holly and was tempted to stop and ask how she'd got on with Patrick's girlfriend, but in the end she only waved and drove away. She felt she was being sucked back to the valley where the bodies had been discovered. As if it was a vacuum and there was no resistance.

The place was quiet. It was about the same time of day as when she'd first visited in response to the discovery of Patrick's body. That had been two days ago, and they still hadn't found the place where he'd been killed, though the search team had been working from dawn until almost dusk over the past two days. Costing a bloody fortune in overtime. They'd finished for the evening and Vera drove past the entrance to the Carswells' house, the house that the locals called 'the Hall'. Percy's Mini was parked outside the bungalow, but here too everything was quiet. As she approached the front door there was the faint murmur of the television. She rang the bell and heard the sound of it inside. It took a while for anyone to answer and Vera thought that Susan must be out. Percy's daughter was so curious that she'd have the door open immediately.

The old man looked a little dishevelled and she thought he must have fallen asleep in front of the TV.

'Oh, it's you.' He stood aside to let her in.

'Your Susan not around?'

'She's gone into Kimmerston to see some friends. Regular date, once a month.'

'Ah well,' Vera said. 'It was you I wanted to see anyway.'

He took her into the living room and switched of the television. 'Just rubbish anyway.' Then he offered her tea.

'You're all right,' Vera said. 'I'm awash with the stuff. I'm not sure what I'm here for really. Only a chat, and to get out of the office.' She sat in an armchair by the window and waited for him to take his place. 'Do you have much to do with the folk up at Valley Farm?'

It took him a while to gather his thoughts. She thought he'd probably been to The Lamb for a couple of pints, then eaten a big supper. He'd have been fast asleep within minutes of his daughter leaving, the doorbell jolting him awake, leaving him a bit confused and dazed.

'I see them around.' She thought he *had* been to the pub, because he was dressed in proper trousers and a shirt, a grey cardigan, just as he had been when they'd first met. 'They seem decent enough. I've known Sam Redhead all his life, of course. He grew up on the estate farm. He's always been a quiet kind of chap.'

'Did you ever meet their daughter?'

He shook his head. 'I heard stories. It's hard being a parent. You have to stick by them, even if you don't always like the way they carry on.'

There was a moment of silence. 'Does Susan clean for all of them?'

'Aye. Mrs Carswell recommended her to the Prof. and his wife, and then the other houses took her on.'

'Handy.'

He nodded. Vera waited. 'She likes some of them better than others. The Prof. can be a bit particular. He doesn't like her moving the stuff on his shelves, then complains because there's a bit of dust left.' Another pause. 'He's a proper writer. He's had real books published. Not fiction. Historical stuff.'

'What about Janet? His wife?'

'Susan says she's a bit of a doormat. It's almost as if she's scared of him.' He looked up. 'But you don't want to take too much notice of what Susan says. She's never been one to let the truth stand in the way of a good story.' He gave an awkward little laugh. 'I tell her she should be a writer herself.'

Vera smiled too. 'You must remember the farmhouse up there when it was still working. The place where the Lucas family lives now.'

'I used to work there. Contract mostly. And my dad before me. He was a moudy man.'

Vera grinned. 'Eh, I haven't heard that word for years! You'd get in the moudy man to clear your land of moles and pests.'

Percy nodded. 'You wouldn't recognize the house now. It's all been tarted up. You'd never guess it was ever a working farm.' A pause. 'A chap called Heslop used to be the tenant farmer. Spent all his adult life there, struggling to make a living from the place. He only gave up when his wife couldn't stand it any more and forced him to shift to the town. He died six months later. He'd be turning in his grave if he could see what they'd done to the place.'

'You've been inside?'

'Nigel Lucas had a party last Christmas and invited most of the village.' He gave a wicked grin. 'I think they were hoping the Carswells would show, but the major and his wife were down south visiting their daughter. So Nigel had to make do with the plebs.'

'He's a bit of a social climber, is he?'

'Cash is no object,' Percy said. 'Susan says their kitchen cost more than a man's wage for a year. But I don't think that's enough for Nigel. He'd like to get in with the county set. It'll never happen, though. Round here you need to be born to it.'

'How did he make all his money?' Vera leaned forward with her elbows on her knees. She thought this was as happy as she got, digging around into the background of her suspects. Perhaps she was a bit of a historian too.

'He had his own business. Burglar alarms. That sort of thing, I suppose. Sold it and made a fortune, apparently.' Percy paused again. 'Susan says he's been accepted as a magistrate. She saw the letter when she was cleaning last week.'

Vera thought that figured. Nigel would see it as a first step to becoming established in the county. Besides, he'd love sitting on the bench and passing judgement on more lowly mortals. 'What does Susan think of the wife? She seems a bonny thing. Younger than him?'

Percy considered. 'She's not that much younger. Not according to Susan. Well preserved.'

Vera thought Susan would probably know. She imagined the cleaner going through desk drawers when she had the place to herself, picking up birth dates and stray personal details. She'd be one to hoard information, loving it for its own sake. *And isn't that just what I do?*

She looked across at Percy. 'Did Susan pick up any useful facts about Patrick Randle, the house-sitter? She'd have been curious – a new man in the valley – but she might be a bit embarrassed to tell us, because she wasn't supposed to go up into the flat. She wouldn't want us to know she'd been prying. But she might have told you.'

For the first time Percy seemed uncomfortable. He shifted in his chair. 'She means no harm.'

'That's not really an answer, is it, pet?'

The old man didn't reply and Vera continued, 'You know this place. Two men are dead. You'd tell me, wouldn't you, if you had any idea what might have caused it? Even if you only suspected?'

'I don't know anything about the murders,' Percy said. 'Really. I hate all this. The police in the meadow and the roadblock at the end of the lane, so I get stopped every time I just want a quick pint in The Lamb. If I knew owt useful, I'd tell you. I want everything back to normal.'

Vera nodded, satisfied at last.

She expected to find the station quiet, but Holly was still there. With a touch of guilt Vera suspected the officer had been waiting for *her*. If it'd been Joe, Vera would have taken him home, fed him something her hippy neighbours had left in her freezer, opened a beer. But she'd learned that Holly disliked that sort of approach, saw it almost as corrupting. So Vera took her to the canteen, bought coffee from one of the machines. That was about as informal as Holly was comfortable with. Their words seemed to rattle around the empty space.

'So, Hol? How did you get on with Randle's girlfriend?

'She'd seen about the murder in the press. Of course she was upset. Although Becky was the one to end the relationship, I don't think she saw the separation as permanent. She always thought there'd be a happy-ever-after ending.'

Vera heard the sarcasm, but ignored it. Holly could do with a bit of romance in her life. It might make her a tad less brittle.

'If she still cared for the lad, why did she dump him?'

'Because she thought he was keeping secrets from her. Maybe she thought if she threatened to dump him, it would jolt him into confiding in her. It didn't work, though.'

Vera became more alert at that. Until then she'd been going through the motions, letting Holly know that she was taking her seriously. But now this was starting to get interesting. 'Come on, Hol. Tell me more. What sort of secrets. Another woman?'

'Nothing like that. At least I don't think so. Apparently Patrick's personality changed at about the time his mother took up with her new man. He became interested in the family history and started researching the past, digging around in the archives of the local paper. He got a bit paranoid about his university research too, talked about people stealing his data. I'm not sure what it was all about. But he sent Becky a text last week.' Holly looked down at her notes. '*Nearly fit to be your friend again. If you can forgive me.* Which Becky took to mean that he'd finished whatever project had been taking up all his time, and he hoped it might be possible for them to get back together. That he might be prepared to tell her what had been going on.'

'Did she reply?' Vera's coffee had been left to go cold.

'She didn't phone him. I'm not sure whether she texted.'

Vera tried to get her head around this. Of course the emotional affairs of two young people might have no relevance at all to the case, but Patrick's obsession with secrecy struck her as significant. What could a young man from his background possibly have to hide?

And where could Martin Benton fit in? She realized that it was starting to get dark outside.

'Get on home.' She made a little shooing gesture with her hands. 'We've got a full day tomorrow and I can't have you off your game. You've done brilliantly, Hol. Thanks.' Then she smiled at the young woman's confusion. It never did any harm to wrong-foot the team by giving a bit of praise. It occurred to Vera, watching Holly walk away to spend the night alone in her flat, that they had more in common than she liked to admit. *She'd* been spiky and defensive when she'd been a young officer, and though there were more women in the service now, Holly didn't have it easy. No family around to support her. And it probably wasn't her fault that she looked like something out of a fashion magazine, with legs up to her waist and American teeth. Holly left the canteen and Vera watched with a stab of sympathy. Then she thought she must be getting soft in her old age.

On the way back to her car she called into her office. On her desk was the brown Manila file she'd seen in Randle's car and a little note from Joe: *This is the file you were asking about. It was empty. No fingerprints except Randle's.* She thought that just about summed up the progress they were making with the case.

The next morning she woke very early. There was the cold grey light of just after dawn, but it was the noise of her phone that had dragged her from sleep. The landline. Everyone knew that her house had crap mobile reception. 'Yes!' She could feel the adrenaline racing through her heart, jolting her, scattering weird ideas in her brain. She thought she must sound as Percy had, when she'd rung his doorbell the afternoon before.

It was a voice she didn't recognize and it took her a while to take in the words. 'We think we've found the locus for the young man's death.'

'Where?' Now she was fully conscious and aware of what was going on. She was already out of bed, the phone tucked between her ear and her shoulder, scrabbling to find a scrap of paper.

'The vegetable garden of the big house. We didn't look there yesterday and it was our first search this morning. There's blood on the wooden rim of one of the seedbeds. Easy enough to miss, but one of my boys picked it up. I'll bet you anything we'll find that the soil on the victim's shoes has traces of compost. There's salad stuff growing in there, and some of the plants have been crushed.'

'Thanks.' Her mind was still racing and that had nothing to do with being wakened suddenly from a deep sleep. If Randle had been killed in the garden, why bother moving him? He'd be just as much hidden there as he'd been in the ditch. Then the thought came, sudden and urgent: *It would help if we knew which of the victims died first.* She realized the officer in charge of the search team was still on the end of the line. 'Tell your people it's my shout next time I see them in the pub.'

'We'll carry on looking. But I thought you'd want to know.'

Chapter Twenty-One

Friday morning and Annie Redhead was counting the hours until her daughter's release from prison. They'd had a phone call from Lizzie and had been told she'd be let out of the gaol mid-morning on Sunday. Phone calls were always tricky. The background noise and the money running out, people in the queue shouting for her to be quick. Annie had offered to pick Lizzie up: 'If that's all right. If you haven't made any other plans.' She'd become used to being careful what she said to Lizzie; always felt it was important not to make assumptions. After all, Lizzie was an adult now. She had to be allowed to make her own decisions. Annie imagined standing in the gloomy prison hall where she waited when she went to visit and seeing the small figure of Lizzie being led along the corridor. Looking like a shadow. In her daydream Lizzie was always delighted to see her and, when she emerged into the hall, lit up through the Victorian stained-glass windows, her face seemed to be shining.

Annie wasn't sure whether she was looking forward to Lizzie's release or dreading it. She'd left behind the social embarrassment of Lizzie's imprisonment months ago. That no longer worried her. The court case had been in the papers and everyone had known about it. The only time Sam ever said anything positive about selling the restaurant was that he was glad they weren't living in Kimmerston when the news came out. 'I couldn't bear it. Customers talking about it and falling quiet every time we got close. The pity.'

Of course their friends in Valley Farm had known that Lizzie was inside, that she'd been charged with grievous bodily harm, but they'd never really mentioned it. Not in front of Sam. They understood that he was a private man. Jan and Lorraine had come to her separately, saying much the same thing: 'I'm really sorry. It must be a dreadful time for you. If ever you want to talk . . .' But the last thing Annie wanted to talk about was Lizzie's behaviour. She was happy to have everyone there when she needed some company, people to share a bottle of wine with, a bit of a party on a Friday night. Even Sam had appreciated that. But she didn't want a heavy conversation or advice. They'd been through all that since Lizzie was tiny – with teachers, psychologists and social workers. None of it had helped. She thought Lizzie was damaged in some way, had been since she was a baby, and nobody could help her.

Occasionally Annie saw a mother with a grown-up daughter walking through the town. They'd have linked arms or be sharing a joke. Then she experienced a moment of intense jealousy, just as she supposed women who couldn't have children felt when they saw a newborn in a pram. The pain of wanting something that would probably always be denied to them.

The great thing about having Lizzie in prison had been that they could stop worrying about her for a while. The relief of that had been immense. Like the bliss of chronic pain suddenly disappearing. Annie knew about chronic pain because of the arthritis in her knees. In prison their daughter was the authorities' responsibility. Annie could go to bed at night knowing that Lizzie was safe, that there would be no frantic phone calls in the early hours demanding action. No mad dashes to A&E. But soon Lizzie would be out, and Annie's deepest fear was that the stress and anxiety would return and they wouldn't be able to handle them this time. They were too old. They'd become used to contentment, a wonderful boredom, and a return to the old way of surviving might break them.

The phone rang again just after Sam had driven away on his routine trip to the village to collect his paper.

'Hello.' Annie hadn't recognized the number and her voice was sharp. It would be someone trying to sell insurance, a new boiler, loft insulation.

'Mrs Redhead? This is Shirley Hewarth. I work for a charity called Hope North-East. It's about your daughter.'

For a moment Annie didn't answer. 'What do you want?'

'Just a chat.' The woman's voice was warm and calm. She sounded like all the other professionals who'd thought they could make a difference. 'About Lizzie's future. I saw her yesterday. Just a short pre-release visit. I can come to you, if you like. Later this morning.'

'No!' Annie didn't want another stranger in the house, and Sam saw any visitor as an intruder. 'I'll come to you. Where are you?' When the woman started describing the office and the pit-village where it was based, Annie interrupted her. 'Yes, I know where that is.' Because it was where she came from. She'd lived with her parents not very far from the charity's office.

Annie didn't tell Sam about the phone call or the appointment. They were both thinking that Lizzie would soon be out, but they hadn't discussed it. Perhaps they were hoping some miracle had happened in the Victorian monstrosity where their daughter had been living for the last few months. That she'd emerge from the big wrought-iron gates gentler and more considerate.

When he walked into the kitchen with his newspaper under his arm, she was already dressed to go out.

'You don't mind, love, do you? I really need to escape the valley for a while.'

'Do you want me to come with you?' He put down the newspaper.

'Nah, I might meet up with Jill. Have coffee. Lunch even. Do a bit of shopping.' He nodded and didn't ask any more questions. It felt strange lying to him. She didn't think she'd ever done that before.

It was weird going back to Bebington. Weird because nothing had really changed. It had been a kind of ghost town since the pits had closed, and she hadn't known it as very much different; there were still rows of houses with peeling paint and occasional boarded-up windows, the bony men sitting on doorsteps, listless, seeming only to wait for their next fix.

In other parts of the country, and the county, the economy had peaked and troughed, but here there'd been nothing but depression. She'd have understood Lizzie's anger and frustration if her daughter had been brought up in this town, but she'd been born when they were living at the farm. Her playground had been the valley. And even when Sam had given up the tenancy and they'd moved to Kimmerston, Lizzie had been loved and given everything she could possibly need.

Annie stood for a moment outside the Hope North-East office and tried to remember what used to be in the building. Suddenly she remembered: a little cafe. An old-fashioned greasy spoon, serving bacon stotties and strong tea. Her grandfather had come here sometimes to meet his pals. She pushed open the door and climbed the stairs to the office.

Three people were sitting at one of the small desks, having some sort of meeting. They had mugs of coffee in front of them. There was a skinny woman who looked middle-aged, but was probably in her early thirties. Lank hair and troubled eyes. A big guy with huge hands and tattoos. And Shirley. From first glance, Annie had realized this must be Shirley. It was the way she dressed and the way she was speaking. She was clearly the person in charge. She stood up. Seeing her close up, Annie thought she was older than she'd first guessed. Late fifties, early sixties. The make-up was discreet, but skilfully applied.

'You must be Annie.' Shirley held out her hand. 'Just give me a moment to finish up here and we'll find somewhere private to talk.'

There was a brief conversation with her colleagues

about diary dates and fund-raising. The big man wandered off downstairs and the little woman returned to her own desk.

'There's an interview room downstairs,' Shirley said. 'We won't be disturbed there. I'll make us some coffee, shall I?' She switched on the kettle, which stood on a tray on the floor, and spooned ground coffee into a cafetière. Annie had been expecting horrible supermarket own-brand instant and was surprised.

The interview room made Annie think of a prison cell. It was small and square with one high window giving very little light. It was comfortable enough – carpet on the floor, two armchairs, a light-wood coffee table between them – but it made Annie uneasy. It was a place where confessions, or confidences at least, would be expected.

Shirley poured coffee in silence, as if she had all the time in the world, and it was Annie who spoke first. 'How was Lizzie when you saw her yesterday?'

'Fine!' That reassuring voice used by social workers everywhere. 'Looking forward to seeing you both soon.' A pause. 'When I went, she'd just had a visit from a police officer. A detective sergeant. He was asking about the murders in Gilswick.'

'Lizzie couldn't have had anything to do with those!'

'Of course she couldn't. But I thought you'd want to know.' There was a moment's hesitation. 'One of the victims worked here as a volunteer. We're all rather shocked. We can't understand how he came to be in Gilswick.' The last sentence came out almost as a question.

'I never met him!' Annie was confused and anxious. She'd thought this interview would all be about Lizzie: where she would live and what work she might get. Now it seemed this woman was more intent on getting information about the murders than on helping her daughter. 'I never met either of them. Why did the police think Lizzie could help?' This was becoming the worst sort of nightmare. How could the police possibly link Lizzie to the killings? Did they think she and Sam might be responsible for the violence?

'I'm sure they're just exploring possibilities.' Shirley smiled. 'Previous offenders are always easy targets at the start of an inquiry.' She paused for a beat. 'The detective asked Lizzie about Jason Crow. Any idea why they might think he's involved?'

'No!'

'Because it's important that when Lizzie comes out she stays away from people who might get her into trouble again. I'm sure you understand that.'

Annie breathed deeply. She'd learned that it was important when you were dealing with professional do-gooders to keep calm. Otherwise they judged you. Wrote things like *anger-management problems* in their reports. Lizzie was always said to have an anger-management problem. 'One of the reasons we moved back to Gilswick from Kimmerston was to put some distance between Lizzie and the crowd she was hanging around with before.'

'Of course. So it must seem very distressing that the criminal activity has followed you to the country.'

'It's horrible,' Annie said. It was starting to feel as if the room was shrinking, as if the air was being sucked out of it, so that she couldn't breathe. She was wondering what excuse she might give for leaving. The woman sat between her and the door, and Annie measured up this distance to it with her eyes.

'I wonder if it's a good thing for Lizzie to return to a community where the police are investigating a double-murder.' Shirley poured more coffee into both mugs, lifted the jug to offer milk. Annie was reminded of all the times she'd drunk coffee with Jan and Lorraine. Sitting in one of the smart houses in Valley Farm, passing on village gossip. Only now *they* were the subject of all the gossip in Gilswick.

'Better that Lizzie comes home with us than that she goes back to her old haunts in Kimmerston.' Annie caught her breath. 'Though of course that has to be her decision. She's an adult.'

'That's what I think too.' Shirley smiled with real warmth and Annie thought the woman was only doing her job; she had been overreacting. The business with the murders had made her panicky since she'd first heard about them, filling her head with all sorts of crazy notions. Shirley continued, 'And I do think Lizzie would like to come back to you. At least to start with. I think she should be considering going back to college. Maybe the FE college locally to get her A levels, then who knows? She's certainly bright enough for uni.'

'She's always hated the idea of studying.'

'I think you might find that prison has changed her. Did you know she signed up for a couple of education classes in Sittingwell? She's joined the writers' group and in the short time she's been attending she's become a bit of a star. I don't believe in the short, sharp shock, but being inside for a while certainly works for some people. It gives them time to sort out their priorities. To grow up a bit.'

'Did she talk to you about what she might like to do?' Annie was finding it hard to believe that this conversation between Shirley and her daughter had actually taken place. All *her* attempts to discuss Lizzie's future had always ended in silence or sulking. Slammed doors and disappearance. On the prison visits Annie hadn't dared bring the subject up. She'd concentrated on being supportive.

'Not in any detail, but I was wondering about the hospitality industry. Didn't you and your husband once run a restaurant?'

'Yes.' She wanted to add: *And Lizzie lost it for us,* but that seemed petty, now that Lizzie might actually have a future. Annie was blown away by the sudden vision of Lizzie as a *normal* daughter with a job and a home. A daughter she could chat with and introduce to her friends. A daughter with whom she could link arms and share a joke.

'I was wondering if I might come and visit you all early next week.' Shirley was pulling out a big diary from her bag. 'See if we might start to put some plans in place.'

'Oh yes!' Annie thought that if Sam didn't fancy meeting the woman he could go out in the morning, go into Kimmerston. She knew she shouldn't build up her hopes for Lizzie's future. She'd done that too many times before. But perhaps Shirley was right. Perhaps all Lizzie had needed was some time away. A kind of retreat from the world. Annie couldn't understand her own initial dislike of the charity worker. How foolish she'd been!

'So shall we say Monday morning at eleven o'clock?' Shirley wrote a note in the diary and then looked up for Annie's agreement. 'That'll give you a day to settle back together again. For you to get to know your daughter.' Now she was writing on a little appointment card and she slid it across the table.

Out on the street Annie felt a ridiculous rush of optimism. Perhaps Lizzie had been changed by the shock of the court case and prison – the few months away from the dealers to get herself clean. The murders in the valley had nothing to do with them, after all. It was the act of a random lunatic. She'd seen occasional cases on the television news. Sick bastards riding down country roads with a shotgun, killing any strangers who got in their way. Glorying in the violence. The police always caught those people.

She drove back towards Gilswick with the car window open, listening to birdsong. Thinking that she would have to explain about Lizzie to Sam. They couldn't put off talking about their daughter any longer.

Chapter Twenty-Two

It was still early when Vera arrived at the big house. She'd phoned the station to set back the briefing for an hour and she'd demanded Billy's presence at Gilswick Hall. He might be a randy old goat, but he was the most meticulous crime-scene manager she'd ever worked with. The officer in charge of the search team was new to her. He was a big bald-headed Scot called Peter MacBride and he was waiting for her by the front door of the Carswell house when she drove up. Getting out of the car, she heard a cuckoo and thought how rare that was these days. When she was a kid they listened out for them every year. She had a sudden sense of nature being knocked out of kilter. A heatwave in April, wasps out of season and the cuckoos disappearing. Two strangers killed in a place people thought of as paradise.

MacBride was apologetic. 'Sorry it's taken so long. It made sense to work our way from the house towards the road and the ditch where the body was found. The veggie patch is at the back, so we've only just got to that.'

'You had an early start today.'

'Aye, well, I'm a persistent bugger. It's been eating away at me that we haven't been able to find the murder scene for the young man. I got the team to assemble just before dawn, so we could make a prompt start at first light.'

Vera followed him round the side of the house. She'd looked out at the vegetable garden from the upstairs windows, but hadn't ventured here. It was big and well tended, almost commercial in scale. Fruit bushes in a cage, strawberry plants under netting, rows of vegetables already starting to push through the soil. Everything labelled and almost weed-free. She wondered again if Patrick had been expected to work out here. Now that was even more relevant and she made a note to ask Joe to check with the house-sitting agency.

A row of cold-frames stood beyond the fruit cage. Solid wooden frames with the glass lids now removed. Inside mostly salad crops – radish, lettuce and spring onions. The lettuce was the cut-and-come-again variety and was ready for harvest. On the corner of the far edge of one frame a dark stain that could be blood.

'Of course we'll need a sample for DNA testing?'

He nodded to show that it was already being sorted. 'And as soon as you've finished here, we'll cover it and let the scientists do their thing.'

'Lorna Dawson's testing the soil from his shoes?' Vera liked the man. His competence and lack of drama.

He nodded again. 'I've been in touch and she says she'll try to visit. It's a long way from Aberdeen, though, and it depends what else she has on.'

Inside the frame the plants were crushed. 'So what's

your theory?' Vera had dozens of scenarios dancing in *her* brain, but none of them made sense yet.

'I think the victim was out here working. Someone came up behind him and hit him. He twisted as he fell into the frame and that's how we have blood on that side of it.'

'Well, I suppose that ties in with the injuries on the body.' But Vera thought it didn't tie in with anything else. They knew that Patrick had picked Benton up from the bus in Gilswick and had driven him back to the big house. There were two mugs in the kitchen in the flat, so they'd had tea together. Why would Patrick leave the older man alone to come out and do a spot of gardening? It didn't make sense.

'There were no defensive injuries.' She was speaking almost to herself now. 'What does that tell us?'

'There's a grass path almost all the way from the house.' MacBride looked back towards the building. 'If Randle was bending over the frame working, he might not have heard the killer approaching.'

Vera didn't answer immediately. She was picturing the scene. Late afternoon. Warm. *Forget about Benton for a while and focus on what was happening here.* There had been no blood stains on Randle's jersey or jacket, only on his shirt, so perhaps he *had* been gardening. He'd taken off his jumper and jacket and put them on the ground close by. 'Maybe.' But why would he work in the garden when he had a guest – Benton – in the flat?

She straightened and paused, hoping to catch the sound of the cuckoo again, but all she could hear were woodpigeons. 'It's a bloody long way from here to the ditch by the road. The killer must have had access to a vehicle. It'd be struggle enough to get him to the drive.' She wondered why the killer had bothered. If there'd only been one murder, she'd have understood it. It could have been an attempt to make the whole thing look like an accident. A hit-and-run. And that might explain why the jacket and jersey had been replaced. But the body in the flat was going to be found eventually and then there was no way the authorities wouldn't link the two deaths. It all seemed too complicated. Too weird. Again she thought that the timing of the men's deaths was the key to this. But she knew there was no way Paul Keating would be able to tell her which of the victims had died first.

She stretched and looked at her watch. She should get back to the station. In Kimmerston the troops would be waiting for the briefing. The sun was almost warm now. MacBride's team were making their way in a line through the small orchard between the back of the house and the hill.

He followed her gaze. 'Just in case someone came down to the house from the footpath that runs along the ridge. But we'll be packing up by the end of the day.'

'Aye, well, thank them. And thank you.' They were almost at the house when she had another idea. 'I don't suppose you've come across a moth trap? Wooden or plastic contraption, with a funnel and a very bright bulb.'

'Is that what they are? We left them *in situ*. This way.' He led her down a beaten path through the trees that separated the house from the road. Sunlight slanted onto the patches of clear fell and the bright-green spears of bluebells. In some places the plants were in flower, giving the undergrowth a bluish sheen. Birdsong everywhere. She thought this was what had brought the people in the new development at the end of the track to live in the valley. They imagined it would always be like this.

'Did you find anything else of interest here?'

'Four sweetie wrappers. Unusual because they're from a local manufacturer. Kimmerston Confectionery. Only sold in a few outlets. They do the old-fashioned sweets – black bullets, pear drops, sherbet lemons. All individually wrapped. No telling how long they've been here, though, and they could have blown in from the road. Or been eaten by Randle when he was setting up the traps.'

Vera didn't say anything. She didn't think Randle was the sort of chap who'd drop litter. And she knew she'd seen a bowl of the sweets recently, though she couldn't for the life of her remember where.

MacBride stopped so suddenly that Vera almost walked into the back of him. By the side of the path there were two moth traps, set quite close to each other. Huge car batteries to power them. 'They were full of insects,' he said. 'We didn't know what to do with them.'

'The traps will be on a timer,' she said. 'They'll only be lit at night.' The light would attract the insects, luring them into the funnel and the soft cardboard egg boxes below.

Vera lowered herself into a crouch, heard her knee joints cracking, then wondered what she was doing down here. She wouldn't know a rare moth if it bit her on the nose. 'Can you get the contents to an expert? The Hancock Museum will have someone. Or one of the unis. And we'll need Fingerprints to look at the traps.'

'What are you looking for?'

'I'm not sure yet. Something unusual. These creatures are the only things that linked the victims.'

'You don't think two men were killed because of these?'

Vera didn't answer. Perhaps the idea was that Benton would stay until the following morning and the victims would examine the contents together. But all this was speculation and probably a waste of time. She pictured what Holly Clarke would make of her theories, as she struggled to get to her feet. MacBride looked away as if he didn't want to add to her embarrassment. 'Eh, pet, give me a hand, will you? Otherwise we'll be here all day.'

He gave a little laugh and pulled her up. She dusted leaves and twigs from her knees.

Back at the cars, she paused. 'You haven't found the murder weapon in your search of the grounds? I mean, whatever caused the blunt-force trauma to the back of Randle's head. It seems that the knife my DC found, when we first came to the house, killed Benton. Dr Keating seems pretty certain about that.' She still thought it odd that the men had been killed in different ways.

'Nothing definite and, trust me, we've looked!'

'I'm sure you have. And that you'd have come across it, if it had been here. Any thoughts?'

'I'm wondering if it had been hidden in plain sight. There's a toolshed. Lots of spades and shovels. We've sent them for analysis. And we're still waiting for Doc Keating to give his opinion.'

When she was in the Land Rover at the end of the drive Billy Cartwright was on his way in. Vera wound down the window and they had a brief shouted chat. To save him having to back all the way down the lane or her pulling into the verge, she turned right out of the drive towards the Valley Farm development. She turned in the courtyard to make her way back to the village, stopping briefly to look up at the houses. Perhaps because it was still early, everything was very quiet. But upstairs in the farmhouse Nigel Lucas was sitting in the window. He'd obviously heard her vehicle and was staring down at her. Next to him on the windowsill stood a pair of binoculars.

Chapter Twenty-Three

Vera was late for the morning briefing and she'd already set it back by an hour. Joe knew she got criticized by her bosses for being too hands-on. They thought she should learn to delegate and have more faith in her team. She'd once read out a comment she'd been given at her appraisal: *You shouldn't believe that you're indispensable. Your role is to pass on your skills to others.* 'Well,' she'd said. 'If they can persuade Holly not to look down her nose at folk who live in dirty houses, they're better senior officers than I am.' He'd laughed at the time, but now he thought the bosses had a point. Vera was the worst kind of control freak.

She burst in just as everyone was starting to get impatient. Holly was muttering that she'd go back to her desk, because she wanted to complete the detailed timeline for the suspects' movements on the day of the murders. She'd just stood up when Vera swept in, full of energy, unstoppable as a steamroller. 'Are you leaving us, Hol? That's a shame, because we've got a locus for the Randle lad's murder and we could do with your input.'

Muttered laughter, while Vera beamed. Holly sat down and the briefing started. Vera didn't even bother to get her usual mug of coffee. This morning, it seemed, she didn't need caffeine to get her going.

'So finally we know where Randle was killed.' Vera was standing in front of them, but she couldn't keep still. She moved up and down the narrow space between the chairs and the whiteboard. If she hadn't been so heavy, Joe would have said she was dancing. The spirit of Muhammad Ali before a title fight was there, even if her weight stopped her prancing on her toes. 'In the veggie garden at the side of the house.' Joe listened to the details: the blood on the cold-frame, the crushed salad plants and the moth traps that had been set, but not emptied.

'So.' Vera threw out the single word like a challenge. 'Let's think what could have happened here. Let's run through some possibilities.' But, instead of pausing to give them all a chance to think, to throw in their ideas, she carried on talking. She was so wired that she found silence impossible. 'We know that Benton and Randle met; we think they had a cup of tea in the flat. Then at some point they must have separated. Why? How did Randle end up in the garden, leaving Benton in the flat? And when did they set up those bloody moth traps? It might be useful to know if they'd been running since Patrick arrived. They're right in the heart of the wood and you can't see them from the road, but you might see the bulbs at night.'

Joe was thinking that all these were small domestic details and there might not be a coherent rationale to link them. During his daily life he sometimes did things that were out of order, not inexplicable exactly, but triggered by a sudden impulse. He stuck up his hand.

'Maybe Randle just fancied some salad leaves to go with whatever he was cooking for his tea.'

He thought Vera might yell at him for being flippant, but she stopped moving and, when she did shout, it was to the whole team. 'What did Randle have in his fridge? Anyone?'

Holly had the notes. 'Two big pieces of spinach quiche, bought from the deli in Kimmerston; some Northumberland goats' cheese and a tub of supermarket potato salad. Some English asparagus. Then the usual bits and pieces. Milk, eggs, half a packet of bacon, a jar of mayonnaise and three bottles of lager. A loaf of wholemeal bread and half a packet of unsalted butter.' She paused. 'There was a bowl of tomatoes on the kitchen windowsill.'

Vera nodded. 'There are tomatoes already ripening in the greenhouse at the Hall. He'll have picked those. The Carswells would have given him permission. They're not the kind of folk who'd like to see food go to waste.' She looked up at them. '*Two* large slices of quiche. What does that tell us?'

'That he was expecting Benton to stay for supper?' Holly again, though by now the whole group had reached the same conclusion.

'And that means?'

'That he could have gone into the garden to cut salad leaves to go with the meal.'

'So let's give Joe a big clap, everyone.' There were a few muffled cheers and catcalls before Vera continued, 'That changes the whole dynamic of the relationship between the two victims, doesn't it? We thought Benton was there for a business meeting or an interview. That was the impression he gave his chum from the charity where he'd been volunteering. But that doesn't quite fit with our scenario. This is more informal. You wouldn't pop out in the middle of a business meeting to get a few leaves to make a salad. They must have been friends.'

Joe stuck up his hand again. 'So why the suit? If it was a social occasion, especially if you were going to be grubbing around looking at moths in the wood, you wouldn't wear a suit.'

A moment of silence. Someone shouted in the neighbouring office and a door slammed. Holly coughed. 'Could it have been a confidence thing? I mean, this might have been the first time they'd met in person, but we know they'd spoken on the phone. Randle would have an educated accent, wouldn't he? Like his mother. We know that Benton was socially awkward. Perhaps the suit was to give him confidence. He'd been invited to dinner and he thought that was the right thing to wear. Otherwise he only had the tracksuit bottoms and polo shirts in his wardrobe at Laurel Avenue.'

Joe thought this was speculation. He expected a blast of Vera's famous sarcasm, but none came. Instead she stopped moving and leaned against a desk. He had a sudden image of an enormous sea-lion stranded on a rock.

'So what was the meeting *for*? Benton told the woman at the dole office, and his mate Frank, that it was business. Randle had set the moth traps at some point. Had he found an unusual species? Were they preparing to write some sort of academic paper about it? Did Randle need Benton's photographic skills? Help me out here, somebody. What am I missing?

What was so important that they needed to meet, instead of making do with a phone call or email?'

Another long silence. Vera launched herself from her rock. 'Okay, let's leave the "why?" for now and move on. The two men arrive at the big house from Gilswick. They chat, Randle goes into the garden. He goes to pick some salad. The murderer hits him hard on the back of the head to kill him.' She looked out at the room. 'Pete MacBride from the search team thinks he might have been killed with a spade. Plenty of those in the toolshed. All being checked. All bright and sparkly, though, so if one of them *was* the murder weapon the killer took the time to clean it. Then he went into the flat and stabbed Benton with a kitchen knife. Is that the way we think it happened?'

'No!' Joe decided that was impossible. 'The killer must have gone to the flat first, expecting to find Randle there. We don't know what he intended at that point. He certainly wasn't anticipating finding a stranger in the place. Benton was killed because he could identify the intruder. Then the murderer went outside to search for Randle. Surely it must have happened that way.'

'So Benton was collateral damage?' Vera closed her eyes for a moment. 'He was never an intended victim.'

She stood, as still as some bloated and ancient Buddha, and then snapped back to life. 'Actions for the day,' she said. 'Joe, I want you to visit Shirley Hewarth, the social worker at Hope charity. What was so urgent that she had to go out to Sittingwell to visit Lizzie Redhead? Hope is for people who don't have support from statutory bodies or from the wider community. I've checked their mission statement.' She rolled her eyes and they chuckled. They all knew what Vera thought of mission statements. 'Lizzie has affluent parents, a home to go back to and more support than she wants. So why is Hewarth so involved?' A pause for breath. 'Hol, I need a bit of action on all the communications we're dealing with here. Phones, laptops and PCs. There must be something that'll give us a hint to the relationship between the two victims. We've got two murder scenes now and plenty to go on.' A brief pause. 'And where's Patrick Randle's laptop? I asked his mother, and he never travelled without it. If we find that, we're close to finding the killer.'

Joe thought they had too much to go on. He stood up, and the others followed. Vera gave a strange, enigmatic smile and disappeared into her office.

Joe phoned Shirley Hewarth to make an appointment. She sounded brisk and efficient. 'Of course, Sergeant. Can we make it early this afternoon? One-thirty? I've got meetings all morning.'

He went home for lunch because Sal always moaned that she never saw him when he was in the middle of a case. He hadn't warned her that he was coming and she was in the garden drinking coffee, reading a novel while the toddler was having a midday nap. He felt a moment of resentment, so intense that it felt close to hatred. If she had time to read during the day, why did she expect him to get up at night with the baby? Then he asked himself if he'd want to be with the kids all day – especially Jess, who was almost a teenager and behaving like one – and he thought Sal deserved a moment's peace. When he stroked the back of her neck it was warm from the sun, and when he kissed her she tasted of the chocolate biscuit she'd just eaten with her coffee. So she'd stopped the diet again. He was about to kiss her again when the baby woke up. Sal grinned and said she'd make him a sandwich. 'You should have come back a bit earlier, so we could have had some time to ourselves.'

He arrived in Bebington just as a meeting had finished in the charity's office and waited at the door to let a group of women come out. He thought Holly would have judged them immediately because of their clothes – market-stall tops over leggings worn thin with washing – their obesity and their poor skin. She'd have labelled them, without even talking to them, as offenders, offenders' partners or possible informants. It would be inconceivable to her that one of them could become her friend. Joe had grown up with women like these as neighbours and he'd been in and out of their homes, playing with their kids. Now, standing on the pavement as they walked past, listening to snatches of their conversation, he felt nostalgic for his childhood, the mucky chaos of many of the houses in the street where they'd lived. The warmth and lack of pretension.

Shirley Hewarth was waiting for him in the office upstairs. She was on her own and saw him look at the empty second desk. 'I'm not a one-woman band, Sergeant, but the others are volunteers and they don't always turn up. Life gets in the way, and I don't blame them. Coffee?'

She was dressed in a short-sleeved white shirt and

a navy skirt. Tights, despite the heat, and smart shoes with a bit of a heel. She looked more like a lawyer than most social workers he'd met, especially those who worked in the voluntary sector.

They sat on two easy chairs in one corner. Joe shifted his seat so that the sun wasn't in his eyes. She set the tray on a low table. 'Isn't this amazing weather for April?' She flashed out an automatic smile; she'd be used to making small talk to put her clients at ease. 'I suppose global warming has its advantages.'

'You went to visit Lizzie Redhead in prison.'

He'd hoped the direct approach might make her uncomfortable, but she answered immediately. 'Lizzie was referred to us by her probation officer. I've visited twice. Last time was to set up plans for her release. She'll be out over the weekend.'

'Do you visit every client referred by the probation service?' Joe was still in his jacket, but he couldn't quite bring himself to stand up and take it off. Hewarth seemed cool and unflustered, though he thought she'd be a good actor. She'd have stood up to thugs and bullies and imperious lawyers. It would be hard to tell what was going on inside her head.

She gave a little laugh. 'Not at all. But I thought it was important to talk to Elizabeth before her release date. She's an interesting young woman.' There was a pause. 'Despite the support from her parents, she has a history of self-destructive behaviour. I can't go into details, but this was one case in which I felt I could make a difference. I used to be a probation officer, and I didn't have so many of those in my career.'

There was a silence. 'Why did you leave the service?' Joe couldn't understand that. Why leave a job with reasonable pay and prospects for a good pension to join a bunch of amateurs in a rundown office in an ex-mining town?

It took her a while to answer. 'When I joined the service our remit was to *assist, advise and befriend* offenders. The system wasn't always perfect, but most of us did our best to help the people we were supervising. That's all changed. I didn't want to be a glorified cop. It wasn't what I was trained for.'

'Tell me a little more about Lizzie Redhead.'

'Ah.' Hewarth leaned back in the chair. The front of her shirt gaped a little and he caught a glimpse of a white lacy bra.

Joe thought she wasn't much younger than Vera, but there was something sexy about her. Slightly provocative. He had to drag his attention back to the conversation, to listen to what the woman was saying.

'You'll know that Elizabeth was charged with GBH after a fight in a bar.' Shirley sat upright again and the blouse fell back into place. Joe thought she was deciding how much she could tell him without breaking her client's confidence. 'Before that she had a history of drug and alcohol abuse. Not a cause of her problems, I think, but a symptom of them. She was a hyperactive child, easily bored, and that continued into her adult life.'

Shirley reached out and poured more coffee.

'Was Lizzie ever admitted to hospital? To get clean?'

'No. I suspect her parents might have tried to persuade her to accept help, but as I explained, I don't think addiction was at the root of her problems. They were looking for easy answers, and Lizzie's anything but easy.' Shirley gave a little smile. 'The bright, sparky ones seldom are.'

'I was looking for a connection between her and Martin Benton,' Joe said. 'You can't think of anything?'

'No!' Her voice was suddenly icy. 'I think you're looking in quite the wrong direction there, Sergeant. Lizzie didn't become a client of Hope until she went to prison. The two of them never met.'

Another silence. Punctuated by a siren in the distance. The phone ringing in the office upstairs.

'Lizzie was mixed up with Jason Crow. You'll have heard of him, if you work round here,' Joe said. He was still trying to work out what motivated Hewarth. She seemed affluent enough. She must be of an age when she could have taken early retirement from the probation service if she didn't like the new regime, could be drinking cocktails and walking her dogs, like the retired hedonists in Valley Farm. She didn't seem moved by the sort of passion for justice that carried his Methodist father to preach in dingy chapels or to knock on doors at election time. But perhaps do-gooders could wear lacy bras too.

'Oh, we've all heard of Jay Crow,' Shirley said. 'Most of the people who come through our doors are more scared of him than they are of you and your colleagues.'

'Have you met him?'

There was a moment of hesitation. 'I knew the family. Supervised his mother on and off, for most of my career. He was intimidating even as a boy.'

'Should Lizzie still be scared of him?'

She paused again. 'I don't think so. I hear Lizzie's parents bought him off.'

'You must hear a lot from all the people who come through this door.' Shirley didn't reply and Joe continued, 'They all knew Martin Benton. Have you heard any rumours? Anything about who might have wanted him dead?'

Joe thought they'd all been assuming Randle had been the target for the murder and that Benton had just got in the way. But perhaps it had happened the other way round. If Benton had been followed from Kimmerston, he could have been the intended victim.

Shirley shook her head. 'Martin didn't have any enemies. He was a gentle creature.'

'But he worked here. He'd have heard a lot too. All those meetings with folk baring their souls. Perhaps he heard more than was good for him.'

'He never took part in any of the meetings.' For the first time the woman seemed uncomfortable. 'Martin worked in the office, making sure our IT was working properly. His only face-to-face contact with clients was running workshops in basic computing, and we used a room in the library for those.'

'He might have had access to confidential information about your clients, though?'

'I suppose he might have done, but he wasn't interested in people. Only in the technology.' She gave a little smile. 'And his moths. I don't suppose he was killed because of those.'

'Where were you on Tuesday evening?'

Her mood suddenly changed and she became girlish, flirtatious again. 'Am I a suspect? How exciting!'

'I have to ask.'

'Of course you do. We all do our jobs. We all follow orders.' The tone had changed once more and become surprisingly bitter. 'I was here until five o'clock. On my own. Sharon, our main volunteer, leaves just before three most days to pick up her little girl from school and we don't have any groups on Tuesday afternoons. Then I went home. I live alone. So no alibi, Sergeant. Nobody to vouch for me.'

Joe stood up. He still felt unsettled because he couldn't quite place her, socially or emotionally. He guessed she must be divorced. This was no confirmed spinster like Vera Stanhope. 'Where do you live?'

'On the coast. Cullercoats.'

That didn't help to pin her down much. Cullercoats had grand homes looking out over the bay, but there were also rows of small terraced houses and Tyneside flats.

They were halfway down the stairs when he turned back to her. 'Why do you do this? Why do you work here?'

'Because I'm nosy,' she said immediately. 'I'm interested in people. I'd get bored alone in the house all day.' Joe thought that was exactly the answer Vera would have given. 'And then there's guilt.' The words seemed to come out before she'd thought about them properly, because he could tell she regretted them as soon as they were spoken. She gave a sad smile. 'Not everyone is as lucky as me.'

Chapter Twenty-Four

Annie got back to Valley Farm in time for lunch. Sam had been baking bread. She could smell the yeast as soon as she let herself into the house. She thought that meant he was troubled. Her memories of the bad times with Lizzie were linked with this smell and with the sight of Sam kneading dough in the restaurant kitchen. He thumped and stretched the mixture on the marble block as if he were committing torture, until the tension went from his shoulders and he began to relax.

'I wasn't sure when you'd be home. I thought, once you started gassing to the lasses, you could be out all day.' There was flour on his forehead.

She took a tea towel and wiped it off. 'I didn't meet the girls.'

'No?'

She'd been married to him for nearly thirty years, but she still couldn't always tell what he was thinking. He put a long oven glove on one hand and lifted the bread out of the oven. Wholemeal. He preferred white himself, but always cooked her favourites. He turned the loaf upside down and knocked the bottom, seemed satisfied and slid it onto a tray to cool.

'A woman phoned earlier. She works for a charity. Hope North-East. She's visited Lizzie a couple of times in prison. She wanted to talk. I didn't like the idea of her coming to the house.'

He closed the oven door and switched it off. 'You didn't say.' No judgement. A bald statement of fact.

'I'm sorry.' Annie paused, took a breath. 'We need to talk about Lizzie. She's out this weekend.' She felt bruised and exhilarated. As if she'd smashed a fist through the glass wall that had separated them for months.

He had his back to her, so she couldn't see his face. He switched on the kettle. 'I expect you could do with a coffee.'

'Sam.' Annie could tell her voice was desperate now. 'We will let her come here, won't we?'

He swung round with more speed than she'd have thought possible from him. 'Of course she'll come here. Where else would she go?'

Then Annie thought that everything would be all right. The two of them would stick together over this. It wouldn't break them apart. They continued the conversation as they ate, and she felt closer to her husband than she had in years. Perhaps even since that time when he'd arrived at her parents' house the week before she was supposed to marry another man. Her parents had both been teachers. They'd lived in the smart new estate on the edge of Bebington, close to their roots, but a little away from the pit-town. They'd had aspirations for her. She'd been away to university and that was where she'd met Michael, her fiancé. Her parents had liked Michael, who was an aspiring lawyer from Surrey. They had even forgiven the fact that his father was a Tory councillor. When Sam had turned up at their tidy modern house, still smelling faintly of the farm, her parents had let him in. He was an old friend of their daughter, after all.

Sam had taken her for a walk along the beach. It was a gusty, showery day and the wind had blown her skirt and her hair, and the waves had been tumbling onto the sand. Later she'd sat in the little front room in her parents' house; she'd cried as she told them the wedding was off, but she'd felt a tremendous exhilaration too. Her parents had tried to understand. 'Are you sure, pet? I mean Sam? He's a nice enough chap, but don't you think he's a bit boring?'

Now, sitting across the kitchen table from him, she thought he didn't look very different from the farmer's son who'd persuaded her that nobody else would love her as much as he did.

'You know I'd do anything to make our Lizzie happy.' There was the same expression as when he'd walked with her along that beach. Stubborn and kind of soppy at the same time. 'She's been nothing but trouble for years, but I still love her to bits.'

'Why wouldn't you go and visit her in prison?'

He gave a little shake of his head. 'I couldn't bear it. She's not a girl who was meant to be trapped. It'd be like seeing a wild bird in a cage.'

'This social worker says she's changed.'

'Oh, aye?' His expression said that just because he loved his daughter, he hadn't lost his senses.

'Lizzie's talking about going to college.'

'Well, she's talked about that before.'

'The woman who works for the charity. Her name's Shirley. She's going to keep an eye on things, support Lizzie once she's come out of prison.' Annie reached out and touched his hand.

'Aye, well, Lizzie's had social workers before too.'

'Young things, always rushing to be somewhere else. Thinking more about their careers than the folk they're supposed to be helping.' Annie was dismissive. 'When you meet Shirley you'll see she's different. She seems to know what she's talking about.'

'When will I get to see her then?' He frowned. He didn't like meeting new people. Even their neighbours in Valley Farm made him feel a bit awkward until he'd had a couple of beers. Then he could be the life and soul.

'She's coming here on Monday. She said that'd give us a day to get settled with Lizzie, a bit of time to get to know each other again.'

Sam nodded. 'That makes sense.'

'We'll need to tell the others.' Annie nodded in the direction of the houses along the courtyard. 'That Lizzie will be coming to stay with us.'

'Why?' For the first time in the conversation he sounded angry. 'What business is it of theirs who lives in our house?'

Annie didn't answer. She knew they had to tell their neighbours that their ex-offender daughter would be landing up in the community. They'd never met her, but Lizzie's face had been all over the *Kimmerston Herald* when she got sent down. Even if she wanted to, Annie couldn't pretend this was a different young relative who'd turned up out of the blue. 'It's none of their business, but best that they're prepared. It'll make things less awkward.' She thought she'd go and tell them this afternoon. Friday night was when they got together for drinks and a shared supper. To mark the start of the weekend, for people who didn't have any other structure in their lives. She didn't want to blurt it out then.

Sam shrugged. 'If you think that's best. You're better at this sort of thing than me.'

She cut another slice of the bread that he'd baked for her. It was still warm and the butter melted and dribbled over her fingers.

'You could be married to that lawyer,' he said suddenly. He'd been thinking of the day when he'd turned up at her parents' place too. The walk on the beach. 'A big house, perfect kids.'

'Nobody's perfect.' She couldn't think of anything else to say, then added, 'But you come pretty close.'

Annie went to Janet's first. She thought Janet would be easier. She'd been a sort of social worker, a bit like Shirley Hewarth. John was in the study they'd made for him at the top of the house, so the house was quiet apart from Radio 4 burbling in the kitchen. The Carswells' dogs were asleep in the sun near the French window at the back of the room. Janet was reading one of the heavy newspapers they always bought. Her glasses had slid to the end of her nose.

'He moved downstairs to work when he got that cold.' Janet switched on the kettle. 'What a nightmare! I had no peace. He kept calling for hot drinks. And there were papers everywhere. I was so glad when he took himself back upstairs. You don't think of that when you retire – that you don't have any space to yourself.'

'So he's feeling better?' Annie didn't really care, but she supposed she should show some interest.

'Much.'

The Archers theme tune came on and Jan turned off the radio. 'I heard it last night. John says that the programme's drivel, but I never miss it.'

'Lizzie's being released this weekend.' Annie hadn't meant to be so abrupt, but perhaps there was no other way to pass on the information. 'I thought you should know. She's coming to live with us for a while.'

'Of course she is,' Janet said. 'You'll be so pleased to have her home.'

'Yes, I will.' And Annie thought she really meant that. It would be exciting to get to know her daughter properly. Perhaps for the first time. She pushed her anxieties about Lizzie getting drunk and wild, and causing a nuisance to their new friends, to the back of her mind.

They drank their coffee sitting next to the dogs. 'I'll miss them when the Carswells get back.' Janet was stroking the back of the old female. Annie could tell she was just waiting to hear whatever Annie had to tell her. She wouldn't ask intrusive questions.

'I'm scared too,' Annie said. 'That we'll get it wrong again and she'll storm away and get mixed up with all those dreadful people. That she'll get bored and cause bother for you. She was always a nightmare as soon as she was bored.'

'Maybe she's just grown up a bit.'

'I do hope so.' But Annie couldn't bring herself to believe that people ever changed that much. 'We won't be hosting drinks next Friday,' she said. 'I know it's our turn, but we thought it'd be a bit much for Lizzie. First weekend out.'

'Well, she's a bit young for the retired hedonists!'

Jan laughed. 'Anyway, of course you'll want to be on your own for a bit. Nigel and Lorraine can come here. I can't imagine Nigel wanting a Friday night without a bit of a party. And we'll all be getting together as usual tonight.' She was still stroking the Labrador at her feet. 'Do you want me to tell next door about Lizzie?'

'Nah.' Annie was feeling more confident now. She was thinking how lucky they were to have chosen to live at Valley Farm, where they'd made such good friends. 'I'll go round now.'

'Have you heard any more about the murders?' Janet threw that out just as Annie was at the door.

Annie shook her head. It occurred to her that she hadn't thought about the dead men all day.

Nigel let her into the farmhouse. 'Hiya!'

He always sounded just a little bit too jolly. He tried too hard to fit in. Perhaps that was because he and Lorraine didn't come from the North-East. Jan had a Scottish voice, but she'd lived and worked in Newcastle for years.

'Can I get you something? One of my famous coffees? A cup of tea?' He had a fancy coffee machine. One of his toys.

'A cappuccino would be lovely, Nige.' Because that was what he wanted to hear. 'Is Lorraine in?' Annie thought it would be easier talking to them both.

'She's working upstairs. I'll give her a shout.'

Left alone in this part of the house, Annie looked around. This was by far the grandest home of the development. She wouldn't want to live here. She thought Nigel had furnished to impress rather than because he liked each of the items. Another sign that he lacked confidence, she thought. He'd obviously been terrific at running a business because he was minted, but once he'd given that up he didn't have anything to define him. A bit like Sam, who still baked bread in their tiny galley kitchen. She did love some of the paintings, though. There was a tiny one of a door leading through a wall into a garden. It held the promise of adventure. Once you walked through the door anything might happen. She'd stood up to get a closer look when Nigel came back with the coffee.

'That's one of Lorraine's,' he said. 'I tell her she should sell them.'

'I'd buy this!'

'You can have it.' Lorraine had been following and Annie hadn't noticed. 'As a present, of course.'

'Oh no, I wasn't hinting.'

But the watercolour was taken from the wall and Annie sat with it beside her, feeling awkward, but still delighted to have it in her grasp.

'I've come to tell you that we won't be having drinks at ours next Friday.' Pause. Big breath. 'Lizzie's coming out of prison this weekend. We'll want her to ourselves for a bit.'

Lorraine was still standing, holding a mug in both hands. 'She's coming to live with you?'

'Of course she will be.' This was Nigel, hearty and kind. 'And of course we understand, don't we, Lorrie? We wouldn't want to intrude on your first couple of weeks together. It'll be very special for you all. We've never had kiddies, but we can see how important it must be for you and Sam to be a family again.'

'Thank you.' Annie realized she was close to

crying. She looked at Lorraine, expecting something more from her too. She'd thought that Lorraine, with her arty clothes and her easy laughter, would be the least fazed to hear that a convicted criminal would be moving in next door. But Lorraine said nothing. She drank her coffee with her eyes half-closed as if the taste and the smell of it were the most important things in the world. Annie wondered if her friend might once have been the victim of a crime. That might explain her wariness. She saw that it wouldn't be so easy to forgive, if you were the person who'd been scarred after a drunken encounter in a bar. Annie had never heard what had happened to Lizzie's victim and didn't like to think about that.

The silence stretched and grew uneasy. At last Lorraine set her coffee mug on a slate coaster on the table. 'Aren't you a bit nervous? About Lizzie offending again? I mean, when she's living with you.'

Annie remembered then that Lorraine had run art classes for people in trouble. Of course she wouldn't necessarily have a rosy opinion of offenders. All the same, Lorraine seemed so upset that Annie wondered if she'd had a more personal encounter with crime.

'We'll get help.' Annie realized her voice was a bit desperate. 'She'll have a probation officer and a woman from Hope North-East, a charity, will be visiting. We won't have to do it all ourselves.'

'I'm sure you'll be fine.' Lorraine seemed to have recovered her composure. She smiled. 'With you and Sam to support her, what could possibly go wrong?'

Chapter Twenty-Five

Lizzie Redhead lay in bed. Her head was exploding with the prospect of leaving prison. The space beyond this place seemed to stretch forever. Scary, and dizzying with its possibilities. Plans fizzed and jolted like she was wired to a power supply. She knew she wouldn't sleep at all. It was because she was so freaked out, and she was frightened of the dreams that seeped into her mind when she was half-awake. *Sodding Jason Crow. You won't leave me alone even here.*

She shared her room with three other women. There was one set of bunks and two single beds. All with flowery duvets, as if pretty linen could turn them into civilized people, good wives and mothers. Lizzie had a bed, the one closest to the window, which was an odd shape because it had been cut in half when the grand house had been turned into an institution and extra partition walls had been built. Outside there was a big tree. When Lizzie had first come to Sittingwell it had been bare and when the wind blew the branches creaked, making her think of an old-fashioned ship in a storm. In moonlight the tree threw strange shapes on the ceiling. It was as if outside had come into the prison.

Now the women were all asking her what she'd do

when she first got out. Two were recent arrivals and she hadn't got to know them well, so she ignored their suggestions.

'You'll go into toon, man. A night on the lash. That club in the Bigg Market, where they do cocktails. A lass like you will pull a fit bloke in seconds.' The two were cousins and had been charged together with a series of thefts from stores. After so many convictions the court had described prison as the only option left, even though they both had babies. The kids were being cared for by grandparents. Lizzie had seen them at visiting time.

The cousins went on to throw out a menu of drinks that they'd go for, when they got let out: lethal cocktails that got crazier and crazier. Lizzie thought she'd moved beyond that. There was more to life than getting pissed. Prison had given her a different perspective. Her world was bigger. She lay on her bed and pulled the curtain aside to see the stars. An owl called somewhere in the garden, and immediately Lizzie was back in the place where she'd lived as a child. The valley at Gilswick. Then it had seemed to her a community of old people. A strict social hierarchy, with the major in the Hall at the top. The only other kids had lived at the big house. Lizzie had been at school with them, until they'd been sent off to private prep schools. She hadn't thought much of Catherine, who'd been dainty and girly, but she'd got on okay with Nicholas. He hadn't boarded until he was older and she'd still played with him at weekends. They'd built dens in the woods and dammed the burn. It should have been idyllic, but it had never been enough for her. She'd still been bored.

The cousins saw that she wasn't listening to their plans for a big night out and they shut up. The other room-mate was older. She had school-age kids. She'd worked in a care home and had started nicking things from the old people. Money and jewellery. In one room she'd found a credit card, the PIN jotted down on a scrap of paper in the same drawer. The man she'd stolen from had been dying. 'He wasn't going to use it, was he?' Rose had said. 'And his relatives never visited, and they only lived south of the river. Why did they have more right to his cash than me? I wiped his bum and washed his face. I made him smile.'

Lizzie hadn't had an answer to that. She wondered whether she'd visit *her* parents if they didn't recognize her any more.

The room fell quiet then, so she supposed the others were sleeping. She started thinking about Shirley Hewarth. When they'd first met, Lizzie had thought Shirley was as tough as her. There was something steely about her, a refusal to be conned. Lizzie had tried to lie about the offence and her relationship with Jason, and Shirley had tilted her head to one side and said, 'Well, I don't think that's *entirely* true, is it?' She'd peeled back Lizzie's pretences until Lizzie felt raw, exposed. She'd found herself confiding in Shirley. Making herself vulnerable. She hadn't even allowed herself that luxury with Jason.

Now Lizzie wasn't sure that Shirley was as hard as she seemed. They might share the same secret, but they had different interests. The thought worried her. It was one of the reasons she was scared about leaving prison: that Shirley might land her in the shit, big time.

Chapter Twenty-Six

Friday evening. Friday was party night for the retired hedonists at Valley Farm and usually at this time Annie would be getting ready to be social. She'd be lying in a deep bath and deciding what she was going to wear. She wasn't usually competitive about how she looked, but Lorraine formed a kind of challenge. Annie had seen the way John O'Kane looked at Lorraine Lucas and wondered if Sam was attracted to the woman too.

This evening, though, she was in the spare room preparing it for Lizzie's return. Lizzie had never spent very long in the house. She'd stayed a couple of days when they'd first moved in, but she'd made it clear that she was bored out of her skull and soon moved back to the town, to the flat they'd rented for her. And soon after Lizzie had been charged with assault and remanded in custody. Even when she'd got bail she'd preferred to keep away.

Annie opened the window to air the place. It was almost dark, but still unseasonably warm. No wind at all. She heard a car drive up the valley and watched as it pulled up outside the farmhouse. Nigel and Lorraine, obviously already in party mood. They could see the light in the bedroom and the open window, and Nigel shouted up to her.

'See you soon! We just popped into The Lamb for a quick one, but we'll be ready in half an hour or so.'

Now the last thing Annie wanted was to go into the big house, to drink too much wine. She knew exactly how it would be: John O'Kane, brooding but somehow predatory. Janet, who became girlish and giggly after a few drinks, so the age seemed to fall away from her and she was an irresponsible student again. Nigel full of good cheer, bad jokes and stories from his past. Lorraine dreamy and distant as if her mind was somewhere else altogether. Annie wondered sometimes if Lorraine had a lover. Not the professor – that would be too obvious – but a younger man outside the valley, to distract her when Nigel became too boring.

'I'm not sure. We might give it a miss this evening. You know what Sam is like, and we're not feeling very sociable.' Annie was thinking of Lorraine's chilly response to the news that Lizzie would be coming home. She wasn't sure they'd really be welcome.

'Come on! Don't be a spoilsport.' Lorraine was right under the window now, her eyes glittering like a cat's in the light that spilled out from the bedroom. 'Come out to play. It's Friday night.'

Annie couldn't say no. She'd never been very good at saying no, and Lorraine's personality was so fierce and she seemed so used to getting her own way that Annie couldn't stand up to her. 'Give us half an hour. I need to jump into the shower, and Sam has been in the garden most of the day.' It occurred to her that Lorraine was almost as manipulative as Lizzie.

In the end Sam didn't take too much persuading. 'We've all been a bit uptight,' he said. 'These murders on the doorstep. Lizzie coming home. Perhaps it'd do us good. And it is Friday night.' He fetched a bottle of wine from the pantry and a flan that he'd made the day before. Annie went upstairs again to have a shower. The water on her body seemed to clear her mind, but later, sitting at her dressing table to do her make-up, she found her hand was shaking as she tried to apply the mascara. She saw that she was as tense and nervous as she'd been all day. Perhaps Sam was right and they needed an evening with their friends to unwind. Perhaps she needed a couple of drinks too.

They could hear the music from the farmhouse as soon as they went out of their door. The Who singing about their generation. Inside Lorraine was moving across the room with a glass in her hand. She'd thrown her shoes into a corner and was barefoot, dancing with an invisible partner. Nigel had pushed the table back against the wall and was setting out plates, a cheeseboard and glasses. It seemed to Annie now that he never dressed like someone from *their* generation, but as someone much older. He could be a character in a Noël Coward play in his blazer. All he needed was a cravat.

Sam stepped aside to let Annie in first. They'd tapped at the door and then gone straight in. Lorraine came up to greet them, hugging them and kissing them on both cheeks. Sam, who was usually very careful about his personal space, didn't seem to mind the hug. And almost immediately Jan and John were there too, appearing through the back door as if by magic. Jan wore a white cotton tunic over wide linen trousers, long silver earrings and actually looked rather glamorous. John was in a collarless shirt over jeans. Today these details seemed very clear and sharp. The background music, the clothes, the food on the table were all branded into her mind. Tonight, Annie thought, they'd all become caricatures of themselves.

Nigel was pouring drinks. He'd made a jug of some sort of cocktail and insisted that they try that first. It was syrupy and very alcoholic. She drank it too quickly and already the room appeared to spin. Everyone seemed to be talking too quickly and laughing too loud. John O'Kane came up behind her and pulled her into a dance. The music was slower now. One of the soppier Beatles numbers. She found herself enjoying the touch of his hand on her back and realized she must be even drunker than she'd thought. There was something flattering about his attention. Usually he talked about himself, his book, his work. Today he asked about her, murmuring so that she could just catch his words over the music.

'Are you okay?'

'Yeah,' she said. 'Yeah.'

He moved his hand from her back to her neck. The sensation of bare skin on bare skin, even here, in front of all these people, thrilled her. She glanced at Sam, who sitting next to Jan on the sofa. They seemed to be engaged in an intense conversation. Annie wondered if it was about Lizzie or if there was a sexual attraction there too, if Sam felt so relaxed with Jan, who was competent and easy to speak to, that he wanted to pull her towards him and kiss her.

We're all getting old and desperate. We can't believe we're no longer attractive.

She pulled away gently from John. 'I need some food to soak up some of the booze.' She walked over to the table and cut herself some French bread and cheese. John followed her.

'Is Jan okay?' Because, looking at Janet more closely, Annie thought she looked tired and tense. She was still listening to Sam and giving him her full attention, but she'd been holding the same drink for the past hour and the fingers clutching the glass were rigid. Annie thought they all took Jan for granted. They all went to her with their troubles. Perhaps she needed someone to listen to *her.*

The professor shrugged. 'She's been moody for the last few days. When I ask her, she says it's the murders. Something about being aware of her own mortality.'

The music changed again and Nigel and Lorraine were on their feet doing some elaborate jive, twisting and swinging, until Lorraine stumbled and they ended up in a giggling heap on the floor.

We're too old to behave like this, Annie thought. *We should have more dignity*. *We're bad for each other. It'll be good for us to have Lizzie at home. Someone younger to put our lives into proper perspective.* All evening people seemed to come and go, swinging into her line of sight and then out of it, disappearing from the room and coming back with no explanation.

It was late. The music had stopped and nobody had bothered to put on a new CD. The room was lit by candles. Nigel had made coffee and they were drinking it with his malt whisky, beyond caring about the next morning's hangover. Only Janet seemed relatively sober. She got to her feet and said she'd have to let the Carswell dogs out.

'Shall I come with you?' Sam, not John. John was slumped on the floor next to Annie, his head so close to her shoulder that she could smell his shampoo.

'No,' Janet said. 'I won't go far. Just down the track a little way.'

Sam started to get to his feet.

'Really, I'm fine.' Janet already had her hand on the door handle. 'I could do with some time on my own. Send out a search party if I'm not back in quarter of an hour.'

They all laughed, but Annie made a note of the time on the clock on the wall. If Janet wasn't back, she'd go and look for the woman herself.

Ten minutes had passed when they heard the scream. Distant, but clearly audible through the open window. There was no music in the room now and the noise cut through the silence. They were on their feet, running outside. There was the sound of their footsteps on the gravel, they were calling out Janet's name and it was impossible to tell where the scream had come from. By now it was quite dark. No moon and no street lights.

'Be quiet!' It was the professor yelling over the chaos. Suddenly they were all still, listening.

Annie could hear the water in the burn below them. Then there was another sound. A dog barking. And footsteps on the track. The light of a small torch, moving in rhythm as the person holding it walked towards them.

'Janet!' The professor again.

'Come here,' she shouted. 'You have to come here.'

Then they were all in motion again, tumbling down the track, stumbling like children racing down a grassy bank. Annie thought it was like a nightmare. The scream had sobered them a little, but not enough for this to make any sense.

When they reached her Janet was standing still. She had the dogs beside her. John put his arm around her. Annie thought it was the first time that the couple had had physical contact all evening. 'Are you okay? I thought something dreadful had happened.'

'It has.' A pause. 'At least I think it has. Perhaps I imagined it. Come with me and check.'

She walked back down the track a little way and shone her torch along the footpath that branched from it and led to the hill. Something was lying across the path. A sack of rubbish, Annie thought at first. Fly-tipping wasn't unknown here in the valley.

'We'd better stay here,' Janet leaned forward as far as she could reach without losing balance. 'I suppose the police will find things difficult if we all get too close, though the dogs have been there. They found her.' The torchlight showed a woman. She'd been slashed by a knife. Over and over. There was blood all over her clothes. One of the shoes had fallen off and rested at a distance from her feet.

'Who is she?' Nigel seemed calm, almost detached. 'I don't recognize her from the village.'

Annie pushed her way to the front of the group so that she could get a better view. The clothes were familiar. The patent-leather shoe with its small heel.

She felt suddenly bereft, as if a relative had died. 'I know her. That's Shirley Hewarth. She's the social worker who's been visiting our Lizzie.'

Chapter Twenty-Seven

Holly had been asleep for an hour when she got the call. She recognized Joe Ashworth's voice immediately, even before she looked at the caller ID, and was awake and alert. She'd switched on the bedside lamp. Her bedroom was mostly white. White linen, white walls. Pale-green blinds at the window. One ex-lover had called it antiseptic. *Like living in a hospital.*

She always kept a notebook at the side of her bed and she was writing as she pulled clothes out of the drawer with one hand. The name of the victim brought her up short. '*Who?*'

'Shirley Hewarth. The woman from Hope North-East.'

Holly was thinking fast now, making connections. 'Martin Benton's boss.'

'Aye, and supervising the daughter of one of the Valley Farm families.'

'But no link to Patrick Randle.'

'Not as far as we know.' Joe spoke slowly, but she thought he was running through the possibilities in his head too.

'I don't suppose she's a moth expert?'

He gave a little laugh. 'The boss wants us all out

there to talk to the witnesses. She doesn't want to leave it until the morning.'

Of course not. That would be far too easy.

'Who found the body?' Holly held the phone between her ear and her shoulder so that she could pull on a pair of jeans. The great thing about women was their ability to multi-task. Sometimes she thought that was Vera's only feminine attribute.

'Janet O'Kane. She was walking the Carswells' dogs last thing. The body was just off the track, lying across the footpath that leads to the hill.'

'Not hidden then.' She put the phone on the bed while she pulled a jersey over her head. 'Sorry, I missed that.'

'Hewarth was close enough to the track to have been dumped from a car,' Joe said. 'Billy Cartwright and Paul Keating are on their way. No information yet about whether she was murdered where she was found.'

'Where are you?'

'Outside the boss's house. She asked me to pick her up on the way to the scene. I think she had a few drinks last night. With her neighbours.' Joe's disapproval was obvious. He disliked the couple who farmed the smallholding next to Vera's house. He thought they were feckless and that they led Vera astray.

'I'll see you there then.' Holly was going to add: *Race you*. But Joe would have disapproved of that too. She'd never before met a police officer who was so law-abiding.

*

When she arrived at the scene Vera and Joe had just arrived. Vera was wearing strange baggy trousers tucked into wellington boots and looked even less like a senior detective than usual. Holly wondered if they might be pyjama bottoms, because she couldn't believe Vera owned a tracksuit. All the cars had been directed to park next to the Valley Farm development. Big arc lights had already been set up where the footpath joined the track and the crime-scene team were just erecting a scene tent over the body. Everything was in monochrome, with sharp shadows and black silhouettes, all the officers and CSIs in their white suits and masks. It looked like a film set. For a horror movie perhaps. Something about a deadly virus infecting the world.

Vera was struggling to get into the scene suit, moaning as she always did that they were never big enough. 'Do they think all police officers are bairns? Or anorexic?'

Holly followed her through the cordon and into the tent. She recognized the victim from her clothes and the little pearl earrings, but thought Shirley Hewarth looked older in death than she remembered, when they'd talked in the charity's office.

'Will anyone be waiting for her at home?' Vera's words were muffled by the mask.

Joe shook his head. 'I don't think so. I'm not sure why, though. Perhaps she said. She lived in Cullercoats. I checked the actual address, because I was curious to know what sort of place it was.'

'And?'

'A Tyneside flat close to the sea front. Nothing flash. It doesn't sound like a family home.'

'She's not wearing a wedding ring.' Billy Cartwright was squatting next to the body. 'Not that that means anything.'

Vera turned suddenly. 'Hol, would you go? Better you than some plod knocking on the door, if there is anyone in the place. You'd met her at least. She's of an age to have grown-up kids and they seem to bounce back these days, don't they? The boomerang generation.' A pause. 'So even if she doesn't have a partner, there might be someone at home who needs to know what's happened to her, before they read it in the press. See if you can get into the house, even if it's empty. It'd be good to get your opinion of the place before we get a search team in. Anything that might tell us what she was doing out here tonight.' Vera paused again. 'Or why she was dumped here.'

So Holly found herself back in her car, driving towards the coast, along the empty night-time roads.

The flat was in a quiet street, narrow and tree-lined. At the end of it was the main road that led along the coast, and beyond that the sea. There were no lights in any of the houses. It was early morning, so everyone was asleep. Classic Tyneside flat-layout: it looked like a standard 1930s terrace, but with two doors side by side at each house. One led to the ground-floor flat, and one to steps and the second flat upstairs. Shirley Hewarth lived on the first floor. Holly rang the bell. No answer.

There was a small window open at the front of the flat, but that wouldn't help her get in, unless she was prepared to climb the drainpipe in full view of any passer-by. And it wasn't long until dawn now. There'd be joggers and dog-walkers making their way to the sea front. She felt along the lintel of the door. No key. The small front garden would be the responsibility of the ground-floor flat. It was overgrown. Rubbish had blown into the borders and the grass was almost knee-high. There were no curtains at the window and there was enough light from the street lamp to see that the place was empty. No furniture. Perhaps it had just been sold or was being prepared to rent out.

Outside Shirley's door two pots had been planted with brightly coloured annuals. They were too heavy to lift, but Holly ran her fingers through the compost, which was almost dry. A couple of inches below the surface of the second pot she found the key. Shirley might once have been a probation officer, but she hadn't been very good about security. Holly pulled on her scene suit and let herself in.

There was a light switch just inside the door and she turned it on.

'Hello! Is anyone at home?' Holly was a light sleeper, but she supposed a relative or lover might have slept through the bell. No response.

The stairs led up from a narrow hallway. It was uncluttered. No junk mail or free newspapers waiting to be dumped in the recycling bin. There was carpet on the stairs and it had been hoovered so recently that there were still stripes in the pile. Had Shirley cleaned because she was expecting guests? Or was she always so house-proud? Holly suspected the latter and wondered briefly how Hewarth could have worked for the charity in the mucky office in Bebington. And her work would have taken her to even more scuzzy houses, when she was interviewing her clients. *But my work takes me into places that make me feel filthy just stepping in through the door. Perhaps that's why we both kept our homes so clean.*

At the top of the stairs there was a hall with four doors leading off. A coat-stand and shoe-rack. Everything orderly, everything in its place. The first door led to the bathroom. Holly found only women's toiletries in the wall cupboard and only one toothbrush in the glass mug by the sink. So it seemed Shirley had lived here alone. Like Holly and Vera, she'd been a single woman.

There were two bedrooms, one looking out over the street, with a double bed, and a smaller room with a futon that could be let down for visitors. Holly already had the impression that this wasn't the home of a lonely woman, even if she had lived alone. Surely Shirley would have friends. Her room had a bay window that would give her a glimpse of the sea. The furniture was old, without being special or antique, inherited perhaps from relatives. On one wall a series of watercolours. Holly opened the dark-wood wardrobe. It contained work clothes – smart but sober skirts, shirts and jackets, a couple of dresses that might have been worn to weddings or functions. A row of shoes on the floor underneath. Nothing expensive or unusual. In the chest of drawers chain-store underwear and jeans, T-shirts and jerseys. All neatly folded. This was a woman of a certain age with a limited budget, who didn't want to stand out from the crowd and took care of what she had.

The room with the futon had a built-in cupboard. It was empty apart from a man's denim jacket and a suit. Holly tried to work out from the style if they might belong to a son, or if they'd been left behind by a former husband or boyfriend. In the end she gave up. By now someone would have found out about Shirley's next of kin and they should have the family details. They would know about an ex-partner or children.

The final door led to a living room and then to a tiny kitchen, which had been built as an extension to the back of the building. The living room was small and square. There was an original grate surrounded by shiny green tiles, and the walls had been painted a paler shade of the same colour. It looked as if Shirley had lit fires here in the winter – a copper bucket of smokeless fuel still stood next to the hearth Bookshelves in the alcoves each side of the chimney. A lot of work-related non-fiction: criminology, sociology, child-development. The rest contemporary paperback novels. Still nothing unexpected or out of the ordinary. Nothing to allow Holly to explain to Vera why the woman had been killed.

A pine table was folded against one wall and a sofa stood against another. Four Ikea chairs were stacked. Again Holly imagined friends, pictured them sitting round the table for supper. Other women sharing gossip and food. People with whom Shirley had worked in the probation service perhaps. Holly felt a moment of regret. Perhaps she should make more effort with *her* friends, invite them to a meal in her home. But her flat was her refuge and she couldn't imagine it rowdy with laughter, wine spilt on the table or scraps of food on the floor.

A single step led down to the kitchen. This space

was so narrow that Holly could almost touch both walls by stretching out her arms. The sink and cooker stood on one side and a workbench on the other. At the far end was another door that led to stone steps and down to the back yard. A street lamp lit up a paved area with more pots of herbs and flowers, a small wooden garden table and chairs, a rotary washing line and, tucked into one corner, a wheelie-bin. No moth trap. Beyond a brick wall an alley. Most of the adjoining yards would be identical. Holly tried to recapture her response to the living Shirley Hewarth, but the woman seemed to slide away from her. Wandering around her home had brought her no closer.

Standing at the top of the step between the kitchen and the living room, Holly looked around both spaces. There was no television. Unusual surely, for a single woman of Shirley's age. How did she spend the time when she wasn't at work? Her friends wouldn't visit every evening. Or did work take up most of her time? On the back of the door that led to the steps down to the yard there was a cork noticeboard. For the first time Holly caught a sense of the victim. There was a recent photo of the woman with a young man who looked so like Shirley that it must be a son. Shirley with a group of women in anoraks and walking boots, grinning outside a country pub. An invitation to a sixtieth birthday party, and another to a retirement bash. Holly made a note of the names and addresses. A couple of scribbled recipes. The programme for Sage Gateshead, the music venue. Ticks beside the classical concerts. A ticket for a drama at the Live Theatre a couple of days later. So Shirley liked her culture.

Perhaps she was snobby about her entertainment and that explained the absence of a television.

Remembering what they'd learned about Patrick Randle's movements from the food he'd bought, Holly opened the fridge. No meat or fish. A tub of hummus and some cheese. Milk, eggs, salad. A packet of supermarket raspberries. Not even Vera could tell anything about Shirley Hewarth from that. It was starting to get light. The strange grey light of dawn. But still Holly was reluctant to leave without something to show from the visit. Her eyes wandered back to the noticeboard. With the invitations and tickets there was a shopping list. It was curiosity about the woman that made her unpin it and take a look.

In her own mind she'd decided Shirley was a veggie. And, indeed, the list seemed to confirm that: olive oil, basil, pasta, green peppers, mushrooms. No meat. No wine, either.

The list had been written on the back of an envelope. Holly turned it over and saw Shirley's name and address. And a postmark, unusually clear: Wychbold, Herefordshire. Where Alicia Randle lived and where Patrick had grown up.

Chapter Twenty-Eight

Joe was heading up the briefing because Vera was at Shirley Hewarth's post-mortem. Everyone was scratchy and wired: lack of sleep, an overload of caffeine and the excitement that comes with a possible break in the case. An underlying sense of failure because they hadn't caught the killer before another person had died. He'd been home to snatch a couple of hours' rest and a shower, and now he stood in front of the team trying to order his thoughts. To wonder what Vera would do to get them to focus, if she was standing in his place. There was a mumble of chat as people got more coffee, found places to sit.

Holly slid up to him. He hadn't seen her since she'd been sent to Shirley's flat to notify any possible next of kin of the woman's death. A thankless task. She looked cool and refreshed, though she'd probably had less sleep than him. She waved a clear plastic evidence bag in front of his nose.

'What am I looking at?'

'A shopping list. I found it in Hewarth's house.' Her hair was still damp from the shower. She turned over the plastic bag so that he could see Shirley's address written on an envelope. 'Look at the postmark.'

'Herefordshire.' Now his mind was racing.

'Wychbold, Herefordshire. Where Alicia Randle lives.'

'Could be a coincidence.' But he didn't really believe that.

'It's a very small town. I checked. So it'd be a very big coincidence.'

'I don't suppose you found the letter that was inside it?' Because understanding why Patrick Randle, or his mother, had written to Shirley Hewarth would make all the difference to the investigation.

Holly shook her head. 'I had a quick look, but the boss told me to leave it for the search team. They're going in first thing today.'

'So you told Vera?' Of course she had, Joe thought. That'd be the first thing she'd do. Like a kid wanting a gold star. To be recognized as top of the class.

'She said not to phone you, in case you were managing to get some sleep.'

He didn't know what to say to that, so he just nodded and called the briefing to order.

'Now we have another victim, and this has to stop before anyone else dies.' He felt the need to say that, though Vera wouldn't have bothered. She'd have taken it as read. 'Of course this killing will be part of the Gilswick Valley investigation. Hewarth and Benton were obviously connected. She'd been his boss and, when his contract ended, he worked at the charity as a volunteer. Besides, Hewarth's body was found only a mile or so from the first scene. Now I'd like to concentrate on Hope North-East. We need to find out everything there is to know about the organization. It's run by a group of trustees. Who are they? Let's get the forensic accountants to check out the finances. And we want a detailed list of the clients. Most of them will be known to us. Did anyone have a grievance? What was going on there, to make two of the workers so vulnerable? And why the time gap between the two murders? That doesn't fit the profile of an offender with a grudge suddenly taking it into his head to wipe out the people who'd pissed him off and going on a killing spree.' Joe paused for breath.

Charlie stuck up his hand. 'Where does Randle fit in then? Are we saying that the intended targets were Benton and Hewarth all along, and Randle got in the way? That the moth-trapping connection was just a coincidence?'

'The moth-trapping brought them together.' It was a new young officer, cocky. 'That's why Benton was out at Gilswick. Like you said, Randle might just have got in the way. Bloody unlucky.'

Joe raised both hands to catch their attention. 'We think this might be a bit more complicated than Randle being collateral damage. Last night Holly found a connection between him and Shirley Hewarth. Tell them, Hol.'

He listened while Holly explained about the envelope and the postmark. There was silence as they tried to take in the implication of the link.

'Of course there are other connections between the victims.' Joe had been leaning against his desk and now he pushed himself to his feet. 'Shirley Hewarth was involved with the Redhead family, whose daughter Elizabeth will be released from prison this weekend. Hewarth's body was found very close to the Redhead home. Also close to the big house where Randle was acting as house-sitter, so we have geographical proximity on all sorts of levels.' He felt suddenly overwhelmed. There was too much information and too many complications. Vera might enjoy the challenge of a labyrinthine investigation, but he preferred things to be straightforward

Holly stood up. 'Any idea how Shirley got to the valley at Gilswick?'

'We found her car, tucked into a farm gateway close to where Randle's body was found off the track. No idea whether she drove it there or if that was the work of the killer.' Joe thought they had very few ideas about what might have happened the night before.

Holly was still on her feet. 'Do we have a next of kin yet? When I looked round the flat I had the impression there was a man in Shirley's life. A son?'

That gave Joe the chance to leave the speculation behind and to pass on the concrete details that had been gathered overnight. He stood in front of the whiteboard and pointed to a photograph of Shirley.

'Shirley Hewarth, aged fifty-eight. She was divorced from Jack Hewarth ten years ago. He was a journo with *The Journal* in Newcastle until he was offered redundancy several years ago. He hasn't worked since, but he's older than her and now lives off his pension. There's one grown-up son, Jonathan, now twenty-one. When the couple first divorced, Shirley stayed in the marital home, but when Jonathan went off to uni they sold it, split the profits and Shirley's been living in the flat in Cullercoats ever since. At around the same time she left the probation service and started work for Hope North-East.'

'Have we tracked down the ex and the son?'

'Jack Hewarth still lives in Kimmerston with a new partner, who has her own business, that classy dress shop on Front Street. He seems to go in for younger women. Jonathan is a third-year student at Northumbria University. Doing drama and music. Living in a student flat in Heaton. They've both been informed of Shirley's death.' Joe paused for breath. 'Obviously we'll need to talk to them at some point today, because they could give useful background to the victim, but I don't see either of them as potential suspects.'

The door banged open and Vera sailed in straight from the post-mortem, scarf trailing behind her like a pennant, bags in each hand.

'We don't talk about her as "the victim",' Vera said. On her high horse. 'Her name's Ms Hewarth. Or Mrs Hewarth. Or Shirley. She's entitled to a bit of respect.' A pause. 'She was killed by stabbing, like Benton. Is that significant? Not killed where she was found, so we're looking for yet another murder scene. Hol says there's no sign of violence in the flat where she lived, but we've got the CSIs checking that now. There's no weapon yet, but Paul Keating did go so far as to say it looked like another kitchen knife. How far have you got, Joe? Have you told them about the envelope? Which would indicate that all three of the deceased were connected. Find the connection and we've got the killer.'

Easy.

Joe drove to the Hope North-East office in Bebington. The visit had been at his suggestion, when Vera had planned the action for the day. Shirley's name hadn't been given to the media and he hoped word hadn't got out yet. He wanted to tell the volunteers himself that their boss was dead. He wanted to see their reaction. 'They run some sessions on a Saturday, so the volunteers might be around.'

He was surprised to find the office open; he'd assumed that Shirley would be the only key-holder and had expected to find people waiting for her on the pavement. Upstairs the skinny volunteer described by Holly was filling the kettle. She heard his footsteps on the stairs and sang out, 'Just making a brew.' She obviously hadn't heard about Shirley's death.

When she turned and saw him, she was thrown. Suddenly anxious about having to deal with a stranger. 'Shirley's not in yet. She shouldn't be long. I thought you were her.'

'I'm afraid she won't be coming in.' Joe was speaking to her as if she were a child. He'd grown up with women like her. Nervy and fragile, surviving on antidepressants, afraid of the world.

'Why? What's happened?' She was trembling. He thought anything out of the ordinary would scare her and that she'd known he was police from the moment she saw him.

'I think you should sit down.'

She was used to doing what she was told and took the seat at her desk.

He pulled up another chair, so that he was on her level. 'There was an incident last night. I'm afraid Shirley's dead.'

'No!' It came out as a wail of grief. One thing was certain. This woman had had nothing to do with

Hewarth's murder. He'd seen people less upset by the death of a close relative or partner.

'When did you last see her?'

'Yesterday afternoon.' Sharon was ripping a tissue into shreds. The pieces formed a small mound on the desk in front of her and she gathered them up in her palm, trying to roll them together like a snowball. 'She asked me to lock up, because she had a meeting.'

'You weren't in when I came to chat to Shirley.'

'No,' she looked up at him. 'Our bairn had a hospital appointment. He's got terrible asthma. Usually his nana minds him, but I wanted to take him for the tests myself. I'm only a volunteer, so there's never any problem about taking the time off. I came in later.' Her voice tailed off as if she realized that, in the scheme of things, none of this was important.

'What time did you get back?'

'About three-thirty.'

'And when did Shirley go out?'

'Not long after. It was as if she'd been waiting for me to come in so that she could get off.' Sharon looked up at him. 'What happened to her? An accident in her car?'

Joe shook his head. 'We're treating her death as suspicious.' He paused for a moment. 'Where was she going?'

'I don't know.'

'Was that unusual?' Still Joe kept his voice gentle. He had the sense that the woman was on the verge of an emotional meltdown, that Shirley and her work at Hope was all that was keeping her together. 'I mean, did she usually tell you where she was going?'

'She wrote down the addresses of all her visits in

the big diary,' Sharon said. 'Health and safety. Some of our clients could be aggressive. I wanted to know where she was going. Just in case.'

Joe thought the volunteer might be emotionally frail, but she wasn't stupid. 'And did you have a system where she phoned in after the visits? So you'd know she was safe?'

'She didn't phone,' Sharon said. 'She'd always text. After each client. *Visit over.* Then the time.'

'So she must have texted yesterday then. Because you didn't panic and call us out.' He gave a little smile to show it was almost a joke.

'No!' Sharon looked at him as if *he* was stupid now, as if he'd got hold of the wrong end of the stick altogether. 'Shirley wasn't going out on a work visit yesterday afternoon. It was personal. When she left, she said, "That's me for today. I'm taking back a bit of lieu-time. See you tomorrow." And she collected her coat and went out.'

'You don't know where she was going?'

'We didn't have time to chat.' Sharon looked up at him and her narrow face seemed more pinched and grey than ever. 'I was sorry about that. I'd wanted to tell her about Aidan and the asthma tests. She's the only person I can talk to about stuff like that. My mam just says he'll grow out of it and that I'm ruining him by fussing.' A pause. 'I don't know what I'll do without Shirley – what any of the folk at Hope will do without her.'

'How did she seem last week?'

There was a long pause before Sharon replied. 'Not herself.' Joe didn't say anything and at last she continued, 'Before she was always such a laugh. I mean, she was serious about her work, but she could have run this place standing on her head, so she never stressed about it. She'd been a senior probation officer, managing a whole team. She'd worked in a prison with lifers, and had to stand up in court to give evidence about hard-core clients. Nothing threw her. Nothing worried her. Not usually.'

'But recently she'd been worried?'

'At first I thought she was just upset, like. With Martin dying. We all loved Martin. I mean he was a bit weird. A bit of a geek. But he had a good heart.'

'But later you thought something else was troubling her?'

There was another silence as Sharon chose her words carefully. This was a witness who needed patient handling. 'After Martin died she got snappy. The least thing and she'd fly into a temper. And that wasn't like Shirley. Like I said, usually she was a laugh. Easy to get on with.' She looked out of the window. A small group of teenagers had gathered for a smoke on the pavement. Presumably soon they'd try to come in for a session, expecting to find Shirley here to run the show.

'And she didn't give you any idea what was bothering her?'

'I did ask her,' Sharon said. 'She said it wasn't anything she couldn't handle. "And nothing that's not my own fault."'

'What did she mean by that?' Joe was finding this conversation tantalizing. All second-hand. All the impression of a woman who had plenty of problems of her own.

'I don't know. She wouldn't say.'

The crowd on the pavement was growing and he

knew he'd soon have to go down and tell them that the centre would be shut for the day. The CSIs would want to come in for a search. The computers would be taken. Then Sharon would lose concentration and start telling herself stories about Shirley, trying to make sense of the woman's death by forming a narrative. There'd be gossip all over the town. The first response to news of her death would be lost.

'Any of her clients have a grudge against her?'

'No!' Sharon was on the verge of tears again. 'We all loved her.'

You all loved Martin, and he's dead too. What does that tell us?

'Can I see the diary, the one where Shirley wrote down her appointments and the addresses of her visits?'

Sharon reached under the desk and pulled out a big hard-backed notebook. She was pushing it across to Joe when there was a sudden noise on the stairs, the clatter of boots, the door pushed open. Frank appeared; his face was red and his huge tattooed fists clenched, as if he was about to hit something or someone.

'I've just heard that Shirley's dead. That some bastard's killed her.'

Chapter Twenty-Nine

Vera was on the phone to Alicia Randle. Before making the call she'd planned a gentle enquiry about any possible reason why Alicia or her son might have written to a former probation officer who ran a ragbag charity in an ex-pit-village in Northumberland. But when the phone was answered, Vera found herself asking a very different question.

'I wonder if I might come to visit you?'

'When?' The veneer of politeness was being slowly eaten away by grief.

'As soon as possible.' Vera thought if she could get a decent pool car and start at once she could be there in five hours. 'I'd like to come today.'

'If you have news, Inspector, you could give it over the telephone.' The voice was icy. Perhaps Alicia didn't want her pleasant home, and all the memories of her son as a boy, sullied by the arrival of the woman who was investigating his death. But surely her elder son had already contaminated the place by committing suicide there.

'There's been another suspicious death,' Vera said. 'We think it might be related to Patrick's murder. I know this a difficult time, but I have to talk to you.'

When she put down the phone Vera felt suddenly

overwhelmed by exhaustion. In a conversation with Alicia Randle every word had to be chosen with care. She picked up her bag and went out to the open-plan office. 'Charlie, you're with me. I need you to share the driving. We can't have the North-East losing its best detective because she's fallen asleep at the wheel. Let's go and see how the other half lives.'

She slept most of the way and woke when they had pulled off the motorway and had started driving down country roads. The satnav had a posh southern voice not very different from Alicia Randle's. The hedges were high and lush and everything seemed very green. In cottage gardens and orchards, fruit trees were already in blossom. There was a village with ancient black-and-white houses tilted towards a green and a squat stone church.

'Eh, pet!' As soon as she'd spoken Vera wondered if she were emphasizing the accent because she was nervous, very much out of her comfort zone. 'It's all very *Midsomer*, isn't it?'

Charlie chortled, but she saw that he was very tired. 'You have a kip in the car while I talk to her. Probably best not to go in mob-handed anyway.'

The house had once been a rectory. It was old red-brick and seemed to hold the heat of the afternoon sun. There was a garden, not as big or as organized as that of the Hall at Gilswick, but plenty of space to keep the neighbours at bay. For a small child to set his moth traps. There was long grass in an orchard that still had a rope-swing tied to one of the trees. Vera thought of Simon, the boy who'd committed suicide, and thought *she'd* have got rid of that. It reminded her too much of a gallows. But perhaps Alicia had been looking forward and was still thinking of a grandchild. There'd be no hope of that now.

Alicia had a man with her. 'This is Henry.' Her lover and intended husband. He was just as Vera would have expected: tall, grey-haired, distinguished. He spoke with the sort of voice that had once commanded obedience through half the globe. And it seemed he had been a diplomat of some sort. 'I was posted to every continent in the world, but I've never been to north-east England. Shameful, I know.' Then he gave a little laugh that made Vera think that he wasn't ashamed at all.

They had tea outside on the lawn. Scones that Alicia must have knocked up while she was waiting for Vera to arrive. Unless she had someone to help her in the house. Vera couldn't quite imagine her cleaning her own toilets.

'How can we help you, Inspector?'

'I'd prefer to talk to you on your own, Mrs Randle. If you'd be comfortable with that.' It was more a way of Vera establishing that she was in charge of the situation than because she objected to the man's presence.

The diplomatic Henry was already on his feet. 'Of course, Inspector, I do understand. There are procedures to follow.' He rested a hand on Alicia's shoulder. 'I'll be inside if you need me.'

'What is all this about, Inspector? Henry's been helping me to organize the funeral. Patrick had so many friends. We're trying to track them down, and most of them will need places to stay.' Alicia was finding her own way of coping with her son's death by focusing on detail. Keeping busy. Now she sounded a little petulant and overwrought.

'I explained that there'd been another murder.' Vera took another scone. She couldn't remember the last time she'd eaten. Charlie would be starving too. She'd treat him to a pile of grease, in the services on the way back. 'Apparently there was no connection between Patrick and the new victim. She was a retired probation officer called Shirley Hewarth.' Vera looked for a reaction, some sign that the name was familiar, but Alicia just seemed confused. Vera continued, 'Shirley had moved into the voluntary sector and worked for an organization called Hope North-East.'

Still no flicker of recognition. 'So you've come all this way to tell me that my son's death was completely random and meaningless – the act of a psychopath. That doesn't bring any comfort, Inspector, and you could have told me that over the phone. I'd rather you were spending your time finding the killer, before he commits another act of violence.' Alicia picked up her cup and sipped at the tea.

The sun was still hot and the sound of woodpigeons in the trees reminded Vera of childhood summers and made her feel drowsy. She forced herself to concentrate. 'I said that apparently there was no link, but in fact we *have* found a connection between Patrick and our new victim.' A pause. 'At least between this place and the new victim.'

'I'm sorry, Inspector, but you'll have to explain. I don't understand.' That iciness again, as if the failure was entirely Vera's for not being sufficiently clear.

'We know that Shirley Hewarth received a letter from this village just over a month ago. We don't have the letter itself, but there was a postmark and date stamp on the envelope.'

Alicia set down her cup. She was struggling for control. Glancing back at the house, Vera saw that Henry was standing by an open French window staring out at them.

'What are you saying, Inspector?'

'That somebody living in Wychbold wrote to Shirley Hewarth.' Vera looked up. 'It's too much of a coincidence to suppose that any of the other residents were connected to a woman murdered so soon after your son. Did you write to her?'

There was a moment's pause. Alicia's gaze turned to Henry, who was still looking out across the lawn, but he was too far away to help her. 'No! Of course not. I've never heard of her.'

'Then I must assume that the correspondent was Patrick.' Vera knew she sounded pompous, but this woman brought out the worst in her. She had always been chippy around the landed classes. Something to do with her father, Hector, being disinherited by his family. 'You don't know why Patrick might have written to a woman running a small charity for ex-offenders in south-east Northumberland?'

'No! I can't imagine why he would have written to anybody. The young don't, do they, these days? It's all email and texting. I never receive a letter now, not even from my older friends.'

Vera thought the woman had a point. What did the post van deliver to her door these days? Bills and the occasional Christmas card from relatives she'd lost touch with years ago. She thought they should find out when Shirley Hewarth last had a birthday; perhaps

Patrick had sent her a card. 'Could I look at Patrick's room?'

Alicia looked horrified. Vera saw that she considered the request as a violation. She couldn't imagine the large and ugly detective in her son's space. Or perhaps she was frightened what they might find there. Did she worry that her golden boy might have been fragile and damaged, like her first son?

'I haven't been in since Patrick died,' she said at last. 'I can't face it.'

'We'll go together then, shall we?' Vera got to her feet. Her head spun for a moment. Too little sleep and not enough good food. If she didn't get some fruit and veg inside her, she'd end up with scurvy. Her young doctor would have a fit if she could see what the team consumed in the course of an investigation.

Alicia led her through a small back door, not the French window. Henry had been watching their progress and was waiting for them in the hall. He stooped slightly towards Alicia, but didn't touch her. They stood awkwardly for a moment. 'All done? That's good. I expect you want to be on your way, Inspector Stanhope. You've got a long trip north. Or shall I organize more tea?'

'The Inspector wants to look at Patrick's room.' Alicia reached out and took the man's hand, clung to him.

'Well, I can see the sense in that.' Henry spoke easily. 'No need for you to go up though, Allie. Not if you don't feel up to it. I can show the Inspector the way.'

There was a silence broken by the heavy ticking of

an old clock in the hall. Vera waited with interest for Alicia's response.

'No, I'll go too.'

'Why don't you come with us, Henry?' Vera thought the last thing she needed was for Alicia to go all faint and wobbly on her, if they were on their own up there. It seemed oddly informal to be calling the man by his first name and she realized she'd never heard his surname. 'You can give Alicia some moral support.'

So they trooped together up the main stairs and into a huge room at the front of the house. Vera stood at the door and was swept again by a tide of exhaustion. This was a waste of time. The room was full of stuff: bookshelves covered the long wall, there were fitted cupboards in the alcoves on each side of a chimney breast, boxes of paper, a pile of prints of moths and butterflies stacked against a wooden chest and all the debris of leftover adolescence – posters of rock bands, a cricket bat, photos of young sportsmen grinning into the camera. The late-afternoon sun streamed through the long sash windows and was reflected from a mirror on the wall, small glittering objects like pencil sharpeners and paperclips scattered over Patrick's desk, a microscope lens. A trained search team would take weeks to look through it properly.

'We spoke to Patrick's girlfriend.' Vera realized suddenly that she'd forgotten to ask about this, and that it was important. 'She told us that he'd been engrossed by a project, but that it was almost over. Do you know anything about that?'

'No, I didn't even know that Patrick and Rebecca were still in touch. I told you, he hasn't been very communicative with me recently. I asked him what I'd done to upset him, but he didn't give any sort of coherent answer.' Alicia stood just inside the door as if she was reluctant to engage with the memories of the room. 'I suppose we'll have to clear all this out.' And then, with a little cry, 'I can't bear it.'

'No rush,' Henry said. 'All in your own time. If you can't face it now, we can leave the inspector to it. I'm sure we're both ready for a stiff drink.'

Vera supposed that he'd dealt with crises before, imagined his reassuring plummy voice notifying relatives of sudden deaths, arrests, accidents overseas.

But Alicia didn't answer. After a brief hesitation she walked further into the room and began to pick up items that had been thrown onto the floor. She hung a dressing gown on a hook on the back of the door, gathered up a pile of newspapers and dropped them into a large black plastic box already half-filled with rubbish. 'It's all such a mess. Patrick was always very keen on recycling, even as a young boy. It was a kind of obsession. He wasn't always as good at bringing the paper downstairs to go into the special skip in the lane.'

'If you want to leave me to it,' Vera said, 'I won't be very long now. A quick peek and then I'll join you downstairs. I'll need to be going back again soon anyway.'

If Alicia was surprised by the detective's change of tone, she didn't show it. Henry put his arm around her and led her away. As soon as they'd gone Vera sat on the bed, put on a pair of latex gloves and pulled the recycling box towards her. Carefully she took out each piece of paper and laid it on the floor. Newspapers, junk mail, adverts for credit cards and holidays in the sun. Empty envelopes. Vera studied the postmark on each one. Nothing from north-east England.

Then she came across the letter. Printed on headed paper: Hope North-East and then the address in Bebington:

Dear Mr Randle,

Thank you for your letter and your request for further information. If you feel it would be helpful for us to meet, I'd be glad to see you in my office. Do feel free to phone me when you're settled in Northumberland.

Yours sincerely
Shirley Hewarth

Vera leaned back on the bed and looked at the patterns caused by the shadows of the trees outside dancing on the ceiling. Another connection between Hewarth, Benton and Randle. But she still couldn't see what information a posh lad from the South could want from a social worker living in a deprived part of the North-East. And why that information had led to the deaths of three people. She slipped the letter into an evidence bag and then into the briefcase her team had given her for her last significant birthday, in an attempt to improve her image and, by association, theirs.

Henry and Alicia were waiting for her in the room that looked out onto the garden. The French window was still open and there was a breeze. They came out to meet Vera in the hall – eager, Vera thought, to get rid of her, worried that if she moved further into the house they'd never get her to leave. Henry opened the front door, and the French window in the room looking out over the back garden slammed shut with a bang.

'I'm sorry to have disturbed you.' She hesitated for a moment on the doorstep. She wanted to be away too, but had the sense that the right question now would solve the entire case.

'Goodbye, Inspector.' Alicia seemed to have recovered her poise. She held out her hand.

Vera couldn't think of the right question to ask and walked away to the car, suddenly desperate to be away from the quiet and elegant house.

Charlie was still asleep. She rapped on the window and he woke suddenly, obviously unaware for a moment exactly what was happening. She got into the passenger seat. 'You've been asleep all afternoon, so you can drive back too.'

She didn't close her eyes, though. There was too much to think about. Charlie saw that she was awake and started chatting. 'Pretty round here, isn't it? Would you ever consider a move south?'

'Nah!' She looked at him as if he was mad. 'Not here. It's too far from the sea.' She paused for a moment and tried to work out why she was so horrified at the prospect of living in the middle of the country. 'I never feel safe away from the edge.'

Chapter Thirty

Holly had been detailed to talk to Shirley Hewarth's close relatives. The ex-husband and son had already been informed of her death, but Vera had wanted them spoken to in more detail. 'I need you to bring back a clearer picture of Shirley. I can't get any sense of her. What was she? Some sort of saint, spending her time with wasters and sinners? Or was she one of those women who feels the need to mother the world?'

So Holly found herself standing in a corridor in Northumbria University, outside one of the rehearsal rooms. Inside, a show seemed to be in the first stages of planning. Half a dozen young people were blocking moves to weird music Holly didn't recognize. Jonathan was expecting her, and when he saw her looking through the glass door he took his leave of the group. They gathered round and hugged him in turn. He was a tall, gangling young man, dark like his mother. She could see the resemblance.

When he emerged into the corridor she held out a hand. 'I'm so sorry about your mother.' She never knew exactly what to say in these circumstances. Vera had banned *Sorry for your loss*. 'We're not characters from an American cop show,' she'd yelled at one of the briefings, 'and the bereaved haven't just mislaid their car keys.'

Jonathan led her to a tiny room where three desks were crammed into a space hardly bigger than a cupboard. 'My tutor said we could use her office. She doesn't need it because it's the weekend. She came in specially because of what happened to Mam.' His voice was even, and Holly thought he was still in shock. He hadn't yet accepted the reality of his mother's death. He leaned against one of the desks and nodded that she should take the chair.

'But you're here, even though it's a Saturday?'

'We're working towards our final performance and there's a lot on.' He paused. 'Claire, my tutor, tried to send me home, but what good would it do me to be moping in my room? Dad's going to pick me up in a bit. I'm going to stay with him and Mandy in Kimmerston for a few days.' He looked into her face. A fierce stare. A challenge. 'Do you know who killed my mother yet?'

Holly shook her head.

'I'd assumed it must be one of her clients.' He had the sort of face that gave everything away. Emotion was reflected in it like the shadows of moving clouds on a still lake. In a few seconds Holly saw disgust, anger and affection. 'She loved working in that place, but when I saw some of the men she was dealing with . . . They'd have scared *me*.'

'You went to the office in Bebington?'

'A few times. Mum and I went to the theatre a lot, and once I'd learned to drive I'd pick her up to bring her into town.'

'Can you think why she might have been in Gilswick yesterday?'

He gave a little laugh. 'That area seems a bit upmarket for most of her clients, but I suppose it might have been work. She did lots of home visits.'

'Your mother didn't have friends who lived in the valley? She told the volunteer who worked with her in the office that she was taking time off yesterday afternoon, so the visit was nothing to do with the charity.'

He paused. 'We were close,' he said. 'I lived in her flat before I got the place at Northumbria Uni and decided I needed a bit of independence, and I can't remember her talking about anyone from Gilswick. But we didn't live in each other's pockets, even when I was still at school.'

'Had there been anyone special after the divorce?' Holly was feeling her way here. She still had no idea what she was looking for.

'Probably.' He grinned. 'But she wasn't going to tell me. We were close, but some areas were off-limits. I never chatted about my love life, either. But I don't think she had a long-term relationship. She liked her independence too much.'

'Was that what caused the break-up of the marriage? Your parents had been together for a long time.'

'Perhaps. Though I didn't ever see Dad cramping her style. She was always her own woman, even when they were married.' He paused again. 'Sometimes I think my mother had a kind of self-destruct button. She couldn't quite accept that things were going well, and made life so difficult for my Dad that he left in the end. Found another woman. Someone less complicated.' There was another silence. 'It was almost as if she didn't believe she had the right to be happy. I don't blame my dad for leaving. They were both more relaxed after the separation.'

It was lunchtime, and through the window Holly could see students in groups on a piece of grass, chatting. It could have been midsummer.

'The local news is linking my mother's death with the double-murder that happened in Gilswick last week.' Jonathan shot another intense stare in her direction. 'Is that true?'

'One of the earlier victims worked with Shirley as a volunteer,' Holly said. 'It seems too much of a coincidence not to be some sort of connection. Did you ever meet Martin Benton?'

'I don't think I ever met him when I called into the office to see my mother. She did talk about him, though. She said he was brilliant at all things technical.'

There was a silence. Vera would have known how to fill it, would have elicited confidences and useful pieces of information. Yet again Holly felt inadequate in comparison. *I'm not even good at this, so why do I put myself through it every day?*

'Patrick Randle, one of the earlier victims, wrote to your mother from his home in Wychbold. That's a town in Herefordshire. Do you know what that might have been about?'

The student seemed bewildered. 'I have absolutely no idea. Mum worked all over the place when she first qualified, but I don't think she ever lived that far south. Besides, that was years ago, long before I was born, and I don't think she kept in touch with anyone she worked with there. Except maybe on Facebook.'

Holly made a mental note to get the techies to check Shirley's Facebook page. Perhaps that had been how Patrick found her. Or how she'd found him. 'When did you last see your mother?'

'Just under a week ago. It was Sunday lunchtime. She cooked for me in her flat. Roast lamb. My favourite. Veggie pie for her. Then we walked along the front to Tynemouth and had a couple of drinks in a bar there, before I got the Metro back to town.'

'How did she seem?'

'I'm not sure.' He seemed lost in his thoughts. 'My memory is coloured by what's happened since. Looking back, she seemed a bit distracted, not quite herself – a bit quiet maybe. I asked her if everything was okay and she said she thought she was going down with a cold. I accepted that. She wasn't a woman you felt you had to take care of.'

'Have you been in touch with her since?'

'Only by text. Some mail had come to the flat for me. Should she post it on or keep hold of it? Did I fancy the new play at the Live Theatre? She was an absolutely perfect mother. Supportive when I needed her, but never interfering, never in-my-face.'

There was a tap at the office door. A woman stood outside accompanied by an older man in jeans and a jersey. 'Your dad's here.'

The woman was obviously Jonathan's tutor. The man put his arms round his son and they clung to each other. Jonathan, who'd been holding things together well until now, seemed to collapse into his father's arms. Holly felt awkward faced by the show of affection. The tutor walked away without another word. Jack Hewarth was crying silently and without fuss, allowing the tears to run down his face.

'This is a detective, Dad. She's investigating Mum's murder.' Jonathan had pulled away.

'Would you mind if I asked you some questions too, Mr Hewarth? Background stuff.' Holly wished they would both sit down. She felt at a disadvantage in the low chair.

'Aye, why not? If it'll help. It'll be the same madman that killed those two people in Gilswick, though, won't it? That's where her body was found.'

'We're not ruling anything out at the moment.'

The man took a seat opposite to her. He was unshaven, untidy, and Holly thought that was his natural state and not a reaction to grief.

'We were still friends,' he said. 'I didn't hate her. Nothing like that. And she came along to the wedding when I got married again and gave us her blessing.'

'Where did you meet?'

'Staffordshire. Two Geordies out of their comfort zone. She was with a bunch of friends in a bar and I recognized the accent, went over for a chat.' He leaned back in the chair. 'It was my first job. Cub reporter on a small-town local rag, but I loved every minute. She'd just qualified as a probation officer and seemed a bit overwhelmed. I couldn't see it was right, a young thing like her dealing with murderers and rapists. They'd send her out to interview men on council estates where the police would only go in pairs. After a day like that she just wanted fun, and nobody can let their hair down like people from the North-East.'

'When did you come back north?' Holly supposed she'd been a young thing when she started working with murderers and rapists. She'd never been one for letting her hair down much, though.

'Soon after we married. I got a job on *The Journal* and stayed there till I took early retirement. She found a post easily enough and worked her way up to team leader. She ended up in the prison. Sittingwell. She'd worked in institutions before and I think she liked it there. It's an open nick, and she thought she could do positive work with the girls. Then there were all sorts of changes to the probation service, plans to privatize, and she got disheartened. She couldn't see a future for herself under the new regime. Retirement wasn't for her, though – I'm an idle bastard, but she always had enough energy to power the National Grid.'

Holly thought the information that Shirley had worked at Sittingwell was new. Another connection between her and the Redheads, though she would already have left the prison by the time Lizzie was convicted. 'So she got the job at Hope?'

'It was just a bunch of volunteers, before she took it on. She was approached by the trustees and asked if she'd consider doing it. It meant a massive cut in salary, but she was always up for a challenge, our Shirley.'

Jack Hewarth seemed to find some comfort talking about his former wife and Holly would have let him continue without interruption. This was the sort of information Vera loved to have. But Jonathan turned away from the window and joined the conversation.

'She always said she'd never work at a job she wouldn't do without pay. That was why she encouraged me to do the drama degree. Most parents would have advised against it, but she said I'd regret it if I didn't give it my best shot.'

There was a moment of silence, broken by the wail of a saxophone from one of the practice rooms further down the corridor. Holly thought this had been a strong family; despite the divorce, the couple had maintained a good relationship and had brought up their son together. She couldn't imagine why anyone would want Shirley Hewarth dead; surely her killing must be the result of the double-murder in the big house. Shirley had known something, or guessed something, that had made her death inevitable.

'Does the name Patrick Randle mean anything to you?' She directed the question to Jack, expecting an immediate denial. Instead there was a hesitation.

'Something about it is kind of familiar.'

'He was one of the earlier victims at Gilswick.' Holly leaned forward across the desk towards the man. 'You probably heard the name on the news.'

'Aye, maybe.' But he didn't sound entirely convinced. 'I thought I knew it from a different context, though. Something that happened a while ago. It's the journo in me. You never forget a contact.'

Another silence. The musician along the corridor was playing scales.

'Did Shirley ever talk to you about Martin Benton? He worked with her at Hope.' Holly was going through the motions now. The Hewarths might have parted on amicable terms, but they'd been separated for years and she didn't think they'd share confidences.

'The geek volunteer?'

She was surprised that he'd known the name. She nodded.

'Just that she'd never met anyone who could find their way round a computer system as well as him. She said he could make a fortune if he took up hacking. Just as well he was on the side of the angels.'

'When did you last see Shirley?'

'She called last week and asked if I fancied a drink. She said she'd had a crap day and needed to bend my ear about something.'

Again Holly was surprised. She dismissed former partners from her mind and from her life. She wondered what Jack's new wife made of the arrangement. 'Was that usual?'

'Not recently. Not since I'd married.' Jack gave a sudden grin. 'Shirley said Mandy wouldn't appreciate it. So I knew she must be a bit desperate.'

'And did you meet?'

'Yes, in the Rockliffe Arms. A little pub behind Front Street in Kimmerston. It's usually quiet in there and we arranged to meet early, straight after she finished work. That time of day it's mostly old men playing dominoes and the odd person calling in for a quick pint on their way home.'

Holly was taking notes now. If Shirley had needed to confide in someone, this might be significant.

Jack continued, 'I could tell something was bothering her as soon as she got there. She looked as if she hadn't slept properly, as if worry was eating away at her.'

'When was this?' Holly looked up from her iPad.

'Thursday.'

'So after the first Gilswick murders.'

'Aye, I remember it was all over the news. People in the pub were talking about it. Because it was so close to home and nobody had been arrested.' Jack seemed to replay the events of the evening in his head and began to describe them as if he could still see them. 'I went up to the bar to get the drinks, and then I asked her what had happened. Martin had just been mentioned on the news as a victim. She was obviously shocked, but she was anxious too. "The police will be poking into our business now. I don't know what they'll find." I was just saying that she shouldn't worry when a gang of her old mates came in. People she used to work with. They joined us and it was impossible to chat after that. Shirley was drinking a lot and ended up leaving her car and getting a taxi home. That was the last time I saw her.' He put his head in his hands. 'I should have dragged her away, found somewhere else to talk. But I thought she was just upset because someone who worked with her had been killed. I thought she needed cheering up, and her friends could do that as well as me.'

'Did you speak to her after that?' Holly tried not to show her disappointment. The man felt guilty enough.

'I texted to ask if she wanted to try for a quiet chat again.' Jack paused. 'She said she was fine. *Nothing I can't deal with*. That was classic Shirley. She thought she could take on the world all by herself.' He looked up at Holly. 'Trouble was, none of the rest of us could keep up with her.'

Chapter Thirty-One

Joe went straight from the Hope office in Bebington to the valley in Gilswick. Less than a dozen miles in distance, but as far removed from the ex-pit-village as it was possible to be. Vera had phoned him from the car just before she arrived at Alicia Randle's house.

'Go and talk to the retired hedonists! I don't want them dismissed as possible suspects because they read books, keep hens and make jam.' Shouting to make her point, although he could hear her perfectly. He thought she'd always be in charge, even though she was at the other end of the country.

It was just after midday and he'd already decided that would be a good time to catch the residents at home. After the fuss of the night before they might have slept in, but it wouldn't be unreasonable now to expect them to be ready for interview. He sat for a moment in the car planning his strategy; and because he was nervous. He might have been brought up to believe that all men were equal, but he found himself awestruck by people with degrees who used long words. Up until now Vera had been the point of contact with the Valley Farm residents. She didn't think anyone was cleverer than her. Joe hadn't even met them and he felt slightly daunted.

He went to the Redhead house first. Shirley Hewarth had visited their daughter in prison, and the police knew that there'd been contact between her and Annie Redhead. A man opened the door. Joe recognized him from the photo pinned on the whiteboard in the operations room. Sam Redhead. Big, balding and a bit tongue-tied. Joe introduced himself. 'Could I come in? I know you talked to officers early this morning, but everything was a bit rushed then. You'll have had time to gather your thoughts.'

Sam showed him into a living room. The original barn walls had been whitewashed and the curtains were white and blue, patterned with small flower prints. Joe wished Sal could see it. She loved all the makeover programmes on daytime telly. A woman, Annie Redhead, sat on a small sofa covered with the same material as the curtains and grasped a mug of coffee. She was plump too, with a very pretty face. Heart-shaped. She might have just got up, but she looked as if she hadn't slept at all.

'This is a detective,' Sam said. 'He wants to talk to us.'

'Of course.' The woman turned and managed a smile. 'Can we get you anything, Sergeant? Tea? Coffee? We don't have a fancy machine like Nigel next door, but you'd be very welcome.' She must have realized she was rambling because she fell suddenly silent.

Joe thought her grief seemed too personal for the death of a stranger, however shocking it must have been to see the slashes on the body. 'You knew Shirley Hewarth?'

'I only met her once. Yesterday morning. She asked me to see her in her office.' A pause, and then a kind of confession. 'She'd been visiting our daughter Lizzie in prison.' Annie turned to face him. 'She had plans for helping her. I'm not sure what will happen about that now. It seems very selfish, but that's all I can think about: that we'll be left to deal with Lizzie coming home, without any help or support. I trusted Shirley. It's crazy, but I almost feel that she's let us down by dying.'

Sam sat awkwardly beside his wife. As he put his arm around her shoulder, Joe was reminded of himself as a teenager; the party when he'd got it together with Sal, sliding his arm around her back, the very first physical contact. There was something innocent about this couple. They could have been teenagers too.

'Was that why Shirley was in the valley yesterday?' Joe thought this might be a breakthrough; it could explain the victim's presence in Gilswick. 'To talk to you about Lizzie?'

'No!' Annie sounded impatient. 'I told you, I went to her office in the morning. She wasn't going to do a home visit until next Monday. Lizzie will be released from prison tomorrow, and Shirley said she'd give us a day to get settled. If Shirley had wanted to talk to me before that, she had both my phone numbers. She wouldn't have dragged herself all the way out here.'

'How did she seem at the meeting?'

'Professional,' Annie said. 'Efficient. Kind. I thought she had Lizzie's best interests at heart.' There was a pause. 'You don't think about people like that having personal problems, do you? I mean doctors and social workers. I can't imagine their lives away from work. I just think they're there to provide a service.'

Like the police. We're not supposed to have personal lives, either.

'What did you do after you'd seen Shirley?' Joe thought none of this was helping.

'I came straight back here. Had lunch with Sam. Then I thought I'd better tell our friends here in Valley Farm that Lizzie would be coming to stay with us for a bit.' There was another pause, then an attempt at humour that didn't quite come off. 'That we'd have a convicted offender in our midst.'

'And was everyone at home when you went to call?' Joe found he was speaking gently, as if to an invalid.

'Yes. I didn't see John O'Kane. He was working in his office upstairs, but he was there.' Annie set her mug carefully on the floor beside her. 'Janet was lovely. So kind. Then I went next door to tell the Lucasas . . .'

Her voice tailed off and Joe had to prompt her. 'How did *they* react to the news of Lizzie's release?'

'Nigel was fine.' A hesitation. 'They've never had children. It's easy to judge, isn't it, if you've never had any? You think the parents must be to blame if a child goes off the rails. I used to do it myself.'

'And what about his wife?' For a moment Joe struggled to remember the name of the Lucas woman. 'Lorraine?'

'She found it harder to accept. She worked in prisons at one time. Education. She taught art and crafts. Maybe you're used to all the sob-stories if you work with offenders every day. You become less sympathetic.'

Not me, Joe thought. *I'm still a soft touch. According to Vera, at least.*

Annie was still talking, trying to explain her friend's reaction. 'I suppose she moved to the valley to escape screwed-up kids, and the last thing she'd want would be to have one turn up here. This is their idea of paradise.'

'What time was that?' Best stick to facts. He was more comfortable with those.

'Oh, I'm not sure.' She frowned. 'I don't wear a watch. We don't need to, out here. Mid-afternoon sometime.'

'Did you see or hear anything unusual while you were out visiting?' Joe knew he was clutching at straws now. If Annie had seen a stranger she'd have mentioned it by now.

She shook her head.

'Mrs Hewarth drove a black Golf. Did you see that along the track at any time yesterday?'

Another shake of her head before she turned to her husband for confirmation. Joe turned to him too.

'Where were you all afternoon, Mr Redhead?'

'Here, in the house. In the kitchen. Listening to a play on the radio. Then I pottered in the garden for a while.' The man shrugged. 'Time seems to pass without me noticing, and some days I wonder what on earth I'm doing with my life.'

'And later you all went round to the Lucas house?' Joe found himself overtaken by the same lethargy as the people he was questioning. He'd always envied people who could afford to retire early, but now he wondered what he'd do with his time all day if he wasn't at work. He'd always been crap at DIY. 'Was it a special celebration? A birthday?'

'I think we were all feeling a bit strange,' Annie said. 'It was those two killings at the big house. Right on our doorstep. The fat detective poking into our business. I suppose we thought a bit of a party would be a way to relieve the tension. Besides, it was Friday night. We always get together on Friday night.'

'Can you talk me through the evening?' Joe thought it was pretty weird, these three couples living on top of each other. If they'd wanted to escape the horror of what had happened in the big house, wouldn't Sam and Annie have chosen to get away from Gilswick altogether? The pictures in town followed by a nice meal perhaps. By themselves, so they had a bit of privacy before Lizzie landed up. The last thing he'd want, in their position, would be to spend the night with the same people he'd see every day.

'It turned into a bit of a session,' Sam said. 'Nigel had made one of his lethal cocktails and the evening went downhill from there.'

Joe couldn't imagine the man enjoying a party. A play on the radio seemed much more his sort of thing.

'Did anyone leave the house during the evening?'

They looked at each other. Joe wondered now if their pallor and confusion were the result of a hangover rather than distress at another killing.

'I can't be certain,' Annie said. 'People came and went all evening. At one point Nigel came in and said how beautiful the stars were. I knew then that he must be seriously pissed. John might have gone out for a couple of sneaky fags. He pretends he doesn't smoke, but we all know that's not true. What I do remember very clearly is Janet leaving later, to take out the dogs. She told us to send out a search party if she was gone longer than a quarter of an hour. I was watching the clock then. And suddenly she was screaming.'

'You could hear her from that distance?' Joe tried to picture where the body had been lying. 'Over the noise of a party?'

'We were all quiet by then. There wasn't any music and the windows were open.' Annie must have sensed that Joe still wasn't convinced, because she added, 'It was definitely Janet screaming. We all heard it and ran outside. Perhaps she'd come down the track towards the house to call out to us.'

Joe made a mental note to ask Janet O'Kane, but let the subject go for now. 'What time was that?'

'A quarter past midnight. As I said, I was watching the clock.'

Joe tried to picture the scene. The five adults at the end of the day, sitting in companionable silence. The scream coming from a long way off. 'You must have panicked.'

'We all ran outside. Almost tripping over each other. It was dark. No street lights, all the way up here.' Annie shut her eyes briefly.

'You had no sense that anyone else was about?' Joe thought it unlikely that the pathologist would pin down the time of death with any real accuracy. Paul Keating was scathing about theories that suggested such a thing was feasible. It was possible that the murder had been committed not long before the body was found, and that the killer had still been in the area while the party-goers were looking for Janet O'Kane.

The Redheads looked at each other. 'It was just confusing,' Annie said at last. 'I have no sense where any of us were. I caught a glimpse of Nigel at one point, and I think Sam was right beside me all the way down the track. Other than that . . .'

'Did you hear anything? A car in the distance?'

This time Sam answered. 'All I could hear was screaming and the dogs barking, people slipping on the grass in the dark. It was like a nightmare.'

'But you grew up round here.' Joe remembered the details written in black marker pen on the whiteboard in the operations room. 'Your family farmed the land. You must be able to find your way around the valley blindfolded.'

There was a moment of silence. Joe could feel the hostility coming from both people on the sofa. They stared at him.

'What are you saying?' Sam's voice was very quiet. 'That I'm telling lies? Our farm was on the other side of the valley. And besides, last night the shouting and the dogs and that poor woman lying there covered in blood – it was my idea of hell.'

Chapter Thirty-Two

It was gone ten when Vera and Charlie arrived back at Kimmerston and the team was still waiting for the evening briefing. No energy now. Everyone desperate for bed and food. She sat on the desk in front of them.

'Right. Quick as you can and no messing. Just the important stuff. We'll go into more detail in the morning. Joe?'

'Everyone at Valley Farm has the same story. They'd got together for supper and drinks in the Lucas house. Everyone had too much to drink. Janet O'Kane went to take out the Carswell dogs. The dogs sniffed out the body. She screamed and they ran out to see what was going on.' Joe paused and looked up at her. 'It's a long way for a scream to carry, but they'd all have to be in collusion if they're not being straight about that, and why would they lie?' Another brief pause. 'Annie Redhead's the only person who admits to knowing Shirley Hewarth – they met up yesterday morning to discuss Lizzie's release from prison.'

Vera felt like a spider in the middle of a web of information. A very large, black spider. Who needed the Internet? 'OK. Hol, how did you get on with Shirley's ex-husband and son?'

'I met them both at the university. All three seem

to have been on very good terms, even after the divorce. A nice family. Jonathan last saw his mother a week ago for Sunday lunch. He said she seemed quiet, but put it down to her feeling a bit under the weather. She contacted Jack during the week and asked if they could meet for a drink – she'd had a bad couple of days and needed to chat to him about something. In the end a crowd of her friends came into the pub and they didn't get the chance to talk.'

'Pity.' Vera tried to assess the significance of that. Shirley obviously had other friends and colleagues. Why would she turn to an ex-husband if she wanted a shoulder to cry on? 'Well, Charlie and I have had a very pleasant day out in the country visiting Alicia Randle and her bloke. Who is very classy, if not exactly my type. Some kind of representative of Her Majesty's Government overseas. Or he used to be, before he retired. Alicia couldn't shed any light on how there was an envelope with a Wychbold postmark in Shirley Hewarth's kitchen, but luckily it seems that Patrick was very green. He saved all his paper for recycling. And in the box in his bedroom I found this.' Vera waved the letter in its transparent evidence bag. She already knew it off by heart and recited it word-for-word. 'So it seems the correspondence between Patrick and Shirley went both ways.' Now she spoke almost to herself. 'Why on earth would this pair be writing to each other? If we know that, we'll know who killed them.'

Vera was alone in her office. The team had dispersed for the night, but she was still fizzing and not ready for home and sleep. Listening to her voicemail – the requests for statistics and completed overtime forms, replies from technicians and scientists to her own demands for speedy updates – she felt a little calmer. There was nothing new. Nothing that needed immediate action. Then she was surprised by another voice. This was someone unused to leaving a voicemail message, very different from the rattled-off information from a colleague who no longer expected to speak to a real person. The caller didn't even give his name, but after a couple of seconds she recognized the hesitant voice: Percy Douglas, the old man who'd stumbled across Patrick Randle's body.

'Inspector, you asked me to call you if I came across anything. Well, it wasn't me, like, but my Susan. It's probably not important, but it's secret, like. I can't see it can have anything to do with these murders, but I thought you'd be interested in anything secret. Can you come along in the morning? I'll stay in until I've spoken to you.'

Vera replaced the receiver and smiled. *Oh yes, Percy Douglas, I'm interested in anything secret.*

It was another glorious day, more like June than April. Early sun slanting across the valley. In the big house's garden the bluebells had opened even more, forming a lake under the trees. Vera found Percy and Susan eating breakfast. A smell of bacon that made her mouth water as soon as she opened the door. Susan was on her feet, sticking another couple of rashers under the grill. 'You'll manage two eggs? Janet's hens are doing so well she's giving them away.' No offer of coffee, but a big pot of tea in the middle of the table and a mug set down beside the guest. Vera's idea of heaven. *Why would I ever want to retire from doing this?*

'I feel bad.' It was Susan again. Percy still hadn't said a word, just given Vera a quick grateful nod when she walked into the kitchen. 'Dad dragging you all the way out here, when you must be so busy.'

'It's worth coming for the breakfast.' Vera knew Susan couldn't be hurried and she couldn't be made to feel guilty. Let her tell her story in her own time.

'It's not that it's anything sinister.' Susan stood by the sink and put the frying pan to soak, then finally turned to face Vera. 'And it's not as if I was snooping. But nothing's been said. I'm not even sure that her husband knows. I mean, I can understand her wanting a bit of privacy, but not telling your husband . . .'

Vera's mouth was full of bread and egg and she didn't say anything.

'Just get on with it!' Percy was almost yelling. 'Let Mrs Stanhope know what you found.'

Vera smiled, but didn't correct him.

'When I was cleaning last week—'

'Before the murders at the big house?' Vera thought it had been a mistake to interrupt, but she needed to make the facts clear.

'Yes. Tuesday morning's when I do Valley Farm, so it would have been the day Dad found young Patrick's body.' Susan came to a stop again. Her father nodded for her to continue. 'I found a letter.'

'Where?'

'In the Lucas house. Nigel and Lorraine were out and I thought I'd give the place a bit of a blitz. It's that time of year, isn't it?' Another hesitation. 'There's a room upstairs that Lorraine uses as a studio. For her art. She tells me not to bother doing in there. "It'd only get mucky again and, besides, I don't like my things to be disturbed." Not even Nigel goes in without knocking, and that's always seemed weird to me. I mean, a married couple – it doesn't seem right.' Another pause.

'But you thought you'd take the opportunity to give it a proper spring-clean.' Vera had finished eating and pushed her plate to one side so that she could sit with her elbows on the table. 'While they were both out.'

'Yes!' Susan sounded grateful. 'I thought there wouldn't be any harm just going in. See if there were any cups that needed washing. Lorraine often took her coffee upstairs.'

'So this letter?'

Susan had begun to blush. 'It was in the drawer of the big pine table she uses for her paper and stuff.'

'And what did it say, this letter?'

'It was a hospital appointment. The Department of Oncology at the Freeman in Newcastle. Inviting her in to discuss her options. It must have come a while ago.'

'So Lorraine Lucas has cancer.' Vera pictured the woman she'd seen in the old farmhouse. Skinny and pretty. Still all her own hair, as far as Vera could tell, but that didn't necessarily mean anything. 'Why do you think she hasn't told her husband?'

'Because it's never been mentioned. I remember her going into town the day of the appointment. It was a couple of weeks ago. Nigel didn't go with her. Lorraine said she was going shopping; she wanted to buy some summer clothes because the weather was so warm.'

'Do you remember the name of the consultant?' Vera didn't think this could have anything to do with the murder of three people. Cancer brought its own terror. But Douglas had been right. Secrets were always interesting, and it might say something about the couple that Lorraine hadn't confided in her husband.

'Robinson,' Susan said. 'I think that was it.'

'What did you do then?'

'I put the letter back in the drawer and went downstairs. I knew I shouldn't have been in there. It was only me being nebby.' The blush deepened. 'I didn't tell Dad about it until yesterday. I knew he'd be angry about me snooping.'

'Then I phoned you.' Percy looked at Vera, wanting to be reassured that he'd done the right thing.

Vera nodded. 'Quite right.' She turned to Susan. 'Is there anything else you've come across?' Trying not to accuse the woman. It seemed almost like an illness itself, this need to pry into other people's business. 'Best to tell me now. You've already said that Nigel had applied to become a magistrate.'

Susan only shook her head.

'You'll probably know those people as well as anyone,' Vera said. 'In their homes every week, and I expect they take you for granted and hardly realize you're there. They probably say things in front of you that they wouldn't tell anyone else.'

'I'm like the dust-fairy.' Susan gave a small, sharp smile. 'You'd think their houses get clean as if by magic. Never any thanks. Not like Mrs Carswell, who'll sit down for a chat when I'm finished.'

'So is there anything you can tell me about them? Do they really all get on as well as they say?'

Susan shrugged. 'They put on a good show.'

'What do you mean?'

'Well, it's all sweetness and light in public. In their own homes it's a bit different. Professor O'Kane's the worst. He doesn't have anything nice to say about anyone. He's arrogant; thinks he's better than the rest of them because he knows about the past. All snide comments.'

They sat for a moment in silence.

Vera got to her feet. 'Nobody else must know about Lorraine's illness,' she said. 'It's private. Not our business.' *At least not your business*.

'I don't gossip. Not really.' Then a confession of sorts. 'I don't have much of a life here, just me and Dad. I'm just interested in other people's lives.'

'Ah, pet, you and me both.'

As Vera was pulling away from Percy's bungalow she was met by a car driving down the track towards Gilswick. Nigel Lucas. Maybe he was just on his way to the village to pick up the Sunday papers, but it seemed like a sign. Lorraine would be in the house on her own.

It took Lorraine a while to open the farmhouse door, and she was still in her nightclothes with a dressing gown pulled over the top. It was the first time Vera had seen her without make-up and she looked grey and very tired.

'I'm sorry.' Vera was sympathetic, but she was inside the door already, taking no chances. 'I got you out of your bed. I wanted to chat to you on your own.'

'What's this about? Your sergeant was here yesterday to take statements. We told him everything we know about that poor woman dying.'

'Shall I put the kettle on? Make us some tea?' Vera walked through to the kitchen, letting the woman follow. There was a granite breakfast bar with ridiculously high stools. She wasn't sure she'd be able to hoist herself onto them. Or get off, once she was there. 'Let's take the tea up to your studio, shall we? We know we won't be interrupted there. Why don't you lead the way?'

Lorraine shrugged. She seemed to have no fight in her. Vera wondered if that was down to the illness or the cure. They walked up the polished wooden stairs to a landing with a view of the hall and the kitchen, and then Lorraine pushed open a door into her studio. It was the size of a double bedroom, with one long window looking north towards the hill. An easel and a set of white-painted cupboards. The scrubbed pine table that Susan had described. Along one wall a chaise longue in faded grey velour. 'I noticed that, in the Kimmerston saleroom when we first moved up here,' Lorraine said. 'Nigel saw that I liked it and went to the auction and bid for it. A surprise, until it was delivered.' She paused for a beat. 'He's such a kind man.'

'Is that why you haven't told him you're ill? Worried he'll kill you with kindness?' Vera took a seat on a chair that looked as if it had once belonged to a teacher in a village school. Lorraine sank onto the chaise longue.

'How did you know?'

'We poke around into everyone's business in a

murder inquiry. That's our job. Not all the secrets we dig up are relevant to the investigation, but we can't ignore them.' From her seat Vera could see into the back gardens of the houses on each side. Janet was feeding her hens. Annie was hanging washing on her line. It occurred to her that Lorraine had kept the secret of her illness because nothing else could be hidden here. She had so little control over what was going on in her body; at least she could take control of the how and when she shared information about being ill.

'I told Nigel when I was first diagnosed with breast cancer.' Lorraine gave a little smile. 'I couldn't really hide it from him; he found the lump, dragged me off to the GP.'

'That was before you moved here?'

'It was what prompted the move. Nigel's business had grown since he first started it. I thought he liked the success, setting up branches all over the country. Then, when I was ill, he decided to sell up. "Someone's made me an offer I can't refuse, Lorrie. Let's call it a day and give ourselves a bit of quality time." I was going through chemo and didn't have the energy to think it through. So I said: why not? A move to the country, more time to paint. All that sounded great to me.'

'Did it live up to expectations?'

'At first. Nigel loved planning the renovations to the house. Now, I'm not sure. He's used to the challenge of problems at work. Having the power to take decisions.' She looked at Vera. 'He's just been accepted to be a magistrate. He'll be good, I think. He's got all the right experience. That might help give his day a bit of focus and make him feel more useful. I encouraged him to give it a go. At the moment I can tell he's bored, fidgety, looking for projects. He doesn't say, because he knows I love it here. It's a beautiful place to die.'

'When did you find out that the illness had come back?'

'Six months ago. I still had to go for regular checks. At first everything seemed fine; then it seemed that, despite the surgery, they hadn't got rid of the tumour. It's spread. It's just moved into my spine. They've offered more chemo, but there's no chance of a complete cure. I'd just be buying a bit more time. I feel remarkably well at the moment, and I'd much rather enjoy the life that I have than keep dragging back to the hospital for unpleasant treatments. Inconvenient and time-consuming, and taking more than the life I'd gain.'

Vera thought she'd probably have made the same decision. 'But you decided not to tell Nigel?'

'He'd be devastated. And as you said, he'd kill me with his fussing. I will tell him, but when I've reached a state when I can't pretend any longer.'

'Isn't it a strain, all this pretence?'

Lorraine gave a little laugh. 'All couples pretend about something. We'd go mad if we were honest all the time. Successful relationships are made up of white lies, small attempts at flattery, aren't they? We want our partners to be happy, so we tell them the stories they want to hear.'

There was a sound in the house below. The front door opening. 'That'll be Nigel back from the village. You won't tell him, will you?'

'Not unless I have to.' Vera couldn't see how Lorraine's illness could be relevant to the inquiry, except that it gave an insight into a relationship she'd previously struggled to understand.

They went downstairs together. Nigel was still in the hall. 'I was just showing the inspector my studio,' Lorraine said. 'She was wondering what I might see from the window. I told her only the neighbours' gardens.'

The words came easily. She even sounder brighter, less tired. Vera hoped that the other residents of Valley Farm weren't such proficient liars. Otherwise she shouldn't believe anything that she'd been told.

Chapter Thirty-Three

Holly had moths on her mind. She'd been reading up about them in the brief time she'd had at home the night before. Sitting on the sofa with her laptop on her knee, drinking mugs of camomile tea, she'd stared at photos. There were huge creatures as big as butterflies, brightly coloured and fascinating, tiny micros that you could only identify by studying their genitalia under a microscope. It had come to her suddenly on the drive home that they'd forgotten about the part moths played in the case. They shouldn't forget the natural-history connection. It had been more than a shared interest for Randle and Benton: more like a passion or an obsession for both of them. The set traps in the Gilswick Hall garden suggested that moths had drawn the first two victims together.

Now, back at her desk in the station, she was continuing the search. This was the sort of work Holly did well, and she found herself relaxing as she checked photo credits and the names at the head of abstracts for scientific journals. It was still early and the office was calm. The reward came with a question on an enthusiasts' website. The heading was *Query from a beginner* and there was a request for assistance with a detail of identification. The query had come from

J. Hewarth. Holly found herself grinning. She walked through the busy open-plan office to Vera's room, but the door was shut and nobody was there. Holly knew it was pathetic, but she felt ridiculously disappointed that she couldn't share the information now, wouldn't have the immediate payback of a hoot of pleasure from the fat woman and a shouted 'Great work, Hol' in front of the whole team.

Back at her desk, she looked at the website in more detail. It hadn't been recently updated and the query was several years old. Holly had assumed the moth-hunter had been Jonathan, but thought now perhaps Jack had taken up the hobby. She looked at the clock on the office wall. Eight o'clock. By the time she arrived at their house it wouldn't be an unreasonable time to call on Shirley's next of kin.

She drove through Kimmerston to a background sound of church bells. The streets were empty but for a small group of elderly women in flowery dresses on their way to Morning Prayer. The Hewarths' house seemed quiet and the upstairs curtains were drawn, but when Holly knocked, the door was opened by a woman in her forties. Blonde from a bottle, but with the colour professionally applied. Curvy, well dressed, in a rather showy way. Make-up, a chunky necklace and a gold bangle. Bare legs covered with a smooth fake tan and sandals with small heels. Over her shoulders a cardigan and in her hand a leather bag. Jack Hewarth's new wife was on her way to work.

Holly introduced herself. 'Is your husband in? And Jonathan?'

'They're in. Not sure if they're awake. They were up late last night talking about Shirley. You know . . .

I thought they probably needed time to remember her, so I left them to it. Just give them a shout. You won't need me, will you? Only I've got a shop in Front Street and I'm the only key-holder. We open at ten on Sunday, but I need to be there to get set up.'

She was friendly and warm, and Holly, who had dismissed her as a tarty airhead, felt a moment of shame. The woman's heels clopped over the pavement as she walked to her car with her keys in her hand. It was a pleasant, tree-lined street of large 1930s semis. Respectable. Polished cars stood in the drives. From the neighbouring property there was already the sound of a vacuum cleaner. A jogger moved easily along the pavement. Holly thought Joe Ashworth would love to live in a street like this. She supposed the house had belonged to Mandy; perhaps she'd been married before too. It wasn't the home of a single woman.

Inside there was no sign of life. Ahead of her an open door led to a tidy kitchen and a window looking out over a garden. 'Hello!' No response. Holly walked through to the kitchen and looked outside. The garden was narrow and long and beautifully tended. Borders had been freshly weeded. Close to the house a patio with tables and chairs. At the far end the square contraption that she recognized as a moth trap. For the first time since she'd got the call about the murders in Gilswick she remembered why she'd joined the police service. She heard footsteps on the ceiling above her and went back to the foot of the stairs. 'Hello! Is anyone there? Your wife let me in.'

'Just a sec.'

The splash of water, the scuffle of clothes being put on and Jack appeared at the top of the stairs. His eyes were bloodshot and he looked more grey and scruffy than at their meeting the previous day. Holly assumed that father and son had spent much of the night before drinking farewell to Shirley Hewarth.

'I need coffee. Sorry, I didn't hear the door.'

'How's Jonathan?'

Hewarth shrugged. 'He's a good lad. He'll survive. But he's sad. In shock. Only natural.' He switched on the kettle and spooned ground coffee into a pot. 'So am I. I was a journalist before I retired. Covered stories like this all the time. But then they were just stories. I never thought I'd live through one. I'm surprised the press aren't still camped out on the pavement.' He gave a hard little laugh. 'They've got no staying power these days.'

He waved the coffee pot at Holly. 'Fancy some?'

She shook her head. The coffee was almost strong enough to stand a spoon in. She could smell it from where she was waiting and thought she could feel the effect of the caffeine from there.

They were still standing in the kitchen and Holly nodded out into the garden. 'You're into moths.'

'The trap? It was a phase Jonathan went through when he was a young teenager. Before he got the acting bug. I got into moth-trapping with him. There's something primeval about catching things. Even tiny beasts that are a nightmare to identify. When Shirley and I separated, I brought the trap here. I thought it'd be something Jon and I could do together when he came to stay for weekends, but we only set it a few times. He'd already joined the Youth Theatre by then and all my time seemed to be taken up ferrying him to rehearsals. Mandy's always at me to get rid of it. I should bring it in and stick it on eBay.'

'It's a connection between all three victims,' Holly said. 'Martin Benton and Patrick Randle were into moths too. Seems like a weird coincidence. You're sure you never had any contact with them?'

'Never.'

'What about Shirley? Could she have met either of the men through their hobby?'

'Shirley was never interested.' Jack drank more coffee, peered at her over the rim of the mug. 'She couldn't see the point – said they all looked the same anyway. She encouraged Jonathan, but it wasn't her thing at all.'

There were footsteps on the stairs. Jonathan had pulled on a pair of tracksuit bottoms and a T-shirt, but looked even more hungover than his father.

'The detective was asking about moth-trapping,' Jack said. 'I told her you had other interests these days. Like prancing on a stage, girls and booze.' The gentle tease took him an effort, and Jonathan managed a smile to show he understood that. He sat at the table with his head in his hands. His father reached for another mug, poured coffee and slid it towards him.

Holly was remembering their last conversation in the office in Northumbria University. She turned her attention to Jack. 'When we last spoke, you said Patrick Randle's name was familiar. Could you have come across it because he was into moths too? He's written a couple of articles.'

'Maybe.' Jack sounded doubtful. 'But like I explained, it was only really a second-hand hobby for me. Jon was the one who followed the stuff online and got the magazines. I helped out in the garden to support him.'

'Jon?'

The younger man lifted his head and she saw he'd hardly been following the conversation.

'Perhaps you came across Martin Benton and Patrick Randle when you were moth-trapping. You might have seen Martin's photographs. They're brilliant. He lived in Kimmerston, just up the hill from here. He's the computer wizard who worked for your mother.' Holly was thinking there were just too many connections now for Martin's employment at Hope to be pure coincidence.

Jon was staring at her now and making an effort to concentrate.

Holly tried to speak slowly and clearly. 'When I asked you about Martin yesterday you said you'd met him in the office in Bebington, but I wonder if you'd come across him previously. Because of the shared interest.'

'Yes!' It was a light-bulb moment and came out as a shout. 'He taught me. Just for one term; he was filling in for someone on maternity leave. He was a pretty crap teacher actually, and maths was never my favourite subject. But he was brilliant on moths and butterflies. We got talking one break and he said I could go and see his set-up.'

'Did you go?'

'A couple of times over the summer. I must have been about fourteen and we still all lived together in Kimmerston then. Mum came with me when I first went. She had a suspicious mind and spent too much of her time working with perverts. She thought I was in danger of being corrupted or groomed.'

'And were you?'

'Nah. Martin was a bit weird, but there was nothing dodgy like that. He was completely harmless.'

'Weird in what way?' Holly couldn't work out the significance of this. It meant that Shirley Hewarth had known Benton for much longer than anyone had realized, but why would that be important?

'Very precise. A bit obsessive. He lived with his mother, who treated him like a kid. We'd be out in his garden checking the trap and Mrs Benton would come out to check he was warm enough, or she'd appear with mugs of coffee and bits of cake. With Martin, everything was recorded and written down and then he'd transfer the data to a file on his computer. He was a great one for lists.' Jon seemed brighter as he relived the memories of his early teens. Perhaps the toxic coffee was working its magic. 'At first I thought all that was brilliant, but Martin expected me to keep the same detailed records and in the end I just found it tedious. I didn't have that sort of brain. I loved the experience: being out late at night to set the trap and early in the morning to see what we'd caught. He'd put them in jars in the fridge overnight to make them still, and once I went up to his house the next morning to watch him photograph them. He was a brilliant photographer. But it was very passive and I soon got bored.'

'You don't remember all this, Mr Hewarth?' Holly turned to the older man.

He shook his head. 'Like I said, I just helped Jon out when he was trapping in the garden. When I was around. I was still working then of course, covering stories all over the region, away a lot.'

'And neither of you made the connection between Martin Benton the moth-trapper and the guy who was working with Shirley?'

'I didn't,' Jonathan said. 'It was a long time ago and it's an anonymous sort of name, heard in a different situation. When I knew him Martin was a teacher, not an unemployed guy looking for work experience.'

Holly thought that made sense. She remembered Vera's first description of Benton as the 'grey man'. It seemed sad that Benton had been so easily forgotten. But perhaps Shirley had remembered, when Martin had turned up at her office looking for work. Perhaps she could still picture a kind teacher who'd spent time with her son and tried to encourage his interest in natural history.

'He was ill.' Another memory had returned to Jonathan. 'It wasn't just that I got bored with going out with him. I went to his house one day and his mother said he wasn't there. He was in hospital. I felt kind of relieved. It gave me a way out and meant I had an excuse for dropping the whole thing. I was one for brief enthusiasms in those days. Phases. I'd already moved on to something else and joined the Youth Theatre. But Martin wouldn't have understood that.'

There was a moment of silence.

'Did you ever see him again?'

Jonathan shook his head. 'My mother asked if I wanted to visit him in hospital that summer. But I'd found out that he was in St David's. You know, the loony bin. Mum said she'd go with me, but I couldn't face it.' A pause. 'That seems so mean now. Callous.

I'm glad he wasn't alone when he died. It was a double-murder, wasn't it? I read it in the paper. He was visiting a friend.'

Holly didn't like to say that the bodies hadn't been found together, that Randle had been killed in the vegetable garden and Benton inside the house, or that they still didn't have any real idea of the relationship between the two men. She stood up. Jack stood too, but Jonathan was still, frozen in the past, reliving memories of his youth when the worst thing he had to face was the awkwardness of telling a former teacher that he no longer shared his passion for the natural world.

At the door Holly stopped for a moment and turned to Jack Hewarth. 'You still can't remember why Patrick Randle's name seems familiar?'

'Sorry. I have been trying. But the more I think about it, the further away it slips.'

'If you do, will you give me a ring?'

'Sure.' But he seemed disengaged again and she could tell he had no hope of the memory returning.

Chapter Thirty-Four

At mid-morning the weather started to change and a blustery wind from the west made it feel like spring instead of summer. Joe had tracked down the chairman of the trustees of Hope North-East and had arranged to meet him. He'd stuck his head into Vera's office before setting off and had found her in a philosophical mood. She got that way sometimes.

'This case is full of people worried about dying.' She'd leaned towards him, her eyes gleaming as if she was fascinated by death, not worried by it. 'They can feel their time running out. The murders must have made the fear more real. Daft, isn't it? We've all got to go sometime.'

Joe wondered how *he'd* respond to news that he had a terminal illness. He didn't think he'd be able to keep it secret. He'd even like the fuss and attention. And it might be exciting to be so close to death. He'd be reckless for the first time in his life. Drink too much. Take risks.

'Perhaps fear in the abstract is worse than facing the immediate reality.' Vera had still seemed preoccupied by morbid thoughts, but her voice had been cheerful. She probably wasn't afraid of anything. Joe hadn't bothered answering.

Hope's chair of trustees was a labour councillor and former union man. He lived in a miners' welfare cottage on the outskirts of Bebington. Joe knew of him through his father. They'd been comrades-in-arms, the same post-war generation. John Laidlaw had been a kind of hero in their family. The cottage was neat, the garden tended. A handrail had been fixed close to the front door, and through the window Joe saw an elderly woman sitting with a piece of embroidery on her knee, a walking frame propped beside her. She seemed to be drowsing, but the man who opened the door was spry and fit and looked younger than his wife.

'You'll be Bobby Ashworth's son. This is a terrible business. Come into the kitchen, so we don't disturb Doreen. She had a stroke last year and hasn't been herself since.'

John Laidlaw was dressed in his Sunday best, shirt and tie and shining shoes. Joe thought he'd probably just come back from chapel. They sat on plastic chairs across a Formica table.

'Shirley Hewarth was the best thing that happened to Hope. I got to know her when I was a magistrate. I knew she wasn't happy with the way the probation service was going. Nobody in their right mind would be . . .' The last was thrown out as a challenge. The former miner still saw a police officer as a potential enemy. 'I offered her the job as director. Never thought she'd accept.' A quick grin. 'Then we had to find the money to pay her.'

'Why do you think she *did* accept?' That had been bothering Joe since he'd first encountered the woman.

'Because she had principles and a social conscience.' To John Laidlaw the answer was obvious. 'She knew people coming out of prison are more likely to reoffend without support.'

Joe remembered the woman he'd met, the glimpse of the lacy bra. He thought there'd been more to Shirley Hewarth than a social conscience.

'What did she bring to your organization?'

'A professional approach. Before that, we were a glorified self-help group. Ex-offenders providing advice for their mates. And I'd use my contacts to drag in some volunteers to run occasional sessions. It was more like a drop-in centre. It served to keep lads off the street, but not much more than that. Shirley knew her way round the funding system and managed to pull in pots of money from a variety of sources. That meant we could run training courses, evaluate the work we were doing, provide individual counselling to clients who needed it. Then, because we had some credibility, statutory agencies bought in our services.' Laidlaw stopped for breath.

'I take it you had the accounts properly audited?'

'What are you suggesting, man?' Laidlaw's voice was quiet, but he was angry enough to bunch one hand into a fist on the table.

'Two people involved in your organization have been killed. I'm trying to find a reason. If someone had been fiddling the books, that might provide a motive.'

'Nobody's been fiddling the books. We run that place on a shoestring. The people working there put in more than they took out. I know damn fine that Shirley worked double the hours she was contracted for.' When Laidlaw spoke, Joe pictured his father preaching. Both men full of righteous indignation, fuelled by class resentment.

'What about Martin Benton?' Joe asked. 'Did you know him?'

'I was on the interview panel that appointed him for the temporary IT post. That was Shirley's idea. She said they were wasting time on admin when they could be working face-to-face with clients. I saw him in the office a couple of times after that, but I never felt I knew him.'

'He was your chosen candidate?' Joe was finding the interview trickier than he'd expected. Laidlaw had years of experience as a local politician. Not giving a straight answer was wired into his DNA.

'He seemed to work wonders in the place when he was on the short-term contract, and had the commitment to come back as a volunteer.' Laidlaw frowned. 'Besides, Shirley vouched for him and that was good enough for me.'

Joe wondered if Laidlaw had been distracted by the lacy bra too. If, in his later years, he'd seen the possibility of a different sort of life, one not restricted by Christian socialist morality. 'But what did you think of Benton when you interviewed him?'

'Why, he seemed a nondescript man,' Laidlaw said. 'No personality. As soon as he walked out of the door I'd forgotten what he looked like or how he'd answered his questions. But he was the best qualified and Shirley wanted him, so we gave him the post.'

'When did you last see Shirley?'

'About a fortnight ago. A trustees' meeting.' Laidlaw paused. 'I had a call from her since, though. Friday lunchtime.'

Joe looked up sharply. 'What was that about?'

'She wanted to fix up a meeting. Nothing urgent, she said, but she could use some advice.' Laidlaw paused again. 'I felt flattered, you know. Usually she was dishing out advice, not asking for it.'

Joe thought there was the beginning of a pattern here. Shirley had set up a meeting with her ex-husband too. How had she thought these older men could help her?

Laidlaw was continuing. 'I told her I was free that afternoon. Doreen has the Women's Guild on a Friday afternoon, so I could call into the Hope office after I'd dropped her off at the chapel. But Shirley said she already had a meeting and could we make it early next week.'

'Did she tell you who she planned to visit on Friday afternoon?' Joe tried to keep his voice easy, but could hear the excitement in it.

Laidlaw was scathing. 'Do you think I'm daft, lad? I'd worked out she might have arranged to meet her killer. If she'd given me more details, don't you think I'd have told you?'

In the silence that followed Joe's mobile rang, startling them both. Joe thought Laidlaw was more tense and nervy than he was letting on. He answered his phone. It was Vera, chirpy. 'Can you get yourself back here? Billy Cartwright's got some news.'

Driving back to the police station Joe found his mind wandering to the first time he'd met John Laidlaw. It had been at his grandfather's funeral. His grandad had been ill for months: lung cancer, probably caused by smoking Capstan Full Strength tabs and spending his early years underground in the pit. Joe had been a young boy and could just remember the occasion. The chapel full of old men. John Laidlaw had done a reading. On the way to the crem, Joe had asked his father what it was like to be dead. 'We can never know for sure,' his father had said. 'It'll be everyone's last big adventure.' Even as a child Joe had been surprised. He'd heard his father preach about life in the hereafter and had expected something more positive. More certain.

Back in the station, Vera was in the office with Holly. 'Billy's pretty sure he knows where Shirley Hewarth was killed. He thinks she was stabbed in her own car. There's blood on the driver's seat and the wheel. And then more blood in the boot.'

'That doesn't mean Shirley was stabbed inside the car.' Holly was frowning. 'The blood on the driver's seat and wheel could have come from residue on the murderer's clothes.'

'So it could, Hol.' A wide smile from Vera to show them she'd got there already. 'But the important point is that she could have been stabbed anywhere, then the killer stuck her in the boot and dumped her in the valley.'

Joe wondered why it had been done that way. 'Could we be looking at a different murderer? Could the body have been left in the valley so that we made the connection with the first two victims?'

'Eh, pet, that's a bit elaborate for me. I'm a simple soul. A body turns up a spitting distance from two other murders and I assume they're connected. Especially when there's already a link between the victims.' Vera suddenly got to her feet and grabbed her bag from the desk. 'Come on, you two. Let's get out there before the rain comes. Let's a have a ferret around the valley and see what we come up with.'

'You think that'll help?'

She grinned at him. 'It can't do any harm and I'm going stir-crazy in here. Think of the time when we worked together on that case in the National Park. It was years ago, Joe. The one with those women doing an environmental survey. They talked about ground-truthing. Checking that their data matched what was actually happening in the field. Sometimes it's important to do that in policing too.'

Joe said nothing. He could remember the case, but he wasn't quite sure what Vera was on about.

The three of them squeezed into the front bench-seat of the Land Rover. A bank of cloud covered the sun as they drove out of the town. When they reached Gilswick there was a sudden downpour, the rain bouncing off the dry soil, forming a pool of water in the road close to where Randle's body had been found. He wasn't surprised when Vera turned into the drive of the big house. Under the trees it was almost dark. Joe sensed Holly, tense and uncomfortable, beside him. He thought briefly that she seemed even more uptight during this investigation than usual.

Vera was speaking again. 'I think the killer used Randle's car to dump his body in the ditch. No other vehicle's been reported in the valley.'

'Have Forensics come up with anything to support that?' This was Holly's first contribution since they'd left the station.

'No blood in the boot, but maybe the murderer was more careful the first time. He'd had time to plan it.' Vera grinned. 'And as the car belonged to Randle, we *would* expect to find evidence that he'd been in it.'

Holly didn't reply and Vera went on. 'My theory is that after getting rid of Randle's body, the killer brought the lad's car back here and left the keys in the ignition. We always thought that was a bit odd. Even out in the wilds, most of us lock our cars and it would have been a habit for Randle.' She brought the Land Rover to a sudden stop, so it skidded a little way in the gravel. 'The big question's this: was Benton already dead by then? And if so, why move Randle's body to the ditch?'

She looked across at them, but didn't seem to expect an answer. She shoved the gearstick to reverse and turned the Land Rover to face the road.

'Let's take a look at where Shirley Hewarth's body was found, shall we? It was hard to get any sense of it on Friday night, with the dark and the chaos and all those people milling around.'

She brought the Land Rover to rest by the gate that led onto the hill. Remnants of the investigation remained: blue-and-white crime tape caught in the wind like kite tails, tyre tracks and footprints. Vera got out of the vehicle and Joe and Holly followed. It was unlike the inspector to move unless she had good reason. And in fact she only walked a couple of steps to the gate.

'You can't see the new conversions from here.' She leaned against the Land Rover so that she was looking down to the valley. 'There's the dip in the hill that hides them. If that body had been dumped anywhere else, you'd see the car stopping.'

'You think that's why Shirley was left here?' Joe

was starting to see the sense in this trip now. It wasn't just one of Vera's weird ideas. 'They must have known that the body wouldn't go undiscovered for long, though – not that close to the footpath and at the start of the weekend.'

'Maybe they didn't mind her being found. They just didn't want an audience while they were lifting the body from her car.'

Despite herself, Holly was starting to get engaged. 'That might tell us something about the time of death. At least about the time the body was carried onto the hill. Because you wouldn't care if you could be seen from the house, if it was nearly dark.'

'You'd be taking a chance to do it in broad daylight, though!' Joe thought the idea was crazy.

'Would you?' Vera looked away from the hill again and across the valley. 'You might not be able to see the houses from here, but you'd hear any car coming from the development. You've got a view of the footpath right to the top of the hill and down to the burn. I'd say you'd be prepared to take the risk. Especially if you knew the habits of the folk at Valley Farm. Like when Janet O'Kane was most likely to be out with the dogs and when she'd be inside, pandering to that husband of hers.'

'You think one of the Gilswick residents killed three people?' Joe thought Vera was mad. 'They're old!'

'Not much older than me.'

'But they've got no motive.'

'Then we'd better find one.' There was a rumble of thunder in the distance. Vera opened the Land Rover door and climbed in before them. 'That means it's back to Valley Farm to talk to the retired bloody hedonists.' She slammed her door shut and started the engine. 'But I can't face them again today. All that respectability in one place – it gives me the creeps.'

Chapter Thirty-Five

Lizzie woke early when it was still dark and lay still. She'd woken with a start in the middle of a dream: a prison officer screaming at her, his face so close to hers that she could only see his open mouth and yellow teeth, yelling at her that she'd never be let out. It took her a while to realize it had been a dream and she'd still be released that morning. The relief made her feel like laughing out loud, but she didn't want to disturb the others. There were so few times in prison to feel alone.

She sensed the emptiness beyond her window. The space was like pressure on her skin, her eyes and ears. She imagined herself as a diver or someone in deep space. Of course in an open prison there was more freedom; it was possible to be outside, and her work on the farm gave her plenty of fresh air. But in a way that had just made her confinement more disturbing. It was as if she was constantly being told: *You can go this far, but no further.*

It started to get light. There was the bright song of a blackbird. Other noises. The day-shift screws' cars arriving. A shouted greeting. *This is the last time I'll hear this.* Not knowing whether she was terrified or exultant. Then she remembered the photos in the book she'd found in the library and decided that the hugeness of the world was a pool to dive into, not somewhere to drown. She loved the image, repeated the words in her head so she wouldn't forget them, and wished she had time for one more meeting with the writers' group so that she could share it. She knew the teacher would be impressed.

Rose worked in the kitchen and was already getting dressed. Lizzie lay in bed and watched. Not in a voyeuristic way. Rose always turned her back to the others and scrabbled into her underwear to maintain an illusion of privacy. Lizzie never bothered with that stuff. She didn't mind the others seeing her body. She knew she was fit. She'd never had kids, didn't have stretch-marks or flabby tits. Before she headed out to work, Rose bent and kissed Lizzie on the cheek. The gesture was so unexpected that Lizzie sat up, startled.

'I won't see you again before you leave.' Rose was whispering. The cousins were still sleeping. Nothing woke them.

'I'll be at breakfast.'

'But everyone's there. It's not the same.'

Lizzie climbed out of bed and they hugged. Lizzie wasn't usually into casual physical contact, felt it like insects crawling over her skin, but Rose had looked after her inside. Taken care of her when the first few days had been a nightmare. Lizzie could see how she'd have been gentle with the old folk in the home, thought it was a shame Rose would never get to do that sort of work again.

In the canteen everyone wanted to come and say goodbye. Queuing at the counter for breakfast, Lizzie found herself almost in tears. Wondering what was making her so upset about leaving, she decided it was because people weren't on her case all the time here. If you followed the rules they let you get on with things. There was none of that prodding and prying she'd got from her mother. The meddling with her head. The wringing of the hands. *How are you, Lizzie? How can we help? What did we do wrong?* Perhaps things would have been different if there'd been other kids for her mother to mither over. If her mother had been younger when Lizzie had been born. If her mother had been more careless in living her own life. More selfish. That would have been easier to handle.

When breakfast was over, one of the officers came to find her. There was a procedure for getting out of here. More rules. In her room she got into her own clothes and put her other few belongings into a black bag. Then she went to the governor's office for the exit interview.

The governor was a very tall woman with a long neck that seemed to curve like a swan's. She always wore blue. Today it was a blue mid-calf skirt in soft wool and a cashmere sweater that was almost grey. A string of pearls round her neck. She could have belonged to the place when it was a grand house.

'So, Elizabeth, you're on your way. I hope you've learned something from your stay here.' She had a very deep voice with an accent that Lizzie had never been able to place. Scottish? Irish?

'Yes, thank you.' This was what the woman expected, but Lizzie thought it was true.

'These days we do our best, you know.' The woman stared out of the window. A cloud of rooks was blown by a sudden gusty breeze. 'We hope all our women take something from the experience of being at Sittingwell.' Then she was on her feet and holding out her hand for Lizzie to shake it. She might have been the headmistress of an exclusive private school. 'Good luck.'

Lizzie picked up the bin bag and left the room. At the end of the corridor she saw that her mother was looking out for her.

Chapter Thirty-Six

Annie Redhead had sat in her car outside the prison waiting for her daughter to be released. She'd arrived early. For a while she listened to the news on the radio, then there was an item about the killings in Gilswick and she switched it off. She couldn't bear to hear about that. The police had stopped reporters coming all the way up the valley, but they were camping out in the village, bothering anyone who went into the shop or the pub. When she'd driven past the church they'd been there too, waiting for parishioners who were starting to make their way inside. Janet said she'd bumped into a journalist on the hill when she'd been out walking Dipper and Wren, but he was frightened of dogs and had run away when they started barking at him.

'They're just cowards,' Janet had said, her bright eyes like sparks because she was so angry. 'Parasites feeding off other people's grief.'

Annie had asked Sam if he'd like to come with her to Sittingwell, but he'd decided against it. 'Best not to crowd her right at the start. She won't want a welcome party or a lot of fuss.' Annie had almost said, 'I'd like you there. I don't want to face her on my own. Please come with me.' But she'd never been very good at making demands of Sam. She was too passive. Perhaps that was a mistake and he'd realize more that she loved him, and depended on him, if she asked more of him.

At last it was time to go inside. A cheerful officer said Lizzie was just with the governor and wouldn't be long. 'How are you planning to celebrate? A big Sunday lunch?'

Annie smiled and said her husband would be in the kitchen now, preparing something special. Then she thought of the woman Lizzie had scarred with the bottle in the bar in Kimmerston. She hadn't appeared in court, because Lizzie had pleaded guilty. Annie didn't suppose *that* woman would be celebrating today, if she'd been told that Lizzie was being released. Her family wouldn't be sitting down to a celebratory Sunday meal.

Then suddenly Lizzie appeared, as if from nowhere, walking down the corridor towards Annie and it was just as she'd imagined. Except that, as she got closer, Lizzie's face didn't light up. It was closed and blank, as it had always been. She just nodded at Annie, called goodbye to the officer at the desk and walked out of the big arched door ahead of her mother.

The weather had changed overnight, and when they emerged into the garden there was a sudden rainstorm that caught them unawares and sent them running for the car. Annie found herself giggling – the result of tension, and because she thought they must look ridiculous. She was still dressed for the heatwave in a light chiffon frock and sandals. She imagined the women watching from the long windows. Lizzie joined in with the laughter and for a moment they stood together on the gravel, their faces turned to the rain, not moving. Then Annie found her keys and they tumbled into the car, both of them drenched.

Annie drove for a while without speaking. She knew she made Lizzie feel hemmed in; it would probably be best to stay cool and keep an emotional distance. She wished she could ask Lizzie what she wanted from her mother, but Lizzie hated those in-depth conversations. They'd tried family therapy once, and Lizzie had taken the piss throughout. So Annie drove out of the gate into the road without a word. Lizzie glanced back at the prison as they pulled away and then stared in front of her.

Another burst of rain spattered the windscreen.

'Have they found the killer yet?' The question from Lizzie came suddenly, but Annie had the impression it had been on her mind from the moment she left the prison.

'No.' Annie paused. 'There's been another death in the valley. Did you hear about that?' She thought there must have been rumours. Shirley Hewarth would have been a regular visitor at the prison. Surely the officers would have talked.

'No.' Lizzie turned to face her mother. They were stopped at traffic lights and Annie glanced back. Her daughter looked very pale in the strange thundery light. 'Who?'

'Shirley Hewarth, the woman who came to visit you.'

A silence, broken by the swish of windscreen wipers, regular as a metronome.

No response from Lizzie. Her face was quite blank and closed again.

'She seemed a lovely woman,' Annie said. Then:

'I was there when Janet O'Kane found her body. She screamed. We were in the Lucas house, and we all ran out to look.'

'She was killed in the valley?' Now there was a reaction from Lizzie. Shock and something else. Anxiety?

'I suppose so. Or her body was dumped there. The police have been nosing around, but they don't tell us anything.' The rain stopped as suddenly as it had started and the wipers squeaked on the dry windscreen. Annie shot another quick glance towards her daughter. 'Where shall we go? Straight home or to Kimmerston? We could have coffee.' She realized the last thing she wanted was to go straight back to the valley. 'Dad's doing a special meal, but he was planning it for later this evening. We know you don't like to eat early. And you need new clothes. We left most of your old ones in the flat. What about heading into Newcastle for the shops?' She stopped abruptly, hearing an edge of desperation in her voice.

There was another long silence before Lizzie answered. 'Let's go home. I've got used to eating early in the prison. And besides, I could murder a proper cup of tea.'

They were driving up the lane towards home when they passed the detective's Land Rover coming the other way. Annie hoped they hadn't been in their house bothering Sam again. He'd be tense enough about Lizzie coming home. Anxious about saying the wrong thing and not giving her proper support.

'Whose car's that?' Lizzie had just looked up as they squeezed past, the Land Rover almost in the ditch.

'They're part of the police team.'

When they opened the door Sam was already in the hall. He must have heard the car. There was a moment of hesitation, then he opened his arms and Lizzie ran towards him. It was all better than Annie could have expected. After all, Lizzie hadn't seen her father for several months and she wasn't one for being held. Never had been. At the back of Annie's mind there was a niggle. *It can't be this easy. Lizzie has conned us before. Why should I trust her this time?* She thought they'd been hurt so many times before that it was sensible to limit her expectations. But she wanted to enjoy this moment too. Lizzie sober and clean, and home from prison. Lizzie being normal.

They'd got the room ready for her. Flowers in a jam jar on the windowsill. A new duvet cover on the bed. A small TV. Everything bright and clean. There was an arched window, formed from part of the old barn door, and the room was full of the sulphurous light.

'Is this okay?' Annie stood at the door and showed Lizzie in.

'It's lovely!' Lizzie stood at the window and looked down at the river. 'Where did you find Shirley?'

'You can't see the footpath from here.' Annie was pleased about that. 'The other houses must be in the way.'

'I might go out for a walk later,' Lizzie said. 'That's something else I've been looking forward to. The freedom to go wherever I like. Clean air.'

'Not on your own!' Annie realized, as soon as the words were out of her mouth, that they sounded controlling and bossy. Not at all how she'd hoped to be with her daughter. Not this time. She took a deep breath. 'There's a killer out there. I just want you to be safe.'

Lizzie turned from the window and stared at her. 'If I stay indoors I might as well be in prison.'

'Of course. I understand. You're a grown-up and you have to make your own decisions. Take responsibility for yourself.' A pause. 'But let Dad come with you. At least for the first time this afternoon. He'd love to be asked. Otherwise I'll spend all the time you're out worrying about you.'

Lizzie gave a sudden smile. 'Oh, Mum, you do try so hard.'

'I'm sorry. I can never quite get it right.'

They stood for a moment, separate and apart, looking down at the valley.

Lizzie waited until early evening before heading outside. The rain had stopped and there were occasional bright bursts of sunshine. Everything looked fresh and green. Sam had started cooking the meal. There was a joint of lamb covered in rosemary waiting to go into the oven and a bottle of champagne chilling in the fridge. Lizzie had spent most of the afternoon on her own in her room with her phone. Annie worried that she was catching up with the friends who had caused her trouble before, but resisted the temptation to call Lizzie down for cups of tea and slices of home-made cake, to ask who she was talking to.

She was relieved at first when her daughter emerged into the kitchen and leaned against the bench, watching Sam stirring a pan.

'I'm going out for that walk now.' It was a kind of challenge and they both knew it.

Annie took a breath and kept her voice calm. 'And you don't want either of us to go with you?'

'Next time. First time out, I want to enjoy it for myself. Don't worry. I've got my phone.' And she waved it. 'I can look after myself. I won't be long. I'll be back at seven to eat.'

Annie wondered what numbers were stored in the mobile; even whether Lizzie had arranged to meet someone. Perhaps a car was waiting for her at the end of the track, where the trees hid the road from Valley Farm, and she'd be driven away back to her old life. Perhaps they'd never see her again. Then Annie told herself she was being paranoid and this relationship would never work if she couldn't trust her daughter. If she kept up this level of worry she'd lose her mind.

Lizzie was already wearing a jacket. 'I won't be late. Promise.' As she walked through the door, Annie thought she should have offered the use of her wellingtons because the grass would still be wet.

Annie stayed with Sam in the kitchen for a while, not helping with the cooking, but enjoying the company. The rhythm of his work relaxed her. 'How do you think she seemed?'

He was chopping an onion and stopped, the sharp knife poised above the board. 'Well. She's put on a bit of weight.'

'I mean in herself.'

He smiled. 'Too early to tell, isn't it? And we can't watch her as if she's a specimen in a jar. That would put anyone off.' The knife sliced through the onion again, so fast that it was just a blur.

Annie laid the table and then went upstairs to take towels into Lizzie's room. Not meaning to pry, she told herself, but because she'd forgotten to do it earlier. And she didn't look at any of Lizzie's things. But that room with its arched window gave the best view of the valley in the whole house. She moved the flowers from the windowsill and perched there. She stared out, hoping to catch sight of her daughter, of the blue Berghaus jacket she'd been wearing, realizing only then that had been her intention all along.

The valley was spread out beneath her. To her right there was the bungalow where Susan lived with her father. Annie didn't know what to make of Susan. She was a good cleaner once she got going, but she talked too much. Gossip about people in the village. People Annie scarcely knew. Percy's old Mini was in the lane, making its way to The Lamb. He was there every evening for an hour before his tea.

It occurred to Annie that The Lamb might have been Lizzie's destination too. She'd grown up in the valley and had been to school with the few young people who remained. The thought comforted her. She'd be safe in the pub, and Percy might give her a lift back.

Annie still didn't move from her perch. She thought she was like Nigel, staring with his binoculars, pretending to be looking at birds, but following Lorraine's every movement. There was the sound of barking and the dogs ran out of the O'Kane house into the courtyard. Not Jan with them, but John, hunched into a waxed jacket, calling them to follow him. Annie ran downstairs, into the kitchen and out of the back door. 'Just popping in to see Jan.'

Sam looked up and gave her a little wave, but didn't say anything.

The garden smelled of wet soil. Dark clouds covered the sun. Annie tapped on Jan's kitchen door and went straight in. The room was in shadow and for a moment Annie thought her neighbour wasn't there. Then she saw her in the rocking chair where Jan always sat to read. Annie walked further into the room.

Jan, who was usually so controlled and sensible, was crying. Annie had wanted to confide in her, as she had many times before, to tell her about Lizzie's homecoming, but Jan was wrapped up in her own grief. Her eyes were red and she held a handkerchief and was dabbing at them. Annie crouched beside her and took her hand. 'What's happened? Whatever's the matter?'

'Nothing. Nothing at all.' The woman stood up.

Annie felt as if she'd been pushed away physically. 'But you're upset. Can't I help?'

'No,' Jan said. 'Nobody can help.'

At the front of the house there was the sound of dogs barking, a key in the lock. 'You must go now.' Jan walked towards Annie, so that she was backing towards the kitchen door. Annie saw that the hand holding the handkerchief was trembling. As she turned and fled she thought that she knew nothing of her neighbours at all.

In her own kitchen Lizzie had just arrived. She'd taken off her soaking shoes and was laughing at the wet footprints that her stockinged feet had made on the tiled floor.

'We were waiting for you before we opened the champagne,' Sam said.

Annie was about to ask Lizzie where she'd been to get so wet, but thought better of it. It was none of her business.

Chapter Thirty-Seven

Back in the police station Vera was reassessing the case. There were no notes on the desk. This wasn't a formal meeting. Anyone looking in at her office would think she'd fallen asleep. She lay back in her chair and her feet were resting on a low stool covered with bilious-green velour. Nobody could remember how the stool had come into her office and usually it sat in a corner covered with a pile of files. The weight of her feet in their walkers' sandals had caused a permanent dent in the cushion. Vera shut her eyes. She thought concentration was the skill most required of a good detective. Concentration and an innate nosiness.

She picked apart the elements of the inquiry in her mind to see if there was a line of investigation that had been missed. It was too easy to rush forward in a case, especially if new details came to light, and to forget incidental facts that had come to light earlier in the process. An investigation couldn't be a route march. More a meander, and that had always been Vera's preferred way of walking. After fifteen minutes she got to her feet, walked to the door and shouted out into the open-plan office where her detectives were working, 'Joe. A minute!'

He came into the office, pushed aside the stool and took the chair on the opposite side of her desk.

'Did anyone ever go and take a statement from Jason Crow?'

It took him a moment to place the name.

'Jason Crow. Charlie's Teflon man. Former employer, and probable lover, of Lizzie Redhead,' Vera said.

'Charlie went out to see him.' Joe struggled to remember the details. 'Crow said he hadn't had any contact with Lizzie since he sacked her, and he'd never met Martin Benton.'

Vera looked up. 'Did you see Lizzie by the way? In Annie Redhead's car when we were on our way out of the valley.'

'No.'

'I thought you and Holly were half-asleep.' She knew she sounded smug, but didn't care.

'Why didn't you say at the time?'

Vera didn't know how to answer that. Sometimes she liked to hoard facts. Secrets made her feel superior. It had become a habit. A bad habit. She'd bollock any of her team if they tried it.

'I can't see how Crow can be relevant,' Joe said. 'Lizzie was inside when all the murders happened. Jason might be a scumbag who got the Redheads' business on the cheap, but he had no connection with Randle or Benton.'

'Has he been inside? I know the name, and that he's been in bother in the past. He could have come across Shirley Hewarth when she was a welfare officer in the nick. She wasn't only at Sittingwell.' Vera was thinking this probably wouldn't lead anywhere, but there was an itch in her brain and she had to scratch. A bit like when the eczema on her leg was particularly bad.

'I'll have to check.'

'Well, run along and do that then, bonny lad.'

He returned a few moments later. 'Nothing since he was a juvenile, and that was just a bit of shoplifting. He got three months in a detention centre.'

She nodded. The detention centres had been another failed attempt at tackling youth crime. The short, sharp shock that just made the lads bitter. And much fitter, so they could run faster from the scene of their burglaries.

'I might just go along and have a word with him all the same,' she said. That itch again. Impossible to ignore, but probably nothing to worry about.

Crow lived on the outskirts of Kimmerston in one of the executive developments that Hector had railed about every time he saw them. *Shoddy, pretentious blots on the landscapes*. Sitting in her Land Rover outside the house, Vera could hear her father's voice in her head and couldn't help smiling. Hector had delighted in coming across a smart new estate so that he could vent his anger and display his prejudices.

She rang the bell. It was mid-afternoon on a Sunday and she thought Jason was unlikely to be there on his own. Despite any fling he might have had with Lizzie, there'd probably be a wife, older kids. This wasn't the home of a single man. If Jason had been on his own he'd have gone for one of the flash new apartments on Newcastle's Quayside. Rumour had it that he could afford to buy one in cash, if the fancy took him, and one of his companies probably owned half of them anyway.

The door was opened by a man. Middle-aged. Sandy-hair that might once have been ginger. Freckles. A naughty schoolboy, grown up.

'Sorry, we don't buy at the door.' An unexpectedly pleasant voice. Vera was starting to see how he'd slid away from so many criminal charges. This wasn't a thug or a bruiser. Crow would be charming and plausible, and he probably had friends in high places. She could imagine he'd be a good golfer.

'And I'm not selling.' Vera didn't bother looking for her warrant card. She hated scrambling in her bag to find it. It looked unprofessional. 'Detective Inspector Vera Stanhope.'

He raised his cyebrows. A gesture of amusement. *They'll let anyone join the service these days.* 'Sorry, Inspector. You'd better come in.'

Inside, the place was less flash than she'd imagined. Classier. A lot of wood. Uncluttered. Plain painted walls with some pieces of art that drew her in and made her stare. Photos of two daughters, one on her graduation throwing a mortar board in the air. A piano. 'Sorry to disturb you on a Sunday.'

'I was at my desk,' he said. 'I work mostly from home now. One of the perks of being boss. I don't keep regular hours. Come into the office.' He walked ahead of her and she realized that despite being middle-aged, he had the body of an athlete. His shirt sleeves were rolled up and his arms were muscular. Her glance followed his spine down to his legs and she realized why Lizzie had been attracted, despite the difference in their ages.

The office was at the back of the house and looked out into the garden. A long lawn with a pergola at the end. Closer to the house a trampoline that looked as if it was no longer used. Inside the office there was custom-built furniture and a rack of heavy-duty filing cabinets. Jason was old enough to prefer paper. He sat on the desk and nodded for her to take a seat so that she was looking up at him. 'I hope this won't take too long. I have to leave in ten minutes. I'm meeting a friend.' An apologetic smile to take the aggression from the words.

'Your family not about?'

'They've been in France for Easter. I'm joining them next week and we'll travel back together.' He paused. 'What is this about?'

'Lizzie Redhead,' Vera said.

'Ah yes, Lizzie. One of my more spectacular mistakes.' A boyish grin that didn't quite convince.

'Tell me.'

For a moment he said nothing. 'She came to work for me.'

'And then?'

'And then I fell for her, Inspector. Hook, line and sinker. Not my usual style. I'm happily married. If I stray occasionally, it's recreational. No strings on either side. But Lizzie was different.'

'In what way different?' Vera really was curious to know.

There was another silence. Vera thought that he'd been sitting here, his family away, thinking about Lizzie. And now he wanted to talk about her to the only person who would listen. Even if that person was a cop.

'She was wild, funny and very beautiful. Most women I meet are attracted to me. Or attracted to my money. Lizzie didn't seem to be. I fell for her. I'd have done anything for her by the end. When we first got together I couldn't quite believe it.'

Vera wasn't sure she believed this story even now. It felt like something she chuckled over in a women's magazine while she was waiting to see the dentist. But what would she know about relationships? Like Holly, she was a loner. 'Then Lizzie ripped you off.'

'At first I couldn't accept that she'd done it.' He paused and played with the wedding ring on his finger. 'It sounds daft, but I thought we were soulmates.' A pause. 'I grew up too quickly, got into bother because that was the way my family earned a living. I'd never had anything like a romantic encounter. Sex was almost always a financial arrangement. Even my marriage felt a bit like that. I was ready to settle down and have kids, and Kate could give me stability and a family. And a bit of respectability. Her background's very different from mine.' He paused again and stared out of the window. 'With Lizzie, it was like falling in love for the first time. She was bonkers, you know. Fearless. We made love in places I wouldn't have dreamed of. On building sites, in half-built houses, in the car by the side of a busy road. It wasn't just the sex. I told her stuff I hadn't told anyone else in the world. And all the time she was stealing from me. Fiddling the books and sliding cash into her own online accounts.'

'So she had to pay.' Vera pulled his attention back into the room.

He shrugged. 'In my position you can't be seen to let people take the piss. Even if you want to.' He paused again. 'If she'd asked for the money, I'd have given it to her. I'd have left my wife and married her. But she made a fool out of me and I couldn't let that go.'

'You could have come to us. She'd have been prosecuted.'

'And got a fine that her parents would have paid! Or a suspended sentence.' His face was red and she saw how Jason might get, if he was angry. Mad. Violent. Even against someone he claimed to love.

'So you persuaded her parents to sell you their business.'

'I've got a brother who works in that field. Not the sharpest tool in the box, so occasionally he needs a hand. He wanted to expand into Kimmerston. It seemed a good way of helping him out and showing people it wasn't a good idea to mess me about.'

'You threatened Sam and Annie Redhead.' Vera's voice was quiet.

'I didn't need to.' The words came back at her immediately.

'Of course. You have a reputation.' She hoped he could hear the sneer in her voice. 'You're a hard man.'

There was a moment of silence before Vera continued. 'Then Lizzie got into a fight in a bar and was sent to prison anyway.'

'That was nothing to do with me.' He paused. 'I heard that she went crazy when we separated. Perhaps I was good for her and kept her sane for a while.

She shouldn't have ripped me off. We'd have been good for each *other*.' Another pause. 'How is she anyway?'

'Out of prison,' Vera said. 'Released today.' Looking up, she could tell this wasn't news to him. He'd been keeping tabs on Lizzie. He was still obsessed with her. Vera thought she should check to see if Jason had visited her in Sittingwell.

'Why are you here?' As if it had just occurred to him to ask. 'She can't have got into trouble already, if she was only released today.' His voice light, as if he didn't give a toss.

'I'm investigating the murders in the valley at Gilswick. You'll have seen the story all over the news. I don't suppose you knew any of the victims?'

'I'm afraid not.' The answer came quickly, without thought. Even if he'd been best buddies with Martin Benton, or Shirley Hewarth had been one of his recreational shags, he'd have denied it. Not cooperating with the police would be a habit, like Vera's need to have secrets.

'You hear things,' Vera said. 'You have contacts all over the county. Anyone saying anything about the murders in Gilswick?'

'I'm a businessman.' Jason pushed himself off the desk and looked at his watch. 'I don't have those kinds of contacts.'

'Can you think why someone would want to murder three people? Different people. A young graduate, a teacher with mental-health problems and a social worker.' Because Jason might not mix with contract killers, but he'd make sure he knew what was going on in his patch. His livelihood depended on it.

This time he seemed to consider the question before answering. 'Someone screwed up,' he said. 'An angry ex-con. People get sent to prison to sort them out, but it often makes things worse. Plays with their minds.'

'Was that what happened to you?'

'Nah.' He grinned. 'I was one of the people detention worked for. A success story. Inside once and never in trouble again.'

'Never convicted at least.' Now, she saw, the conversation was becoming a game again. Perhaps he was already regretting being so frank. 'How do you think Lizzie will have handled being inside?'

'She's like me. A natural survivor. And she was in an open nick, wasn't she? A doddle.' Jason looked at his watch again. 'Look, I've enjoyed the chat, Inspector, but I've got to go.'

They walked together through the house. Some of the finishes, and the way the rooms were laid out, reminded Vera of the Valley Farm conversions.

'Did you have anything to do with the development in the valley at Gilswick?'

'The two barns? And then the renovation of the farmhouse? Yes, that was done by one of my companies.' He was standing by the front door, impatient for her to go.

'A bit of a coincidence,' Vera said. 'You built the house where Lizzie Redhead's parents live.'

'Not really. Anything high-end, built in this part of the county, I've probably got a hand in it.'

She walked through the door. He grabbed a jacket from the bottom of the stairs and followed her out. So it seemed he really did have a meeting; he didn't just want to get rid of her.

'Lizzie Redhead,' she said.

'What about her?'

'How do you feel about her now?'

She expected another flip and sarcastic comment, but this time Jason considered before answering. 'I still dream about her. I lie beside my wife at night, but I dream about Lizzie.'

She took her time walking down the path to the road where her Land Rover was parked. Jason climbed into a sports car standing on the drive in front of the house; there was the sound of screeching tyres and he drove away. Vera looked after him, wondering who he was in such a hurry to meet.

Chapter Thirty-Eight

Holly escaped back to her flat for a couple of hours. Once inside she shut the door and double-locked it, stood with her back against it and took a deep breath. Felt her pulse slow and her mind calm. She tried to work out what was happening to her. She'd never reacted this way to a case before. Usually she was the last person standing. Physically fit and mentally alert. Competitive. She could distance herself from the violence and grief she encountered. She'd trained herself not to get emotionally involved, to the point where her colleagues thought her heartless. Now she only felt clean and safe in her own home. Outside there was death and decay. And even here she realized she was haunted by a fear of dying. The image of the elderly woman with the smeared lipstick and rag doll, whom she'd seen on the Kimmerston pavement, stalked through her dreams. The brief moment of triumph that had come when she'd found the Hewarth boy's name on the moth enthusiasts' website had faded long ago.

She moved into the kitchen and switched on the kettle. Saw a mark on the worktop, got out the disinfectant and wiped it off. Opening the fridge to get milk, she saw a bottle of wine, was overcome by the temptation to undo the screw top and pour a large glass. Perhaps that would dull the anxiety, help her through the rest of the shift. She reached out for it, felt the icy bottle on her fingers and then changed her mind. Not even Vera Stanhope drank in the afternoon when she was on duty. With a flash of insight Holly thought pride might be her enemy, but it was also her saviour.

She took her tea into the living room. The rain had blown over and there were sudden bursts of sunshine. Outside all the colours seemed very sharp, as in a child's painting. In the cemetery a young family was laying flowers on an old grave. The wind pulled at their hair and clothes as they walked back towards the road.

She tried to unpick the strands of her anxiety. What had happened during the day to send her rushing back to the safety of the flat? She was tired of course, but she'd learned to cope with exhaustion. She thought the news of Lorraine Lucas's cancer had thrown her. Of all the residents in Valley Farm, Lorraine had seemed most alive.

Perhaps I'm having a kind of mental breakdown. Or a religious experience. Holly's parents were religious. C of E, but on the evangelical side of the church. Hands in the air swaying and inspirational preaching. They'd been disappointed when Holly had shown no interest, but philosophical. 'You might come back to it, darling. We'll pray for you.' Holly had made a comment to Joe once about the problems of being an atheist in a family of believers. He hadn't said much and she'd wondered if he was a believer too.

Her phone rang. She was tempted to ignore it, but it was Vera.

'Where are you?'

'I've just called in at home to collect a few things.'

'Only I've got something that needs digging into and you're the best person to look into it.'

Vera was waiting for her in the station. By now it was evening and the big, open-plan office was nearly empty. Discarded Coke and Red Bull tins showed how the team had kept going through the day. Only Vera seemed to have the energy to carry on thinking straight.

'I hadn't realized how late it was – I sent most of them away a while ago, and Joe's just sloped off. His missus calling in the three-line whip. He lets her get away with murder. Are you okay to have a go at this? We can leave it until tomorrow if you like.'

Holly shook her head. 'I can make a start.'

'No hot date then?'

Holly was surprised. Vera didn't ever ask about her personal life. 'No hot date.'

They sat in Vera's office, and Vera told her about the relationship between Jason Crow and Lizzie Redhead. 'Something about the woman has got under his skin. Something weird.'

'I don't suppose he's obsessed with moths? Has a trap at the end of the garden?'

Holly had meant the question as a joke, but Vera took it seriously. 'Well, that's a thought. I forgot to ask. Something else to look into. But he's more obsessed by the woman, I think. She's got him trapped all right.' Then Vera came out with a list of instructions, sharp and detailed. One after the other, so that Holly, making notes, struggled to keep up with her.

Later Vera came out of her glass fishbowl to chat. 'I've had Lorna Dawson's report. There are traces of soil in the wound to Randle's head, so it seems Peter MacBride's right about the murder weapon there. Must have been a spade. But it doesn't match the sample taken from the vegetable garden close to the locus. It's richer, and it contains animal matter.'

'What kind of animal matter?'

'Chicken shit.' Vera paused. 'And we know the O'Kanes keep hens. It looks as if we'll have to go back to Valley Farm. Not tonight, though. Tonight we're both going home.

'I think I've found some interesting details.' Holly tried to keep the excitement from her voice. She never knew how Vera would react to pieces of information. Sometimes stuff that Holly thought new to the case, Vera had already filed away in her giant brain. 'I've been digging into the past of all the suspects and come up with some connections.' She turned the computer screen so that Vera could see.

Chapter Thirty-Nine

Over breakfast they scarcely spoke. Annie wasn't quite sure what to say. This morning it was like having a stranger in the house. Lizzie was like a paying guest who needed to be appeased. Sam had been out earlier to get the paper. He said he'd passed Vera Stanhope's Land Rover on his way out and now it was parked on the drive at the Hall.

Lizzie looked up then. 'Who's Vera Stanhope?'

'The inspector in charge of the murder investigation.'

'What's she like?'

'Fat,' Sam said. 'Nosy.'

Lizzie gave a faint smile.

'I think she's rather clever.' Annie didn't want her daughter to get the wrong idea. She wanted Lizzie to see that Vera Stanhope was somebody to be wary about. 'She has a way of making people confide in her.'

'What are your plans for today?' Sam's question was directed at them both. Annie thought he hadn't sensed their awkwardness. He imagined they might have a girlie day together, pictured them with their heads bent together as nails were painted; trying on clothes in the same changing room. Annie and Lizzie had never had that kind of relationship, but Sam had wanted to believe his wife when she'd said that prison could have worked a miracle.

'I might go into Kimmerston.' Lizzie put the emphasis firmly on the *I*.

'Shall I give you a lift?' Annie thought that might work. She could go to the library, do some shopping and perhaps they could meet up later. At least she'd know where Lizzie was and could bring her back safely. She felt as she had when Lizzie had been seven and had demanded to walk down the valley to the village school in Gilswick on her own. Annie had followed her at a distance, just to be sure she'd got there. *All this is my problem, not hers. I'm a control freak – always have been.*

Lizzie seemed to be considering. 'I think I'll walk into the village and get the bus. I could do with the exercise.'

'Okay.' Annie knew she'd been outwitted, but there was nothing she could do about it. 'Give me a shout if you need a lift back. There's only one bus in the afternoon.'

'Will do!' A bright, brittle smile.

Sam beamed. He seemed to be unaware of the careful words, the dance around the unspoken questions: *Where will you be, Lizzie Redhead? What will you get up to, and who will you meet?* 'More toast, anyone? And I'll make another pot of coffee, shall I?'

Lizzie left the house at the right time to catch the bus. For a moment Annie was tempted to follow her down the road, as she had on the first lone walk to school, then realized how ridiculous that would be. Hiding behind bushes, skulking in gateways. Lizzie was fitter than her and would soon leave her behind.

Still, Annie might have done it if she hadn't been aware that Nigel Lucas would probably be upstairs with his binoculars, staring down at the valley. She hated the powerlessness of staying at home, waiting for Lizzie's return.

After breakfast she'd heard Lizzie on her phone, arranging to meet someone. Annie told herself that it was probably an old school friend, but in this febrile mood everything seemed sinister to her. It was as if they were all spies, telling half-truths, planning deception. Lizzie's phone wasn't out of her possession for a second. If she'd been able to sneak a look, Annie might have stooped to checking out the call record. *Why can't I relax? Why can't I just accept everything she says?*

She went upstairs as soon as Lizzie left the house. Not into Lizzie's room. That would have seemed an intrusion too far today, but to the window on the landing, which still had a reasonable view. It wasn't raining, but the day was overcast and gloomy and Lizzie's jacket provided a patch of colour. Annie saw her daughter walk down the lane until she disappeared from view behind a clump of trees. Lizzie seemed to have a very jaunty stride, defiant, as if she knew her mother was watching. She only carried a small bag over her shoulder and that gave Annie some comfort. But as the slight figure disappeared, Annie felt suddenly bereft. She could believe that her girl was disappearing from her life forever. At least when Lizzie had been in prison she was contained and safe. Annie told herself she was overreacting. It was these murders. Everyone was on edge; even Janet, who was usually so calm and motherly. They were all given to strange outbursts of emotion. She couldn't stare down the valley after Lizzie every time she left the house.

Sam was still doing the crossword. He at least seemed not to feel the need to change his routine. He looked up when Annie came into the room. 'Shall we go into Newcastle? Have a spot of lunch somewhere nice?'

'No!' Her response was immediate and violent. She couldn't leave the valley until Lizzie was back. Then she thought that she was being quite ridiculous. Why shouldn't they go into Newcastle? It might help her put things into perspective, and if she waited here she'd only fret. She kissed the top of Sam's head. 'But why not? That'd be fun. Give me a couple of minutes to change.' When she looked down the valley from the landing window on her way to their bedroom she thought she saw a speck of blue, right at the end of the lane. When she came out of her room later there was no sign at all of Lizzie.

They had a pleasant day in the city, though anxiety rumbled at the back of Annie's mind. On the way in, she'd texted Lizzie: *Dad and I in Newcastle. Can still give you a lift later if you need one.* There'd been an immediate reply. Laconic. *OK.*

They wandered round the stores in Eldon Square. Sam wanted to buy Annie a gift – clothes, jewellery, something to cheer her up – but she was intimidated by the choice. She preferred browsing in the few shops in Kimmerston. 'Really, I'm happy just looking.' Time seemed to go very slowly. She wondered if she'd be less stressed about Lizzie once the murderer had been caught. Perhaps it wasn't so crazy to be anxious, when the killer of three people was on the loose. But she knew she wasn't seeing Lizzie as a victim. She was worried about what Lizzie might do, rather than what might be done to her. She was pleased beyond belief that Lizzie had been in prison while the murders were committed. It wasn't too hard to imagine her wielding a knife, slashing into someone's flesh. After all, she'd attacked another woman with a broken bottle.

While Sam was looking at the kitchenware in Fenwick's, Annie's phone rang. She answered it quickly, hoping it might be Lizzie, but it was the young sergeant who looked scarcely more than a boy. Inspector Stanhope wanted to speak to them. Nothing urgent. She explained that they were in Newcastle. Then Ashworth asked about Lizzie.

'She's with friends in Kimmerston. And I really don't see how she can help you.' Knowing she sounded almost rude.

Sam wandered back from inspecting cast-iron pans to ask who'd called.

'The police again. Nothing important. I said we'd be in later.'

They had lunch in a French restaurant near the Quayside. The chef had worked for them in Kimmerston for a while and seemed pleased to see them. The food was simple and well prepared. Annie found she was hungry and drank more than her share of a bottle of wine. Sam kept topping up her glass. 'I'll drive, and I can go into Kimmerston later if Lizzie needs a lift.' When they came out into the city afternoon there was a grey drizzle, so they could hardly see the far bank of the Tyne. The Baltic art gallery was a block of shadow and the reflective glass of the Sage Gateshead was a faint shimmer in the gloom.

'Perhaps that's it,' Sam said. 'We've had our summer.'

In the car he asked Annie to phone Lizzie. 'We might as well pick her up on our way through.'

'Oh, I'm not sure. Perhaps I should just text.'

'Don't be daft. All this texting. Why don't folk just talk any more?'

So she dialled Lizzie's number, but it went straight through to voicemail. She didn't leave a message.

'Not answering? Halfway to getting pissed, maybe.' Sam stared at the road. He put most of Lizzie's troubles down to booze. Annie remembered Lizzie's tempers when she was still a child, the yelling and the swearing. She hadn't been drinking then. Annie thought her daughter's problems were more complicated than either of them had realized. She sent a text: *On our way back if you want a lift as we go through.* This time there was no answer.

When they arrived back at Valley Farm, Vera Stanhope's Land Rover was parked in the courtyard. 'Blasted woman!' Sam was mumbling under his breath. 'I thought we might have escaped her.' There was no light in their house, and Annie had worked out that Lizzie should be back in Gilswick and they should have passed her as they drove up the lane, if she'd got the bus.

She opened the door and shouted up, just in case she'd got a lift from a mate or a taxi, 'Lizzie, we're back!'

No response.

'I told you,' Sam said. 'She'll be pissed. Or worse.'

His belief in the miracle of prison seemed to be fading already. 'Ring her again.'

Annie pressed redial on her mobile, but there was still no reply. Sam switched the kettle on. There was a tap on the back door. 'Come in!' they shouted together, but when they turned it wasn't Lizzie, who would have come straight in anyway, but the huge bulk of Vera Stanhope.

Chapter Forty

Monday morning and they were back in the valley. On her first visit Vera had seen it as idyllic. Now the steep hills rising on either side of the burn and the fact that the lane disappeared into a dead-end made her feel trapped, so claustrophobic that she felt like screaming. The drizzle had closed in behind her as she left the village and now she could see no way out. She hoped the case would soon be over and that she'd never have to come here again. She waited outside Gilswick Hall for Joe and Holly. The Carswells had been in touch saying that their first grandchild - a little girl - had been born and they'd be home the following week. She imagined that they'd slide back into their routines and responsibilities. The garden and the dogs. The magistrates' bench and the WRVS. They'd remain aloof from their neighbours in the farm conversion. Still lords of the manor in spirit, if not in name. As distant as if they were still in Australia.

Joe and Holly arrived in the same car. Vera thought Holly looked pale, frozen. They stood for a moment on the gravel outside the big house. 'Let's go into the kitchen.' Vera started for the door. She had no real plan and a reluctance to venture further up the valley to face the retired hedonists. 'The CSIs have finished downstairs, and it's daft to get wet before we start.'

Inside there was the background warmth of the Aga. Vera stood with her back to it, toasting her bum. There was still fingerprint powder around the back door and the window ledges. 'They didn't find any sign of a break-in.'

She nodded to the chairs by the table. 'You might as well take the weight off your feet.' Now, in the warm room, she'd lost any sense of urgency. The cosiness of the place made her think of tea, hot crumpets dripping with butter.

'What's all this about?' Joe was scratchy after a whole evening at home. He pretended to love his time with the bairns, but he could only take so much. Vera knew he used work as an excuse when Sal started making demands.

'We decided last night our killer must be someone who knows the valley well.' She paused. 'Hol did some digging for me, while you were off playing Happy Families. She made some interesting connections.' She moved away from the Aga and joined them at the table. 'Show him, Hol.'

'A connection's not a motive, though, is it?' Joe was at his most churlish. He'd looked at the records and seen this was a breakthrough, but was too childish to congratulate Holly on her work. 'What's the plan?'

Vera didn't like to admit that she had no plan. 'It's too early to make an arrest. I want to speak to our respectable friends in Valley Farm again. Let's make it a bit more formal this time. We don't have the grounds to take them to the station, and anyway the press would have a field day if we interviewed them there.

But let's bring them down here. One at a time. Get them out of their comfort zone.' Making up a strategy as she went along. Lazy policing. She turned to Joe. 'Nip back to the village, would you? Get some essential supplies. Tea, coffee and milk.' She could tell he was starting to sulk because she'd asked him and not Holly. It served him right and she shouted after him, 'And biscuits. But not Rich Teas. I can't stand Rich Teas.'

They called Nigel Lucas in first. Vera phoned him. It was hard to tell when he answered what he made of the summons. He had a veneer of good humour, slick and shiny, that he never seemed to lose. 'Of course, Inspector, if you think it would help.'

He knocked at the kitchen door and looked around him as he came in. Vera could tell he'd never been in the house before and that he was disappointed. He'd been expecting something grander, more in keeping with the squire's residence. They'd set out the big kitchen table as if they were conducting an interview: the three of them on one side and Lucas on the other. There were glasses and a jug of water. Vera had already said they wouldn't be wasting the chocolate biscuits on the witnesses. Holly was furthest away from Lucas and she was taking notes. Vera had decided on Lucas first because she'd thought this would be the most difficult conversation. There was a confidence she couldn't break unless she had to – and she still couldn't see that Lorraine's illness was relevant – so it would all be about choosing the right words.

He sat, waiting for her to break the silence. The room must have seemed warm to him, coming in

from the cold, and he'd taken off his jacket and was sitting in shirt sleeves. There was a sheen of sweat on his forehead.

'We're confused about the latest killing.' Vera gave a little shake of her head. 'Shirley Hewarth. She wasn't stabbed where she was found. So why bring her to the valley? I'm wondering if the murderer was trying to tell us something.'

'To implicate us, you mean?'

'Aye, maybe. Any reason they'd want to do that?' Vera leaned forward, her elbows on the table. She could feel the grain of the wood on her skin.

'None at all. We get on very well with other people in the village.'

'Had you met Shirley Hewarth? Had you seen her in court? She used to go sometimes with her clients. I understand you sit on the bench.'

'I've not long completed my training,' Lucas said. 'I've been in a few times to observe. It's fascinating, I must say, Inspector. I certainly don't remember meeting Mrs Hewarth.'

'Perhaps in another context then?' Vera poured herself a glass of water and sipped it.

Lucas shook his head. 'I'm sorry, Inspector, I don't think I can help you.'

'Your wife worked in prisoner education. That might have been a point of contact between you. When she was a probation officer Mrs Hewarth was in the welfare department of a number of institutions.' Vera maintained a polite persistence. Stubborn. Hoping to make him so irritated that he'd give something away.

'That was when we lived in the South,' Lucas said. 'And Lorrie certainly didn't bring her work home.' He

paused. 'She was ill not very long after we married. Breast cancer. She took early retirement. Part of our decision to move north and settle in the valley. Luckily she's well now.'

Vera didn't respond to that. 'Tell me about your relationship with Jason Crow.'

'I'm sorry?'

'Jason Crow. The builder who worked on your house. He'd converted the barns and you employed him to do the renovations. So I understand. According to the inspector who checked the building regs.'

'Is that what the boss is called? The company's name is Kimmerston Building Services. That's what's on their letter-heading and written on the side of their vans.' Lucas tried a small smile. 'That's who I wrote the cheque out to. Cost me a bloody fortune.'

'So you never met Mr Crow?'

'Not to my knowledge.'

'Friday afternoon.' Vera changed the subject without a beat, and for a moment Lucas looked confused.

'What about it?'

'Let's go through your movements again.'

'I've already given a statement. Someone came to the house on Saturday afternoon.' He took a handkerchief from his trouser pocket and wiped his forehead.

'I know, pet. I've got it here.' She set the document in front of her. 'Just humour me, eh? Go through it again. Starting at lunchtime.'

'Lorrie and I had lunch at home. She stayed in her studio to finish a painting. We were having our friends round that evening, so I popped into Kimmerston to buy the booze and some nibbles. I showed your colleague the supermarket receipt. It's timed at 4 p.m.'

He was starting to get exasperated. In her head Vera cheered.

'And later?'

'I came home. Lorrie and I had a cup of tea together. With some of Annie's biscuits. She and Sam bake as if they're still running a restaurant business and give most of their stuff away.' He paused. Vera let the silence stretch. 'Then we went to The Lamb in the village. Percy Douglas was there and we had a chat. Always full of stories about the old days, is Perce. He'll tell you he was chatting to us. We had one drink. It was just to get Lorrie out of the house because she'd been in all day. Then back to prepare to party.'

'What time did you arrive back from the supermarket?'

'About quarter to five. I didn't have time to kill anyone!' He looked round at them as if he'd cracked a joke and was waiting for the laughter. None came.

'Did you leave the party for any reason?'

'Once, to look at the stars. That's still a novelty, Inspector. It's the first time I've lived anywhere without street lights.'

'Were you alone?'

'I called Lorrie out to see them. I love my wife. We were middle-aged when we got together and I'd given up finding anyone to share my life with. Standing there outside our dream house in the company of Lorrie, surrounded by the darkness, was pretty special.'

Lorraine Lucas looked frail and insubstantial. Her skin stretched tightly over her cheekbones. She wore a thin blue smock laced with silver thread, but had wrapped a hand-knitted jacket over the top. Even here in the warm kitchen it seemed she felt cold.

'Can we get you anything?' Vera thought the woman needed feeding. She had the ridiculous notion that if they gave her wholesome bowls of soup, hearty and warming, she'd get better.

Lorraine shook her head. Even that seemed to take an effort. 'Sorry. It's not such a good day.'

'Maybe you should tell your husband that you're not well?' They could have been on their own at the table. Holly and Joe seemed part of the furniture, along with the rush mat in front of the Aga and the crockery in the dresser.

'It might come to that. In days, rather than weeks. But I'd prefer to wait until things are back to normal, until you've caught your killer. Do you think that might be soon?'

'Very soon. But I need your help first.'

Lorraine didn't answer, but gave a little shrug of acquiescence.

'Tell me how you came to work in the prison.'

Lorraine leaned back in her chair. 'I was a teacher in a big comprehensive in Essex. Coping. Loving it, actually. The performance. I managed to hold the students' attention and occasionally there was a star. A kid with passion for art, who saw the world differently from the rest of it and managed to capture the vision.' She looked up and grinned, self-mocking. 'Listen to me! I sound like one of those adverts to persuade gullible young people into the profession.'

Vera said nothing. Outside, water dripped from a

leaking gutter and she saw that it was raining more heavily.

Lorraine closed her eyes briefly. 'Then there was a divorce. Nothing unusual. My husband fell for a younger woman, a colleague. It was all rather banal. But it knocked my confidence. Suddenly I couldn't stand up in front of a class and control the little sods. The anxiety kept me awake at night. I needed a more amenable audience.'

'And prison provided that?'

'Offenders are unlikely to kick off, if there's an officer standing in the corner.' She paused. 'Usually it was the adult equivalent of child-minding. Providing meaningful activity, in the jargon, though actually it was pretty meaningless. Sometimes there was a man with a spark of interest. But it was a way of earning a living without the stress of being in a school.'

'How did you meet Nigel?' Vera thought the question was hardly necessary. Lorraine was telling her life story, was glad to have the chance perhaps, as her time ran out.

'It was at a social event. An awards-do for arts and crafts created in prison. Nigel's company was one of the sponsors and I had a student shortlisted. It was one of those dinners where the food's dreadful and the speeches go on forever, and everyone survives by drinking too much cheap wine. We sat next to each other and started talking. He was very charming and thoughtful.' She paused for a moment. 'It wasn't love at first sight. Not for me. But I'd had that with my first husband, and look how that had ended.' Another pause. 'Honestly, it helped that Nigel was rich. I liked everything that went with that. The lack of worry.

The treats, like weekends away in Paris. Meals in the very best restaurants. I got used to being spoiled.'

'What's not to like?' But Vera thought she couldn't sell her independence so cheaply. 'You carried on working, though?'

'Until I was ill. It was a matter of pride, I think. I didn't want to be entirely a kept woman. And there was no question of children. We were both in our mid-forties when we met.'

Another silence. Outside the drip of water, regular as the ticking of a clock.

'Did you ever meet Jason Crow?' The question sounded rather brusque after Lorraine's gentle telling of her life story, and Vera added, 'He owns the company that renovated these buildings.'

Lorraine looked up and stared at Vera. Her eyes blue and glittery like her blouse. 'No, I don't think so, but Nigel dealt with all that. He's the practical one in the relationship. He looks after me very well.'

Chapter Forty-One

Janet O'Kane looked old. The white streaks in her wire-brush hair seemed more pronounced. Vera decided it had been a stroke of genius to bring the witnesses to the big house. At home it had been possible to define them by their surroundings; here the layer of domesticity had been stripped away from them. Janet seemed tired but very alive, rather wired. And now that she was without her talk of hens, dogs and garden she was clearly fiercely intelligent. Vera saw the woman she'd been before retirement.

'Is there any news?' Janet ignored Holly and Joe.

'I'm afraid we can't talk about the progress of the investigation.' Vera realized she sounded just like one of her bosses, a man called Potter. Whenever Vera saw him she had an irrational but almost overwhelming urge to hit him.

'Does that mean there's *been* no progress, but you won't admit it?'

Vera didn't answer.

'This is dreadful. You don't know how it's affecting us all. Whenever I go to the village now, people avoid me. Or they want all the gruesome details of that poor woman's body, and that's even worse. It's as if we've been touched by the plague.' Janet pushed her hair back from her face. 'As if they're all just waiting for somebody else we know to die.

'I understand it's hard for you, because you found her.'

'It's hard for all of us.'

'Can you take me through that day again? I know you've given a statement, but it's important that we know exactly where you all were throughout the afternoon and evening.' Vera heard the despised Potter's voice in her head as she spoke. The precise, rather nasal intonation.

'John and I were at home all day. John was working in his office upstairs. That's what he calls it. Work. He's planning another book. But the sales of the last one were disappointing and I doubt very much if he'll find a publisher.' The woman's voice was hard. Vera wondered what had gone on between the couple to change Janet's attitude to her husband. Perhaps her proximity to violent death had made her see him more honestly.

'And you?' Vera asked. 'What were you doing?'

'Do you really want to know, Inspector? It's intensely boring.' A pause. 'I took washing from the machine and put it on the line. It dried very quickly, so I brought it in and ironed it. I put clean sheets on our bed – taking care to do it quietly, so John shouldn't be disturbed. I prepared lunch, ate lunch and washed the dishes.'

'Did you go out at all?'

'I took the dogs for a walk. The highlight of my day.' The words were hard, sharp as slate.

'Did you go up onto the hill?' Vera was thinking of the footpath, hidden from the development by a dip in the land, where Shirley Hewarth's body had been found.

Janet realized the implication of the question. 'No. I went the other way. Down towards the burn. Are you saying she might already have been dead by then? That her body was already on the hill?'

'It depends what time you went for your walk.'

'I went just before lunch. John took the dogs out later in the afternoon.'

'Then Mrs Hewarth wasn't on the hill when you went out. She was in her office all morning.' Vera kept her voice matter-of-fact. 'Why did your husband go out in the afternoon? Was that usual?'

Janet didn't answer for a while. Vera saw that she was gripping the arms of her chair and her knuckles were white. 'No,' she said at last. 'Not usual.'

'So why the change of routine?' Vera used her quiet voice, her psychiatrist's chair voice.

'Because I'd threatened to leave him, if things didn't change.' Janet looked up. 'I said I was bored rigid and he couldn't treat me as a domestic slave. I reminded him that I had a good degree from Cambridge and, if I didn't leave this bloody valley and escape these bloody neighbours and start using my brain, I might go very noisily mad. And that might disturb his life and upset his writing routine.'

Outside, the rain continued to drip from the broken gutter. Vera thought the Carswells would have to get that sorted as soon as they got back or *they* might go mad. 'I thought the move to the country was your idea,' she said. 'The good life. Returning to nature.'

'It was. That's what's so infuriating. John would

have been happy to stay in the city. I thought a change was what our relationship needed. That we might become closer. More honest. But when we got here everything between us stayed the same. Life's just much more inconvenient in the valley. And rather boring. I pretended I loved it because it was my idea. I couldn't admit the experiment was a total failure.'

'Who dealt with the negotiations of buying your house?' Again Vera changed subject quickly.

'What do you mean?'

'Once you decided you wanted to live in Valley Farm, how did things proceed?'

'Oh, I saw to all that.' Janet pushed her hair back from her face again. 'John hates the detail of everyday life. And he was still working then. I suppose he had an excuse.'

'Did you deal directly with the developer?' Vera looked up at her.

'I met him once, to discuss the final finishes. Tiles, paint colour – that sort of thing.'

'Where did you meet Jason Crow?'

'Onsite. He walked us through the place.'

'So John was with you then?' Vera slid a glance at Holly to make sure she was still keeping notes.

'No, he got held up at the university. Annie and Sam were with me. Jason showed us round both houses. It was the first time I'd met our neighbours.'

Vera imagined how that would have been. Sam and Annie shown round the house they'd just bought, by the man who'd ruined their business. Had they been aware, before they turned up, that Jason Crow was the developer? Surely they must have known the name behind Kimmerston Building Services.

'You and John never had children?' Another swift change of direction, but again Janet didn't seem thrown.

'No.' There was a long silence. 'I would have liked a child. In fact I was quietly desperate, as the biological clock ticked away and I approached my forties. But John had made it clear before we married that he didn't want a family. I went into the relationship knowing that, and didn't feel I could change the rules.'

'Why *did* you marry him?' Vera had wanted to ask the question since Janet had first started talking.

'He was the most beautiful man I'd ever met.' It came out as a cry. 'And he needed me. I suppose he became the child I never had. How can I complain that he's too dependent, when I made him that way?'

'Tell me about your work.'

'After my first degree I trained to be a social worker. I specialized in fostering and adoption and more recently worked as a mediator for the family court.' The words came out easily. The standard answer given at dinner parties. No emotional engagement. Then: 'I loved it. I really loved it.'

'Did you ever meet Shirley Hewarth professionally? She worked as a probation officer before she took over the ex-offender charity in Bebington.'

Vera was expecting an immediate answer, but Janet seemed uncertain. 'I don't think so. When I worked in fostering and adoption it's possible that our paths crossed. I might have placed one of her clients' children with a foster family. Offenders often have multiple problems and lead chaotic lives. There can be safeguarding issues. But really I don't remember.' There was a long pause. 'When I saw her body, I only saw her face briefly. Even if she'd been a close friend I don't think I'd have recognized her.' A pause. 'Last night I had a nightmare. I was on the hill and I came across the body again. But in the dream *I* was lying there with the stab wounds in my chest. And it was my face that I saw.'

John O'Kane had decided to be charming. He slid into the chair opposite and gave them the smile with which he'd been seducing women since he was a student. 'The last time I was in this kitchen I was drinking the major's very good malt.' Letting them know he mixed in the best circles.

'But this isn't a social occasion, Mr O'Kane.'

'Of course not.'

He still dressed like a younger man. Expensive jeans. Designer stubble not grown long enough to show the grey. Vera wondered if he dyed his hair. She wouldn't be surprised. He must miss his audience of attentive students and young lecturers.

'This is a terrible business. I'm not entirely sure how we can help, though.'

'What attracted you to the house in the valley?' She couldn't see why he'd have given up his coterie of friends, the bars and restaurants that seemed to be his natural habitat.

'Janet felt we needed a move, and I could see the attraction. I needed to concentrate on the new book. Where we lived before there were too many distractions. I had the feeling that this was my last chance to write something of value. Something that might outlive me. A book to define a place and a period in time.'

He frowned. 'That probably sounds ridiculous to you, Inspector. Overblown. But it's been my ambition since I was a young man and I've never achieved it. If I could focus on the writing, I have a sense this book might just come close.'

'So you were happy to move.' Vera wondered what her legacy might be. She'd locked up a few criminals. Trained a few good coppers. Perhaps that was enough.

'It was a joint decision,' O'Kane said. 'Jan has always had a romantic hankering after the good life. She saw the site first, when it was still not much more than a barn, and came back raving about it. The view. The peace.'

'How do you get on with your neighbours? With your fellow retired hedonists?'

'We rub along very nicely on a superficial level. Socially, you know. A few drinks on a Friday night. Major Carswell's an amateur historian, so perhaps I have more in common with him than with the others.'

Snob.

'These murders . . .' Vera looked at him. 'Are you certain you haven't come across any of the victims before?'

'I saw the house-sitter once in The Lamb and we had a bit of a chat.'

'You didn't tell us that before.' Her voice so sharp that he seemed almost chastened.

'Didn't I? Sorry. But perhaps you didn't ask.' He paused. 'I escape to The Lamb sometimes after a day at the computer. I need other company. Background noise. I've decided I'm more of a city boy after all.' He made another attempt at the winning smile.

'What did you and Patrick talk about?' Vera thought this was the first person she'd met, besides Patrick's mother, who'd had any real conversation with the young man.

'Academic life. He was hoping to return to Exeter to do postdoc research and I asked him why he'd decided to take a break. I wondered if he had aspirations to be a writer too. There was something about him. A way he put words together.'

'What did he say?' Vera tried to imagine herself in the pub. Gloria would be behind the bar gossiping. Percy and the other old boys would be huddled over their domino board. Patrick was in a strange place where he didn't know anyone. The retired professor might seem the closest he'd get to a kindred spirit in his new home.

'That he might write something one day,' O'Kane said. 'That he had a brilliant story to tell. But that wasn't why he'd come to Gilswick.'

'Did he tell you what *had* brought him to the place?' Vera found she was holding her breath.

'Not really. He said he was doing his own kind of research.'

'Did he mention Martin Benton?'

O'Kane shook his head. 'No, I'm sure he didn't.'

'Can you tell us anything else at all about your conversation?' Vera was losing hope that she'd gain anything useful from the man. She looked out of the window. There was still a fine rain blocking the view of the garden.

'He said he was going to set some moth traps under the trees here. He invited me to come down one night and see what he'd caught. I said I'd like that.

I wasn't really bothered, but it sounded like a diversion. And he was so keen. It seemed a real passion. I could tell it would please him.'

Chapter Forty-Two

Joe sat next to Vera in the kitchen at the Hall and watched her perform. This was a masterclass in witness interrogation. The individuals who'd seemed little more than puppets previously – the dutiful wife, the jolly husband, the dying artist, the grumpy academic – seemed to become real in front of his eyes. Her words blew life into them. He resented the skill, which seemed to come to Vera so easily.

When John O'Kane had left the room Vera sat back in her chair. 'What did you make of that? Not just the professor, but the whole bunch.'

'It makes the "retired hedonist" thing sound a bit hollow,' Holly said. 'A sham. They all seem pretty miserable.'

'The effect of having three murders on your doorstep, do you think?' Vera was bright-eyed. She knew she'd conducted the discussions brilliantly. 'You can see that might be a bit of a downer.'

'If anything, you get the sense that the killings just provided some relief from the boredom.' Holly was looking down at her notes. 'Janet O'Kane seemed genuinely upset, though.'

'What have you got to contribute, Joe?'

He turned to his boss and his mind emptied, all

rational thought flushed away. Sometimes Vera had that effect. He'd described the experience to Sal and she'd laughed. 'Sounds like a kind of intellectual enema,' she'd said. 'Like colonic irrigation, only of the brain.' Now the vacuum in Joe's mind didn't seem so funny.

'They all had some contact with Jason Crow, even if it was only through his company,' he mumbled at last. 'Seems another weird kind of coincidence.' He knew his offering was pathetic.

'Aye, well, you know what I think about coincidence . . .' Vera looked at her watch. 'Where are Annie and Sam? And it'd be good to chat to the terrible Lizzie, if she's there too. I'd like to meet her for myself. You did phone and ask them to get their arses down here?'

'They were out,' Joe said. 'I left a message on their answerphone.'

'Well, phone again. Let's talk to them while I'm on a roll. And if there's nobody there now, try their mobile number. With a fair wind, we could have this over by this time tomorrow.' She shut her eyes. A fat, complacent Buddha, keeping her own counsel and her thoughts about the case to herself.

Joe went outside to ring the Redheads. He'd visited a demented elderly aunt in a care home once and the calls of the woodpigeons in the trees sounded like the moaning of old people there. Gentle and plaintive. He stood in the shelter of the house. Through the window he saw that Vera hadn't moved. There was no reply from the Redheads' house phone and so he tried Annie's mobile. She answered immediately, obviously not recognizing his number. 'Yes?' The voice almost panicky.

He explained that the inspector would like to see them in the big house at their earliest convenience.

'We're in Newcastle for the day, Sergeant. I'm afraid we won't be back until later this afternoon. That *is* alright? Nothing else has happened?'

'No, nothing else.' Because what more could he say? Vera might have demanded their presence, but he couldn't insist that they return to Gilswick immediately just to suit her. Annie was about to end the call. 'Perhaps we could talk to your daughter?' he said. 'Will she be at home?'

'No.' The answer came quickly. 'She's visiting friends in Kimmerston. And I don't know how Lizzie can help you. She wasn't even here when these dreadful things happened. I think you should leave her alone.'

They ended up in the pub for a late lunch. Joe thought there were other things they could be doing; it was ridiculous to be hanging round in the valley just to wait for Sam and Annie Redhead to return. Vera had gone gnomic on them. Turned in on herself. Uncommunicative. They sat in the corner of the lounge and he could tell she was earwigging the conversation in the bar. Percy Douglas was there with an elderly mate, talking about the good old days when the Carswell estate still sustained tenant farmers and there were decent EU headage payments for sheep. Holly was rereading the notes she'd made during the interviews. Joe felt excluded. If Holly hadn't been there, Vera might have talked to him.

When they left The Lamb, Vera suddenly seemed to have a change of heart. 'No point you two hanging around here, twiddling your thumbs. Get back to Kimmerston. Hol, get those notes in a form that we can present to this evening's briefing. We've got a bit more background on them all now. Joe, have a little wander around Kimmerston. Places where young Lizzie might be hanging around with her friends. I want to talk to her, so give me a shout if she comes to light. And I'd really like to know if Jason Crow headed off to France to meet up with his family, as he told me he would, or if he's still in town.' Vera bundled them into the Land Rover and dropped them off at the big house to pick up Holly's car. As they drove off, Joe saw the boss was still sitting there in the driver's seat, her eyes closed once more.

From the station Joe phoned the offices of Kimmerston Building Services and asked to speak to Jason Crow. A middle-aged woman answered. 'I'm afraid Mr Crow is in meetings all day. Can anyone else help?'

'Will he be free tomorrow?'

A pause, the sound of pages being turned. An old-fashioned diary. 'I'm not sure of Mr Crow's movements for the rest of the week.' So Crow hadn't joined his family for a perfect holiday in the French countryside. Not yet at least. Joe thanked the woman and hung up.

He headed out into the town. He wasn't sure where young people hung out in Kimmerston during the day. He tried the bus station first and tracked down the driver who'd driven from Gilswick that morning. It was the same man who'd carried Martin

Benton to his death. Joe described Lizzie. 'Pale. Red hair. Bonny.'

'Aye, she was waiting at the first stop in Gilswick.' He was outside in the designated smoking area, sucking on a tiny roll-up as if it would save his life.

'Did she come all the way into town?'

'Not quite. She got off two stops before the bus station. That posh estate on the hill. What's it called? Something naff. Heather View.' He threw the remains of his cigarette onto the floor and stamped on it. 'They changed the whole route to take in the estate, but there aren't many buggers from there who use public transport.'

'Was anyone waiting for her?' Because Jason Crow lived in one of the palaces on the edge of Heather View.

The driver shook his head.

'Did you see which way she walked?'

'Aye.' A slow, conspiratorial smile. 'She was worth watching. You know what I mean?'

'And?'

'She walked up the hill, away from the town.'

Joe phoned Vera and had the sense that he'd woken her up. He imagined her still in the Land Rover outside the Hall, rain from the overhanging trees rattling on the vehicle's roof.

'I think Lizzie's at Jason Crow's house. What do you want me to do?'

There was a silence. She was going through the options.

'Go there. You've got a reasonable excuse. Ask him

about his dealings with the Valley Farm folk. How he found them to work with. All useful stuff anyway.'

'And if Lizzie's there?'

Another long silence.

'See if you can persuade her to come back to the valley with you. Offer her a lift. I'd rather know where she is.'

Joe remembered Lizzie as he'd met her in the prison. Amused and defiant. He thought it would be very hard to persuade her to do anything she didn't want to do. He drove to Jason Crow's house and sat outside for a moment, intimidated despite himself. The big house and the memory of Lizzie Redhead sapped his confidence. He got out and rang the doorbell. Crow appeared, looking older than the photos they had of him in the operations room, but still fit. He was barefoot, in jeans and a sweater. It didn't look to Joe as if he'd been in meetings all day.

'Is Lizzie Redhead here?'

'Who wants to know?' Crow was old enough to be Lizzie's father, but there was the same arrogance, the same air of superiority.

Joe showed his warrant card.

'Of course. I should have guessed. That jacket comes straight from central casting.'

'Lizzie Redhead?' Joe was wondering how he could get inside to have a look.

'You just missed her,' Crow said. 'She left half an hour ago.'

'What was she doing here?'

There was a moment's hesitation. 'I suppose,' Crow said, 'she came to make her peace.'

Joe didn't ask what the man meant. He knew he wouldn't get a straight answer.

Crow seemed to be losing patience. 'She's not here. I told you. Come in and check if you like. I don't want my neighbours getting the wrong idea, seeing the filth on the doorstep.'

There was an expensive suitcase in the hall at the bottom of the stairs.

'I'm going to France to catch up with my family tomorrow. An early start, so I'm prepared.' Then: 'Help yourself, Sergeant. Go wherever you like. I'll be in my office, if you need me.' Crow seemed suddenly amused by Joe's discomfort. The irritation had dissipated.

Joe started at the top of the house. He had no expectation of finding Lizzie now, but he wasn't going to walk away without looking. He was curious too. He imagined going home and telling Sal about the grand bathroom in the master bedroom, the kids' rooms, each with their own shower, the fitted furniture and the flat-screen TVs. He opened wardrobes and saw suits that must have cost more than he earned in a month. On the ground floor he looked in the utility room and found a door into the garage. Nothing. Crow's office door was open. He was sitting at his desk, looking at a computer screen, the bare feet on a chair. Apparently relaxed.

'Did Lizzie tell you where she was going?' Joe asked.

'Back home to the valley, I think. She said she had some shopping to do, then she'd catch the bus.' Crow kept his eyes fixed on the computer screen.

'You didn't offer her a lift?'

'I'm a busy man and she's a grown woman. She could make her own way home.'

Joe wasn't sure what else to ask. He felt stupid standing in the office doorway, an uninvited guest in the rich man's house.

'You can see yourself out, Sergeant.' Crow didn't turn round when Joe made his way to the front door.

Chapter Forty-Three

Holly had never been a rule-breaker. At school she'd been close to the top of the class, but she hadn't had the spark of genius or the willingness to take risks intellectually that might have set her apart. She'd won her place at university through dogged hard work and had joined the police force because she'd understood that those traits would be rewarded.

Vera had sent her back to Kimmerston to write up the notes from the day's interviews for the evening briefing, so Holly sat at her desk preparing to do just that. Then, her fingers resting on the keyboard and without any conscious effort, suddenly she was inside Lizzie's head, seeing the world through her eyes. She knew precisely what the young woman was planning. This flash of intuition was dizzying and was so unexpected that Holly sat for a moment without moving. She picked up her jacket and shouted to the team remaining in the open-plan office that she was going back to Gilswick. A middle-aged DC looked up and waved to her, but nobody else took any notice.

Holly arrived in the village at the same time as the bus from Kimmerston. She pulled in close to the pavement outside the post office and waited to see the passengers get off. Three people: two elderly women with baskets of shopping and Lizzie Redhead. Lizzie was last off and hesitated before setting off on foot up the lane towards the valley. Holly waited until she was out of sight, switched her phone to silent and followed. The rain was lighter, hardly more than a damp mist, but the visibility was poor. Lizzie was a shadow glimpsed occasionally in the distance; the copper hair that was so distinctive in the photo pinned to the incident-room whiteboard was drained of colour. Everything in the landscape looked grey.

Close to the gates to the big house Lizzie seemed to disappear. Holly stood and listened. Nothing. Holly was accustomed to the silence of the city where there was always distant traffic noise, the occasional blast of a siren. This was real silence, dense and a little frightening. Behind her she sensed movement. Perhaps it was the rustle of waterproof clothing or a careful footstep on wet grass. Holly looked behind her, but only saw the lane leading back towards the village. To her left stood the big house, invisible from here, hidden by the high stone wall and the trees where Randle had set his moth traps. To her right was a patch of scrubby bushes leading down to the river. Both provided hiding places. Holly remained still and strained to listen. It didn't seem possible that Lizzie could have shifted position without Holly seeing. But if it wasn't Lizzie moving behind her, then who was it?

There was silence again. Nobody was following her. The sound had been caused by an animal in the undergrowth. Vera would laugh if she could see Holly's unease: *Not really cut out for work in the big outdoors, are you, pet?* Holly turned through the pillars that marked the entrance to the big house. Lizzie must have come this way. There was no other explanation.

Chapter Forty-Four

Lizzie walked slowly up the valley. Her hands were in her pockets and she had her hood up against the drizzle. She could have phoned her parents for a lift when she got off the bus, but she had other plans. She wouldn't be going straight home. Not now. In her right pocket was the Stanley knife she'd bought earlier in the day in the cheap hardware shop in Kimmerston. She'd unscrewed it so that the blade was exposed and she rubbed her thumb against the metal.

Jason Crow had been disappointing. He seemed to have got old while she'd been in prison. He'd lost his edge. Become soft and sentimental, talking about his family as if he cared about them. Gutless. Saying he loved Lizzie, but he couldn't run away with her, not while the kids were at university. Not until he'd sorted out the business and released his assets. Too many excuses, so she didn't believe any of them. Then: 'You're playing with fire, Lizzie Redhead. Just let it go. Do you want to go back inside? You won't get such an easy ride next time.'

If she'd had the knife then, she might have been tempted to use it on him. She shut her eyes briefly and imagined how that would feel. The rip of the blade through the skin, like scissors through fabric.

That would bring Jason Crow alive again. He wouldn't ignore her then.

Lizzie opened her eyes. She'd reached the turning to Gilswick Hall and paused for a moment, remembering childhood teas with the Carswell kids. Chaotic affairs in the kitchen: sliced white bread with honey or Marmite, mucky jars on the table, cakes from a packet. Stuff she was never allowed at home. The major had fought in the Falklands and had told stories that entranced her. If she'd been brought up in that house, where adventure was encouraged, she might be a different person. She turned into the drive and her feet crunched on the gravel. She walked slowly now and moved away from the drive, keeping to the trees. The detective's Land Rover had been parked in here when she'd walked out to the bus in the morning, and the last thing she needed was to meet a bunch of cops. The rain wasn't heavy, but water dripped from the branches. No Land Rover. No sign of life in the big house.

Shirley Hewarth had told Lizzie about the moth traps during that last conversation in Sittingwell. They'd talked about Patrick Randle and Martin Benton at an earlier meeting. Two dead men who'd shared a passion. And a secret. Lizzie knew what she was looking for and walked through the trees until she found the traps. Her shoes were wet from the long grass, her socks sopping. She looked at her watch. Not long to wait.

She flicked a switch and the lights came on. Long neon strips, so bright they hurt her eyes if she looked directly at them. So white that they appeared tinged with icy blue. They'd attract more than bugs that night. She squatted beside them, pulling her waterproof under her bum so that she didn't get too wet. Then she began to rehearse the words that she'd use to the person she'd arranged to meet here. The words that she'd been planning since she'd come across the book published by the *National Geographic* in the prison, rehearsing them while she was lying awake in her room, listening to the other women's breathing. She'd repeated the phrases over and over again while she dreamed of deserts, forests and wide, open skies.

Chapter Forty-Five

Vera sat in the Redheads' living room and watched the light drain from the valley. Annie and Sam were with her, so tense that the air seemed to crackle with their anxiety like static electricity. Annie couldn't keep still. Every few moments she got to her feet and ran up the stairs. Vera knew what she was doing: staring out of the landing window in the hope that she'd catch a glimpse of her daughter making her way up the lane. But now it was almost dark and there was nothing to see.

Vera had got Joe to check with the bus station again, to see if Lizzie had been on the last bus back to Gilswick. He hadn't got back to her. Sam had already driven down the road to look for his daughter. Now he wanted a search party in the valley. Blue lights and sirens. 'There's a killer on the loose and my girl's missing. And you're sitting here and drinking tea.'

'She could be in a bar in Kimmerston,' Vera said. 'You told me yourself that was the most likely thing she'd be up to. No need to panic yet.' But she *was* panicking. Back in the station Holly was supposed to be tying up loose ends, but nobody seemed to know where she was. Joe was in Kimmerston, in case Lizzie had switched off her phone to stop her parents nagging and was celebrating six months' sobriety by going on a bender with her mates. And Vera was here, having to make a decision about what to do next. Feeling indecisive, which was unlike her. So close to making an arrest, but not quite ready. And Lizzie Redhead primed like an unexploded bomb, out and about in the wilds of Northumberland.

Vera's phone rang. She left the room and took the call in the kitchen. Joe.

'We've tracked her movements through CCTV. When she left Crow's house she headed to the town centre. She went to a couple of shops – one hardware store and one travel agent – then to the bus station. She got on the three-thirty bus to Gilswick. I've sent someone to check the shops to see what she was up to.'

'So she should have been home an hour ago, even if she was walking slowly.' Vera's mind fizzed and sparked, and she thought again there was a charge in the air that was blocking rational thought.

'What do you want me to do?'

She paused. If they brought in a large search team, the killer would go to ground. There'd be no evidence and no resolution. No real explanation. The most frustrating end to an investigation. 'Come to the village and park there. Walk up the valley. Slowly. There might just be enough light, if you're quick. Sam has already driven down, but he'll only have been looking at the road. Try the footpaths that lead to the burn and the ones that go onto the hill. I'll start from this end.'

'Okay.' She could tell that he was already moving.

'Come quickly,' she said. Now she'd decided on a course of action, she wanted to bring the thing to a close. The panic that overwhelmed the house was still making her jumpy. She had never been so uncertain. When she finished the call she stood for a moment, before heading back to talk to Sam and Annie. They'd be waiting for her, expecting some explanation. She wasn't sure she wanted to leave them in the house on their own.

'Good news,' she said briskly. 'Lizzie got on the bus in town and headed out to Gilswick. It's possible that she met up with a friend from the valley, don't you think? That she's in The Lamb, catching up. Or in one of the houses in the village. Waiting for the rain to clear. She probably has no idea that you're worried.'

They stared at her. Annie just looked distraught. Vera couldn't tell what was going through Sam's mind. 'Maybe you'd like to check?' Vera said. 'Drive down to the pub and see if she's there.'

'We could phone Gloria.' It seemed Sam had decided that Vera had nothing useful to contribute. 'That makes more sense.'

Annie tugged at his sleeve. 'No. Let's drive down to the village. I can't stand waiting. This house . . . And there might be other people there who were on the bus. We might even bump into Lizzie on the road.'

Vera stayed where she was until she heard their car drive away, then she went outside. In the other houses facing onto the courtyard the curtains had been shut against the weather. Everything was quiet. The rain was gentle and persistent. She pulled up the hood of her jacket and started down the track, allowing her eyes to get used to the gloom. She had a torch in her pocket, but didn't need it yet.

She turned onto the footpath leading to the hill where Shirley Hewarth's body had been found and stood for a moment, listening. Again she was struck by the fact that it was impossible to see the Valley Farm development from here. It was only a few minutes' walk away, but she could be miles from human habitation. There was no sound. No movement. She started on down the lane towards Percy and Susan's house, walking on the grass verge so that her footsteps made no noise. When she got to the trees there was less light and it was only the gleam from an elaborate lamp on the outside wall of the bungalow that kept her on the road. The couple hadn't drawn their curtains and she stood very still, looking in. Percy was standing in the kitchen with a mug in his hand. Vera couldn't see Susan. The rain had stopped and the sky seemed to be clearing a little.

She walked on more quickly, seeing her way more easily. The next turn-off was the drive to the Hall. Because of the twist in the track and the trees, it was impossible to see the house. But in the distance there were lights. Blue-white and ghostly and close to the ground. Patrick Randle's moth traps. It was the last thing she'd been expecting to see, as if the young man had come back to haunt them.

Vera stopped again and listened. Voices. Indistinct and too far away for her to make out the speakers. At this distance they were more like whispers. Lovers' caresses. At first she wondered if the sound was just caused by the wind in the branches.

She didn't move. She wished she knew where Joe was. She didn't want him stumbling along the road, all heavy boots and shouting. This was a delicate situation. She thought again that Lizzie was like an unexploded bomb. A sudden movement or a loud noise might set her off. Vera took her phone from her pocket and switched it to silent. Then she tapped out a text to Joe: *Lizzie in Gilswick Hall close to the moth traps. Approach carefully. No fuss. No noise.* She hit 'Send' and the message disappeared silently into the ether. Vera listened again, but the conversation under the trees seemed to have stopped.

She was a heavy woman, but years of acting as Hector's lookout had made her quiet on her feet. The damp undergrowth cushioned her tread. Still the violet lights of the traps seemed to dance in the distance. She walked, but she didn't seem to come any closer. Then suddenly she could see them in a clearing ahead of her and the voices had started again. Intense. Two figures were standing just beyond the traps. They were of a similar height. Both dressed in waterproofs and boots. Dark shadows in the fading light and impossible to identify. Vera slid behind the wide trunk of a beech and listened.

'It's up to you.' A woman's voice. Apparently reasonable. Persuasive and clear. Loud enough so that Vera could hear. 'Your choice. You can afford it. Who need ever know?'

Silence.

Vera felt the rough bark of the tree against her back even through her coat. She didn't dare move to see the figures more clearly. She didn't need to look.

'You don't understand.' The shadow was bulky, bull-headed, thick-necked.

'Just give me the money and I'll be away. You'll never see me again.' Her voice was still reasonable, but Vera could tell that the speaker was losing patience now. There was a scuffle and a little scream. At that moment the security lights at the big house went on. The timer must have been triggered and the whole grounds were flooded with a white light.

As if lit by a spotlight and like a character in a Victorian melodrama, Nigel Lucas stood at the centre of the clearing. He had one arm round Lizzie Redhead's throat and the other was raised to strike. He had a Stanley knife in his hand; Vera thought he must have grabbed it from Lizzie just before the lights came on. Everything seemed to happen very slowly. Vera came out from behind the tree, but she was too far away to stop the attack and Lucas seemed so angry that he appeared not to hear her yelling. It was like a nightmare; she was running, but seemed rooted to the ground. Tied down. Impotent. She knew she wouldn't get there in time. She imagined the conversation with Sam and Annie: *I'm really sorry. There was nothing we could do.* The parents' pale faces and their staring reproach.

Then, still as if in slow motion, another figure appeared. A dark shadow silhouetted against the bright security light. It took Vera a moment to recognize Holly. Lucas released Lizzie and lunged at the newcomer; the thin blade of the knife reflected the light and then disappeared, buried into Holly's clothing. Or into her body. Someone was screaming, and it took Vera a moment to realize the sound came from her own voice. Panic pushed her on. She'd almost reached the group, when Holly kicked out with her feet. Lucas fell to the ground, his face in the sodden leaves, and Holly was sitting on top of him, twisting the knife from his grip. Lizzie Redhead started running away through the trees.

'Stop her!' Holly's face was white in the unnatural light. Vera looked for blood, but saw none.

'Never mind Lizzie bloody Redhead. Joe'll get her. Did he hit you?'

Holly seemed not to hear. *Am I really here?* Vera thought. *Or am I some sort of ghost? Invisible and completely powerless. Can they all manage fine without me?*

She helped Holly pull Lucas to his feet.

'I'm fine,' Holly said. 'A scratch.'

Lucas looked up at Vera. Even with his face smeared with mud, he managed to turn on the automatic smile. There was still the need to be believed. 'Inspector, please don't be misled. Did you see what happened? These young women assaulted me.'

'Is that what happened when you were a prison officer?' Vera was still panting after the run, still shaking with anxiety, and she couldn't stop herself. 'All those lads you abused in the detention centre. Had they assaulted you too?'

She was aware of footsteps to her right and saw Joe Ashworth making his way from the drive. He had grabbed Lizzie by the arm and was pulling her after him.

'Read him his rights and get back up, then take him to the station, Holly.' Vera felt suddenly very tired. 'Joe, get Lizzie to her parents. They're in Gilswick. If not there, then back at the house. I'm going back to Valley Farm to tell this man's wife that her husband's a triple-murderer.' She thought it was the least she could do.

Chapter Forty-Six

Vera found Lorraine in her studio at the back of the house. She was working at an easel and an anglepoise lamp shone straight onto the painting. Lorraine looked up as Vera walked in. 'Is it over?'

'Did you know?' Vera sat on a wooden rocking chair with a patchwork cushion.

'I didn't know. I didn't want to know. I think I guessed. Then I told myself I was being paranoid and tried to forget about it. What reason could Nigel have for killing two strangers?' She paused. 'I wondered if the cancer had spread to my brain, eating away at it, making me imagine things. If I was going quietly mad. It's been a horrible week.'

'You're one of the sanest people I know. When did you suspect?'

'Friday afternoon, just before the party. Not that Nige was the killer then, but that something was wrong. He'd been in town shopping, stocking up on drinks and snacks.'

'He showed us the receipt,' Vera said.

'He seemed to be away a long time. And when he came back he changed and put all his clothes in the washing machine. He's pretty domesticated, but that seemed odd.' She turned away from the painting and wiped her brush on an oily rag. 'And he seemed very wired and hyper, insisting on dragging me down to The Lamb for a drink.'

Vera didn't speak and Lorraine continued.

'Also I knew there was something in his past, something that he wanted to forget. He refused to tell me about it. Once there was the start of a news item, and he switched off the television before I could see what it was about. "Why can't they leave all that alone, after all this time?" he said. "What good does it do now?" He wasn't himself for days.'

'He'd worked as a senior prison officer,' Vera said. 'Before he set up his own security company. One reason why the business did so well. He had contacts. People trusted him, just at a time when a number of the prison functions were being put out to private tender.'

There was a noise in the next-door garden. Janet O'Kane locking the hens in for the night.

'I knew he'd worked in the prison service,' Lorraine said. 'He never liked to talk about it. I thought it was a kind of snobbishness. He wanted people to think of him as a successful businessman.'

'He worked in a detention centre for young offenders in Staffordshire. Shirley Hewarth was a recently qualified probation officer based in the same institution. It took us a while to make the connection. Perhaps we didn't really know what we were looking for and we got distracted by other things.'

'What could possibly have happened there to make Nigel kill three people?'

Vera was surprised by how calm Lorraine seemed.

Her interest in the story was almost academic. Perhaps she had her own death on her mind.

'It was a different time,' Vera said. *Though perhaps not so different*. 'The Home Office thought the answer to youth crime was a short, sharp shock. Military – everything done on the run. No excuses and no compassion.'

'Like a US boot-camp.'

'Maybe. A few of the officers took the idea too far. Even enjoyed the cruelty, perhaps. The power. There was abuse. Some lads tried to break their own limbs to get invalided out.' *Like soldiers in the First World War, though surely the regime can't have been that horrific.* 'Many of them lived with the effect of their sentence for years. There've been some recent court cases, lawyers representing the kids and demanding justice, a public inquiry. The inmates were young. Some boys only fourteen and fifteen. Lots of them were screwed up and disturbed.'

'So that was the news report Nigel turned off.' Lorraine stretched. She seemed uncomfortable and rubbed her back.

'One of the lads was from a well-to-do family. A bit of a tearaway who'd got involved with drugs. Name of Simon Randle.'

'A relative of the Carswells' house-sitter.'

'An older brother. He never got over the experience. Went off to Oxford, but then committed suicide halfway through his first year. The parents never told Patrick that Simon had been inside, but he must have found out about it somehow. Got obsessed and started digging into the past to find out what had happened. Resented the fact that his parents hadn't told him the whole story about his brother. He was a bright boy and he knew about research.'

'He came to the valley because he'd tracked Nigel down?' Lorraine got to her feet and went to a small fridge in the corner of the room. She took out a bottle of wine and found two glasses and a corkscrew on a shelf. 'Will you do the honours, Inspector? I don't have the strength in my arms any more. Some days I can't hold a paintbrush.'

Vera opened the bottle and poured two glasses. 'Nigel was the officer that Simon Randle hated most.'

'I can't imagine Nigel as a sadist.' Lorraine looked up at Vera. 'Are you sure about all this?'

'Perhaps it wasn't about being a sadist,' Vera said, 'but about not wanting to stand out from the crowd. Obeying orders. Doing what was expected. Being good at his job. He'd have been a young man then.'

Lorraine gave a little smile. 'That does sound more like Nigel.'

'It was premeditated.' Vera couldn't quite give Lucas an easy ride, even to please Lorraine. 'He killed Randle with a spade stolen from the O'Kanes' house and he scattered a few of John's sweet wrappers on his way. Laying a false trail. He'd have been happy for someone else to be convicted.'

'I suppose he was desperate.'

Vera thought this was a surreal conversation. She was chatting quite calmly to a woman who was about to die, about a man who'd killed three people.

'He must have felt trapped,' Lorraine went on. 'He wanted so much to be respectable and to make me proud. He'd just become a magistrate and thought that would be the opportunity he needed to meet the right sort of people.' She drank half the glass in one go. 'I love it here. It's my idea of paradise. I wouldn't have wanted to move away.'

'Another of the lads in the centre was a local lad called Jason Crow. He was there a few years after Randle.' Vera kept her voice even. The woman deserved information. It was quite dark outside now and the whole room was lit by the single spot from the anglepoise lamp. 'Builder and businessman. Lover of Lizzie Redhead, before she went wild and ended up in prison.'

'So Lizzie knew about Nigel?'

'Jason recognized him when they negotiated the work on your house. He must have told Lizzie.' Vera paused. 'Jason survived the experience of the detention centre very well. Says it was the making of him. It didn't stop him offending, but he was never convicted again. But Lizzie remembered the stories he'd told about the abuse there. And Jason still had nightmares about it. When we arrested Nigel this evening, she was trying to blackmail him.'

Lorraine reached out and topped up her glass, waved the bottle at Vera, who shook her head. 'What about the older man? Martin Benton. Was he in the detention centre too?'

'No. Martin was a computer geek. A bit sad. Patrick Randle was employing him to dig around in the old Home Office files and find out what the government knew about the regime at the centre. He was planning a big story in the press about his brother's suicide. Martin and Patrick had come across each other because they shared a passion for moths. Not exactly a coincidence, but a weird connection that threw us for a bit.' Vera thought how thrilled Martin must have been. His first job as a self-employed computer consultant and Patrick had asked him to be an ethical hacker. It would be the most exciting thing he'd ever done in his life. He'd told his friend Frank that the work was secret, and that Frank would be proud of him.

'And the woman? The social worker?'

'As I told you, she worked in the same detention centre. Benton must have come across her name when he was digging around in the records. He admired her and was grateful to her because she gave him work, but he passed on her name to Randle and they corresponded. She'd always felt guilty about her time at the detention centre, the fact that she hadn't done anything to stop what was happening. It was what drove her to work for practically nothing at the charity for offenders. I think she suspected that Nigel was involved in the murder and confronted him.' Vera knew this was all guesswork. She hoped Nigel would be filling in the gaps to Joe and Holly now. 'I shouldn't be telling you this,' she said. 'The CPS would go ape if they found out. But I thought you should know.'

'Don't worry, Inspector. I won't be around when this comes to court. The CPS need never know.'

'Aye, well, that's what I thought.' Vera shut her eyes for a moment and then she drained her glass. 'Are you okay on your own?'

'When will I be able to see Nigel?'

'Not tonight. Tomorrow maybe.'

Lorraine looked up. 'He did all this for me, you know. He'd have toughed out the press and the lawyers, if he was still on his own. He was trying to protect me from the publicity. It wasn't just his own reputation that mattered to him.'

Vera nodded. She thought that was probably true. Nigel believed in himself as a good husband and protector.

'I might go and see Janet,' Lorraine said. 'She's a good friend. I can't face Annie and Sam.'

'I'll walk round with you.' Vera followed Lorraine down the stairs and out into the darkness. The sky was clear in patches and there was a faint moon and a smattering of stars. She stood by the Land Rover while Lorraine tapped at her neighbour's door. She watched the women embrace, backlit by the house, and then she climbed into the vehicle and drove away from the valley. It occurred to her as she passed the big house that she'd have nobody to comfort her in a tragedy. She thought it was probably simpler that way, and besides she'd never been able to cope with sympathy.

Chapter Forty-Seven

Holly found herself in Vera's house in the hills for the second time during the investigation. Outside it was completely dark and the lights in the village below were hidden by the drizzle. Vera had conjured a meal out of nothing. Lamb stew and home-made bread. 'Joanna seems to know when I'm busy. She's a good neighbour and she looks after me.' Holly had given up red meat years ago, but the smell was so delicious that she took a bowl. Vera poked at the fire. They sat with their food on their knees, the hunks of bread on a plate on the floor between them.

'I never liked Lucas.' Vera had dribbled lamb fat down the front of her jersey. She sounded smug. 'Never trusted him.'

'He wasn't a bad man, though. Not at the start.' Holly thought Lucas hadn't ever been a villain like Jason Crow. After all, Lucas hadn't been the person to decide that young scrotes needed a brutal regime to sort them out. That had been dreamed up by the politicians, and journalists weren't threatening the Home Secretary of the time with exposure and legal action. The newspapers had gone for the easy targets, the men and women doing their jobs. 'Not until Patrick Randle started hassling him.'

'Just following orders, do you think?' Vera kept her voice amused, but her eyes were sharp. 'Not his responsibility if a few lads were so screwed up by their time inside that they went on to commit suicide, become alcoholic or violent themselves?'

'Not unless he crossed the line.' Holly supposed she should let this go, but she was tired of Vera's bullying.

'Ah, that line . . .' Vera leaned back in her chair with her eyes half-closed. 'If only we knew exactly where it was.'

There was a moment of silence so that Holly wondered if Vera had fallen asleep. The big woman roused herself to set her bowl on a table behind her and continued talking. 'In terms of this investigation, it doesn't matter what really happened all those years ago. What matters is that Patrick Randle believed that Nigel Lucas had caused his brother's suicide and wanted the world to know what had gone on in the detention centre. And Lucas made up his mind to stop him going public.' She looked at Holly. 'That was premeditated murder – the worst crime there is. So do I personally think Nigel Lucas was capable of beating up the lads in his care? Tormenting them until he drove them mad? Yes, I do.'

Joe shifted uncomfortably. He'd never been much good at confrontation. 'Talk us through the details,' he said. 'Tell us what happened.'

Vera beamed at him. She knew he was distracting them. 'Aye, why not? If we go all philosophical you'll be here all night, and I need my beauty sleep. Though maybe we should get Holly to tell it. She got to the answer before the rest of us.' The comment was barbed, so Holly squirmed in her seat and expected a lecture on following direct orders. But Vera sat up straight in her chair and began her lecture. Holly found herself impressed by the crisp delivery and by Vera's sharp mind.

'Patrick came across details of his brother's suicide, and the fact that Simon had been inside. That caused a breakdown of communication with his mother, Alicia – Patrick resented the fact that she'd kept the whole thing from him. He tracked down Shirley Hewarth and Nigel Lucas. Shirley had been Simon's welfare officer, and Nigel the prison officer in charge of Simon's wing. Shirley had obviously been distressed by her ex-client's suicide and must have discussed the case at home. If you remember, Jack Hewarth thought Randle's name was familiar.'

Vera paused for a moment to collect her thoughts before continuing.

'Patrick wrote to Shirley and she was sympathetic. She understood that he wanted to gather more information about his brother's experience inside. But she must have been scared about being implicated in covering up the abuse.'

'How did Martin Benton get involved?' Holly had always wondered about the grey ex-teacher.

'Patrick had been in communication with Benton online for some time to discuss the finer details of moth identification. He knew Benton had the computer skills to dig around in the official records to find evidence of what had happened under Nigel Lucas's regime, and who else knew. Patrick didn't hide the fact that he was in the valley at Gilswick. He wanted to scare Lucas and make him feel uncomfortable. He'd already written to him to demand details of Simon's stay in the centre. It would never have occurred to him that Lucas might contemplate murder.'

Holly thought about Patrick Randle. Life had been easy for him. He'd had a loving mother, a good education, research that he enjoyed. Why had he felt the need to dig around into the causes of his brother's suicide, disturbing the lives of all these strangers? Would it have been different if his mother had been honest with him from the start? The story would probably all be made public now anyway. In his obsession he'd lost Becky, the girlfriend who'd adored him.

Vera continued talking. 'Lucas watched what was going on in the valley. He was obsessive about his wife and liked to know where she was, but he had a voyeur's curiosity about everything that happened there. He was especially interested in the house-sitter, of course. He understood the rhythm of his days. The afternoon of the murders Lucas saw Randle's car drive up the lane to the Hall. He wouldn't have known that Benton was there too, though. From that distance he couldn't have seen inside the car. Lucas prepared. He knew that Randle usually spent his afternoons working in the Carswells' garden. That was part of the house-sitting arrangement. He made his way to the Hall, waited until Randle came out of the house to go into the vegetable garden and hit him as he was about to pick leaves for the salad. He dragged him to the drive and used Randle's own car to dump him by the track. Randle's jacket was in the car, and Lucas put that on him so that it would look more like a hit-and-run accident. Then he went back to the attic flat to pick up any evidence that Randle might have on the regime in the detention centre. Of course he had no idea that Benton was there.'

'So that killing wasn't premeditated,' Holly said.

Vera shook her head. 'Lucas must have been scared shitless when he walked into the place and saw a middle-aged man working on a laptop on the table. Benton recognized Lucas from photos he'd seen during his research, so Benton had to die. Then Lucas took the laptop and got home by the footpath along the burn, before his wife got back from her walk and the other women returned from the WI.' Vera paused. 'We found Randle's laptop in that fancy new kitchen of his, hidden in the drawer where he keeps the coffee.' She gave a sly grin. 'He was the only person allowed to play with the all-singing, all-dancing coffee machine, so he knew it would be safe in there.'

'Shirley Hewarth must have worked out Lucas was the killer.' It was Joe again. He leaned forward to warm his hands at the fire. 'Why didn't she tell us?'

'Perhaps she just couldn't see an old colleague as a double-murderer,' Vera said. 'Or she had a weird sense of loyalty. And, of course, if she pointed us in the direction of Lucas, her role in the cruelty at the centre would become public too. She didn't commit the abuse, but she must have known what was going on and she kept quiet about it. That was a sort of cowardice at least.'

'But she did suspect Lucas, didn't she?' Holly was becoming engrossed in the story now. 'She tried a couple of times to get advice about what she should do. She set up the meeting with her ex-husband in the pub, and then she arranged to talk to the chair of trustees.'

'But by the time she was due to meet him,' Joe said, 'Lucas had already killed her.'

'Shirley talked to Lizzie Redhead too.' Vera looked out of the uncurtained window, but it was still misty outside and there was nothing to see. 'Jason had told Lizzie what had happened at the detention centre and had mentioned Shirley's name. It was a shared secret between the women.'

'What will happen to Elizabeth?' Holly hadn't liked Lizzie Redhead. Somebody else with doting parents and a comfortable life, who'd felt the need to make life difficult for other people.

'I don't see much point in charging her with blackmail,' Vera said. 'Lucas would be the only prosecution witness, and who'd believe a man convicted of a triple-murder?'

Holly was about to argue the point – she'd heard Lizzie's attempt at blackmail – but looked at Vera and thought better of it.

'I don't think Lizzie will be sticking around to bother us anyway,' Vera went on. 'If she's desperate to see the world, I suspect her parents will fund her adventures. Life will be much easier for them if their errant daughter is on the other side of the planet. And maybe when she comes back she'll be a bit older and wiser.' She paused. 'Lizzie will have to learn a bit of responsibility on her own in the big, bad world. Sending her back inside would be an easy option and she'd never grow up.'

They were quiet again. The fire was just embers now and Vera made no move to throw on another log. Joe stretched, got up and said goodbye. Holly stood up and followed him to the door, but Vera called her back.

'Are you okay, Hol?'

'Yeah, just tired.' What could she say? *I'm not sure I want to do this any more. This investigation has got under my skin and sapped my confidence. I don't want to end up like you.*

'Some cases bother us more than others,' Vera said. The light was so dim that Holly could barely make out her face across the room. 'That's just the way it is. It's not a bad thing to get involved, no matter what the textbooks say.'

'I'm not sure I did a very good job.' It was the closest Holly could get to an explanation for her unease.

'Nonsense!' There was a pause. 'You cracked the case for us. You found the connection that mattered: that Crow, Lucas and Hewarth had all been in the same institution.' Vera got to her feet. 'And you saved a young woman's life. Nothing more important than that.' A pause. Her voice changed, became loud and hard. 'But if ever you put your life in danger like that again, you'll be off my team before you have time to make a pot of that disgusting herbal stuff you call tea. Now get off home. A good night's sleep, a decent meal and a couple of days' leave and you'll be ready to start on the next investigation. We'll forget the rest.'

Outside Vera's house a breeze had blown holes in the cloud, and the lights in the valley were visible again. Holly found herself grinning. She thought that Vera was probably right. As usual.